CW01494683

Olaf's Saga

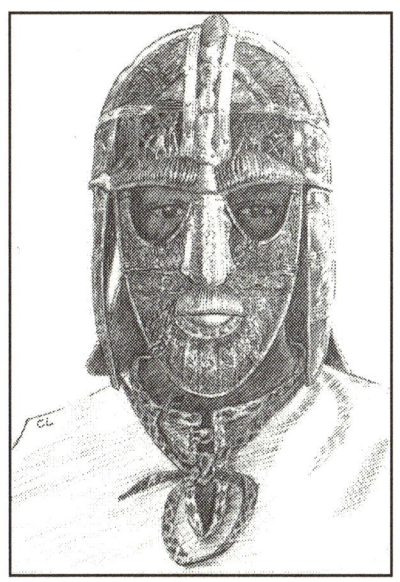

Stephen Liley

authorHOUSE®

AuthorHouse™ UK Ltd.
500 Avebury Boulevard
Central Milton Keynes, MK9 2BE
www.authorhouse.co.uk
Phone: 08001974150

© 2007 Stephen Liley. All rights reserved.

No part of this book may be reproduced, stored in a retrieval system, or transmitted by any means without the written permission of the author.

First published by AuthorHouse 6/28/2007

ISBN: 978-1-4343-2033-9 (e)
ISBN: 978-1-4343-2031-5 (sc)
ISBN: 978-1-4343-2032-2 (hc)

Printed in the United States of America
Bloomington, Indiana

This book is printed on acid-free paper.

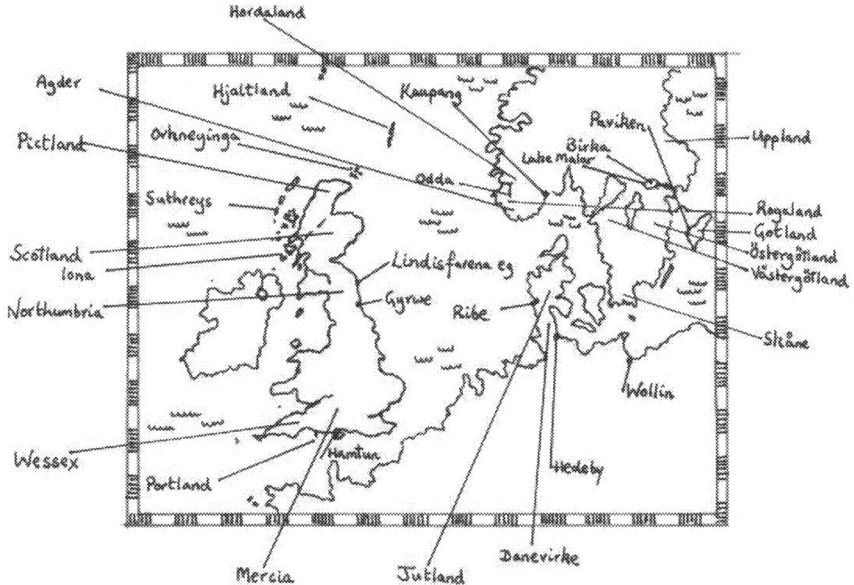

Hardaland

Agder

Hjaltland   Kaupang

Pictland   Orkneyinga   Paviken

Uppland

Suthreys   Odda   Lake Malar   Birka

Scotland   Rogaland
Iona   Lindisfarena eg   Gotland
                                                              Östergötland
Northumbria   Gyrwe   Ribe   Västergötland

                                                              Skåne

Wessex   Wollin

Portland   Hamtun

                                          Hedeby

Mercia   Jutland   Danevirke

Bretland and the Norse World
789 ~ 795

Olaf's Saga

is for

Rachael, Elli, Tom, Charles, Gisela, Adrian, Geraldine, Paul,
Bronwen, James, Christopher and Eve

Characters
Anglo Saxon

*Alderman Wulfherd	Reeve to Beorthric (Beaduheard)
*Billfrith	Metalwork binder of famous Lindisfarne Gospels
*Bishop Eadfrith	Lindisfarne Bishop, creator of Lindisfarne Gospels
*Bishop Eathiwold	Lindisfarne Bishop, binder of Lindisfarne Gospels
Bishop Elstan	Bishop in realm of Wessex
*Beorthric	King of Wessex
Brother Agilbert	Monk at Lindisfarne
Brother Alcuin	Monk at Lindisfarne
Brother Cathwulf	Monk at Lindisfarne
Brother Coelfrith	Monk at Lindisfarne
Brother Eadric	Monk at Gyrwe
Brother Ealdred	Monk at Lindisfarne
Brother Egbert	Monk at Lindisfarne
Brother Godric	Monk at Gyrwe
Brother Oda	Monk at Lindisfarne
Brother Wilfred	Monk at Lindisfarne
*Cassiodorus	Roman who founded two monasteries including Vivarium
*Coelfrith	1st Abbot of Gyrwe A.D. 685 (4th year of abbacy when church of St. Paul's dedicated)
Eanfrith	Prior of Gyrwe
*Ethelbald	Abbot of (Gyrwe / Donemouth) & Wearmouth monastery
*Higbald	Abbot of Lindisfarne
Hulda	Wife of Sviðbalki (AS name not known)

*Offa		King of Mercia, Bretwalda of England
Sister Cecily		Nun at Lindisfarne, Ingvar's slave
*St. Benedict Biscop		Abbot who founded both Gyrwe and Wearmouth

ꝺorse

Adúlfr	m	Ulf's youngest son (wolf)
Ægileif	f	Ulf's daughter (terror / fate)
Alfarinn	m	Ulf's second son (eagle)
Alþrúðr	f	Heilfúss's woman, (strength, þrúðr – daughter of Thor)
Ámóða	f	Bodvarr's stepmother, (edge, wrath)
Ásgauta	f	(inhabitant of Gotland)
Ásmóðr	m	Young oaf killed by Skjaldbjörn, (madness)
Ávarr	m	Ulf's eldest son (defender)
Bers	m	Olaf's childhood friend, (little bear)
*Bjarni	m	"Buna" Veðra-Grimsson, King of Sogn (760-mid 800's)
*Bjorn	m	Ironside (I) of Sweden (794-804)
Bodvarr	m	Olaf's father (from Hordaland), (752-775)
Bodvarr	m	Olaf's friend / fellow raider
Bröndólfr	m	Olaf's childhood friend
Bröndólfr	m	Mardöllson, second son of Mardöll
Brynhildr	f	Mardöllsdottir, third daughter of Mardöll
Eilíf	f	Olaf's woman on Orkney (always, one alone)
Esja	f	Ingvar's woman (clay)
Farþegn	m	one of ÓþyrmiR's younger brothers, (traveller / merchantman)
Fastaðr	m	weapon dealer in Kaupang, (fast fight)

Folkaðr	m	crew on 'Mjollnir', crew on Gjálfrmarr (warrior)
Fóthraðr	m	Norse boy at Lindisfarne massacre
Fugl	m	crew on 'Mjollnir', crew on Gjálfrmarr (fowl bird)
Gagarr	m	bailer on 'Mjollnir', crew on Gjálfrmarr (hound dog)
Gedda	m	one of ÓþyrmiR's younger brothers, (pike fish)
Geirhjálmr	m	bailer on 'Mjollnir', crew on Gjálfrmarr (helmet)
Geirlaug	f	Mardöllsdottir, first daughter of Mardöll
Geirraðr	m	bailer on 'Mjollnir',crew on Gjálfrmarr (counsel)
Gjafvaldr	m	Crewman on Ulf's boat, Svana's man, (give)
Gnauðimaðr	m	boy killed by Olaf in a fight, (noise / alarm)
Gnúpa	m	young crewman on one of ÓþyrmiR's knarrs, (mountain side)
Gormr	m	crew on 'Hamar', (worm, serpent)
Gunnfríðr	f	Ragnarr's wife, Olaf's adopted mother
Grima	m	One of Óðinn's guises – an old man
Grímr	m	Necromancer in Egersund (one of Óðinn's names for disguise)
Gríss	m	crew on 'Ormr', (piglet)
Groa	f	witch or seiðkona
Grubbi	m	crew on 'Ormr', (wrinkled face)
Grúmr	m	crew on 'Mjollnir', (cruel one)
Guðbjörn	m	crew on 'Mjollnir', crew on Gjálfrmarr (god-like being)
HættingR	m	crew on 'Hamar', RagnalfR's man, (hat, hood)
Hallgríma	f	Mardöllsdottir, second daughter of Mardöll
Hár	m	alias for Óðinn
Hælga	f	Wife of Hjorleif, Queen on Rogaland, died in Egersund (790)

Heiðr	f	Brewer in Odda
Heilfúss	m	crew on 'Hamar', Alþrúðr's man, (lucky)
Hjalmlaug	f	Olaf's mother, first wife of Bodvarr
*Hjor	m	Jossurasson, King of Rogaland (c756-c790)
*Hjorleif	m	Hjorsson the Fornicator, King of Rogaland (c790-c805)
Hónefr	m	crew on 'Ormr', (nostril)
Hugi	m	bailer on 'Hamar', (mind thought)
Hulda	f	Anglo Saxon wife of Sviðbalki (deceased)
Hvíthöfuð	m	Old man (grandfather of Bodvarr (709-769)
Hvítkárr	m	Crew man recruited in Birka, (curly white)
Ígull	m	crew on 'Hamar', (sea urchin, hedgehog)
Ígull	m	Olaf Hvíthöfuðarson's friend, (sea urchin, hedgehog)
Ingvar	m	ÓþyrmiR's adopted son
Ingiþóra	f	Rorik's elderly sister
Jólgeirr	m	Olaf's friend recruited to Ormr in Hordaland (Yule spear)
Ketilbjörn	m	husband of the Odda brewer Heiðr, (chieftain with helmet)
Ketilbjörn	m	crew on 'Hamar', (chieftain with helmet)
Leikfroðr	m	crewman on Ormr, (weapon-play/battle, bird's nest)
Lofnheiðr	f	Olaf's vision whilst drowning, (Lofn – Goddess of love: one of Frigga's handmaidens, heiðr- heath)
Magnhildr	f	Þórfastr's woman, (might, power)
Mardöll	f	Olaf's woman, Veddellemettis' woman (Mermaid)
Oddr	m	Master smith – now a draughrinn
Ofæti	m	crew on 'Ormr', (glutton)
Olaf	m	Bodvarsson. Norse leader (from Hordaland - son of Bodvarr) (770 -)

Olaf	m	Hvíthöfuðarson. Father of Bodvarr (735-788)
Ótama	f	Óþyrmirʼs renamed Orcadian wife (untamed)
Ótama	f	Rorikʼs wife (untamed)
ÓþyrmiR	m	Merchant, boat owner, helmsman on Ormr (a merciless ruthless man)
RagnalfR	f	HættingRʼs woman, (counsel)
Ragnarr	m	Olafson. Olafʼs adopted father, Bodvarrʼs older brother (750-) (power of the gods)
Rorik	m	Father-in-law to Bodvarr (trader from Kaupang)
Rúnfastr	m	crew on ʻOrmrʼ, (hidden knowledge)
Særða	m	crew on ʻMjollnirʼ, crew on Gjálfrmarr (to hurt)
*Sigurd I	m	King of Haithabu (750-798)
SkarfR	m	crew on ʻMjollnirʼ, (mountain pass)
Skógi	m	crew on ʻOrmrʼ, forest
Snæbjörn	m	Olafʼs friend recruited for Ormr in Rogaland (snow bear)
Smiðkell	m	Mardöllson, third son of Mardöll
Smiðr	m	Olafʼs friend recruited for Ormr in Rogaland (craftsman)
Spjall	m	crew on ʻOrmrʼ, crew on Gjálfrmarr (spell, curse)
Sviðbalki	m	crew on ʻHamarʼ unofficial navigator, later on ʻOrmrʼ, later on Aðalríkr, AS wife Hulda deceased (to singe wood)
Skjaldbjörn	m	Beserker nicknamed Shield-biter (shield-beserker)
Svana	f	Gjafvaldrʼs woman (swan / lady)
Svana	f	Young girl known to Olaf and Bers when living in Odda
Sveina	m	Olafʼs (Bodvarrʼs father) old friend
Thorkell	m	Bodvarrʼs younger brother (756 -)

Thyri	f	Bodvarr's first wife, mother of Olaf (754 - 770)
Tubbi	m	bailer on 'Hamar', (Þórr bear)
Ulfr	m	karl of Hesthamar Hutne, boat owner (wolf)
Viðbjörn	m	crew on 'Ormr', later 'Ávarr', (tree, forest, bear)
Þengill	m	ÓþyrmiR's & Otama's first son, died as a baby
Þiálfi	m	crew on 'Ormr', (over powers)
Þjóðbjörg	f	woman friend of Gunnfríðr
Þjóðgeirr	m	Mardöllson, first son of Mardöll
Þórormr	m	crew on 'Ormr', (Þórr dragon)
Þórbjörn	m	crew on 'Hamar', (Þórr bear)
Þórfastr	m	crew on 'Hamar', Magnhildr's man - (Þórr strong)

The words in brackets denote the literal meaning of the Norse name

Írísb Kíngs

*Aedh Oirdnidhe	792-817, the son of Niall Frasach
*Domhnall	738-758, son of Murchadh, son of Diarmaid (1st King from Clann Colmain)
*Donnchadh	765-792, son of Domhnall, son of Murchadh
*Niall Frosach	758-765, son of Fearghal resigned to pilgrimage (died 773)

Orcaðían & Píctísb

Brude	m	petty Orkney chieftain of Irish descent, father of Veddellemettis
Drosten	m	petty Orkney chieftain
Itharnan	m	petty Orkney chieftain

Nehhton	m	Celtic, Ogham inscription
Peanfahel	m	petty Orkney chieftain
Uirolec	m	petty Orkney chieftain
Veddellemettis	m	Boatman from Orkney, son of Brude

*next to a name indicates this to be a real person

Norse Boats

ÁdiarfR	Knarr built 788, 'Courage'
Aðalríkr	Knarr built 781, 'Might'
Ávarr	Knarr built in 789, 'Defender'
Gjálfrmarr	Drakkar built 789, 'Steed of the sea'
Hamar	ÓþyrmiR's knarr, originally called 'Ormr'
Hrókr	'Crow', ÓþyrmiR's knarr which sank
Ormr	'Dragon', name of ÓþyrmiR's knarr later renamed Hamar
Ormr	'Dragon', name of Olaf's drakkar
Mjollnir	ÓþyrmiR's custom built drakkar to the same specifications as Ormr – (Mjollnir was the name of Þorr's hammer)

Introduction

I am called Jón Loftsson and I am the son of Loftur Saemundsson, who in turn is the son of seal rider, Saemundur 'the Learned' Sigfusson, the first of the Oddaverji. I can trace my forbears all the way back to before the time of Óðinn. The year is 1191. It is the slaughtering month of Gormánuðr, in the season or misseri of vetr and it is already cold as we should all expect in winter. I am alone and have all the time I now need to think. A simple wooden seat is the only luxury in my small, damp and dark turfed house in little and all but forgotten Oddi; a thinly spread out community in Ragnárvellir near to the southern coast of Thule. The weather is as bleak as the treeless wind blown scenery. My father, Loftur told me that our sheep are to blame for the lack of trees, but where would we be without their wool or their meat?

Páll's wife I tell you must take full blame for the story that will presently unfold and she can also take the blame for any mistakes or deviations from the truth that I am bound to make in this journey of the mind. It was she and she alone who took the iron dagger to the boy's father's face to rip it open. That incredibly is a full nine long years ago now. So much has changed in the years that followed; you and you alone can decide whether these changes were for the better or the worse.

I no longer see anything of Sturla Þórðarson, the boy's father, or for that matter his mother, Guðny Boedvarsdóttir. On reflection, I think Páll was lucky in some way, for he was weak. His wife's clumsily wielded blade which aimed to pierce or cut the eye from the socket of Sturla did him no favours either. The poor man initially had a good claim. Why couldn't he have sorted things out more amicably? Why for Óðinn's sake did he let his wife take matters into her own hands? By attempting to commit such a facile and hopeless deed she ruined any serious claim they may have had.

And by mocking the greatest of our gods, Óðinn, his woman won him nothing but scorn and humiliation at Althing. What could she have been thinking of, attacking Sturla in that way? Óðinn may have gained his great wisdom from the giant Mimir's spring after sacrificing an eye, but did she genuinely believe she could reflect the glorious ways of the gods within the humdrum and mundane lives of mere men? I think not. She would have done well to have remembered that Mimir's head was cut off by Óðinn!

Alas, Sturla and Guðny may have done little wrong, but they lost their three year old son to me, an old man, as part of the decision made at Althing. Yes and before you ask, gold and silver still pass hands regularly and the boy ever grows in my care. He has now seen twelve summers and possesses an unusual and apparently unquenchable thirst for knowledge. The past is his playground and words are his toys.

ᛉ   ᛉ   ᛉ

My old oil lamp flutters now and then and its moss wick grows ever brighter as the light outside begins to fade once more into the complete darkness of a long night on this island which sits astride the top of the world. Snorri, the boy, has come in out of the cold and is sitting beside me in the dim light, waiting patiently for me to begin. I have recounted so many tales to him of myth, legend and truth, but still he craves more. The settlement of our island, the people, the feuds, the development of Althing; our government, nothing it seems satisfies his need to know.

I have told him of my family, of my boys, Saemundir I Oddi and Þorsteinn, who themselves now grow old. They should take care of the boy, as their children are about the same age as he is, but no matter. Snorri always craves something new; an account he has not heard before, an anecdote of people or a legend of ships, a narrative that tells a complete story, a chronicle that is true.

I do not pretend to be either the poorest of skalds or a scribe of sagas or eddas. After all I received no formal teaching in the art of words. Unlike my illustrious forbears I have no real way with written or spoken thoughts. All I boast is a memory; but what a memory it is that I possess; it is full to brimming, bloated with all sorts of details, stories and accounts given to me by other far greater men and women than I. Some say I am fortunate, because I can bring to mind so many wondrous tales from a bygone age. As a small boy I listened, open mouthed to so many from my parents, Loftur Saemundsson and Þora Magnúsdóttir. My mother was, remember, none other than daughter to Magnus the Barefoot, King of Norway and direct descendant of Harald Fairhair, the first true king of Norway.

I can recall even a few extraordinary and dark yarns from many, many years ago, told beautifully to me by my grandfather, whom many say was and a few say still is a wizard, Saemundur fróði Sigfusson. The man with no shadow some called him. What he didn't know of the beginning of the world and of the old kings of Norway and Denmark wasn't worth knowing. As a boy I had to recount to him the family lineage; back through the forgotten ages to Haraldur King of Denmark, to Halfdan King of Jutland, to Skjold the first King of the Danes, even to Óðinn in Asgard and to times believe me, even earlier than that, to Sceaf.

I also remember lesser every day tales and stories that teach or instruct and others of the way of the world that simply entertain. Some of these sprang from the lips of his two sisters, Elín and Halla Sigfúsdóttir and yet others still I can recollect from the merest shadows of people who now barely live in the memory. In my mind, I can still see each and every one of their faces, some faded, some crystal clear and what is more I can hear their voices deep or shrill as if they were speaking to me at this very moment in this humble dwelling.

The tale I have settled upon is a new one, but one that is deep rooted in the distant past. It is a story that to me will always be called 'The Saga of Olaf Bodvarsson', but that is much too grand a title to be given to anything created by a lowly story teller such as me. To Snorri, it will assume the name, 'The Curse of the Drakkar'. The boy will listen to my poor words and muddled thoughts, which I have had to change often, so they may become the words and thoughts of the characters that live within the fabric of this history. Sometimes I have included words exactly as I believe they were spoken (1) and at other times I have not. My memory is as I have stated sharp, but my mind is growing feeble, so like Snorri, you must forgive this wretched story teller if he strays too far from the plot or moves forwards and backwards in time too much (2). These are the failings not of the tale, but of the orator. I tell it how I consider it to be; true to the way of real life, as I alone see it now and how Vemundur would have seen it. Remember that my lineage back to Vemundur is unbroken, back to the time of this offering. Some people in this tale will inhabit many of its vellum leaves, whilst others may just come and go, a number will return quietly and a few gloriously, others still may never return.

I make no apologies, why should I? The act of living as all who have been put down in Midgard know, can be cruel, but can also be kind. The world alas is changing and the old ways; my ways pass from it to be lost forever. The cross and the one god take over, but this way is not of my choosing. The old well-trodden paths, the true ways of our great gods; they live in my tale. If truth be known, the old gods still find a way into the lives of those even today and will so until the fury of Ragnarok. Tell me that Yggdrasil with its three great roots, one in the past, one in the present and one in the future is not the tree of life!

(1) Some of the speech is in Old Norse, after which a translation is included.

(2) To help the reader various notes have been compiled. There is a glossary

of Old Norse words and various appendices offering information on such things as runes, oghams, number systems, telling the time and date, the festivals, and a list of more technical words. All these things have been placed at the end of the book, making reference to them easier than if they were to be buried in the text somewhere. There are also a number of different maps that can be referred to, as well as family trees.

Part 1

~~~~ ODDA ~~~~

Chapter 1

Vetr, Gói
Odda, Hordaland

A.D. 769, February - western region in Norway

Frost had dusted the landscape white, to leave blades of grass crisp with ice and spiders' webs frozen in delicate symmetrical patterns. The quietness of early morning was unbroken, save for the far off cry from a solitary wolf. Its melancholy howl somehow managed to penetrate the gossamer like sea mist that hung magically above the still black waters of the wide and deep fjord.

A small bundle had been carefully placed near to the entrance of one of the smaller long houses in Odda the previous night. Any tiny movements or the slightest of noises coming from it had ceased as the grip of the cold night took its terrible toll.

Bodvarr Olafsson had only seen sixteen or perhaps seventeen summers; he wasn't really too sure, whilst his woman, if you could call her that, had seen at least two summers less than him. He was the first in Odda to see the light of this new day. Pushing his way past the weighted down heavy woollen flap that covered the entrance to the longhouse where he lived, he emerged into the cold and instinctively yawned. Then, through his nostrils he drew in a sharp burst of cold air as though in an effort to wake himself fully. Still stiff of limb from his recent slumbers, he staggered a few steps away from the door flap, to rest his bare hands on the hoar-frost covered fence that abutted the wall of his simple abode. Two large and immobile steaming swine looked up at him as though in expectation of some morsel or perhaps in anticipation of a cursory greeting on this new day in Hordaland.

The boy; he was just a boy, showed no overt outward signs of manhood, being both painfully thin and of nothing less than a weedy disposition. Further to this, he was also unfortunate enough to be in possession of a slightly pinched, stubble-free and rather grubby and spotty face. This made any first time acquaintances of him to think he looked startled for no apparent reason, or at the very least consider him to be of an anxious disposition.

The only other thing that would surely have struck those who happened to come upon him, were the curious pair of ancient leather boots adorning his feet. They had in an unusual act of generosity been handed down to him by his father. These, the cheapest of family heirlooms were far too big for his feet and as a consequence they drew the eye unerringly, for they seemed wholly out of proportion to the rest of his emaciated and gangly physique. He had, because of the boots' enormous size consequently stuffed them with straw; but in truth not very well. Bodvarr had forced handfuls of the stubborn material into the toe ends in an attempt to make them fit better, but in spite of his best efforts, both boots remained painfully uncomfortable and inevitably they let water seep in. Logic would dictate that this would have made his feet permanently cold and consequently make him feel miserable, but the water and straw somehow created a little unexpected warmth in his boots. This coupled with the tiny amount of heat retained by his nalbanded socks, did actually make his feet feel comfortable; they gave him the impression the frozen ground on which he walked was warmer and that may be, just may be spring had arrived. In spite of the gnawing cold, he did feel quite good about himself though and was at least from a physical aspect reasonably comfortable. A pair of tight-fitting woollen trousers hugged his spindly legs over which a rough cotton shirt hung down rather untidily. In a habit that appeared to be born out of nerves, these trousers were periodically adjusted with a quick upward and slightly sideways jerk. Each of these instinctive checks seemed to satisfy his seemingly distracted mind for no more than a few moments. Even when there was no actual or immediate danger of his trousers falling down, Bodvarr would every so often pull on the thin leather cord which had been passed through a series of small holes and check the small knot he always tied after pulling them on, shortly after the first light of each and every day.

The girl lay inside on a bed of straw covered in animal pelts and she still slept fitfully. In stark contrast to the lad, she was spotlessly clean, but even so she gave the impression of being somewhat dishevelled, having just about enough flesh on her little body to avoid being termed haggard or waiflike. Neither, the girl or the boy for that matter appeared to have any real permanence about them.

Norsemen and women in their community took only a passing interest in either of them. Invariably, they would shake their heads sadly and if they had chanced to speak about them would say something like, 'Both of them are just about hanging on; life is hard and more than tough on the sick and weedy. Scrawny young 'uns, like them, well they just don't make good parents and by *Þorr's* chariot that's good, that's very very good! It couldn't be better. It would have been better if as babies they'd been left outside their long house overnight in the way all the deformed and weedy babies are. If that pathetic sort start filling up Midgard with their feeble sort, we might as well by *Óðinn* and all of the other gods, give up and invite the terrible fury of Ragnarok and allow Fenrir to take us all!'

They were after all an unlikely young couple and their first meeting just so happened to turn out to be a terribly contrived and more than unsatisfactory affair. He hadn't much liked the look or demeanour of her, his 'wife to be' and to be honest, who in their right mind could have blamed him. Nothing since this first meeting had given him even the slightest cause, to change his mind. She had in contrast almost not noticed him, because although she was facing him, standing right in front of him, she existed somewhere else, or at least she did so in her head. This 'elsewhere' was a sinister, dangerous, dark and unwelcoming place for her to inhabit and it may possibly have explained the lost, staring, wild expression on her young face.

Their betrothal took place in spite of any one, or indeed of all the combined differences between the prospective partners. In fact, just six days afterwards, on the great and magical Feast of Vali, the girl and boy symbolically made their vows to each other. Bodvarr had dutifully done what he felt he must, that is, what his apparently ailing father, Olaf Hvíthöfuðarson, had in no uncertain terms instructed him to do, several weeks before the couple had met for the first time.

'My son it is best for us that you take this girl, as she will bring you wealth and she'll set you up well with some good and much needed coin,' he explained.

'But, I may not like the look of her, she may be a dog,' came Bodvarr's well thought out and rehearsed reply. But most unfortunately for the boy, his father's rejoinder was equally well practised as well as being much more powerful.

'It doesn't matter to me, not even for a single tiny bloody coin or even the smallest of debased silver bars. She may not just look like, but really could be the back end of a well tupped ewe! What's more, you ungrateful sod, far more important than you could ever imagine, by all our gods is the fact that I don't give a shit what you think. You will take her and you, by all the gods will take that money, her money. Remember that! You can always marry another, if you think you'll be rich enough, one day, or you could do what the rest of the men who are married to dogs do. Forget her now my boy and you can forget me when it comes to any inheritance you ungrateful whelp!'

Olaf was and always had been in most respects, something of an enigma to his son. He had from his earliest memories appeared to be far older than he should have been; old before his time in so many ways, but intriguingly not in all of them. He could still be quite active at times, when it suited him. He still worked at splitting logs with his trusty axe, helped build the frames for longhouses or barns, constructed wattle panelling and thatched roofs with reed or straw. Alternatively, like the more elderly and possibly wiser men, he could say he was too old or ill and sit down and watch the work being done with a broad and satisfied smile on his face. When he did this and it was becoming far more frequent of late, he would enjoy criticising those carrying out the work for their lack of skill or common sense. Usually with a horn of mead to hand, or a bowl of potent beer, he looked on at the work being carried out as though it was some kind of performance arranged for his benefit.

'I've had it,' old Olaf would grumble. 'These bent fingers, these calloused hands and these bloody arms of mine have done more than their fair share of work, down the years and now by the gods of Asgard, I need a well earned rest,' he continued.

'Yes, you, you have had it and you, you old lazy sod, you'll have plenty more I'll wager! You'll have more than enough time to rest in Asgard, in that favourite hall of yours, you old 'running' dog. You have enough strength for two if truth be told, you wrinkled old cur.'

Ígull, Olaf's oldest and closest friend never minced his words. 'Perhaps Sveina and I should have words with that beautiful Ámóða of yours and see if you're lazy with her as well,' he continued. 'We are your friends as you know and I'm sure we can manage to be *kveldúlfr*, both of us. We'll more than help you out, if you need it!' With that he exploded with self generated mirth and then rather mockingly outstretched his arms as though inviting Olaf to some kind of childish reconciliation.

Ígull revelled in the crudity of his banter, possibly because he knew that this particular and much used ploy of his would more than likely needle his old friend in the way a sharp wooden splinter has the unnerving ability to irritate. Igull's jibes and comments made this particular splinter feel to Olaf as though it had been cunningly pushed up, in such a way as to work its merry dance behind an unsuspecting and wholly susceptible finger or thumb nail.

'You know Ígull; I like you in spite of what you are. You are truly an old dog, but when all's said and done you're a dog turd, nothing more than a stinking dog turd. I don't trust you at all, not as far as I can piss against the winter wind or for that matter as far as my lame old dog can shit!'

'Ha! At least you've still strength enough in your ancient body to piss and your dog, ha, call that filthy matted fur ball a dog; it's a dirty great shit maker that's all it is. By *Sleipnir's* arse, it can shit all right. You say you like me, don't make me laugh will you? Olaf Dvergarson, you are as cunning as old Grima himself, get off your fat arse and try bending your fragile little back for a just while longer!'

ꙅꙅ   ꙅꙅ   ꙅꙅ

Olaf dressed as all the other men of Odda happened to; wearing a long black woollen robe that was securely fastened together near the shoulder with a very shiny golden pin. This was the only visible sign of any affluence afforded by the old man. His other clothes were in stark contrast to the fastening and were so well worn and grubby that they made people who didn't know him believe that the pin itself must be of a lesser metal. Under his tatty outer robe he wore a pair of threadbare, smelly woollen trousers and a sweaty and stained old white linen shirt that had been ripped both near his neck and below his left armpit to a lesser degree. To keep himself warm in the severe cold, because he carried not a pinch of excess fat on his body, he also wore a knitted smock-like top that had several deep pockets, which had many years before, on his instruction, been cunningly fashioned to be hidden on the inside of the garment. These, he put to good use; hiding a tiny iron hammer, the odd spare coin or even a small silver bar from which he parted all too grudgingly. When he did so, it was usually the result of a trivial wager that had been lost or possibly for a horn of strong ale or mead; he was more than partial to either drink.

Many a time, Olaf would be heard moaning about the quality of the metal in others' ingots or coin. 'My silver's all pure all right; there's no muck, nothing in my stuff, *'brannt silfr'* (pure silver), that's what you expect from me and that's what you get, nothing more and nothing less. Not like the shit the merchants always try to palm on us, day after sodding bleeding day! All that lot do, is to mix what little good stuff they can get hold of, with their own bad low grade muck. What do you end up with? I'll tell you what, stuff you don't bloody well want, because no sod has any fucking idea whether it's good, or whether it's shit. Imagine a world full of *'bleikt silfr'* (silver that has been debased), that's what we're going to bloody well end up with! Then what'll we use? I know what you'll say, you'll say gold and I'll say yes to that, but there's not enough of it to go round.'

He would always spit on the floor or at a door post or even on one of his hounds after finishing his well repeated but still acrimonious diatribe. Then rather more forlornly he would pull an anguished expression whilst scratching his head or arse as if to disturb some hidden louse or flea. He would usually conclude the well rehearsed ritual by muttering to himself about how things were not what they used to be. Olaf still had a full head of long wavy, but thin hair and was also in possession of a bushy golden beard with just the faintest traces of silver. His entire appearance suggested that of a man, whose body was still defiantly clinging albeit not that successfully to the vestiges or more accurately last remnants of youth. His delicately lined and leathery face was of a ruddy colour that more than hinted at two particular facets of his being; firstly his life was generally spent outdoors even in the more harsh of weathers and secondly that he possessed a penchant for fermented liquor; beer, mead or any other mind numbing substances and that this was not a passing indulgence of his.

Olaf's highly impressionable son had out of a sense of duty adhered to the strict paternal brief; the Norse tradition had been completely and utterly ingrained in him. He had even endeavoured to engage albeit half-heartedly in as near as to a polite conversation with the girl as he could possibly manage. However, he was soon to learn that any attempts of his were to be in vain; they were destined to have absolutely no effect on her, either for the good or bad.

She was well dressed, tidily turned out in a plain white linen dress that hung down or rather drooped rather shapelessly from her rounded shoulders to just below the tops of her brown leather boots. Over the top of this, she had pulled an over large hooded brown woollen cape, which had for the moment bunched untidily and you would have thought somewhat uncomfortably, at her waist. This circumstance had come about no doubt as a result of the thinness of the biting leather cord that she had securely tied about her middle. In fact, the girl had knotted it wholly unevenly and then pulled it far too tight and needless to say, too quickly; in fact everything she had done had been achieved without either any practical ability or any due care or attention.

Her hood was down. It had been pushed or pulled back some time before to expose her long brown hair that now hung limply down to her waist in a single forlorn plaited ponytail. Whatever the boy, Bodvarr had said to her, it had singularly failed to elicit even the slightest of responses from her; she just looked at and through him with a total indifference. He could not and had not failed to notice those staring, penetrating and hollow, yes that was it, hollow eyes. None of the questions he posed were capable of penetrating the mantle that seemed to enshroud and protect her detached persona. This made it extremely difficult for Bodvarr; he felt totally helpless, because she hadn't taken even the most fleeting interest in him. Instead, at all times she had remained wholly and utterly indifferent towards his approaches, issuing not even a half-whispered syllable of encouragement in his direction. It appeared that she was completely and utterly preoccupied.

Periodically and wholly unprompted, she would explode into laughter and gibber loudly in a tongue that defied any comprehension. Olaf muttered something about it being Pictish and then shook his head in complete disbelief.

Speaking out loud, but to himself, because he was far enough away from his son to hear and also because he knew that the girl wouldn't be listening, Olaf began a heartfelt diatribe. 'Bloody Picts! Sometimes they copy our language and sometimes they simply jibber to one another in a tongue that beggars belief. Their writing from what I've seen is even worse,' he paused to laugh to himself. 'It's as mixed as walrus offal, made up of all those stupid little scratchy lines. Sometimes the upright scratches just about reach the 'middle line' from above, sometimes up from below, and sometimes they simply cross it. There seems to be nothing to it; there's no logic or reason behind it if you ask me. No wonder they're always fighting with each other, they probably get their scratchings mixed up. Somes says they can write down our words in Ogham, yes that's it, that's what they call it, but I says, runes is best for proper folk, folk who carve runes knows things, thank *Óðinn*, not them stupid folk with all their bloody silly little scratches. But why in Asgard's name is this girl going on in Pictish anyway? The gods may full know, but I for one don't. I suppose we, or should I say the boy should be grateful she's not speaking our language. At least no one can understand a blind word she harping on about. Who'd want to know what's going on inside her funny little head, no one I'd wager, it's enough to bloody well frighten me' manhood, if yer' get me drift. If those eyes of her can really see elves and trolls and other things that normal folk can't, then she's welcome to keep her weird visions to herself, 'cause I just don't want to know and I'm sure my son Bodvarr won't. Her eyes look full mad, you know, she's got the same eyes as that nasty shaggy coated old horse of Sveina, the one called, 'Thunder', you know, the one that makes the children laugh cos' it keeps farting, but by *Þorr*, can it bite by buggery, I'll say it can, it'll take a lump out of anything, child, man or beast anything that'll go near it. I wonder if she's the same, I wonder. My son'll soon find out if she is!'

Nothing quite nearly as sophisticated was being conjured up in the confused and pained mind of Bodvarr. Before attempting to speak to his prospective bride, the young man had been wondering if she had been specially washed, dressed and then he winced, even scrubbed for the occasion. In his mind's eye he had the most fleeting glimpse of this girl as she might really be, within months of leaving the care of her family. The stark image he was presently conjuring up in his imagination was not a pretty one; she was wearing the same clothes, but now they were filthy, having been splattered with mud, sweat, grime and he grimaced, even blood. Her face was a deathly, grimy, greyish colour with only the skin surrounding her eyes appearing to be clean, giving her a truly gaunt and perplexed look. Her hair was now startlingly unkempt and the gusts of wind moved strands of it randomly and freely about her head making it resemble a nest of angry and hostile serpents. With considerable effort, the boy shook this unfortunate image from his mind and forced himself to concentrate.

'Go on, she won't bite! Talk to your bride.' Olaf's brief instruction leapt from his lips with such enthusiasm that his hypocrisy remained quite remarkably, almost wholly hidden.

'What is your dwelling like?' Bodvarr responded to his father's prompt, but even so his first nervous question was delivered in a terrible monotone and he knew full well his attempt was quite simply feeble.

'Where are your sisters and what are their names? You have four I believe, is that not so?'

His second and third questions were dispatched so quickly that there wasn't any opportunity for the former one to be answered. Unsure exactly of what to do, he nervously pressed on.

'Have you been to Odda before?' So it continued, until Bodvarr finally realised he was to elicit no real responses from the girl, who was now blankly staring at the clouds; this girl who was to be his bride. He in contrast, looked down to the straw covered earth and said nothing, pausing for quite some time. All of the time, he was thinking about his mute bride to be and how she would undoubtedly affect his life, for the worst. 'She'll be not much use in or out the sack or in or out of the longhouse. How by *Loki's* teats am I going to keep this mad bitch? May be I'll have to drown her in the deep waters of the fjord, when it's dark.'

'I knew you'd think of something son, you always were good with ideas.' Olaf was genuinely impressed and touched by his boy's sensible and practical response.

ℬ   ℬ   ℬ

It had begun to rain; great unpredictable blustery gusts of wind now sent unwelcome bursts of spray over the small heavily cloaked and shivering crowd who had dutifully assembled outside old Olaf's small and dilapidated longhouse. The turf sods at one end were attempting to prise the very frame of the house apart. Heavy and wet, they attempted to bend and warp the wooden timbers further that tried vainly to keep the house in shape.

It seemed as if only the closely knit roots of the stubborn grass that carpeted the entire roof in a shaggy green mantle were the force that kept the far end from falling in completely. Even the rain, for it was still rain in spite of the biting cold, seemed reluctantly slow in making the decision to become sleet or snow. It felt more than cold enough for the lashing drops of water to change into great snowflakes. In a short time though, the rain finally shook off its lethargy and the drops magically changed, to dance and whirl in twisting flurries of whiteness, whilst kissing the guests and their longhouses indiscriminately.

The bony and blanched hands of the bride and groom's fathers had been shaken in symbolic agreement over the proposed wedding and more importantly over the associated financial arrangements. The solemn procedures had been completed at the front of Olaf's longhouse, so that any interested onlookers could bear witness to the proceedings. The *mundr* or bride price had been paid in full, not a particularly large one, bearing in mind the status of the girl's family, but even so, one which had been quite difficult for Bodvarr's father to pay.

Olaf had in an overtly grand gesture handed to the girl's father, Rorik, a small black woollen bag, which had been tied tightly at the top. He had never been troubled with much gold and any spirit he had had for life in general or for that matter in accruing any reasonable quantity of gold or silver, had left him when his first wife, Hjalmlaug had died. This occurred when his son, his second of three sons, Bodvarr was no more than six summers. His wife had developed a burning fever whilst working in the fields, had come back to the longhouse and simply curled up on a bed of straw and died after shivering uncontrollably during the long dark hours of that night.

He had of course re-married, by necessity, but he had had no further children by his second wife Ámóða, with whom he shared what appeared at best, a brother-sister relationship. At least that was how the rest of his family and friends viewed his second marriage. Olaf surprisingly had not sent his first son Ragnarr away and some folk had it that his wife's early death had been the result of this.

'No good'll come of it, I'll tell ya,' had been said dozens of times by a good number of well meaning people commenting on poor Olaf's strange decision to raise his eldest son himself.

Wealth had never troubled any of Bodvarr's more recent ancestors and even before their time, there had been little enough gold, silver or coin of any consequence to speak of in his more distant family. For a great many generations, strife and hardship were the only guaranteed heirlooms for Bodvarr and his kin. Apart from their longhouse, all the family currently possessed was a comparatively small strip of poor land upon which a few animals spent their wretched lives and an indomitable, defiant spirit that had helped them through the most difficult of times and of late these had unfortunately become the stock standard fare.

Part of the problem relating to land ownership stemmed from the ancient laws of inheritance. Olaf had tried with little success to explain the intricacies of these to Bodvarr the previous summer.

'You see, the way it is, in fact the way it has always been, is quite straightforward.' Bodvarr being impatient at his father's long drawn out words interrupted his father rather rudely.

'If you don't get on with what you've got to say to me and keep dressing up whatever it is you mean to say in your fine language, it'll too late, 'cause soon I'll be old as well and I'll be the one looking to pass my longhouse onto my son and you father will be just a memory, looking down on your ancient son from somewhere over the other side of the rainbow.'

'When I leave Midgard', Olaf ignored his son's petulance and continued, 'to wherever I am destined to venture, my house will pass to your older brother, my eldest son Ragnarr. Thorkell and you, as my other sons will inherit an equal portion of my land, meaning what I've got will be split into three pieces. On your plots, you can build your own longhouses, only Ragnarr of the three of you, can sit back, whilst you two, chip away at wood and fashion something that'll keep you and your families warm. You'll have equal land all right, but I can't hide the problem. Decent land as you know is in too short a supply. What I've got here is just about enough for me and my family's needs. It makes our crops, fattens our horses, pigs and cattle at the moment, but if I had fewer fields, you know full well that we'd all be hungry! I was lucky all right. I was my father's only surviving child. You can't fault the old man, he tried for more of the likes of me, who wouldn't?' He stopped to laugh briefly, at his weak joke, before carrying on. 'But all of 'em died, each little perisher, either inside my mother's womb, or when they were just knee high or less. So I got the lot, so to speak. You boys aren't in that position, you will have a big problem in the years to come. You cannot grab more land further down the fjord as it has already been claimed, settled and farmed since before my father was a boy. Up there, they're already spoiling for a fight for more land. You know what trouble we've had with them in the past, just keeping them in their place, away from our land and our women! They only keep their distance because they think we'd given 'em a bloody nose or worse again. But they'll coming creeping back when it suits them and they'll try to surprise us.'

'But what about all the other half decent families up and down the fjord, is it the same for them?'

'I'm afraid it is my son. If you look at all the longhouses, they are for the most part spread out, because they sit on their own little patches of land. The ones that are closer together tend to belong to the bigger families. Their houses are a bit smaller and they have less land. It just doesn't add up at all. In time they'll all be fighting each other for a miserable scrap of land that will hardly grow two or three stalks of rye. I tell you it'll mean hardship, starvation and disease for many. It'll be the weak and the old like me that gets it first, you mark my words. It may also mean that the time has now come for some, not necessarily the weak to look for new land, there's a thought for you!'

Ignoring this remarkably profound statement from his father, Bodvarr as any child of his rather tender age would, thought of what would happen to him. He cared only for himself, not for the plight of others, whom he had the greatest of difficulty empathising with. The world was a huge place; so large as to be beyond his comprehension, but Bodvarr still very much believed himself to be at the very middle of it. The world for the moment seemed to him to turn about his being.

'But, but there is no point in having your own longhouse and being married, if you have no land for your beasts and crops.'

The dilemma had finally reached and then slammed into the boy's mind, like a wild boar charging at full speed into its chosen target.

'Yes, it is a problem and one which is not going to go away. I can give you no solace. The odal land allocation idea has always been and even today seems good in principal, as long as there is enough land to go around. As you know, you will have a third of my land and so will each of your brothers. But, it'll do you no good, because the three of you simply will not have enough. You should be grateful though, that you don't have more brothers or even a sister.' Olaf replied almost cheerily, before unexpectedly breaking into a laugh.

'I don't see why me having a sister, when I haven't, is anything to do with it,' came Bodvarr's sullen reply. 'And I don't see what you're laughing at.'

'Well the law has it,' Olaf seemed almost enthusiastic about the problem now and seemed to have forgotten the difficulties his sons would be left in, at some not so distant point in the future, 'that a sister of yours would be entitled to exactly half of what you would get, so think yourself lucky.' Olaf suddenly appeared worn out by all this thinking and instead, now furrow browed, focused on the floor and became silent.

The small-holding of Bodvarr's family or rather his father's, lay hidden in a remote and even by Norse standards, very isolated place, by the name of Odda. Being hemmed in at the head of a deep and extremely long and winding fjord in Hordaland, it was huddled between the icy water's edge and the imposing and sheer black mountains that seemed to reach down from the sky at a precipitous and dangerous incline. The fertility of the land was clearly poor and its barren loam produced barely enough plant matter to support the family's few miserable sheep, goats and bony cattle. All year round the unfortunate beasts just about managed to eke out a tardy existence on the scrubby, dry grass and few stubborn weeds that somehow grew, wind blown and stunted, between boulders and stones in this inhospitable and gods forsaken place. A good proportion of the reasonably flat land at the base of the mountains was also unfortunate enough to be covered in a thick layer of ever increasing and shifting stones, which appeared because of their vast quantity to be trying vainly to reach back and up towards the changing skies in the form of a rough scree, rendering it less than useless for grazing. Sheep and goats of the family thus wandered far and wide, often scrabbling amongst the barren rock detritus in vain, foraging for anything at all that could be eaten.

The cattle, being slightly less hardy were tended rather more closely by the farmers and allowed on the better pasture as well as being brought under cover during the winter months. This arrangement worked well, but it meant that all the folk of the small community spent long, hard hours at harvest time, working in the ribbon like *tún* or field that stretched far down the side of the snaking fjord, collecting the precious hay for the beasts. Pitch forks worked tirelessly, throwing the sickle harvested hay onto wagons dragged by unwilling oxen to barns or longhouses.

Bodvarr like all his contemporaries had learnt as a youngster that each animal needed some two tons of hay to keep it in condition through the winter. His father used to say to him, 'Feed the ground and the ground will feed you'. The trouble was that there never seemed to be enough to feed the ground with, unless of course you decided to feed it with numerous pebbles from shingle beaches or sharp rocks that leapt from the mountain sides, to form irregular piles, which the inhabitants referred to dismissively as *urð*.

And all the time, high above, the slumbering giant, the great ice sheet by the name of Folgefonn creaked, grumbled and groaned, whilst looking down disdainfully on the tiny, neglected and unloved Odda. The massive glacier had over many hundreds of years become a living and breathing legend in Odda and it figured prominently in many of the supernatural tales of trolls, elves, dwarfs and dragons, which were carefully told and retold to the young and open-mouthed children, keeping them spellbound on dark wintry evenings.

Folgefonn also lived in the minds of the adult population as well and permeated the sleep of all. It gave to Odda's folk uncomfortable dreams that made them twist and contort in their straw filled wooden or stone-lined cots. Visions of mystical, dangerous and grotesque creatures would suddenly and worryingly appear, dance in jerky fashion between negatively coloured hues and then veer disturbingly into a screaming nightmarish abyss of sudden black obsidian. These visions were punctuated with greatly contrasting yellow and orange ectopic shapes that contorted hideously to dance with bizarrely perfect zigzag patterns that floated disconcertingly in 'mind space', before darting hither and thither, before disappearing quickly and unexpectedly.

Hjalmlaug had been not dissimilar to the other children's mothers, who lived around the sides of the fjord at this time. She had, when Bodvarr was very small, filled her son's heads at sleep time, with dark tales of Folgefonn, the mysterious and powerful. Her favourite tale would begin thus.

'Þér mun ek þó segja, en þú munt hlyða. Stórr var hann sem risi...'

I shall now tell you and you shall listen. He was large as a giant the greatest troll there has ever been,' she began, 'he arrived a long time ago, on a particularly dark winter's night, when the snow had been falling heavily in the valley, where we now live. Would you believe it? Yes, in our own little valley. He had come from a terrible land far off to the east of Midgard, called *'Jötenheim'* and his name was,' and here she whispered quietly as though his name might conjure up some unspeakable demon, *'Jötnar'*. She paused momentarily before continuing, 'The great troll didn't come alone, for it brought with it, its two brothers, *Nýi* and *Niði*, because the dreadful quest it was to attempt, could not it believed be accomplished alone. Now, I can hear you ask, why had it come at all, with its two dreadful brothers to our tiny valley in the first place, hidden away in a forgotten corner of the world of men? Well the answer is as simple this. It came to kill the evil serpent which dwells to this very day beneath the ice blanket of Folgefonn. Yes, it is still there, there's no mistake. He, if you dare call him that, is still there.'

At this point the boy's eyes opened wide to betray his great anxiety, whilst his mother pretended to be locked in a seizure of terror herself. Hjaumlaug knew her son well and this ploy of course had the desired effect on Bodvarr, who was now desperate to hear the end of the story, but at the same time was almost too frightened to listen.

Beginning again, but more slowly now, she went on. 'The fire-breather had quietly left his lair of ice the previous winter and flown all the way to *Jötenheim*, for it had dreamed one night of a hidden hoard of magical golden weapons. Sure enough, the worm's dream was true, for dragons it is said always dream the truth and this particular dream surely guided it well. The beast found what it sought deep within *Jötnar's* stone hall. A helm of gold, a magical golden spear and a great sword with a jewel encrusted golden handle, which it was said could not be defeated in battle. The great worm carefully carried off these trophies in his poisonous jaws, back to our valley without challenge of any description.

The shrill and deafening cry let out by *Jötnar* when he returned to find his precious things missing sent splintering rock flying into the air and caused gaping cracks to open in the ground's surface. It is said that the land ran with liquid red rock and the air was full of burning ash, sulphur and choking smoke, but remember little one,' she hesitated and let her eyes roll, 'it is only a tale.'

'Well', she appeared now to suddenly have regained her composure and the tale leapt from her lips once more, '*Jotnar* learnt of the dragon's visit from other giants and more importantly which direction the dragon had flown off in. The trolls sailed many a day in a huge boat to arrive at our shores. It is said that they saw the great and terrifying Midgard serpent from afar; the one *Þorr* once caught using an anchor as hook and an ox head for bait, but that belongs in another tale. Anyway, they wasted no time at all in finding our precious valley and with nothing but their bare hands they dug into the side of the mountain for nine whole days and nights, before breaking through and reaching an immense hall, the roof of which was made of living and moving ice! There were fantastic arches of transparent blue ice, as smooth and shiny as that hammer of iron you are now clasping. You can still see the damage the trolls did to our mountain, to this day. When dawn breaks, if you dare, go and look! You'll see huge piles of rock all spilled down the side of the mountain, all those great boulders, some the size of five longhouses put together and that jagged lip at the top, high up there. That's exactly where they toiled and dug into the mountain's heart, so they say.'

As story tellers go, Hjalmlaug was good; never failing to captivate and frighten. She paused now, to allow her elaborate descriptions mix with the reality of Odda's mountains, fields and houses which dwelled in her son's mind. To the boy, it all made complete sense, he could not find fault with a single word he had heard. Bodvarr didn't doubt his mother's story in any way; he lived within its shifting landscape and he believed it and what is more he breathed it. His mother paused as if threatening to say no more, deliberately building upon the tension she had so carefully strived to create. Then just as her wide eyed son was about to protest, she began again. '*Jötnar*, *Nýi* and *Niði* went deep into the serpent's ice lair and without even the most basic plan of any description confronted him, just like that!' As a hushed aside she added, 'As you can see, trolls are not amongst the cleverest of beasts.' Then she began again once more. 'They were so foolish, for they thought their strength would prevail over the enormous and wicked beast. *Jötnar* at first lunged to grab the great dragon by his tail and his brothers unthinkingly and blindly followed him. The serpent had cleverly guessed what they would do, because as with most creatures of his sort, he could see straight into their simple minds. He moved his vast tail in a huge sweeping circle and at the same time gently turned his body, in order that he kept his tail moving and moving.

Whilst the stupid trolls ran to catch up, the worm smiled briefly to show his sharp and yellowed teeth, before breathing his rank and deadly poison over them; a wall of instant death it was, nothing less. *Jötnar* was hurt, but not slain, but the brothers *Nýi* and *Niði* who were closer to the worm were done for. As they crashed to the hard stone floor, the beast in an act of celebration exploded a huge fireball from its golden jaws and the two unfortunate trolls were blasted with such a force out through the side of the mountain. You will find this hard to believe, but we can still see them today, but they are not together and will never be so again, for they landed if in fact they did so, far, very far apart. When the moon is new, there, up in the night sky is *Nýi* and when it is waned and nearly gone, there is *Niði*. Some say when the winter frosts abound and the sky is at its clearest, the magic of the dragon's breath can still be seen around whichever of the brothers happens to be riding in the sky. If you look carefully, you can see a faint ring encircling the hapless brother, it is said it is the dragon's breath. No matter, I digress. The blast as they flew into the sky, made fire rain down on our valley, followed by rivers of liquid rock, which in turn were followed by torrents from of dirty icy water from a huge mountain lake. It nearly did for little Odda. The trees on the lower slopes were at first battered by rocks, then singed by the heat of the angry liquid rock and finally almost swept away by the power of the flood unleashed from the top of the mountain.

Jötnar saw his brothers die and he became most terribly afraid. He immediately stopped chasing the serpent's tail realising that he would soon be done for if he did not. Instead, he changed his strategy and began to try to argue with the beast. In his deep and sonorous voice he began thus, "Oh, greatest and mightiest of worms, killer of my poor brothers and now true owner of my three treasures, I implore you, I beseech you. You have the jewel encrusted golden helm, you have *Geirr* the greatest of spears and you have the powerful sword of judgement. I beg you, greatest worm of all worms; can I not have back just one of my three treasures?"

The serpent was, no I should say is, a crafty beast, make no mistake. He paused for some considerable time pretending to think, before deciding with a wicked grin on his scaly face that he could be lenient after all, even if it went against his better nature. He allowed, after much deliberation and a great deal of hissing, the troll to have back his great golden helm. There was a drawback though, as the helm itself of course had become terribly enchanted, for the worm had used his terrible magical powers and cast a dark and unspeakable spell on it. Of course, the dragon, like all dragons of his type loved his gold much too much and the unbearable thought of someone stealing it away from him and using it, pained him so grievously that he simply could not entertain the merest or slightest notion of it. However, in spite of his misgivings, he felt he could give up the helm, for he knew it would not really be going anywhere. "Take the helm", the worm whispered with the tiniest of smiles forming at the corner of his hideous mouth.'

The mother briefly paused once more before continuing with her tale. 'When the great troll *Jötnar* pulled the golden helm on, he realised at once he had been tricked. The whole helm became part of his living flesh and of course then he was not able to remove it. Naturally he tried to of course, at first violently attempting to pull it off, then ripping at his own being, until trickles of golden blood oozed from terrible self-inflicted wounds. These dropped from his body as orbs of pure and heavy gold to bounce briefly on the cold stone floor of the cavern. They looked like pebbles bathed in the rays of light from a setting midsummer's sun. The dragon smiled with satisfied malevolence as it saw the unexpected gift of gold from its prisoner. If the troll had dared to think about leaving the great hall, the serpent had now persuaded him otherwise. The dragon whispered to him, that if he did so, then the helm would slowly turn his whole being into pure gold as well, thereby killing him in a most agonising way. The worm then assured him that he was welcome to attempt to escape or he could stay there forever, but then if he chose the latter option, he would have to become a mere servant; a servant to the whims and desires of the great breather of fire.'

The story was nearly finished now and the teller was making sure the listener was satisfied with all the minor details. 'To this day, the evil dragon and the wicked troll are up there still, locked in the great ice hall, with nothing to live for but their hatred of each other. The troll continues to argue with the great beast, they say, but he is wasting his breath, for the worm is too strong and too clever for him. You can hear their arguments, even down here. The rumblings beneath the Folgefonn are loud enough for those who truly listen with their ears and their minds. If you dare to climb onto the ice however, high up there, some say you can see the two of them snarling at each other and crashing about in fits of rage. They will not spot you of course, because they are too concerned with their hatred of each other. Just below the surface, there they are, fighting away to this very day.'

Bodvarr was tired, but he was now quite awake. In Odda, sleep did not come easily to most children at night. The question each and every writhing and sweating body was posing in the darkness that enveloped everything was, 'Where does the dream finish and where does the world truly begin?'

Mystical tales of both *Huginn* and *Muninn*, the ravens of *Óðinn* not only kept the young inside at night time, but were also quite enough to scare witless all decent folk of whom there were still a good number. All but the least superstitious took heed. Each night, whole families would huddle round fires in their longhouses, play games, tell stories and try to avoid sleep until it crept upon them and bore them away as it invariably did.

Hjalmlaug, Bodvarr's mother had sternly instructed her son, when he was no more than five years old that the king of the gods, *Óðinn* was all seeing. One day she had whispered to him darkly.

'Hann hefir hrafna, er heita Huginn ok Muninn, ok fljúga þeir hrafnar um heimana. Þat, er hrafnarnir sjá, sér ok Óðinn.'...

'He has ravens called *Huginn* and *Muninn*, and those ravens fly around the world. That which the ravens see, *Óðinn* also sees. *Óðinn* also has something else.' At this point her voice lowered to a level whereby the boy could only just hear her. '*Óðinn* gave up one of his eyes to drink from the giant, Mimir's spring of wisdom. Afterwards, he cut off *Mimir's* head which he keeps in a sack to this very day. He has preserved the head with special magical herbs and *galðr*, because my son, *Óðinn* has knowledge of the ways of *seiðr*. The greatest of our gods is not proud of this, because he knows *seiðr*;

the understanding of magic is the domain of women.'

The poor boy had been made to grow up in a mysterious world in the belief that he was always being watched or more accurately, spied upon and worse still judged. He must have seen at least ten or eleven summers before he finally became numb to the ever present *Óðinn*, god of war, death, poetry and love. At first, he would somewhat cautiously say to his friends in mock bravado, 'If he can see me, then he can strike me down, but he won't.' Later, he would call on *Óðinn* directly and challenge him, 'Can you hear me? Can you see me? Can you thrust your spear, the great spear *Gungnir* through me? Are you still hiding from me, you the great one, *hinn almáttki áss?* (the most powerful god?)

I am here. I am in no *vé*, this in no holy place. So strike me down, in the name of *Ragnarök* itself strike me down now, I command you!'

Some of his friends would run away from him and rush to their parents for solace, when he shouted such frightening things, afraid they may become infected by the spirit that drove the big boy to say such terribly blasphemous words. As they ran off, Bodvarr would jeer and threaten them all in as many different ways he could think of, with many of the other lesser gods and or their terrible weaponry or with dreadful creatures armed with ripping teeth and claws.

In Odda, such things as the unexplained crack of a twig, the eerie far off cry of a wolf or wild dog, the clack of falling stones or rocks from high above were all ascribed to either *landvættir* (land spirits), *Álfar* (elves), the Lord of the Dead, *Hel of Niflheim*, or the mischievous *Loki*, who was capable as all Norse men, women and children knew of anything. Whenever sheep or goats failed to return from their pastures, the unspoken assumption was that either of these two dangerous gods had to be to blame. Tiny iron hammers, amulets of every conceivable shape and design hung from strips of leather cord or twine to encircle the necks of virtually every adult and child. In time, they were, over many years of ownership slowly rubbed smooth by their wearers for the sake of goodwill, luck or more often than not just to be left in peace, until they shone like burnished silver. The distorted reflections given out by the metal's shiny surface, not only frightened away the evil spirits that infested the valley, but also reminded the wearer of the colossal power of *Þórr's* hammer, *Mjollnir*.

Naturally, all children were taught to fear the great god *Loki* for his darker side, but adults feared him also, for his more mystical abilities. He as all knew could change his shape if it so pleased him, to become any wild beast he wished or alternatively, he could if he so desired transform himself into a woman, to trick men. Bodvarr like all his contemporaries was wary of all women he had not seen before and of beasts both wild and domesticated for this reason. Dogs were an especial worry, particularly ones that jumped up at or seemed to take an excessive interest in him; these he treated with great apprehension, because he considered that they might be *fylgjur* (guardian spirits or animals) in league with *Loki*, or could even be the great trickster *Loki* himself, in just one of many his changed shapes.

ℴ   ℴ   ℴ

Bodvarr's new wife had always been extremely superstitious and was particularly frightened and worried by spirits of any kind and of course by all of the gods, especially the mysterious, mischievous and dangerous ones. She also particularly feared *Loki* and was forever praying to and making votive offerings to him and to spirits of all kinds to help her though each and every nerve twitching moment that built one upon the other, to fill her frantic and frenetic unplanned days. There was not a single bush or tree near to the family homestead that wasn't festooned with little scraps of differently coloured wool or linen. In fact, when the girl had first come to the utterly wretched place, which was to become her home, she had momentarily fallen to and muddied her knees, as though struck down by the overbearing malevolence that she seemed to think permeated from the rocky and infertile ground itself. Jumping to her feet in a rapid single movement, she screamed, *"Hvat gøra slíkir landvættir hér?"* ('What are such land spirits doing here?') Then the poor girl began to whirl around, shouting and screeching at nothing but the thin air. Why she asked herself, were 'they' screaming at her? Why did 'they' tease her so, and berate her, a helpless bride. Was this forsaken wilderness she had come to cursed? Her husband's family had somehow survived here for generations, were they cursed as well?

'What has father and mother made me do?' she for once screamed loudly and clearly, but no one was listening. Why couldn't she have lived in the great Kaupang or even in the fashionable Birka, the places her father, the great Rorik Grímsson, was forever disappearing to and returning from, with fantastic stories of travel and wealth, she thought.

The girl knew her father wielded power. She brought him to mind and conjured an accurate picture of him in her head; there he stood, a tall man with long and dark hair. His small tidy, well-trimmed beard embodied his personality; he was of a slightly nervous disposition and above all felt most comfortable when everything was just as he liked it to be. His clothes she remembered were always carefully buttoned up or tied together, they were always clean and unlike most other people's they were all, for the most part fairly new, showing his considerable wealth. Everything about his appearance indicated a man of adequate means and high status. Beneath his kirtle or over tunic, he wore a bleached white linen under tunic. This hung well down and over his baggy woollen trousers to almost hide a rather ostentatious golden brooch like buckle on his broad plain belt. The girl remembered this adornment as if were right there in front of her; the shining bright metal contrasting strongly with the dark tanned leather it sat before. Few people she mused could have wished to emulate such an open display of wealth, which was of course further emphasised by the tight and delicate chevron twill which constituted the almost decadent weave of his kirtle.

His daughter was still able to recall the times when he used to return all smiling, with expensive presents for her poor mother Ótama and for herself and for all of her sisters of course. She could see them all now, in her mind's eye they were so clear that she actually reached out to touch them; delicate silver arm rings, amulets and chunky pendants cleverly fashioned out of richly coloured honeyed amber. These times had passed all too quickly for the young girl, as all good times inevitably seem to. Now, she was left to look back and rue these golden times that to her warped perception strangely constituted most of her childhood. She daydreamed and brought to mind only the happier times, blanking out so many others that would have brought with them upset. Of course whilst she was growing up, each day had seemed to bring with it a host of different jumbled and confusing events; some of which had been mundane, some repetitive, some sad, some happy, but above all many that were desperately frightening. She had grown, some uncharitable folk had whispered, 'been dragged unwillingly' to womanhood in a hard and unforgiving world, a world where she had severe difficulty comprehending not only who she was, but also her own tiny place within it. Some of the less than charitable folk had hinted that her insecurity was deep rooted and that it came from her overbearing father, others blamed her mother, but no one would ever dare to say openly why they thought this.

ℬ   ℬ   ℬ

In spite of all the apprehension on the parts of both the prospective bride and groom and their respective families, the marriage of Olaf's son to Rorik's daughter took place in the early spring. It certainly wasn't a love match, but was instead a solid business arrangement between two families of quite different standing that were now being brought together by a bond of blood.

'Well my old friend, the time for our children to join us or rather our families together has finally come.' Rorik said this in a quiet voice to Olaf, whose reply although quick, was even more softly spoken, almost sullen in its tone.

'It's a time of great joy for me and for the boy of course.'

'Taktu viþ horni ok drekki.' (Take the horn and drink) 'Then, let us drink, you and I, to the union that will join our great families and hope that afterwards, very soon afterwards, we will all grow the richer and have time to enjoy our coin before we finally leave Midgard.' Rorik's elaborate rejoinder came with even less conviction than Olaf's brief statement and was delivered whilst his eyes moved rapidly about whilst looking downwards. He spoke in a most unconvincing monotone.

'I raise this, my special drinking horn and ask you to raise yours, to drink to all of our children, especially these two! Now, let us drink to their children and their children's children!' With that, Rorik raised his beautifully decorated, silver rimmed drinking horn and momentarily paused to admire the craftsmanship that had gone into its creation. Small silver stags chased each other, encircling the horn, just below the golden rim. Below them still, other less clearly discernable but decidedly more abstract and menacing beasts lurked within an undergrowth of delicate interlocked, entwined silver trellis work that contrasted vividly with the dark of the horn behind it. Enthused by the beauty of the vessel, he downed in one great gulp a good quantity of a light coloured beer. This fairly weak brew had been specially commissioned by Rorik for the wedding celebration. As an after thought, he refilled his horn once more from a large brown porcelain jug and raised it with considerably more spirit and enthusiasm, 'And I now I drink to Heiðr, for her ale is surely the finest in all of the land!'

Indeed, the liquor was more than generally approved of by the brewer's nearby residents; it was all agreed of the highest quality. Delicately flavoured with young juniper twigs, it refreshed and sated thirst at the same time. The brewer was well known in Odda for her particular craft; the production of various wonderful brews for every conceivable occasion. Heiðr was indeed considered a marvel. She lived in a large immaculately clean longhouse with her slightly older husband and their great brood of children. Somehow she had managed to raise and educate her surviving children of whom there were seven, make rye bread, spin and weave wool, fashion clothes and keep the nearby families happy with both weak and heady brews to commemorate various festivals and happenings that punctuated each and every year. This she had done, as her mother before her, without fail for as long as the younger folk could remember. Heiðr had seen just twenty six summers, although her many children, the biting cold winters and the never ending hard work that constantly blighted her life meant that she had the appearance and disposition of someone far older. She shuffled about slowly in her nearly worn out leather boots on her permanently aching and arthritic feet. Her knee and hip joints also caused her to grumble and in times when rain was imminent made her curse. Also, her permanently bent fingers bore testimony either to the fact that her bones were possibly diseased or that she had been involved in a multitude of hard repetitive manual tasks over a great many years. These were now beginning to take a heavy toll, on her small frame. The poor woman could easily have been mistaken for fifty summers and frequently was, although she was always cheery and seemed to possess boundless energy. She chuckled to herself, exposing a full set of well worn and flattened teeth, being seemingly impervious to other hurtful comments, '*Tuttugu ok sex.*' (twenty-six) 'That is what I am! You can't change it, only the gods can do that and they do so, each year,' she laughed. 'If I am lucky enough to see next year, you will have more beer for your bellies and I will have another, another year not beer, that is.' She began again, '*Tuttugu* ok sex ok einn (twenty-six and one), that makes *Tuttugu* ok sjau!' (twenty seven) She chuckled knowingly to herself, before disappearing into her rather smoky longhouse that rather invitingly smelled strongly of a mash of malted barley and possibly juniper berries, or alecost or alehoof.

Each year the brews she produced had somehow become smoother and more refined as though she had absorbed extra pieces of information each time she brewed and used these tips to improve her beer to good effect. The art of brewing and baking was in her blood and she had no match in her craft in Odda and she clearly knew it. She enjoyed the attention and compliments and also the status her art bestowed upon her and her man. Ketilbjörn, her husband was a jovial, corpulent, red faced man being some seven or eight years older than she was. He was particularly keen on his food and victuals and forever sang his wife's praises, regularly raising his drinking bowl rather more often than was good for him, to her health.

ℬ   ℬ   ℬ

At the time of Bodvarr and his woman's wedding, rumours had begun to circulate in little Odda and these had it, that Rorik's life had been saved many years before by none other than Olaf himself. He had purportedly intervened in a desperate fight that Rorik had been having with a fellow merchant in Birka. This unfortunate trader had been more or less ruined by an agreement over a large stash of silver of extremely dubious quality that had been struck earlier in that fateful day with the girl's father.

'*Ek vil hann daudan!*' (I want him dead!) The words of the dealer had been all too clear.

The impoverished merchant's henchmen, still clearly in his employ were attacking Rorik with a great deal of uncalled for enthusiasm and were seemingly just beginning to get the better of him, when Olaf, so the tale went had made his timely and crucial intervention, killing three or was it four assailants with his axe and afterwards taking the wounded, bleeding and seriously incapacitated Rorik to the longhouse where he had been staying, to heal. The ruined dealer had mysteriously disappeared after the fight and in spite of a careful search being made was not to be found. Olaf thought the man a worm. He spat defiantly and addressing the small group of people who had emerged from their longhouses to see what all the commotion was about, simply said, '*Ek kalla han ragan!*' (I call him cowardly). The tale had, as happens to all good tales, grown in the telling and the number of attackers was rising steadily by the day, until Olaf took on the mantle of a god come down to *Midgard*. He could do no wrong in the eyes of the village folk and as such a famous fighter he had the attentions of not only the small, but also the not quite so small children who followed him about relentlessly. From a little way off, he resembled a giant of a leader amongst lesser folk. At first, the fuss he received amused him, but very soon all the attention began to irritate and he would snarl at his motley entourage, to discourage them.

A full ten years had passed since this now legendary fight and over that time Olaf had enjoyed many a free horn of ale, whilst enlightening and in the same instant embroidering the story, but the real debt had never been met, at least not yet. A debt to a Norse man, especially from a man of high birth is something that must be met, particularly when it is one that involves the saving of a *jarl's* life; then it lasts, until the debtor leaves *Midgard* for beyond. Giving his eldest daughter to Bodvarr was one of Rorik's ways of paying back a part of what he owed Olaf before he himself went, if he was lucky, to the hall of fallen heroes; the hall of *Valhöll*. Since he had been a young man Rorik had been racked with worry that he may end up in one of *Asgard's* other great halls and not in the hall of fallen heroes. He had mused long and hard to himself which would be the best or worst other options. His insecurity had often led to him playing mind games with himself; counting quietly to himself as he waited for a crow to take flight, a dog to bark or a squirrel to run up a tree. Each time he would present himself with a different scenario. If he reached *tíu*, then he might have promised himself he would go to *Folkvang*, the Hall of *Freyja*. On another occasion, it might have been *Himinbiorg*, the Hall of *Heimdall*, which lay near to the Rainbow Bridge of *Bifrost*, or *Njord's* Hall, *Nóatún* for Norse folk who fell by or in the sea. '*Einn, tveir, prír, fjórir, fimm, sex, sjau, átta, níu*', he would count, then he might pause briefly, to see if he could cheat his promise. If the crow had refused to take off, or the dog had remained silent or the squirrel had refused to climb, before he had finished his count he would extend his pause and then with a fleeting resentment, he would utter, '*tíu*', before sighing and imagining himself permanently left in a vast and beautiful hall, but still a hall he simply did not want to be in. His fascination with numbers had permeated most aspects of his comparatively speaking well-ordered life.

Even before he had met his prospective bride, Bodvarr had been surprisingly reluctant, almost hostile to the idea of accepting Rorik's daughter. He had however more than welcomed the *heimangerð* offered to him and it was this dowry coupled with his father's stern instruction that had finally won him over, even if it had not completely placated him. He duly received his payment in the form of a good number of small irregular shaped gold bars, one particularly beautiful golden penannular brooch and finally two ingeniously crafted matching silver arm-rings in the shape of inter-woven serpents. Having received these articles from his father-in-law, he looked him in the eye and as was the custom spat on his own hand before offering it, not just in friendship, but now as a son. His father-in-law followed the younger man's lead before shaking the outstretched hand of Bodvarr. All matters had thus soon been satisfactorily concluded and everything had seen to be done in the correct way.

Later, within their respective longhouses, members of both families of course pretended to have been the more successful of the benefactors, but in truth, most either cared very little about this match or thought their family had not done particularly well. Now however, the proceedings within Olaf's longhouse had been slightly shaken up by an old man, who sat well out of the light, merging with the shadows that played against the longhouses' walls. Hvíthöfuð was truly old, thin and wizened. After a protracted illness that had robbed him of much of what remained of his energy a number of summers before, he had ceased to speak; not a single word had he spoken for many a year. Naturally, his family, all of them so much younger, now believed him to be completely mute. The old man liked nothing more than to pass his time listening to others engaging in their conversations, whilst he would sit in complete silence and just nod his head slightly and smile. Hvíthöfuð also happened to be Bodvarr's paternal grandfather and to most local folk it was very surprising that he still lived.

The general lack of interest from all who knew the newly wed couple, concerning the match, was summed up quite simply and accurately by several clearly spoken blasphemous words that crossed the longhouse's smoky interior, *'Kuþ hialbi ãn hãns!'* (God help his spirit). The speaker was to the amazement of all present Hvíthöfuð. He said no more, for no more words were necessary. A few folk, scaremongers possibly, said Hvíthöfuð's words were words of warning from the god *Hel* herself, but most just spat defiantly on the straw covered floor, whilst rubbing tiny iron hammers that dangled about their necks. The old man in his dotage had caused no harm, other than stir up fears of both *haugbui* and *aptrgangr.* Some believed him already dead; he was surely far too old for a man of Midgard, others still considered his silence as proof that his mind had already left and a few pointed at him darkly and whispered, 'there walks the after-goer, escaped from his mound.' Fortunately for the old man, he was lucky enough to have a strong family around him to protect him and because of this he lived on for a good many more summers in the little town of Odda without harm. He had no cause ever to speak again though. When, as was the custom, he was finally pulled feet first through a newly created hole in the side of the longhouse, the old man was at last put to rest. The crude aperture was carefully restored and all within then felt safe, for the departed, as all knew would only attempt to re-enter the house they had lived in, by the entrance from which they had departed.

ဢ   ဢ   ဢ

The wedding party took place at one of his new wife's family's smaller longhouses in distant Ringerike and had been a rich celebration; one which had inevitably underlined the gap between the two families' social standing and their inherent wealth. Several days before the wedding, Bodvarr and his family and friends had taken a mountain pass to get to Ringerike, which lay south east of both Odda and Aga. There had been plenty of food and drink for all of the guests and this in itself had to a great extent broken down many of the barriers or hidden concerns the guests possessed concerning the status of the bride and groom and their considerably disproportionate means, or to put it more bluntly the gold or land they owned. The provender and victuals supplied to the banquet had been no mean achievement, because there must have been at least sixty hungry and thirsty folk to provide for after the short and somewhat anti-climatic marriage ceremony. Time and time again people raised their drinking bowls or horns and shouted, *'Taktu viþ horni ok drekk!'* (Take the horn and drink!)

In a short space of time; the sun had barely moved its position in the sky and it was all over. Most of those attending the celebration had become quite drunk on Heiðr's ale which had been specially brought all the way to Ringerike for the celebration. Both families had managed albeit unwittingly to provide several relatives who, with some of the other guests had become rather more than a little intoxicated. Pockets of conversation came and went like gusts and squalls of wind and rain.

'I've always liked dogs me, I have!' One drunkard lurched disconcertingly as he spoke his, what he considered to be, well considered words.

'So you should, you old beggar, 'cos you married one!' This unexpected rejoinder, intended no doubt to ridicule, had quite the opposite effect on the canine friend that a logical mind might have expected. Standing almost still and for some strange reason examining a bush with the greatest of interest, he swayed.

'Yes, that's right I did!' He coughed loudly, before rather disconcertingly laughing almost dog-like at his own weak joke, which somehow betrayed to his fellow drinkers, if they had bothered to listen, which naturally they weren't, a glimpse of a lonely and rather pathetic man who happened to be hiding behind a thick and almost impenetrable mantle of drunkenness.

'You can't like 'em that much, if you've only got the one bitch!' This uncalled for and considerably more barbed attack still failed to draw the dog lover.

'One's enough for me or any man, that's for sure! Some men have two, but well...' He had lost interest by now and turned his back, looking for a place to urinate.

'Pissing dog lover!' The final insult washed over him, but unlike a wave of any substance, it instead left him untouched and simply drifted off into the night with no effect. It seemed that either his ears were not listening or that his drunken mind was so pre-occupied with some other utter nonsense that he failed to decipher the taunting and provocative slur. He staggered a few paces before remembering something that momentarily drew him back. His eyes had indeed returned to the bush that had preoccupied him so, moments earlier. The foliage had to his addled brain magically taken on the shape of various faces to form an intriguing tessellated pattern of grins and smiles.

'Well, will you look at that? I said will you look at....' His voice tailed off once more and when he began again, he instantly stopped, for he had already forgotten what had impressed him so much just a short time before.

Most of the inebriates engaged in conversations that had very little meaning. They concluded their talking and in but a little time staggered off into the darkness of that long ago *annar mánuðr* evening. What they did in the darkness, we will never know and thank the all of the gods for that. Apart from what you would imagine; cursing as they fell over or catching themselves on prickly bushes or pissing into the wind so that their woollen trousers became soaked or simply vomiting their last draught of beer and food violently onto the floor, before keeling over to lie flat on their backs and fall into a fitful sleep. By either jabbering incomprehensively in a comatose state or snoring long and loud, they passed the long and cold hours of darkness on the straw covered floor of one of the longhouses given over to guests.

ℰ   ℰ   ℰ

It had been a mild spring, Ostara had come and gone, the days were noticeably becoming longer and this month in particular had been more than kind to the communities of Hordaland and Rogaland. The chickens had been laying well, lambs were being born aplenty and the month was as a result being referred to by young and old alike, by two of its other more appropriate other names. Some called it *Eggtið,* or 'Egg-time,' whilst others preferred *Stekkið,* or 'Lambfold-time,' whatever it was called; it was a time of plenty.

ℰ   ℰ   ℰ

Bodvarr Olafsson lay in a dark longhouse; blood was seeping slowly, but unendingly from a number of terrible gaping wounds that had ruptured his body. 'Swine, filthy bastard swine!' he muttered, trying desperately to shout out, but only managing a hoarse rattle throated whisper.

In that exact terrible moment, he had managed for some inexplicable reason to lucidly cast his mind back through many years, to that fateful night when his first child and only child had been born. He simultaneously also remembered with little more than a tinge of embarrassment, the time he had taken his virgin bride to the straw filled bed of his father's longhouse on that, the evening of his wedding day. Even as a young man, a youth of not that many years, who had been brought up to sagely respect all of the Old Norse ways of life, he had considered it an intrusion, a strange and wholly unwelcome tradition that obliged him by law to take witnesses into what passed as the bridal bedroom; the partitioned off end to the longhouse. The curtain if it could be called that which acted as a barrier which separated the sleeping area from the rest of the longhouse was in fact part of an old *knarr* sail. The edge of the curtain was skilfully hemmed with a thin rope to stop it fraying; something Bodvarr knew to be called a *rálik*. Most of what was left of it was of a dull pink colour, with what somewhat incongruously appeared to be a decorative and intricate flowery pattern on its surface, but that was in fact the pattern created by the ravages of a creeping black fungus. The musty smell only occasionally managed to permeate the atmosphere and become perceptible when the fire or fires finally died and the accompanying smoke that tended to fill the nostrils and redden the eyes had slowly dissipated.

He could clearly picture them in his mind's eye; it was as though the moment still lived. Each one of them stood there with his own peculiar and individual stance, each one fidgeting, each one rocking on his feet and each doing what he seemed to think best. The older men appeared to be whistling, but whistling in such a way as to produce no sound, whilst simultaneously looking upwards towards the heavens as if for divine guidance. It was as if they somehow expected to see *Óðinn's* great steed *Sleipnir* crash through the very wooden beams and trusses that supported the heavy turf covered roof. In contrast, the younger men appeared to be much more interested in the proceedings. They stared wide-eyed, with their large black pupils fully dilated, enabling them to feast on the visual goings on like hungry birds gorging on over ripe and juicy late summer berries.

His father-in-law, two brothers-in-law the smaller of whom stood disconcertingly with his mouth half open dribbling saliva onto his chin and then onwards to the earthen floor, two of his father's best friends and Thorkell, his younger brother; all of them had stood there. They shuffled from one foot to the other, not really wanting to be there, in that small and stuffy room, whilst he, the groom clumsily pawed at his bride and finally, thank *Þórr* and the other gods, had rather quickly completed his part in the pact of wedlock.

'Get on with it then. Give her, a good seeing to! Will yer? I've got similar business to be getting on with, if yer get me drift', interrupted one of the older men with a sly smile spreading across his leathery ruddy complexion. Sveina, one of Olaf's greatest friends had a dry, rapier sense of humour and he apparently quite enjoyed seeing the youngster's acute embarrassment. He meant no real harm though and in spite of some of his more eccentric behaviours was still highly regarded in his home village. In contrast, the dribbler's older brother, Ásmóðr had made the mistake to offer to take Bodvarr's place and this had made a difficult situation almost unbearable.

'Piss off you shit!' The groom's riposte came immediately and carried the kind of urgency which indicated that some violence was possibly being stored up for a later time. His father-in-law nodded approvingly, almost enthusiastically, 'I think I'll get to like him, he knows a shit when he sees one!' Sveina laughed, for he was about to utter something very similar. It seemed as though all the older men had come to the same conclusion and were now in agreement over Ásmóðr's character.

Several weeks had elapsed, before a further but far more serious indiscretion on this young man's part had proved to be just one too many. *Muninn* it seemed did see and remember everything and *Þórr* with his great hammer to hand, *Mjollnir,* was always listening. Bodvarr wasn't to know it, but Ásmóðr, the oaf of a young man who had made the lewd suggestion, now lay in the cold damp and unforgiving ground in a remote unmarked woodland grave. Or at least what remained of his body did so. His supposed final resting place had been hastily and rather badly dug, possibly deliberately so. Far too little earth had been deposited over the deceased's body; as a grave it was nowhere near adequate. Consequently, the decomposing corpse had became rapidly dismembered and carried off in a number of directions by wolves and then what was left of it was further dispersed by other scavenging and hungry animals of which there were always many.

Ásmóðr had not stood any kind of a reasonable chance in single combat with such a fighter. His friends found out later the man was not just a hardened warrior, but as some in the village had whispered quietly, 'a berserker'. This mysterious man, so it was quietly said, picked and ate dangerous mushrooms, the ones that children are taught to avoid and ones which give men dangerous insights and stark visions usually only seen by the gods themselves. Periodically, he was to be seen moving through the woodland, all by himself, before apparently disappearing into thin air. He would re-emerge moments later at a spot which was seemingly impossible to reach without being spotted. All the village children feared him greatly and consequently avoided him. They kept well away and behind his back rather imaginatively named him the 'Shield-biter.' They had no idea that their nickname for him was very nearly his actual name, which happened to be, '*Skjaldbjörn*', meaning 'Shield-berserker'. No one insulted Skjaldbjörn and lived.

৯০   ৯০   ৯০

Hailing from the prosperous merchant town of Kaupang in southern Norway, the girl's father, Rorik, was a ruling *jarl* and wealthy merchant, with a natural quickness of mind to trade anything that came his way. Almost always, a healthy profit was made by the deals of Rorik. He was an imposing, but likeable man, who had used his money and his brain to good effect, subsequently amassing a considerable fortune. He was supported by a large number of local people, who looked to him for security and more importantly work. As the *jarl*, he was the law and had great sway over the lives of those in his care, but unlike many others in his position, he did not abuse his power too often and was on the whole very fair in all of his dealings with the *Þræll* and their disputes. He was not only liked by the populace, but also highly respected. Using some of his not inconsiderable wealth, he had bought three *knarr* in a good condition and had commissioned the best craft's people in the locality to build three more to similar specifications.

Rorik had now given his eldest daughter away; the first of the five girls he had fathered. In truth, he was beginning to feel rather pleased with himself, because he had idly speculated that his daughter might have cost him a lot more than she actually had. He glanced at Bodvarr, a mere *karl*, with a slight feeling of unease and just the merest pang of regret; having given his first daughter so little with which to start her married life. However, he managed to balance these mildly negative feelings with the slightly brighter consideration which also happened to impart to him an excuse that allowed him to feel that it might just make the couple fight for their place in life. Þórr only knows how she would support him though, he mused, the girl really wasn't quite right in the head.

Rorik was a hard and somewhat unforgiving man with the demeanour of one who had mostly worked for what was his and this ingrained ethic for survival forced his mind to come to the possibly ill conceived conclusion that they could do so as well. After all, he thought scratching his greasy, lice-ridden beard he still had four other daughters still to pay off. Changing his mind, in the blink of an eye he said to himself, 'No we'll make that two.' Musing now on the details he further considered, 'Two only'll marry in the next few years for I'll have my ships and they don't come cheap. The other two can look after me and the longhouse, whilst saving me a pretty pile of coin.' For a moment Rorik's steely eyes glazed as he remembered his young wife Ótama, the woman who had brought all his daughters, but no sons into the world of Midgard. The poor woman had become quite mad after the birth of their fifth child. She had been in labour for nearly two days; it had been just too much for her. She had gone missing no more than half a day after the child's arrival. The disappearance had been blamed on the spirits of the land, *Loki*, the gods and in fact anything that could possibly had the slightest bearing on the poor woman. Several weeks later she had been found dead; a drowned bloated white corpse in the pure crystal waters of the fjord. Her distorted and much changed body could only be identified by the elaborate arm ring she had been wearing. It now cut into the blue pock marked skin of her upper arm, in the way a ligature bites deep to prevent loss of blood from a wound. Ótama's place had never been taken by another woman, leaving Rorik to live alone, but for his daughters. Two elderly sisters of his had appeared at his longhouse quite frequently in the years immediately after the death of Ótama, but these visits tailed off as it became apparent that Rorik wanted to be left alone to cope. His girls had duly taken over all the domestic chores between them as they became older and more able to carry them out.

At least he's too young to have run up gaming debts and he's no bondsman thought Rorik, returning to the immediate situation. He's free to make a half decent life for himself and he could take any number of *þræll* (common folk) to work for him or make money by selling them. The girl's flights of fancy did worry him though and her fanaticism to the gods was somehow too extreme, it would try the patience of the best of men. She carried out her mundane little life in the land of men; almost it seemed with resentment, whilst spending all of her time praying, thinking and more importantly worrying about the gods and what they might do to her. Bodvarr, poor Bodvarr, Rorik thought, would have his hands and head full with all the mind-numbing rituals his idiosyncratic daughter insisted on sticking to.

ᛋᛟ   ᛋᛟ   ᛋᛟ

Bodvarr's woman was named Thyri Roriksdóttir, but alas, this matters no more. On the very last day of the month of *Ylir*, on the night of *Vetrnætr* itself, she had given birth, to a large baby, a boy, but subsequently had become gravely ill. It was perhaps no mere coincidence then that the previous day, when all had appeared well that the heavily pregnant strange young woman had said darkly, *'Svá grunar mik, at bandagr minn muni vera á morgun, Vetrnætr.'* (I suspect that my death might be tomorrow, on the Festival of Winter's Nights)

Her child had indeed come struggling and very reluctantly into a world of momentous change. Some said it would not have come at all, on this of all days, if it had not been for poor girl's elderly aunt, Ingiþóra. She had been summoned the day before, by Bodvarr, when he knew the birth was imminent and had arrived under the cover of darkness. Her presence was deemed necessary, for she was well versed in all manners of *seiðr*. As a woman of magic her attire was unusual;

she wore a long blue mantle fastened with leather thongs. The finely woven woollen material of this had been sumptuously decorated with a variety of stones that periodically caught the light of the fires. Threaded glass beads made up a necklace which she wore around her scraggy neck. Her head was covered by a jet black lambskin hood which had been lined with white cat skin. She carried with her an old wooden staff, the top of which was mounted with a gold coloured metal and finely ornamented with stones. Around her middle she wore a girdle of agaric from which hung a small leather bag, which contained various magical devices. Her feet were covered in calfskin boots, which were neatly tied up with long leather thongs, which had been woven in and out of a series of small metal hooks. Her hands were covered in cat skin mittens, the same colour as the lining of her hood. The old woman was herself well beyond child bearing age, having in her younger days produced a total eight children in as many years, of whom as many as three had survived into adulthood. If anyone knew about the mysteries of giving birth and raising children it was her.

Rorik's thin and pallid daughter had writhed deliriously and screamed in pain that terrible spring night. The young man knew that the dísir had been busy making mischief for his pregnant wife and he knew they were only too aware of his complete lack of feelings towards her. It was they who were punishing him. *Loki* himself may also have been playing a part in the mischief. Thyri had more than confirmed Bodvarr's worst suspicions by screaming out in the night that her child would be cursed along with her husband's family and everything they possessed.

As the long and dark night passed slowly, the prospective father had in his frightened state, in order to please and placate these wicked spirits, commanded his younger brother to carry out a *blot* (sacrifice). Thorkell, a smallish red faced boy of some twelve years, had duly sacrificed a scraggy, ill looking sheep at a nearby pagan shrine and returned early in the early dawn with a cream-coloured stone bowl full of *hlaut* (sacrificial blood). Bodvarr instead of thanking his brother, whose hands and arms up to his elbows were covered in dark congealed blood, had become apoplectic with rage on seeing the ceremonial bowl. He told his shaking and frightened grubby younger brother that his thoughtless and senseless actions would be punished by the spirits.

A small and easily missed recess in a dry stone wall, near to an ancient ivy clad tree was the home to the revered soapstone object that had been taken; not much of a place, but even so it was a powerful shrine to the magical *Vanir*. The removal of such an important object from its sacred resting place is as all Norse children should know, not a wise thing to do. Thorkell Olafsson had acted without thought or due care. In spite of his tender age and the fact that he had been carrying out his older brother's wishes in the early hours, he was to be beaten by his brother and no doubt would be punished by the spirits as well.

The girl was seemingly right after all, she must have been able to see the spirits and she knew full well that she was to die. 'Like mother like daughter, that is what it is. One went the way of the water and the next, only a few summers later taken by childbirth. For your sake my boy, I hope the infant is a boy.' Ingiþóra alone had seemed to sense the infant was losing its battle for life and it was she who by the very gods who made Asgard their home, who had torn the dark blue, shiny and unmoving baby from its withering mother. She spoke quietly, but loud enough for Bodvarr to hear.

'What in *Midgard* are you blithering about?' Bodvarr's aggressive reply betrayed a deep innocence as well as feelings of complete disorientation that had set in, to make his mind feel as though it was expanding to fill his whole skull to bursting point.

The axis of Bodvarr's existence had tilted in an instant; although he couldn't fully understand the words of the old woman, he felt their impact all the same. He had witnessed his son enter the world of men and at the same time watched his superstitious and unloved wife leave it in one violent act. Within the space of a just a few minutes a wife had died and two families only recently joined by blood had been rent asunder. The mother lay perished, killed by both her own innocent first offspring and by the harsh and unforgiving actions of her old aunt. The girl was now rapidly turning to the same pallid deathly hue of her infant, before it had at last rallied and breathed its first few breaths. Slowly, quite slowly at first, the baby had become a ruddy pink and as if to show it would survive after all, it had at last begun to cry, quite quietly as though mourning its deceased mother.

It was no surprise to Ingiþóra, a seeress or *völva* that the death had come at the darkest time of night. Like all her kin, she had as a child been taught that this was the most dangerous hour. It was when all of the spirits emerged from their hiding places and created mischief and wreaked havoc amongst the men and women of Midgard. The sun's place in the sky was not to be seen, but all Norse folk knew that it hid at *óttastað* (early morning place), having disappeared over the horizon earlier that day.

'*Miðn ætti*' ('Midnight'), Ingiþóra said quietly to herself and shook her head. It would have been better, for the child to have been born then, she whispered '*Miðn ætti, ótta, jafn nærri badu*' ('Midnight, early morning, evenly near both'). '*Eigi ótta*' (not early morning), she said hoarsely, her voice tailing off, as the first of many tears slowly welled in her reddening eyes. The first of these made its escape from her now overflowing left eye and dribbled forlornly down her left cheek, before disappearing suddenly into a void of darkness. The light of the fire caught the falling orb ever so briefly and the reflection of the dancing flames made it appear to flash for a fraction of a split second.

Tradition even at such a time of hurt and unrest was upheld and so it was that the baby was put to the breast of the mother, even though in this case to a completely lifeless girl, to suckle. Ingiþóra, now a great aunt to the baby, had insisted this be done. It was a token gesture, but was even so an important one; a part of the ritual of being brought into the Norse world, to establish rights of inheritance. Bodvarr still numb from the shock of losing his wife, had then been instructed by the old woman to take the baby on his knee and in so doing named the baby Olaf, before sprinkling a few drops of spring water on his forehead. So it was that *vatni ausinn,* the naming ceremony had been seen to be done and the new born infant, who had no mother, took the name of his grandfather. Ingiþóra stood up and took a few steps to the door and turned to Bodvarr.

'I will take the child now. You have no need for him and it will be better that he has a true family around him. He shall be Ragnarr and Gunnfríðr's son.'

The old woman had, it seemed made all the necessary arrangements for the child. Bodvarr touched his son's head tenderly for the one and only time before handing the swaddled baby to the old woman. He returned to his longhouse to sleep and puzzle what he would do next. He knew it was for the best for his son, because one of the greatest *völva,* Ingiþóra could not possibly have got it wrong.

છ છ છ

So you see, some things in life are easier than others. Snorri has had enough of this tale after all; he has succumbed to tiredness granted to him by the hard manual work of the day. Those long hours outside in the cold and the darkness that now blankets everything, have more than taken their heavy toll. The boy is now lost to slumbers.

Perhaps it is the story he is weary of? No matter, I am not offended. The tale does not belong to me after all. Ah! See, he wakes after all and surprise, surprise, he asks for more. Who am I to deny him? Just a little more then, it'll do no harm for the night is so long. A deep sleep never fails to beckon afterwards, to be followed once more by yet another day's work and then more words; there are so many, plenty more to fill all the long dark evenings to come.

I have been thinking about the way in which I described the mother's frightening tale to her son. I must confess, although I will not repeat any such confession, that Saemundur my grandfather told me the very same tale. I must have been about five or six summers, but I can still see the mountain he built with words all that time ago as though I had seen it with my own eyes. I learned from my father, in the year he died that my grandfather had added the sleep time story to the tale, to give to Olaf some family history. The exploding mountain seemed real enough to me then, possibly because Saemundur's words rang true. He had witnessed with his own eyes the great earth shattering eruption of Hekla in 1104. Indeed my father and I as well were lucky enough to see for ourselves the same volcano burst into life in 1158 as well as the neighbouring Katla some eight summers before. These visions of my own, burned into my memory, if you'll excuse the play on words, have I think added just a touch more realism to the story. Even now, the tell tale hint of sulphur in the air from a small peat fire or from a fissure in the rocks, from the bowels of the earth itself, as it were, brings this episode to my mind in the sharpest possible focus.

Chapter 2

Vetr, Einmánuðr

Aga, Hordaland

781 AD, March – western region in Norway

Síðan skildu þeir feðgar

Then the father and son went separate ways

Drengskapr ok níðr

Honour and shame

Olaf Bodvarrson had not seen or heard anything at all about his father for over thirteen years. He had been a baby, a tiny child just like any other when his father and his great aunt had completely disappeared from his world. Naturally, he now had no memory at all of the young man and the old woman who were responsible for bringing him into Midgard. He considered his great *foðurbróði* (uncle) Ragnarr, his father's elder brother and his family to be his only relatives. Olaf had in true Norse tradition been taught that as a first born child, he was special and that was why he had been given to Ragnarr and Gunnfríðr by his father. He had grown up instead in their village, Aga; a small community, only about two days sail from Odda.

What he was unaware of though was that his father, Bodvarr had been killed six years before in a *leikmót* (games meeting). The exact details had never been given to Olaf, but Ragnarr had heard that his younger brother and five other men had perished after a particularly nasty game of the violent *sköfuleikr* (scraper). This highly dangerous game, which had acquired its strange nickname of 'the scraper' by those Norse men bold or stupid enough to take part, involved using cow horns as makeshift weapons. It usually lasted all day, as it had on this particular occasion. Needless to say all of the combatants had been extremely drunk on ale and mead. Some however were in a semi-conscious state having deliberately altered their state of perception having ingested a mixture of potent toadstools and mushrooms. First, the fungi had been ground, before being added to an open pot of very hot water. Several minutes later the hallucinogenic liquor was drunk in vast and enthusiastic draughts.

The abhorrent injuries sustained by Bodvarr on the occasion of this particular event were such that he had taken a full week to die. Drifting in and out of violent and disturbing dreams he felt he floated on waves of blackness that surged his body ever upwards as though on a huge ocean swell before crashing suddenly and forcefully downwards, leaving his mind reeling and his stomach churning. He had felt no pain at first, but as his body began to recover from the cocktail of strong drink and hallucinogens he had taken, he had fallen into a living nightmare peopled by brutish, stabbing thrusts of indescribable agony. Slowly, but oh so slowly, steadily, painfully, minute by minute, he bled internally. His body jerked and twisted in torment as he coughed up in wrenching, shaking, excruciating fits, great black gobbets of congealed cruor, until what was left of his lifeblood had finally leeched away and he, what very little there was left of him, mercifully fled *Midgard*, the home of men.

All Olaf had been told was that his father was dead, Ámóða his step-mother, whom he had never heard of before, had remarried and that appeared to be enough for the boy, because he never once asked questions about his actual mother or father and had never shown any desire to discuss his lineage at all. He was also unaware that his grandfather had perished several years before, having been carried off by some terrible illness that had slowly eaten him away from the inside, before he was finally carried across the rainbow bridge of *Bifrost*, to join other fallen warriors in the one and only great realm of *Asgard*, which took men; the hall of *Valhöll*. Ragnarr Olafsson in his role as father uncle had told the young Olaf all about the different halls of Asgard. 'The halls are so great my boy that there is room for everyone, but you don't want to get yourself into the wrong hall. Can you imagine what it'd be like if you ended up with the dwarfs in their hall? Or in *Jötenheim*, the land of giants, that'd be no fun, because they by all accounts throw rocks and boulders about, you'd be crushed flat. Did you know', he would whisper darkly, 'that some of the giants now and again come to Midgard? Did you know that my boy? You've seen the rocks falling from the mountains to the sea before, haven't you?'

'How come we can see the rocks fall down the side of the mountain, but never see the giants? I'd love to see what they look like, why don't they show themselves?' Olaf's replies persistently worried Ragnarr, for he had no real answers for the inquisitive boy. Somewhat exasperated by his own inadequacy, he would attempt to respond to the child, but he sadly considered most of his replies feeble and his suppositions flawed. Between clenched teeth he would swear to himself in the resigned way men do when they know they have failed in an argument.

'Just don't go wishing stupid things like that, because giants and magic are things best left for those folk who know or at least pretend to understand them. I bloody well don't and you certainly don't and never will! So you go worrying about what we do know and not about what we don't know or never will know!' With that, Ragnarr concluded his brief conversation with a snort. Quietly and just to himself he said, 'I wish I knew more to help the little'un, but the truth is, I'm not sure about any of this magic stuff or nonsense or any of the doings of the gods. I must be a right thick 'un me. I always have been and I've never learnt anything, not like the men who are close to *Óðinn*, the ones who craft the runes. They have ideas and they can put words down on wood or stone and go back to them later. They don't have to remember things, so long as they don't lose their little bits of scratching. By *Sleipnir's* teeth, they know a thing or two.'

ᛂ   ᛂ   ᛂ

As a twelve year old, Olaf had grown rapidly to become a large boy, both tall and stocky. He used his size well and in time became particularly skilled at most physical games and contests; his greatest natural ability lay in Norse wrestling or *glíma*. In these bouts Olaf had surprised hardened and far more experienced wrestlers by being able to throw opponents who were four or even five years his senior and who were considerably heavier than him. His ability lay in both his fleet of foot and in his timing. What power he was able to summon was always used in one explosive burst at the precise moment it was needed.

Fighting games had always been one of Olaf's favourites; he had learned quickly to use a staff in numerous ways to disable an opponent. He could use it to trip his opponent, to smack him, to lever him off his balance, to graze and startle him with its edge, to punch him hard with its end and he could even use it to catapult himself to another position from which to begin another assault. In addition, he developed with lengthy sessions of practice, advanced attacking and defending techniques with both a heavy wooden sword and with a real *scramasax*. But these were not all of the fighting skills he learned, he also perfected the two ways of throwing a spear. First, he could launch it with his hand and secondly he perfected using a thin rope, to help him obtain a much greater distance and thus power. After mastering this surprisingly simple technique, Olaf never travelled anywhere without his trusty spear or more importantly his precious *snærisspjót,* the string with which he achieved the throw. The axe in all its forms took up yet more of Olaf's time as he grew. He practised using long handled ones in mock combat and short handled ones in throwing competitions. He learnt to hurl them great distances with either his left or right hand and managed to obtain a remarkable accuracy with both.

A great natural strength appeared to have been bestowed upon the youngster; it was a strength which appeared to increase day by day as he worked at developing hardened muscle and steely sinew. He little realised it now, but he was honing combat skills that would save his life in foreign lands on more than one occasion in the future.

His well developed physique enabled him to master yet another weapon, that of the bow and arrow. Years before he should have been able to draw the bow string back far enough for the weapon to work effectively, Olaf had succeeded in pulling the string back as far as it would go. In spite of this, however, Olaf spurned the bow for some reason and said it was merely a hunting weapon, to be used to bring food.

In any game of physical contact or brute strength, he showed more than a little potential and this had been noticed and contemplated by his peers and his elders. In a swimming contest on one summer's morning, Olaf had to the delight of Ragnarr nearly drowned Bers, a boy three years his senior. Swimming contests it must be said had little to do with swimming, but more with using the water as a weapon itself. Only the somewhat reluctant intervention of the other boy's father had ended the competition, much to the *níðr* or shame of his bedraggled son, who had to be dragged away screaming and swearing all kinds of horrendous vengeance on Olaf.

ಬ   ಬ   ಬ

Olaf had also been taught to play many kinds of board games by Gunnfríðr and her great friend Þjóðbjörg, including the popular, but difficult *hnefatafl*, a game of great strategy and some considerable skill. Gunnfríðr Esjadóttir had discussed young Olaf at great length with her close friend and confided in her that, 'The boy needs to develop his mind with other interests in addition to all that terrible fighting.' The two women were in complete agreement and so it was that they cleverly adapted Olaf's lifestyle to encompass much more than just fighting. The discrete regime was so skilfully introduced that neither Olaf nor Ragnarr ever realised their clever female subterfuge. Olaf found himself inside the longhouse for much greater periods of time and so it was that he played every imaginable game that existed. He was drawn into word and number games, drawing and mime competitions, puzzles of logic using gaming pieces and even poetry contests.

As a result of all this game playing, Olaf had learned to concentrate for considerable periods of time and by so doing had also discovered how to entirely conceal his emotions, thus denying his fellow players the tell tale signs of glee or worry which usually betrayed players of his age. He played *hnefatafl* with a fixed face; a face that betrayed no feeling whatsoever, whether he was the attacker or defender in this game. His eyes were deep as the fjord he was growing up by and as black and as seemingly lifeless as the cold water that swirled in and out on the tides. There was not the slightest flicker of light; nothing, not the faintest hint of anything appeared there, to show or betray any life in those circular pools of darkness. Then when all hope of action seemed lost, suddenly, in less than a blink of those eyes, Olaf had moved his carved whalebone king into the corner of the square board and his broad grin indicated the game had been won and his opponent vanquished.

The boy become expert in the intricacies of strategy, whether defending or attacking and seemed to know instinctively what his opponent's weak spot was. When he had worked this out as he unerringly did, he ruthlessly exploited his advantage. Thus, Olaf rarely lost and when he did, he felt more than a little uncomfortable, for losing was not part of his nature, it felt unnatural to him and caused him hurt. Unlike his peers the youngster usually reached for the darker pieces thus taking on role of attacking the king in the game. He knew that although he had twice the number of pieces, his task was in fact the more difficult and therefore more rewarding, if he won. Although, he assumed command of twenty four drengr, half of these would be needed to guard the four corner squares and the other half to capture the king by surrounding him, after of course defeating his *dróttin*.

After showing such early promise in *hnefatafl*, he had been presented with a set of beautifully crafted amber and walrus tooth gaming pieces by Gunnfríðr's friend Þjóðbjörg Ketilsdóttir. The proportion of games he lost after receiving this wonderful gift became less. The eleven by eleven squares of the board held no horrors at all for Olaf and each time he played he tried to put his own psyche into the defending king's mind. To him it was more than a game, it was real life and the pieces took on spirits of their own. 'How would he, the king feel? What would he do? Would he fight or would he run? Would he be prepared to sacrifice his own men in order to win? Would he worry about the ones he resigned to their deaths? Would he expect his men to be prepared to do his bidding without for a moment questioning his leadership?' Olaf very soon realised that he could never truly win, because there was never really an end to kingship or the game, only a new king, or an uneasy truce before the next game. There was a never ending line of kings stretching both forwards in time to Ragnarok and backwards to *Óðinn*, just as indeed there were finished games, games currently being played and games that had yet to be played.

Þjóðbjörg had played an important part in Olaf's life at this time, because both his step-father and step-mother were hard but kind, whereas his mother's friend accepted Olaf for what he was, even when he wasn't being particularly pleasant, which as it happened was quite a lot of the time. Þjóðbjörg made a great impact on the young Olaf, although he wasn't to fully realize it for a number of summers hence. 'You will find your way, but you may find it later than you would wish my boy. You must be true to yourself, don't be distracted.' She encouraged Olaf in everything and was always there for him if he had a question on anything or a worry that seemed insoluble.

฿ ฿ ฿

When aged twelve, Olaf and almost all his friends played a fast moving game called *knattleikr*. In every possible spare moment they had they were to be found in a circle, with the 'paddler' in the middle. This exciting game involved one player hitting a hard ball with a paddle shaped bat, whilst either his or the other team attempted to catch and carry off the ball to a designated location. The important part of the game was the 'carrying off', where wrestling and fighting skills took centre stage. It was not unusual for players to become quite seriously injured as drink and youthful exuberance often took a severe toll when mixed together in inordinate quantities. Olaf had soon learned to strike the ball thunderously hard and with his excellent coordination, always seeming to manage to place it well away from the players of the opposing team; usually over their heads and onto the roof of some longhouse, or into a field. This made for an interesting chase and one that more often than not resulted in some controversy or other. Late one evening, the ball had been struck particularly hard by one of Olaf's friends, Bröndólfr into the still waters of the nearby fjord and sunk without trace. The game had finished before it should have done and all the young men and boys in their disappointed state slowly turned away from the area on which their game had been played and made their way to their respective own longhouses.

The long seemingly endless summers of Olaf's childhood were however destined not to last for ever. Unknown to him they were to come to a rapid and premature close. Games and play which constituted the fabric of his life were soon to be replaced by the more serious task of survival as an adult in a world where strength and resolution were the character traits that really matter most. Olaf was of course as prepared as he could have been, as much as the next boy, but that really didn't mean much at all in the grand scheme of things. He would have to take what chances he could in life, just as all the other boys and girls would and then he would have to hope beyond hope that *Þórr* and the other gods or spirits would look after him.

Ragnarr and Gunnfríðr appeared to have managed to balance perfectly the upbringing of Bodvarr's boy. Ragnarr had always been close enough to the lad to help and instruct him, but at the same time distant enough to allow Olaf to make his own mistakes and take his beatings. This Ragnarr believed, was how it always had been and should be and how he would have expected any first male child to be brought up. The beatings and scrapes Olaf had periodically found himself in, had happened a great deal more frequently when he was a fresh faced lad, but as the years passed, such incidents grew rarer and rarer, until at about the age of thirteen, they ceased altogether as Olaf became to be unchallenged by any of his contemporaries. None of his peers were prepared to or dared fight him or indeed cross him in any way. It was possibly as a consequence of this that it became a time when the mind of Olaf changed. He ceased to be a just a boy with an inquisitive eye and tenacious spirit and changed almost instantly and most dangerously into a young man, a man at that with no serious rivals of his own age, who could keep him in check.

Gunnfríðr, ever observant, had seen many signs, which betrayed this change in Olaf and had reluctantly taken the boy to one side in their longhouse. Looking at him closely with her pale blue and somewhat melancholy eyes, she now saw her adopted son in a different and not wholly welcomed light. '*Drengskapr*', she said to Olaf, 'remember this, honour is all'. Olaf had looked seriously at the kindly woman and nodded to show he understood. He did however say nothing and with that unwelcome vacuum of sound ringing in Gunnfríðr's ears, he was suddenly gone. She considered, that it was the first time he had failed to respond to any statement she had made and the first time he had ever walked out without any explanation. It was she thought, the precise moment that defined the end of the boy's childhood. Leaving their long house in Odda, with large purpose filled strides, he soon found himself wandering amongst the birch trees that grew in small groups along the shore line of the fjord near to his home village.

Sitting in near complete darkness inside their longhouse, Gunnfríðr and her husband would regularly talk quietly to each other on important issues. Now, they did so in the same resigned way that people discuss things, over which they hold no sway. One would start by saying, 'If only', and the other would reply, 'But'. The result was, as is always the case in such hypothetical conversations the same, with neither of the participants feeling the slightest bit better. At least they felt they had discussed the boy and more importantly at least they had each other. Ragnarr as if to underline the end of the sombre discourse, resorted to one of his favourite and well worn phrases, 'If the boy is big enough, then he's old enough and if he's old enough, then he's big enough'. Gunnfríðr knew her man so well by now, that she chose not to reply, but simply fixed his gaze with hers and smiled, before sighing quietly as the beginning of a tear began to well in each of her eyes. Ragnarr had always been a good man to her and they had enjoyed their lives together, bringing up their own three children and then Ragnarr's brother's eldest as well. When Olaf had been given to him all those years before, Ragnarr had foretold that the infant would be a great leader one day, but he also was wise enough to know the cost such leadership would bring. 'It will be high, very high, may be too high', he said to himself. Then, looking across the smoke filled room he met his wife's glance and after seeing a first single tear make its way slowly down her left cheek, he whispered rather forlornly, 'Who my dear will pay the price, who will pay?'

His wife choosing to ignore this question, instead replied intuitively to another unspoken question that had been gnawing away continuously at Ragnarr for the past five or six summers, 'My dear, we are getting to be too old to be good parents, we are too soft and too caring and we both know that no child in the history of *Midgard* has benefited from that!'

'My dearest wife, you're right as usual. I feel that we have failed not only the boy, but his father and ourselves as well. It'll be up to the boy soon. He'll be on his own and I fear at present he's not ready for what life holds in store for him. My old father used to say to me not to trust a plot sown too early, or to praise a son too soon, as elements rule the land and intelligence the son. Both are in their own way exposed to danger.' Ragnarr finished speaking and went in search of his drinking horn and some mead with which to fill it.

Muttering to himself, he castigated his wife unfairly for hiding his drinking vessel and then did so again after she complained about his drinking.

'It's no wonder I drink he thought, before looking at his woman, he whispered hoarsely, *'þat kann ek at segja þér, at þessa skiptis munu vit iðrask siðar.'* (I can tell you that we will regret this later)

ᛞᚩ   ᛞᚩ   ᛞᚩ

The first real snows arrived today. Dark almost brown skies delivered them in but a short time. From the entrance of my long house, in the early twilight I can make out the distant silhouetted black mountains which seem to bite or gnaw at the very clouds. The flat ground of the valley is lightly dusted white and even now reflects what little light there is. It is cut by a great gash of black though, the wide but shallow river that winds its way and flows steadily unhindered to sea. The sea, yes the dark and dangerous sea that the drakkar in their own way tamed.

Much earlier in the day, I ventured for many hours towards the coast to visit an old friend of mine, Ari Thorgillson, whilst Snorri stayed here to tend the farm. I took Sleipnir, my favourite horse, whose hooves can tame the roughest ground. I paid a lot of silver for him five years ago when he was just a foal, but he was worth it! Without training of any kind, this wonderful horse could and would tolt, I tell you. Sitting on his strong back for many a long hour doesn't sap your energy in the way trotting does, for his long strides land in such a rhythmical and smooth way. He races in the way of the most beautiful of sinuous eddas; four beats, followed by four beats and so on, no rising and falling, just the repetitive beats. It is magical in its own way; to me it is equine galðr.

Ah, where was I? Oh, yes. At great length, I discussed with Ari the long lost days of our youth. We spent more than a little time casting our minds back to the time of our grandfathers; the time of the 'great histories.' My grandfather was of course Saemundur the Learned and his was none other than Ari the Learned, two of wisest men to have ever lived. They knew each other, though not that well I believe.

Looking out to sea, the clarity of the air and lack of mist and cloud enabled us to have unhindered views of the horizon. The thin line separating sky and sea is broken just the once from between where the land meets it to the west and to the east. There are but a few small islands and just the constantly moving waters which change colour and demeanour at the whims of the weather.

Snorri has already eaten the few fish he had brought with him and the last of the fliki I had been saving for myself. It'll be dry rye bread washed down with ice cold water from the stream for me again I fear. No matter, for once it's been eaten and gone from my sight I'll make all the changes necessary in my memory to make it become the grandest of meals possible. A banquet it may well become to me in time; give me just a little time and I'll see. But I'll saviour the delights of my meal later, after I have first satisfied the hungry mind of Snorri.

Chapter 3

Sumar, annar mánuðr

A.D. 785 May

Departure from Hordaland

Vitz er þorf,
þeim er víða ratar,
dælt er heima hvat;
at augabragði verðr,
sá er ecci kann
oc með snotrom sítr.

There is need of wit
to him who travels widely,
everything is easy at home;
he is suited for mockery,
he who knows nothing
and sits with wise men.

The tiny community of Aga had just disappeared from Olaf's sight and for a brief moment the young man wondered if he would ever see his home village again. Suddenly, the sea which had until that moment been quite choppy calmed and great circular pools began appearing in the shifting troughs of the powerful, but now gentle swell. Huge masses of tiny bubbles broke the shiny and effervescing surface of these ever changing swirling bowls giving them, Olaf thought, the appearance of massive concave circular shields, pitted with damage caused by the clash of gigantic unseen swords and axes in some battle between the gods. Heaving slowly in the seemingly friendly waters, 'Ormr' wallowed while vast unseen forces pulled her this way and that, to make her timbers creak and groan.

Olaf looked up at the silhouette created by the square sail of the *knarr*, which momentarily had begun to hang limply from its yard. Periodically it flapped heavily to thud against the sturdy oak mast that supported it; a carefully fashioned tree trunk which had been attached securely to the boat's keel with a number of heavy wooden pins. The mast, he knew was fixed, unlike those on the *drakkars* which could out of necessity be removed. On these boats all that was needed was a heavy wooden mallet, which could knock out the restraining pins, allowing it to be stored flat along the length of the boat.

Looking across at the other *knarrs*, Olaf marvelled at the length of each boat and considered how large the piece of wood would have to be to form a backbone for the vessel. He knew that in the last few years or so, it had become increasingly more difficult for the boat builders to find oak trees big enough to be made into keels for the *drakkars*, and *knarrs*. Across the Norse world many of the boat-builders, in places such as Jaeren, Agder and Nordland in the west and Öland, Östergötland and Uppland in the east and Bornholm Isle in the south had out of necessitude decided to use other large trees, such as pine for their keels. *Knarrs* were similar to *drakkars*, of course, but they were far the more seaworthy of the two types of boats and Olaf was feeling grateful that he was leaning on the reassuringly high wooden top strake of a sturdy sea worthy *knarr*. Also, he considered the fact that *knarrs* were both shorter in length and were broader; being partially covered to give a greater degree of protection for whatever cargo they happened to be carrying.

He imagined the amount of time needed to fashion a keel from a single tree trunk and then also deliberated on the idea of joining two trunks together to overcome the problem of tree size. It could be done, I'm sure it could, he thought to himself.

There were just four *knarrs* making this trading voyage from Hordaland back to Kaupang. Each boat had nine or ten people on board, meaning the journey from a mariner's or rower's viewpoint should be fairly light work. A good sea-worthy *knarr* could easily be crewed by just six men who knew what they were doing. All Olaf knew was that his passage and fare had been hurriedly arranged by his father's brother. He understood only a little about boats and their ways and had over the years done his best to avoid them at all costs. He was fully aware that he was no sailor and from what little time he had spent on the water he had come to realise fully the intricacies of the sickness of the sea.

The time for Olaf to leave had arrived, because it was clear that he was becoming something of a liability to his family. There had been a disagreement, followed by a fight in which a young man called Gnauðimaðr had been killed and all of the talk in the village of Aga relating to the incident suggested that Olaf was to blame. Ragnarr had looked to the youngster and said with a solemn finality, words which were to indicate his fate, '*Ver þu heill ok far vel!*' (Be healthy and fare well!)

Ragnarr had discreetly paid out a small amount of gold to a local boat owner whom he knew well and instructed him to get Olaf to row or help with the sails or do anything else that may be required to make up the rest of the agreed fare. Ragnarr had always been a caring guardian and now felt Olaf was not just a boy whom he had a duty to look after, but that he was truly his own boy. He desperately didn't want Olaf to suffer the curse of *Fjörbaugsgarður* and he rightly or wrongly felt that to a degree he was somewhat responsible for the boy's violent actions.

'I should have been harder, much harder on the boy, or perhaps I should never have taken him on.' Ragnarr looked towards his woman for some kind of consolation.

'Well it's of no consequence now.' Gunnfríðr's lips tightened somewhat, giving her the appearance of someone who appeared to be smiling, as she spoke her well rehearsed reply. Her husband had seen this expression on her face many times before and recognised it instantly as the one that betrayed feelings of worry that she may have been trying to hide. He looked towards her and frowned, as if to demonstrate as clearly as he could that he was being extremely serious and understood her anguish and empathized with her completely.

'If the local *þing* decreed Olaf guilty and he were to be banished, it's possible that I, myself may also lose some of my land and livestock. This is, well, it is so unfair. My brother, the real father of the boy never took any responsibility for his son at all! He hadn't made any arrangements for the boy at all, before he was stupid enough to get himself killed. And what a way to be killed at that!'

'That may be, but Olaf would certainly suffer terribly by being kept away from his own community, it's the only community he knows and I'll wager he'd starve to death without any support. I don't need to tell you what the law in its wisdom has decreed, because you already know. But Olaf doesn't know that anyone, anyone at all found to be offering help to an exile will suffer the same fate of the outcast. Nobody in their right mind would help him.' Gunnfríðr's argument was sound and now she continued with renewed fervour, 'Over the years, Ragnarr, you and I have seen too many young men from Aga, just like Olaf, and from other places too, that we have visited, suffer this terrible destiny. Some of them were just boys, but some were respected men with families, some had pots of gold! This I tell you is the work of *Loki* himself and if it's not, it'll be that damned *Hel* if I'm not mistaken.'

The slightest of nods of Ragnarr's head and a low grunt from him, showed his implicit agreement. 'Those unfortunates more often than not die after struggling terribly to find food and shelter in the harsh winters. *Hel's* work it may be, for she is their only lord now! Or else, if they're the lucky ones, they move away and become outlaws or pirates, leaving their loved ones behind to fend for themselves. If these men, some of whom are hardened criminals and murderers, can't survive banishment, then how would young Olaf, a lad of sixteen summers, possibly fare. The boy simply has to go soon and the sooner the better and that's that.'

'At least a crime committed in a community like ours has no impact elsewhere, so Olaf should be all right.' Gunnfríðr now seemed to genuinely smile having worked out her answer with such infallible logic and then persuaded herself that everything would be all right after all.

'Yes, we should thank the gods that the whole of this country of ours is divided up and ruled by hundreds of *jarls*. Fortunately, for Olaf, nobody knows who has done what!' Ragnarr exploded in a fit of laughter. 'Each *jarl* serves up and dishes out his own peculiar brand of justice as he deems necessary.'

'The problem though, with all these little *jarl*doms or whatever you want to call them, kingdoms as some of those uppish *jarls* would have it, is that there's a growing band of wild and dangerous young men out there,' she waved her arm dramatically, 'who simply have nowhere to go.' Gunnfríðr finished her observation by suddenly becoming very quiet and looking very concerned.

'What will become of them all? By *Sleipnir's* shit they've got it tough and no mistake,' Ragnarr asked and profaned almost simultaneously.

'Never mind that, where will they go and what will they do? No good will come of it, that's to be sure,' came her perceptive rejoinder, whilst all the time she continued to skilfully tie yet another knot in the wool she was cleverly manipulating with a long and delicate hooked bone pin that she clasped between her dexterous and strong fingers.

'Have you seen that horn of mine? Ragnarr asked his woman, before continuing in a slightly quieter voice. 'It has taken itself off again.' Then almost inaudibly his words tailed off to nothing. 'Or, maybe you have put it somewhere so safe that I'm not meant to find it.'

His wife shook her head in sadness and with a hollow feeling of disbelief.

ဢ   ဢ   ဢ

ÓþyrmiR was the helmsman and he knew his job more than well. He was a man of about thirty summers and he was currently pulling gently on the tiller, which for the moment was still fully immersed in and cutting satisfyingly through the water. Changing his usual casual stance, he now became more upright, seemingly mildly apprehensive about some slight change in his immediate surroundings. He growled something at the three men standing near the back of the *knarr* and looked up with his right hand shielding the light from his eyes. The master read the weather instinctively from the slightest signs; signs that were invisible to most eyes. Towards the front of the boat, a white wall of sea mist now visible to all was quickly rolling in and for just a few fleeting seconds only a tiny and wholly unexpected rainbow appeared in the tumbling misty wall. ÓþyrmiR now grumbled to himself, something about a 'weather dog' and that this was a sure sign of imminent bad weather.

'By *Þórr* and by his father, by *Óðinn* himself, I've not seen one of those in at least *atta* (eight) or even *tui* (ten) summers. This is bad, this is a message from *Asgard* itself, to see *Bifrost*, is to see almost into the realm of the Gods. The sun is too afraid to appear in the same sky and I of all folk have to see it, by *Óðinn's* teeth, I have to see the bridge that leads to *Hel's* dominion. This is not good for me.'

Within just several minutes the clinging whiteness had engulfed the tiny rainbow as well as the unsuspecting leading craft and in only a matter of a blink of the eyes or less all of the boats had become hidden beneath an apparently impregnable blanket of sea mist. Instinctively the helmsmen, with the air of someone who had seen everything before successfully managed to get the boats into a tighter formation enabling each of them to see at least some of the other boats. By such action all of the boats had some reference point in a world of tranquil water and swirling eddying cloud, a world where the mind would often begin to play games with the senses. Even the power emanating from the sun had diminished. It seemed as though it had lost all interest in this particular day and was hiding its face from the surface of the sea. It hid in a sky which had now become universally white. The wind had faded to a mere breath by now, seemingly as if in awe of the all smothering fog, which had already subdued the sun. All land had disappeared from sight and now it lived on only in the memories of the crews and their few passengers. It was *undorneykt,* or at least the crew thought it was, but no one on the boats could have proven it.

The master remained wholly unperturbed by the change in weather and with the help of two other men had the tiller lifted to its highest position, allowing the side mounted device to steer the boat in very shallow waters, without risk of it being damaged on the sea floor. Indeed, in this position, held in place by two large wooden upright studs, the boat could be beached with the tiller still in place. This was clearly the intention of the helmsman. Several of the crew became agitated and shouted their concern that they would be lost. However, in contrast, the youngest of the travellers was a boy of perhaps fourteen, who hailed from the tiny island village of Birka and he seemed surprisingly at ease. His parents still lived on the island of Björkö and as was the tradition, he as the eldest son had been brought up by his father's brother's family, in the same way that Olaf had been by Ragnarr. So it was that Ingvar had grown to think of and respect ÓþyrmiR as his true father.

The temperature quickly began to drop and some of the men made their way to their wooden chests which were placed on the deck next to their respective oars, to retrieve oilskins or some other article of clothing with which to stave off the cold and wet. Ingvar pulled out of a *húðfat,* a very large and dirty smock-like overall, which he pulled awkwardly over his tunic. Olaf made his mind up to talk to the boy and seen if he could learn from him what was in the mind of the helmsman. Olaf introduced himself, by saying, '*Ek kalla mik Olafr,*' (I am called Olaf) thinking at the same time about not giving away any details of his necessary and rapid departure.

The boy in reply echoed Olaf's sentence and simply said, '*Ek kalla mik Ingvar.*' (I am called Ingvar) A few moments later, he continued, 'The master knows the ninth rune, the one which shelters ships, calms wind, smoothes waves and sends the sea to sleep.'

After exchanging several polite, but somewhat strained pleasantries about the boat, Olaf learned that the helmsman had believed it safer to land their boat at Hesthamar Utne, a small sea village on a large bend in this particular fjord. Three men on each side of the boat dipped long oars into the water and began rowing, from standing positions. Theirs was not an explosive energy sapping pull of an oar, but a far more sedate standing pull, given energy by the weight of the man hanging on the oar. Ingvar offered Olaf a square piece of waterproofed woollen material which he gratefully took and wrapped around his shoulders.

Ingvar was a real mine of information, telling the quiet and patient Olaf all sorts of things about the boat. Clearly he had a passion for and subsequently a great knowledge about both *knarr*s and *drakkar*s. The red and white crosshatched sail Olaf had been idly examining, apparently represented a massive investment in human labour. Ingvar pointing upwards said, 'As with all *drakkar* and *knarr* sails, it had taken more than a full two years' hard work on the part of five or six women to produce.' He informed Olaf with pride that the women in question were from his family and that they were the best sail makers to be found.

All of their efforts had gone into manufacturing one simple, but beautiful piece of woven material. The wool woven by the women, Ingvar explained, had originally been shorn from a breed of small hardy sheep living on the hills of Gokstad. It had then been washed and carefully combed with bone handled iron toothed combs. The clean woollen fibres were then drawn out by girls and young women, who meticulously spun them onto wooden spindles. These were weighted down with smooth round stone spindle whorls. He went on to tell Olaf this long winded activity had usually occurred and probably was now occurring during the long evenings when other forms of recreation or work had been completed.

Olaf wondered how Ingvar had learned so much about something that to him looked like it could have been completed in just a few weeks. Ingvar was now really excited by his subject, 'Later, vegetable dyes were employed on the yarn and their colours became fixed with naturally occurring mordants, such as salt obtained from sea water. They tried to use piss, because that's salty, but it was a waste of time, because it seemed to bleach the wool it was meant to be colouring and it made it smell like, well like piss!' At this unexpected juncture, Invar stopped briefly to laugh at his own crudity, before continuing. 'These substances, not piss though,' he giggled, 'are used to permanently fix the colour of the resultant yarn, but they're usually only partially successful.'

Ingvar then went into even greater detail about the way the wool was then treated. 'Endless hours, I tell you, endless hours of repetitive weaving on upright looms. Clack, clack, rattle, clack, clack and so on. All those little woollen strings or yarns are held carefully in place by a set of strategically placed stones or clay weights. These hang below the frame of the loom to provide the necessary tension in the wool. One of the sails of this tiny flotilla, can you see it?', he beckoned to Olaf, 'is plain white, two have been coloured with vertical red and white stripes, whilst our sail has been made up of alternate red and white upright squares', he enthused. 'The red in all the sails has faded now though,' he said somewhat dejectedly.

It was true; the red of the sail was now more of a dark pink and the white was really a dirty creamy colour. Suddenly however, Ingvar's interest picked up again and he began extolling the virtues of animal fat and its great and varied properties and multiple uses. He described how a thorough application of animal oils and fats had been needed to complete the production of the sail required for each ship. Once the sail had been completed, numerous walrus hide strips, which had also been meticulously treated in another lengthy process, which surprisingly he wasn't all that sure about, had been used to strengthen the woollen sail. They, Ingvar went on, had been dried and tanned, before being carefully stitched into the sails with a heavy bone needle. 'The strips of walrus leather were arranged neatly in an intricate cross hatched pattern, can you see it, to prevent the sail from being pulled out of shape and thereby making it difficult to manage and more importantly rendering it ineffective. Without such a strengthening device, the effects of lashings of sea water and thunderous gusts of wind, from repeated harsh and unforgiving storms would otherwise stretch and thus destroy this woollen sail in a short space of time.' Ingvar went on to explain that the ropes on the boats, which held the sail in place were either made from walrus skin or were manufactured from the fibres of a variety of different plants such as flax, hemp, oak or more increasingly silver birch.

'The walrus skin ropes,' much revered by these sailors and clearly by young Ingvar had he went on, 'been obtained for 'Ormr' by cutting the skin from the walrus in a single piece. The body of the walrus was rotated while the strip of hide was removed in a spiral. In contrast, 'Ormr's other ropes have been made from the fibres of many silver birch, and were obtained after being bartered for in Birka on a previous trading expedition two years before.' Ingvar went on, 'These trees grow in vast numbers near to Birka and it is said the town took its name from the birch.' Ingvar seemed to be nearing the end of his lecture and Olaf sensing this, waited in silence for him to finish. Gripping a thinner rope, he dug his finger nails into the fibres and examining them closely said, 'These were made by a more lengthy process.' He was off again; he went on, 'The branches, not all of them, were removed from a good tree. If you take too many off, the tree suffers too much and may die.' He scowled, 'The bark is then cut along its length and stripped off with an axe. The single pieces of bark are then cut into pieces about the width of, say my thumb. These are then peeled apart to separate the outer and inner bark. The outer bark is shit; it is too brittle for making ropes or anything and so is discarded and burnt. The inner bark though is boiled in water containing a good quantity of the wood ash from the outer bark. After an hour or so it is taken out to dry and shrink. When still damp it is twisted to form a string from which a rope can be spliced.'

Ingvar became silent and his ad hoc rope making tuition appeared to have concluded as suddenly as it had begun. Olaf fearing a further lecture simply asked his new talkative friend what Hesthamar Utne was like. Olaf was expecting a long answer and was rather taken aback when his companion simply said, *'Í skógum eru oft allillir vargar ok.'* (In forests there are often very evil wolves) Ingvar went on to briefly describe the way wolves fight and concluded that they would make good Norse men if they could shape change at will. Somewhat perplexed Olaf let his mind revert to his companion's earlier statement concerning the magic of the ninth rune. It seemed it had had the effect of calming the sea after all. He asked Ingvar what other runes he knew of and immediately regretted his inquisitiveness as the reply left him more confused than ever.

> Understand how to carve them, understand how to read them,
> Understand how to stain them, understand how to prove them,
> Understand how to evoke them, understand how to scratch them,
> Understand how to send them, understand how to spend them.

As Ingvar concluded this cryptic verse, Olaf noticed ÓþyrmiR carefully tie a piece of twine with an elaborately patterned knot to a crudely made cylindrical piece of iron. The other end of this, had earlier on the master's instruction been covered with a thick layer of a particularly creamy and white glutinous pig fat by a blond boy by the name Farulfr. The master let the iron device drop over the side of his *knarr*, allowing it to fall to the seabed unhindered. When it had grounded, he rapidly pulled it back up, counting hand over dripping hand as he did so. At once, he seemed pleased with the results; his face beamed a broad smile. It appeared that from this procedure he had ascertained that the *knarr* was lying in water just the height of four men and more importantly he now knew where the boat was, more or less. Farulfr had smeared the fat on in such a way that the end of the lump of iron had acted in the way of an effective water resistant glue. When the iron lump had hit the seabed, sand and grit had become deeply embedded in the fat. The colour, size and composition of the grains gave to ÓþyrmiR all the information he needed. These meagre details indicated to the master mariner that the boats were pleasingly close to the trading community he was seeking. Not only did he know the sea from above, but he knew if required where he and his boat were by simply measuring its depth and then examining the grains or small stones trapped in the fat.

Chapter 4

hesthamar Utne
785 A.D.

'Ormr' grounded onto a shingle beach in the early evening. She had been under sail for about four hours and then the men had grudgingly rowed albeit rather slowly for a further eight hours or so. The cry of *víka sjóvar* from ÓþyrmiR had come some fourteen times during the day and the last seven of those had been called in the sea fog. As the crew was so small in number, it meant that some of the men rowed two sets of *víka sjóvar* back to back. This was no mean achievement, as each *víka sjóvar* represented a full *púsund* (thousand) pulls of the oar.

ℰℴ   ℰℴ   ℰℴ

Of course, as Snorri knows only too well, a Norse púsund (thousand) just so happens to be larger than the one universally adopted elsewhere; one thousand two hundred, to be precise. If ÓþyrmiR had wanted one of the thousands other folk are used to, he would have called for, 'átta hundrað fjórir tigir' (eight hundred and four tens) – his hundred would also have been proportionately bigger, being 120!)

ℰℴ   ℰℴ   ℰℴ

Olaf had done his fair share of rowing as indeed had Ingvar, who seemed to want to try to keep up with his older and more muscular companion.

Before they had seen the beach, ÓþyrmiR had called something to the men at the fore stem to remove 'Ormr's beautifully carved dragon's head which looked out menacingly from the prow of the craft. The master mariner still held the thin tightly plaited dripping rope in his left hand and the cylindrical piece of iron with a lump of pig fat on one end in the other. Looking at the sharp but small bow wave ÓþyrmiR turned to Olaf and said, 'Well the bad weather didn't materialise, that's for sure.'

Although not a *drakkar*, 'Ormr' was a remarkably quick boat, with what Ingvar had called 'good lines' and unlike all other *knarr*s, she was fitted with a magnificently carved figurehead. A cry of joy sounded from the crew and Olaf found himself becoming worried, unnecessarily so, because he had misread the meaning of the men's cries. Ingvar quickly explained to him that the serpent's head had to be removed when they approached land in order to placate the *landvættir,* the land spirits, which inhabited rocks, gullies and the forests that seemed to clothe most of the shorelines. Thus, the cry that signified the snarling head's removal indicated the imminent and welcome end of the day's relentless rowing. It had been a particularly hard day, because the men were not yet conditioned to rowing for so long, having been on firm land for some seven days, where their main exercise had been for the most part eating and drinking.

All the crew had enjoyed their time in Aga, taking things relatively quietly. They had of course firstly unloaded their boats on arrival; a frenetic and frantic day's activity, which was followed by five days undisturbed relaxing. During the day the men played games, gambled and during the evenings most drank to excess, told tales which grew in proportion to the amount of beer and mead consumed, gambled and womanised. The community of Aga had taken to the small group of merchant travellers, who were somewhat different to the men who usually visited their community. They had been courteous on the whole and had not tried to charge exorbitant prices for their wares. Also, remarkably few fights and disagreements with the local people had occurred. The gambling games, the wagering on board games and even the drinking games had been carried out for the most part in good humour. ÓþyrmiR explained to a perplexed and slightly drunken Olaf that the use of horns for drinking vessels in such competitions was ideal, for the drinker was unable to put the horn down until he had drained it to the last drop. If a man dropped his drinking horn, in a competition, he not only lost his wager, but also spilt his drink, to add further to his embarrassment.

The men and women enjoyed nothing more than railing a half drunken competitor and of course gambling on the outcome of each contest. Olaf had managed to get into a drink fuelled fight with a large and rather fat man, who in spite of his weight gave Olaf a sound and thorough thrashing. Both men had been wielding staffs and to Olaf's amazement, he had found himself lying on the floor nursing wounds to the head. His nose had been broken high up on its bridge. One blow of his opponent's stick had sheared across his cheek leaving a heavy deep cut, before the end of the shaft had gripped and tugged and finally ripped the bottom part of one of his ear's away from his head. Some time after the melee had occurred, Olaf sat up and found himself to be dizzy and more than a little light headed. The world had suddenly seemed to become lighter, much lighter, with rapid sparks flying from a central sphere of white light that completely filled his view. Only when he lay down did his mind regain control of his body. Sitting up again after several deep breaths, he coughed and half swallowed to feel a huge semi-congealed mass of blood and mucus dislodge itself from the inside of the back of his nose. The resulting bloody mass half filled his mouth and instinctively he spat it out on to the ground.

During the last two days, the men had been carrying and loading goods on to the boats, so the relaxed feel to their trip had more or less ended as soon as it had begun and they were now beginning to prepare themselves in earnest for the journey home. Olaf had helped with the work. He had also been taken by surprise, because he had recognised the boy from Odda whom he had nearly drowned a number of years earlier. It transpired the boy was on one of the other *knarr*s and like Olaf had been forced to leave his community for some or other indiscretion. Olaf couldn't bring his name to mind, but recognized his face and stance instantly, although he was clearly older and bigger, much bigger in fact. At first, Olaf was wary and said nothing, but now it was too late, for the young man had seen him and by his interest clearly recognised him as well. Walking up to Olaf, he spat into his hand and then offered it in friendship. *'Heill, vestu!'* he said. (Hello, greetings!) Olaf echoed the other's greeting and then his name came to him.

'Þu heitir Björn.' (You are called Bear)

'Kalla þú mik Bers!' (You call me Bear)

A pleasant exchange it was and a welcome surprise for Olaf, who if truth be known, had expected trouble from the moment he recognised the lumbering youth. Bers clearly remembered his embarrassment from the years before and his face changed from one that was smiling to one slightly more serious, before asking Olaf, 'You nearly drowned me, you remember?'

Olaf's reply was slightly delayed as he considered what would be the most diplomatic response. 'It was boys' stuff, it's in the past now, we can be friends, can't we?'

'I still remember it well. You seemed determined to sink me for good.' Bers seemed not to have completely forgiven him even though many years had passed since their previous conflict. 'I'm sure you couldn't manage to beat me so easily now, especially if I kept you away from water.'

Bers was clearly spoiling for a rematch of some sort and with more than a little reluctance Olaf felt he must oblige, even though he was all too aware of the reasons why he was on a voyage that led him away from his family home. Two reasons pushed him onwards. First he was as stubborn as ever and never in his life had he considered backing down and secondly, he considered that no-one could match his fighting skills, which he still practised daily as a matter of course. Once his mind was made up and to be truthful it didn't take long, he proposed they have an insignificant wager on the outcome. 'I'll put just one ounce of *'brannt silf'* (pure silver) on the fact that I'll have you lying on your back like a newborn or Svana begging for it.'

'Fine, that'll do me fine! Though I doubt you ever got close to that one. She and her like are too good for the likes of you, but then you were always more interested in arguing and fighting.' Bers clearly had a great confidence in himself, but he was not going to up the wager, because he knew such a tactic could have disastrous consequences. He had seen it too often before, when men covered with blood, sweat and piss, with cracked jaws had pleaded with their victor. It was a truly pathetic sight, not only to be beaten in a bout, but to have to grovel and attempt to bargain with a smug assailant. No, he wasn't going to make that mistake. His father when younger had taught him consummately well and he had learnt his lessons quickly, but his poor mother of course had had the worst of it. She had more than paid for his father's indiscretions, either for the fights he took part in or for the pathetic wagers that he periodically insisted on becoming involved in. These rash and sometimes bizarre bets had usually been fuelled by large amounts of either mead or beer and invariably he lost them. Bers' mother knew his father's drinking companions and those he bet against all too well and she had not been at all pleased with the sporadic arrangements these engendered.

Olaf suggested a fight with no weapons, or a bout of *glíma*, but Bers preferred a contest with staffs. He insisted on staffs, it had to be staffs, staffs and nothing else. He repeated this once more. Olaf being intransigent by nature had decided that he would prefer anything at all, but not staffs, particularly after his recent thrashing. So the argument took off and soon it raged as a fire, with both men shouting insults at the other before randomly repeating his demands for his chosen particular form of combat.

In the end, Olaf succumbed to the request of Bers, possibly after being goaded relentlessly by Bers, who made fun of the bruised broken nose and cut that still retained a good portion of congealed blood. His stubborn streak remained in tact though. His reason for capitulating was that he had tired of shouting and simply wanted to get on with the fight and show Bers that he could still teach him a good lesson, even though he was clearly carrying several recent injuries.

Bers was naturally pleased that Olaf had succumbed to his wishes and soon it became apparent why. Each combatant was handed a staff by another young man who had been appointed hastily to make sure that the combat was conducted as fairly as possible. This independent observer of sorts was actually a good friend of Bers and quickly he proved himself to be more than a touch partisan.

Olaf gripped the staff in the customary manner; his right hand clenched about its shaft some way above his left, leaving the lengthy piece of wood almost at a diagonal angle across his body. By grasping it in such a manner, he allowed himself both the opportunity to strike at his opponent or conversely he could step back and use the stick as a defensive weapon. In stark contrast, Bers held the staff in his left hand only and by its very end. In so doing, he enabled himself to twist his wrist through a series of tight circles and thereby rotate the staff in great swishing loops that threatened to brain his somewhat amazed opponent. As a consequence of the way Bers held his staff, Olaf stepped back, trying to reassess the situation. In all his years of practice, all opponents had stuck to the tried and tested method of holding the staff firmly and attacking and defending when the felt they must. It was an unwritten protocol and this deviation from it was completely unwelcome, almost unfair or at the very least honourless to Olaf's thinking. It was not so much as an unpleasant surprise, as a nasty shock.

'Begin', shouted the youth who had handed out the staffs. His timing was impeccable and it instantly handed an advantage to Bers, who was more than ready to start. He began the bout proper by thrashing the wooden shaft downwards with lightning speed. It caught Olaf's staff with a thunderous blow; Olaf had raised his weapon to just above his leather clad head and he was more than grateful he had managed this in his defence of his skull. Because of the unusual technique being used by Bers, Olaf gripped his staff with a tremendous and nervous power with the result that the blow from Bers' staff was made to glance off rapidly. Olaf instantly took his chance by responding quickly; pushing and jabbing the end of the piece of ash into the face of his now startled opponent. The blunt butt of the staff did not land firmly, but instead flailed in the thin air before just catching the top of Bers' right shoulder, which jerked backwards violently. As Bers attempted to recover his balance and composure, he also took a step back, before rotating the staff once again in great looping circles. Olaf instinctively began to crouch, bending his knees, whilst holding up his staff above his head to protect himself from any attempted downward blow.

At this point in the conflict, Olaf begun to understand why Bers had been so insistent they fought with staffs. It was clear that he had not only mastered fighting with sticks, but had brought his chosen method of conflict to an extremely high competence level. Olaf parried again and again as well he could; waiting patiently for the chance to take Bers by surprise once more. But it was to no avail, for the reason that Bers had trained long and hard and was ready for any clever feints or subterfuge that Olaf may have contrived to hide from him. He had seen trickery of all such types and was well versed in quick and effective responses. The blows continued to rain down on Olaf's staff and perversely he welcomed them as they hit the middle, but was somewhat less at ease when they thumped onto his fingers that held his staff aloft. Time and again the blows smashed uncompromisingly onto his knuckle joints, making him jerk his hands and the attached staff upwards. It was currently a hopeless situation and he knew it. The blows continued to hail down relentlessly, as though Bers had been granted the strength of all *Asgard's* gods. Olaf's knuckles and fingers pained him terribly, they were bruised, and some had split and were bleeding profusely.

Just when Olaf was considering withdrawing and running back a few paces to reconsider what to do, his luck changed, but not because of anything to do with his fighting prowess. A large black brute of a dog seemingly appeared from nowhere and made straight for the combatants or more specifically for Bers. Snapping wildly at his legs with great dripping jaws, it barked with a deep resonant throaty roar. The hound lunged decisively as though it expected to pull great lumps of flesh from Bers' calves. Immediately, the complexion of the fight changed; Bers had become so distracted that his welter of blows slowed drastically, to cease within seconds. He stood there eyes blinking, amazed and disgruntled all at the same time, at this wholly uncalled for interruption. Foul and abusive cursing more than proved his great anger. He bellowed as loudly as he could and grunted at the beast to frighten it off, but all this did was to encourage it to jump up and down in as though in play. Continuing to bark and jump and turn into tight circles, it snapped at Bers again with its flashing dagger like teeth. Olaf, who although seconds earlier had been facing a sound thrashing was now fighting back a great desire to smile, but even so he took his chance, as he knew he must. The large man stepped two paces back, readjusted the position of his hands so they held the staff at one end and in a flash, he brought the ashen pole crashing downwards to the neck of Bers, who by now offered no defence whatsoever. Olaf using his formidable strength managed to stop the staff precisely, so that it came to rest lightly on the exposed skin just below Bers' right ear. Bers froze knowing that Olaf had taken full advantage of his extraordinary misfortune.

The combat had ceased now and both men knew that Olaf was the victor, although the circumstances of that triumph were dubious to say the least. Bers' expression had changed from being deadly serious to one of unbridled mirth even though he knew he had lost a contest that he had been winning. However, he also was aware that most men would have pressed their advantage home and his neck would have been broken asunder with a blow such as the one Olaf had apparently been about to deliver. '*Loki* moves in most mysterious ways. You are in his debt my friend.' Bers smiled as he gasped these words, exhausted from his efforts. The dog had lost any interest it had had in Bers as soon as the fighting had stopped. It ran off between two longhouses before stopping to raise a back leg very briefly as though to mark its territory. Without looking back it trotted away, to bark loudly three times before disappearing.

ᔐ   ᔐ   ᔐ

It wasn't to be a rapid trip. There were to be at least seven or as many as twelve stop offs en route, to collect or drop off various items and of course pay out some gold and to collect a great deal more of course. ÓþyrmiR was a highly skilled and well practised organiser, he had taken orders for items on the way to Aga in nearly all of the small sea-side communities and now on the way back was delivering each and every one of them. No space on the *knarr*s was wasted and every item being moved was accounted for. ÓþyrmiR was very profit driven and because he had heard tales of places where there was wealth beyond dreams for the taking, he had determined to become hugely wealthy.

ÓþyrmiR as helmsman had managed to avoid rocky cliffs and many of the potentially hazardous steep landing places. The beach the *knarr* now lay on with its three other sister ships was about as perfect a landing area as possible. It was shallow and the water did little more than lap the small round, many coloured and irregular pebbles that crunched satisfyingly under foot. Olaf was the first ashore and within only a few minutes the crews seemed satisfied the boats were safe left just where they were. Ingvar made his way towards Olaf and whispered almost inaudibly.

'Í skógum eru oft allillir vargar.' It was the same phrase he had used earlier on the boat, but added rather hoarsely, *'Vér sjám þá ganga um skóginn'.* (In forests there are often very evil wolves, we see them walking around the forest)

Olaf simply shrugged his shoulders and followed the group of mainly men and the few women who had left their boats. ÓþyrmiR was clearly not only the chief helmsman, but also in charge of the landing party and it was clear from the outset he knew exactly where he was leading his people from the *knarr*s. It must have been half an hour past sunset on a late summer's day, meaning that there was only about two hours light left to walk by. The path, for there was one, was little used, but was still quite clearly a path. At first it was simply a cutting through a low sand dune off the shingle beach, but then a short distance inland it led into a dark arch, created by tall and overbearing pine trees.

The walkway once underneath the trees' dark canopy became soft under foot; a multitude of pine needles carpeted the woodland's floor, with the consequence that virtually all sound became muffled. Not that there was much sound at all; the people off the boats had stopped talking and seemed to be ready for anything. All of the men were carrying weaponry of one type or another. Spears were not slung over shoulders, but were held ready for action, bows were to hand, the boys trudged with drawn saxes and even those men who preferred not to walk for long distances holding their chosen weapons, quietly slapped the hafts of trusty axes or *gaflak* every so often, which hung from their leather belts. Of course not all of the crews and their passengers had weapons to hand, because they were carrying sacks containing a wide range of foods and other diverse objects that had been ordered by the community they were now hoping to locate. These men had tied their make shift sacks of merchandise to the hafts of their spears which were balanced over their left shoulders. In such a way two men working together could carry quite large quantities of produce.

It was at this point Ingvar's strange comments on the boat about wolves came into Olaf's mind, because of the distant howling of wolves which he had heard whilst they were on the beach. This was now becoming louder and more and more clear. It seemed that the landing party had attracted the attention of a pack of hungry animals. No one seemed unduly worried and the presence of the animals had to some extent put the minds of some of the party at rest, because it appeared that they believed the wolves had closed in on them, for the simple reason they were the only people in the area.

All of the men and women kept close together and chatted loudly, whilst waving staffs and spears at the wolves, which had now come into view. There appeared to be about thirty or maybe even forty of them. Their leader was a large grey beast with a dishevelled and almost apologetic look about it. Its yellow eyes captivated Olaf and seemed to him to see through him and perceive everything there was to know about his being. Just one harrowing glance that was all and it was gone. Immediately, Olaf considered whether the beast could be *Loki* himself. The animal had felt his presence and known him somehow and had then without warning slowly turned away and disappeared, melting away into the dense pine woodland, shortly to be followed by all those in his troop. Nothing more was heard from any wolf that night.

The company carried on walking in what seemed like an inland direction, but in reality they were in fact trudging along on a semi-circular path, which had left the shoreline to avoid a rocky outcrop before returning to the coast a little further up the fjord. Within fifteen minutes or so of seeing the wolves, they were in the small community of Hesthamar Utne. The locals seemed to expect the visitors and did so with grace. The whole place however stank unmistakably of dog shit and piss. In fact, it was clear from the large number of tanning vessels that this small community was expert in the business of preparing leather.

Olaf and Ingvar were joined by Bers. They followed the men and women into the centre of the community, where a few words were said by ÓþyrmiR to the local people and their leader, of which only *'Heil'* (Hail) and *'Vetsu heill!'* (Hail, greetings!) could be heard from the back with a few polite words being received back. Olaf did also hear the phrase, *'Hvat gøra slíkir menn hér?'* (What are such men doing here?) muttered by a small and rather dirty looking child. ÓþyrmiR and the village leader, a *jarl*, retired to the largest longhouse in the village for talks. It seemed that they knew each other well and the apparent confusion over the route to the village had been caused by their landing at a small bay which had not been used before by the traders.

Olaf wanted to find out about the village and its leader, because it seemed to him to be almost a mirror image of his own home settlement. Ingvar was as usual more than willing to divulge all kinds of information and detail regarding Hesthamar Utne and its residents. Bers simply wanted something to eat and drink.

Olaf Bodvarrson learned from his young friend that the village had always had a number of good shipwrights, who manufactured a great range of different types of vessel. Ingvar told Olaf that they produced a small number of ærings, small narrow boats which allowed each man who was rowing to pull a pair of oars. They made four-oared færings, six-oared sexærings, eight-oared áttærings as well as ferry and fishing boats, as well as the larger coastal and ocean going trading boats or knarrs and of course their beloved long ships. Ingvar was once again on his favourite topic. He enthused about the craftsmanship of these boat builders.

'Some of *drakkar* are built wide enough for two men to man each oar, imagine that. The speed of such ships cutting through the water is quicker than any other fighting vessel! They have no match.'

Olaf grunted approvingly, he could imagine these boats ploughing their way through crystal clear pewter waters and suddenly realised that he admired the knowledge and enthusiasm of his new friend. Yes a friend; Ingvar had become a friend to him. Olaf shook his head and smiled, for he usually only respected older boys or men for their fighting prowess. Yet, the small, puny and very young looking Ingvar had gained as much respect as any of the brawlers or weapons' experts Olaf so admired. He also grudgingly admired the boy's use and variety of language and his seemingly unending supply of information.

Invar, however sensing a change in Olaf's mood suddenly changed tack.

'There is also a small smithy which is renowned for its subtle and intricate metalwork. If you get a chance, ask to see some of the work. The forge specialises in bridle work. Many of the horses' bridles are made in gilt bronze, which gives to them a shiny golden colour and they have within the mounts fantastic pictures of animals and beasts I have never seen. There are curved serpents and dragons with swirling legs and wings and sinuous bodies, but also dangerous big animals which hold onto the edges of the mounts. They seem to either grip themselves or hold the designs together. I can't understand what they are supposed to be doing really. Last time I was here I asked one of the artists who works with the smith and he just shrugged his shoulders before hitting me hard on the arm and telling me to piss off, which I did. I had the bruise from that bastard's clenched fist for weeks.'

Olaf acknowledged his friend by raising his eyebrows and spitting on the ground as he stood quite still, but failed to speak. He thought he might like to try to see some of the magical pieces of shiny bronze, if the opportunity arose, but he doubted he would somehow. He didn't like the idea of being knocked about by a craftsman however skilful he was. His mind now wandered back to his home village and suddenly, without warning, he felt a great sadness come upon him. The melancholy which now enveloped him was perhaps created by the look of the village; it looked, sounded and even smelt strangely familiar. Essentially it was the same place he had left no more than fourteen or so hours earlier, but by a different name. The cosy houses with their turfed roofs, the all pervading wood smoke and the cloying mud and straw, it all jogged and irritatingly needled his memory for home, even though he had left less than a single day before.

This musing had a dangerous effect. It had generated an idea, not a particularly clever idea, but one which popped into Olaf's young head never the less and lodged itself there, stubbornly. What if, he thought, he just so happened to disappear in such a place as this, he need not go all the way to the great trading centre of Kaupang and could live much as he had previously done. Ingvar suddenly looked up at Olaf. To the deeply thinking and unhappy youth, it seemed that his new friend, the happy go lucky young boat man was able to see his very thoughts. Ingvar quickly began describing the great Kaupang in impressive superlatives, and described the other places he had seen on his travels in intricate detail. Hedeby, Ribe and his village of birth, the small but developing Birka, all were exquisitely painted in words by Ingvar and the buildings and atmosphere of these remote and far off places seemed to come alive in the mind of Olaf. Some other place called Wollin was also mentioned and scoffed at by Ingvar. It was clear that he was for some reason less impressed with what this trading centre had to offer.

'It's a piss poor place, I'll tell you. The problem with it is,' and here he paused briefly, 'well it's the people, they're all trying to take every last scrap of silver. When they've got it, they don't want to know you. They treat you like shit. Their goods, well they're not well made, their jewellery falls apart and they use *bleikt silfr* (debased silver). We of course have to pay in *brannt silfr* (burned silver), which is worth much more, because it's purer. They don't make friends that easily, just ask any of the men. Gnúpa a young crew man of some twenty or so years, had obviously overheard Ingvar's less than flattering remarks regarding Wollin.

'Every word he's said is true. Don't bother trading there they'll have too much silver from you for their gold. They weigh it carefully, that's for sure, but their weights work differently to ours. The scale pans work for them all right. If you want to fight for your coin or *eyrir* (ounce), then Wollin's for you young man.

Ingvar's guardian, ÓþyrmiR and the *jarl* of Hesthamar Utne suddenly appeared from behind the curtain covering the door of the longhouse, stifling any further dialogue between the young men. It looked as if things had gone more than well for him. Trading agreements were being finalised by some of the leaders' men and goods had been delivered and payments were being received. Both men marched up to Ingvar and Olaf smiling and appearing very much at one with the world. Olaf couldn't help but stare at the *jarl* and wondered why he felt he knew him. He found it extremely difficult, almost impossible to draw his eyes away from the imposing leader, whose presence seemed to extend through the entire community. All his people, the karls and the *Þræll* of course appeared to look to him for instruction, even though he clearly was not going to address them now. He spoke quietly to the two young men, with a deference and solemnity which transfixed them both.

'Heil! Kalla Þú mik Ulfr, ek veg eigi goda menn. Ragir menn sjá reiðan varg koma.' (Hello! Call me Ulf, I don't kill good men. Cowardly men see an angry wolf come)

Olaf felt an immediate empathy with this well spoken leader, but at the same time shuddered, for he saw in the eyes of this man, the same wildness he had seen earlier in the forest in the eyes of that great all seeing wolf. His particularly uneasy conclusion had already been reached by Ingvar, who now looked more than a little apprehensive. After all, not that much earlier, Ingvar himself had given Olaf some cryptic statement concerning wolves and how they fought and here both of them were addressing a man whose name was taken from the animal of the same name. Ulf put both his hands out, extending them in a gesture of friendship, with his palms turned upwards in the same way a priest or monk may indicate he was about to speak in some holy manner. Ulf however said nothing and seemed about to turn away, but before doing so, he stopped and pointed up at the horizon, just above the gently swaying trees and at the same time, said in his quiet but resonant voice, 'Kaupang is where you are going and now it is also my destination. ÓþyrmiR and I have some serious business to attend to. This work should be the beginning of something great. By all the gods in Asgard, we are going to make *Midgard* shudder more than if the great serpent itself appeared before us. We will show men how great the Norse and their gods are. We are all to be rich if the tales I have heard be true. My sons and my daughter here will have to look after the longhouse and all the affairs of the village, for I will be away for quite some time. I trust you with all I possess, Ávarr, Alfarinn, Adúlfr and Ægileif. Your task is simple, rule and rule well. Ávarr, you are *jarl* in my absence and your decision is final on everything.'

With this, Ulf slapped ÓþyrmiR heartily on the back and strode away. So it was that a new passenger had been recruited onto 'Ormr'. In time, this meeting between two leaders was to have far reaching effects on a number of kingdoms. These far off realms knew remarkably little about the Northmen and their weaponry, but even less about their beliefs and what motivated them. They would learn though and the lesson was going to be a hard one and one which would be remembered for a very long time.

⊗   ⊗   ⊗

That is more than enough of this tale for one night. It makes me feel good though to think about all those wonderful dragon prowed boats of ours, ploughing their way majestically through the wide and dangerous seas, to change Midgard, the world of men forever. I wonder what we Norse folk would have done if we hadn't been so skilled in both boat building and in the art of the mariner.

Perhaps our countries would have lain undiscovered for hundreds may be thousands of years and may be, just may be little Thule would still sit astride the top of the world as unknown to us all as the way of the one god and his cross would have been. The gods of Asgard are and I say this quietly, are the gods for me. You can see and hear the actions of them all; they have no need to live in little wooden or stone buildings. We don't even need to write down what our gods do, because we simply know, we remember because we are descended each and every one of us from them. The papa they seem to think they own their god; they look to tell us what to do, how to think and even what to think. Yes, they purportedly came here first, that's true or at least what they tell us, but they did so I believe, only to get away from their own people. Now, they seem to want to convert the whole world to their way. Well I don't like them or their ideas. It may suit them, but it's not for me and I'm sure it never will be. I may pretend to embrace the new ways and I may even appear to preach them, but in my own time and space I give them no credence whatsoever.

Snorri has been most patient as he usually is; he ponders both long and hard. His mind is I am sad to say keen, or at least sharper than mine is now. I think he puts up with my ways, patronises me, because he knows I can't change. He told me when the sun clawed its way above the horizon this morning that he would never embrace the one god. He senses that the story teller is tired and that his mind is becoming confused and fatigued. Tomorrow I will begin the tale again, hopefully with a fresh mind. Sleep beckons and for once the long darkness of night has too quickly become a good friend of mine. I will lay my head down, but before I do, I will sit for the briefest of moments in the öndvegi, the most honourable seat in the longhouse and remind myself of whom I am, in spite of what I am now. I will afford myself the luxury of bringing to mind Halldora Skegg Brandsdöttir, bless her! Of my four wives, she was my favourite through all the years. She bore me no children, but that matters not. Alas, she like the others is gone as well now.

Chapter 5

Kaupang
785 A.D.

Era svá gott,
sem gott queda,
ol alda sona;
þuíat færa veít,
er fleíra dreccr,
sins til geds gumí.

The ale of the sons of men

is not as good,

as they say;

since about his own mind

a man knows less,

the more he drinks.

The return journey to Kaupang had been quite unremarkable; the weather had been good and the small boats had made excellent time. It had taken some twenty two days since Ulf had become their passenger and now it seemed to Olaf that he had always known the man with the penetrating gaze. During the late evenings, for they sailed whenever it was light, after they had set up camp at the edge of the great fjord which stretched out towards the open sea, Ulf had spoken time and again about the riches to be made in far off lands. To Olaf these seemed to be magical and made up places and it was only when ÓþyrmiR added to Ulf's words, that 'this place was due south' or 'that one was far in the west' did it start to dawn on the young man that these were real villages and towns and that he may one day if he was lucky see some of these places for himself.

On the journey, fare was about as good as could be expected. However, the frequent stop-offs meant that the boat was always well stocked with foods that would have perished on longer journeys. The sailors were able to replenish the stock of water, take on more loaves of coarse rye bread, stocks of cheese, curds and occasionally even fresh meat at each port. Consequently, all on board were in reasonably good spirits as their stomachs rumbled far less frequently than was usual.

From the sea, Kaupang suddenly appeared from around a headland. It looked just like any other small Norse community. A pall of light grey smoke moved very slowly upwards and outwards, but did so, so slowly that it seemed to hang idly over the settlement and to resent having to leave the vicinity of the cosy wooden houses, workshops and stores. The buildings which had come into sight were all constructed on a single level and were thatched from what appeared to be straw or reed. All were made to a similar design, or at least at first sight appeared to be, as indeed were all the houses and buildings that Olaf had ever encountered in his short life. Most houses were about four times as long as they were wide and had been sturdily built, but there existed subtle differences between all of the buildings. The majority of the constructions were rectangular in shape, but others, the ones which appeared to be somewhat shabbier, dirtier and older, were built with tapering ends. From the summit of the mountains that looked down upon these houses, shops and merchants' stores, all would have looked like strange land-locked straw covered boats.

Some of the older and quite a few of the newer houses had been constructed with a solid wooden frame, which had then been filled with panels of wattle and daub. Others still, were made from overlapping horizontal planking. Only some of the much older buildings had been stave built, with solid vertical planks, made from wedge-shapes cut from tree trunks. These had been joined together somehow after having been forced into the ground. The less well off occupied the smaller houses, which tended to be squarer in shape; some of these being little more than huts, measuring no more than three good strides across. These dwellings were however possibly the most cosy and at least kept the householder dry, having been expertly wind and water proofed with dung and locally dug clay.

It was behind these not quite so grand dwellings that the men found themselves staying. After arriving in the port, ÓþyrmiR had taken Olaf, Ingvar and four other similarly aged youths from the boats to a rectangular field that lay behind the permanent buildings. The six young men had been supplied with a good amount of wood, several hammers and a bag full of large, blunt and rather rusty nails. Stone foundations had already been sunk into the ground and it was on these that the men made their reasonably comfortable temporary shelter. A series of wooden uprights were then hammered into the ground down the centre of the stone kerbs and from these wooden rafters were skilfully attached. The rafters leaned against and were fastened to one another to create a high pitched roof, which in the event of a heavy down pour would quickly drain away any water and also prevent any build up of snow if the temperature happened to plummet. Afterwards, a series of battens were fixed to the rafters with the iron nails and these were then covered with freshly cut sods of turf, for insulation purposes. During the construction process there had been a few arguments concerning angle of pitch and whether some of the sods should be cut a deal thicker, but agreement had been reached quickly in all of these. None of the men wished to spend any longer on this work than necessary, because they wanted to get into one of the communal longhouses where they hoped there would be plenty of young women and an assortment of mind numbing drinks.

There had also been a more heated argument, before they had left in search of recreation over which of them was to sleep nearest to the hearth. This had been built into one of the corners of the shelter. As temporary accommodation, it was deceptively roomy inside, possibly because the floor had been excavated downwards giving to it a much greater feeling of space as well as more headroom, which was appreciated by the taller of the men staying there.

Each of the houses and indeed shelters had but one entrance and this, as Olaf later found out, led immediately to a neatly wooden slatted path that cunningly linked up with many other similar paths. Thus, all the houses tended to be aligned towards the nearest path. These criss-crossed the entire community of Kaupang and made it possible for the inhabitants and their visitors to move about without ever muddying their feet. The maze of paths did however eventually stop somewhat abruptly, a short distance from the stone quays. Instead of having to negotiate muddy and difficult tracks, residents had taken great care to install impressively wide paths constructed meticulously from many tiny and shifting stones. Olaf learnt later that the coarse shingle had been collected from the nearby beaches and that the paths were painstakingly renewed every year or indeed more frequently as was necessary.

The *knarrs* carrying their goods had arrived at the great trading centre of Kaupang in the early evening of a day late in July. It had not taken long for the boats to be tied up to the small stone jetties that protruded out into the peaceful fjord, whose waters shone like burnished pewter. Norse boats, now resting, rose lazily and gently up and down in the calmest of water, with the thick ropes which held them secure to the small quays tensing and relaxing rhythmically. As these stretched, they creaked and large bulbous drops of water were squeezed out of and finally released from the tightly knitted fibres, to drip back into the mirror like sea. Most of the boats' yard arms had been taken down shortly after their arrival and they now lay supported by the crossbeams along the length of the boats, as though resting from their long journey. Sails had also been removed and had been taken away to some nearby longhouse for repair and storage. All of the side mounted rudders which had been put into their highest position as they approached land had finally been lifted out of the water to rest dripping and green on the respective foredecks of each boat. The dragon's head of 'Ormr' had similarly been removed some time before they arrived at Kaupang and it too now rested somewhat forlornly on the foredeck alongside the helmsman's steering blade, which it appeared to have taken a great disliking to and was now snarling at continuously. The voyage or more specifically the brine and sea spray had taken its toll on all parts of the boats to a greater or lesser extent. Whilst the *knarrs* were temporarily out of commission they were to be lovingly restored by paid craftsmen, to their original pristine condition using a good deal of the gold and coinage ÓþyrmiR had made from the trading mission he had just completed.

All of the cargo held by 'Ormr' and its companion boats had been unloaded by a small army of men who swarmed hither and thither in a well rehearsed and completely controlled operation. Ingvar pointed to two men who were busying themselves with a variety of different barrels and said to Olaf that they were two of ÓþyrmiR's brothers. The larger of the brothers was called Farþegn, whilst the smaller, who appeared to be in charge was named Gedda. It transpired that the brothers organised all loading and unloading operations at the jetties and as such were regarded as important men. ÓþyrmiR's boat 'Ormr' had been attended to first, followed by the other *knarrs*, which were slightly shorter in length and beam and thus had proportionately less cargo on board.

Olaf had more or less adopted the helmsman and his boy as his family by now and he felt wholly at ease in their company. There had been many stop offs, all highly profitable, at other trading stations before they had finally arrived at their destination. Many villages in Hordaland such as Jondalsora, Arsand, Sundal, Sunde, Fjelberg, Leirvag, Tjernagel and Ryvardenmost were places visited all for different lengths of time depending on such things as the amount of trade to be done, the weather conditions, the tides and whether the particular community was on the coast itself or as was often the case, some way inland. All of these villages lay discreetly hidden in a vast landscape, on the side of the massive Viksfjord, which suddenly and startlingly opened up and became the wild and open sea. Once out of the fjord, the waters became much deeper and more dangerous; the stop offs became far less frequent. All of the boats were obliged to stop each night at small coves that fortunately punctuated the steep and sheer coastline. At first light, they left and travelled carefully, hugging the shoreline, going south at first and then eastwards. Only during the last few days did the weather turn bad, with winds blowing strongly from the west, creating dangerous lurching swells. At this time, the crews created a tent-like structure on the deck, to provide at least some shelter. The boats did however finally enter a remote but huge fjord and in the tranquillity of its sheltered and almost still waters made their way slowly to Kaupang.

Ulf had kept himself to himself all the while, but had always insisted on rowing his fair share. He had asked to travel in 'Ormr', for felt at ease with and got on well with the helmsman and they talked and discussed in great earnest important things every day. Olaf heard parts of phrases and snippets of sentences and in time began to put together in his mind, some ideas concerning what was being planned. He had of course asked Ingvar, but he surprisingly seemed completely uninterested in any such talk, saying it was none of his business. Ingvar was a naturally inquisitive boy and such a response seemed to be quite out of character. Olaf as a consequence, came to the unhappy conclusion that his friend had to be concealing something from him. Surely he was 'in the know', he mused, his adopted father would have confided in him and he must have been warned not to give out any information. Olaf continued to press him on plans for the future, but the responses he received were always irritatingly similar. Ingvar merely said he had no idea, but in spite of this seemed rather irritatingly to relish giving his apparently well rehearsed answer each time he was asked. Olaf was a shrewd young man however and he had, as a result of his friend's lack of cooperation put together pieces of all the conversations he had managed to overhear, in the same way a child assembles its view of the world.

He had quickly learned that trade had been good around the coast and in the fjords of Hordaland, Rogaland, Jæren and Agder, but that ÓþyrmiR and Ulf had other more striking ambitions. Moreover Olaf had learned that Ribe to the south and the far off Birka and also Paviken on the isle of Gotland to the south east were excellent trading centres, where a lot of gold and silver had been made. From what he could gather, all this talk and subterfuge pointed to one thing, that new trading routes were being examined by Ulf and ÓþyrmiR. These routes could potentially bring profits almost untold to those willing to take risks with investment of gold and silver and of course with boats. New expeditions would however mean sailing to distant places in unfamiliar and dangerous waters.

℘   ℘   ℘

The summer was waning and the warm dry weather it had brought was soon to be replaced by the wet and cold of the autumn. The thoughts of most of the folk in Kaupang had turned to the local harvest, because the trading season had more or less ended. Most of the small ribbon-like fields had been planted with a coarse rye-like grain, which was used to make very heavy, dark loaves of bread. The grain heads on the stalks of this crop had swollen and now waved gently in the breeze, as though inviting the smile of the sickle. There were some boats however, which continued to ply their wares late into the autumn, but these tended to be specialist traders whose cargoes consisted mainly of the pelts, skins, bones, teeth and horns of strange animals, both from the land and the sea. In addition, some of the boats carried completed pieces of clothing, such as capes, rough linen shirts and pants, long woollen trousers, hats for all kinds of weathers and mittens and gloves. Some of the items of clothing were crudely stitched animal pelts, which in life must have lived in the most severe and cold conditions. Other pieces of attire were considerably more refined and clearly their production processes had demanded a much greater input of human labour, with the consequence that such objects claimed more coinage, or even silver or gold bars for their purchase.

At one of the regular markets set up in the centre of bustling Kaupang, Olaf had decided to buy himself a pair of hardy woollen mittens for the winter. He soon came across a pair that caught his eye. They had been carefully placed on a roughly cut, thick plank of strongly smelling resin laden pine that was itself precariously balanced between two barrels. Olaf was utterly astounded at the asking price and Ingvar who had accompanied him on this bartering trip simply made matters worse by laughing long and loud at his friend's incredulity. He irreverently prodded Olaf in the ribs and whilst telling him he had expensive tastes; tastes that were not for the likes of him. Ingvar reminded his friend that the mittens were composed of the finest lambs' wool and that they had been manufactured by some poor man or woman who must have needed money quite desperately. Shaking his head, he complained saying that he wished he had time to make other people's clothes. Then, picking up the costly mittens Olaf desired to buy, he said, 'All my gloves and mittens are made by me, nobody else. It takes me forever to tie all those knots and then loop the next line of knots through the first row and then carry on till all the rows are held together securely. By the springs and lakes of Kaupang, nalbanding would have me go mad, if I had to make a new pair of these every year. My mittens have lasted and will last me for years, even when I work at sea on the boats I can't seem to wear the things out, thank the gods. I couldn't imagine making these for someone else to wear. I wouldn't have the patience and I wouldn't make them so well, if they weren't for me. This made a great deal of sense to Olaf and he suddenly realised that the mittens he so desired moments before had now completely lost their appeal to him.

As he walked away from them he thought to himself about the power of persuasion his friend possessed. Shaking his head and grinning to himself, he also understood that he had changed; he had surprisingly learned to listen and take advice, without taking offence or trading blows.

Kaupang also provided Olaf with his first view of trading between real merchants, men whose lives depended on their transactions. Ulf had told him to come with him one morning to see him haggle for a new spear. The young man had been pleasantly surprised to be asked and felt that Ulf had asked him, because he must have had some ulterior motive. Ingvar would probably have accompanied them, but he was still recovering from a night of heavy drinking and now lay senseless on damp straw, which constituted the flooring of the temporary hut. The two of them had walked to a small longhouse situated well away from the stone quays, somewhere at the very edge of the trading community. Walking side by side along the broad wooden planking, they had arrived there within several minutes.

Ulf had shouted out a greeting through the already half opened door and instantly a large smiling man appeared. He was slightly shorter than Olaf, but much sturdier around the middle. His hair was shortly cropped, but he also possessed a very bushy flaxen coloured beard, which he had carefully twisted into three strands and plaited. It seemed the presence of these unexpected visitors had for some reason cheered him no end. Olaf had earlier learned from Ulf that the man's name was Fastaðr, which had made him snigger uncontrollably. Ulf had grunted and reprimanded him by hitting him on the upper arm with the outside of his hand for being cheeky, but even so, Olaf thought he saw a glint in the older man's eye which gave him the idea that he had also found the man's name somewhat amusing.

Fastaðr welcomed both the younger and older man in the same way, by bowing his head to each of them in turn and simply saying, *'Vestu'* (Greetings). Ulf responded by quietly saying, *'Heill'* (Hail), whilst Olaf simply repeated the merchants own greeting back to him.

'Ek kalla mik Fastaðr' (I am called Fastaðr). *'Ja'* (Yes), he said before his voice tailed away. He had clearly spotted the slight smile that Olaf was unable to conceal on his face and before speaking again, he showed an array

of broken teeth as he smiled himself, indicating that he may have appreciated the young man's sense of humour. Fastaðr looked at Olaf and told him that his name was also his way and that for a dealer in weapons that must be a good thing. Olaf, straight faced by now merely nodded. Fastaðr appearing somewhat earnest replied quietly, 'Strong fight, that is what and who I am.'

A short while later all kinds of swords, saxes, cutting knives, spears, shields, helmets and armour of the type Olaf had never seen before, had been laid out on the straw covered earthen floor of the small longhouse. One particular blade, one made by a master craftsman of the greatest skill, did not fail to catch the eye of both Olaf and Ulf. Fastaðr described in great detail the benefits of this particular blade, before saying quietly to himself, so that Olaf alone could just hear the whispered words, 'Hann hjó til Fastaðrs með sverði.' (He struck at Fastaðr with a sword) Without warning, the avuncular man pulled back his left sleeve to reveal a deep crescent shaped scar which ran from his elbow, almost to his wrist. He smiled at his prospective customers and said that the blade cut through his flesh as though it were cutting a fresh apple. 'My arm can say more to you than my words can,' he affirmed, whilst drawing his sleeve down to once more cover the wound.

The blade was enchanting and alluring at the same time and it was one which clearly interested Ulf. However, as is the way with men who like to think they drive a hard deal, Ulf feigned but little interest and chose instead to almost sneer at the exquisite weapon and view it through half closed eyes. 'I have a sword and its blade is thicker and stronger than this weedy looking article,' he scoffed. Not to be put off, Fastaðr demanded that Ulf take the blade and feel for himself the wonderful balance, the magical way the blade cut through the air and the superlative ease of its movement. Ulf begrudgingly did as he was asked before asking the dealer how much silver would be required for the sword, before saying in whispered tones, '*Eru engi álög á brandinum?*' (Is there a spell on this sword?) Fastaðr smiled knowingly, whilst nodding his head; he knew that the big fish had taken his bait. His particular way of closing deals usually worked and now before losing any momentum that he had built up, he launched into a well rehearsed speech about the best had to cost the most. It was of course meant to prepare Ulf, his next customer, for the shock which he was shortly to receive.

To delay proceedings and no doubt to distract Ulf from the momentum his bargaining methods had gained, the dealer picked up a fantastically crafted helmet and offered it to Olaf to try on. 'It is of Anglo Saxon make, rumour has it that only two of this type were ever made. One went to a great king, to be buried with him and his ship far away in Bretland I heard and this one, the finer of the two came to me. How I secured it I will not confess to you. Look at the fine hinges, the way the two metals fuse to become one, the well crafted figures and all that wonderful detail. It is in truth the plaything of a prince or king, not for the likes of you or me.' The ploy had worked, for even Ulf, who was completely captivated by the blade he now held, lost his attention to this other fine piece of consummate artisanship. Olaf needed no second invitation to try the highly polished silver and gold helmet on. He instantly smiled from ear to ear and imagined himself as a fabled and invincible warrior in the centre of a battle wielding a huge double headed axe. He could almost see the faded writing on the vellum pages describing his great heroics and fantastic deeds.

The prospective owner of the sword spat at the preposterous weight of silver required, whilst pretending not to be shocked, although to his core, he genuinely was. Soon the number of ounces had been radically reduced by Ulf, with Fastaðr grumbling and offering his open hands to the sky as if he were being robbed by the sharp edge of the blade itself. The stage had been reached where Olaf in his naivety believed that the merchant was being taken advantage of unfairly by Ulf and he felt sorry for the man whose arm bore such a terrible scar. With a shaking of hands, the deal was all of a sudden struck and Olaf felt a tinge of disappointment that it was so quickly over. It had been so rapid after all! A small velvet bag containing pieces of silver was passed discreetly from Ulf to the dealer, so discreetly in fact that a casual observer wouldn't have noticed the substantial payment being made. Fastaðr immediately dangled the bag between the thumb and fore-finger of his left hand as though trying to work out the weight of its contents by feel alone. He then loosened the draw string about the bag's neck and with well practised relish, poured the contents onto what looked like a worn and tarnished metal plate. Most of the silver from the bag appeared to be just small slivers, or simply grains, but there were several coins, a number of chunky nuggets and even two small rectangular bars. With his stubby fingers, Fastaðr sorted the contents of the bag into several small piles, after which he turned and peered with half closed eyes into one of the darkened corners of the small building.

In this particular corner, perched on top of a woven reed basket containing an obsidian black noisy raven, which jumped about angrily and made harsh calling noises, there was a small set of scales. It was a very carefully crafted and rather beautiful set, because the pans which held the weights and the gold or silver that was there to counter-balance them, hung from three delicate small bronze coloured chains. These in turn were deftly attached to an exquisitely decorated cross bar of a similar metal that sat and balanced carefully atop a pointed upright, that acted as a fulcrum. Clearly, the entire contraption could be dismantled to sit within a small black, velvet-lined and hinged wooden box, which acted when it was being used, as the balance's base.

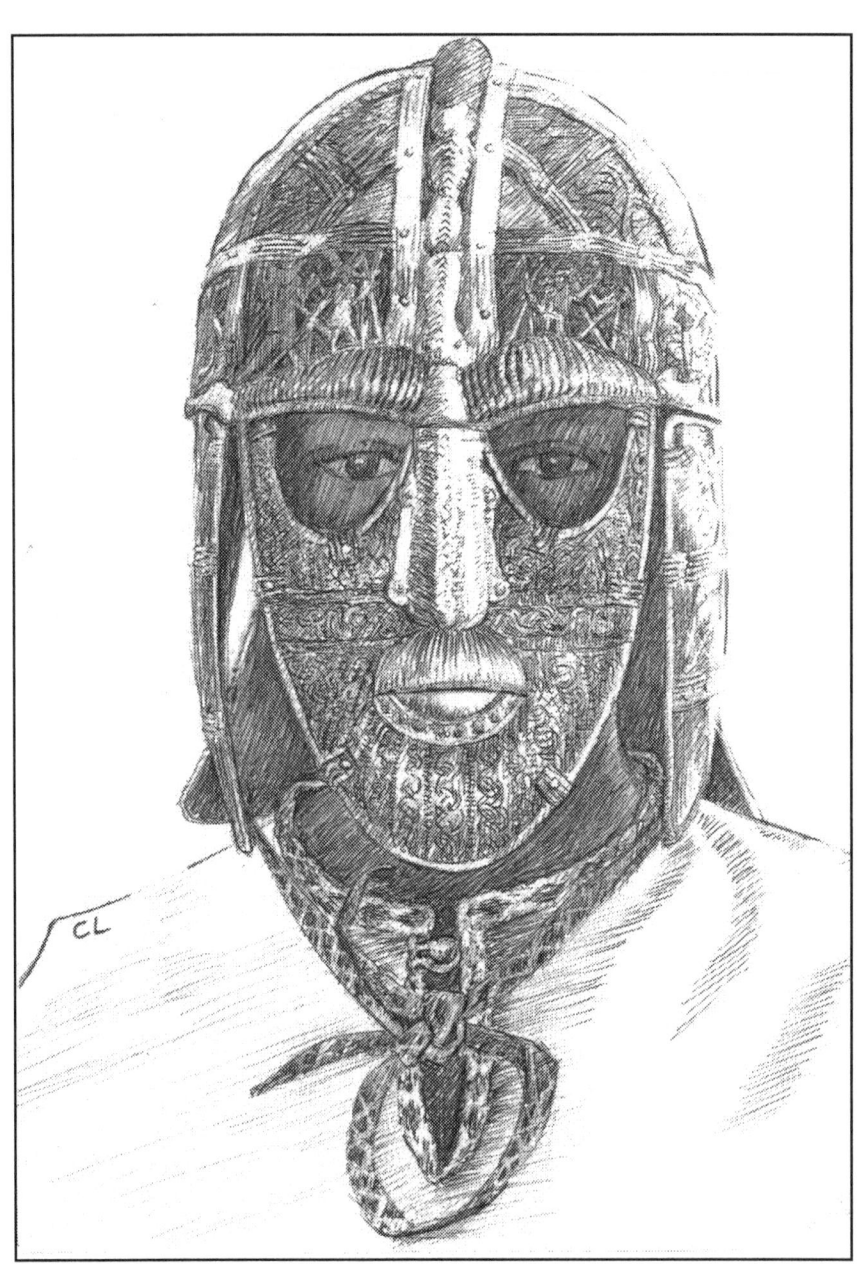

Fastaðr collected the balance with relish and placed it carefully, with well practised movements on a small upturned barrel that looked to Olaf, because of its smooth top as though it was used in normal circumstances as a makeshift seat. The merchant then proceeded to add a number of weights to one pan, before carefully placing the small bars, followed by the coins in the other, nodding his head as he did so each time in a sort of ritual, until at last the small beam was parallel with the box's base and he had reached what appeared to have been the agreed quantity of silver. Then he smiled, raised his eyebrows clearly indicating that he was going to ask the proud new owner of the sword a pertinent question. In a quiet but firm voice, he politely asked if Ulf would like to buy the scabbard for the blade as well.

'*Umgjorðr, umgjorð*' (the scabbard, the scabbard), Ulf said quietly to himself before whistling once, knowingly instantly that he had made a big mistake. In addition, he had made this childish blunder in front of the boy. The scabbard would cost him a good deal too and he, as the dealer knew so well would have to have it. A great sword needs to be cared for, it needs a scabbard in the same way that a boat needs a figurehead. A *drakkar* cannot sail without a snarling beast at its prow and a sword cannot hang at the waist without the scabbard that was made for it.

Ulf ended up paying half as much again for the housing that would look after the blade. However, the scabbard, like the sword was a work of consummate artistry. It was composed of what seemed to be reinforced leather that had been carefully decorated and covered by a cage of two or so precious metals. The entire object was exquisitely decorated with swirling golden dragons whose tails, wings and indeed whole bodies were intricately intertwined, locked in what appeared to be mortal combat. The dragons' talons held on to the edge of the scabbard and their teeth gripped the top edge where the sword would enter and leave. Ulf later confided with Olaf that he thought had got the better of the dealer and that the combined price of both the sword and the scabbard was about right. From that moment on however, Olaf looked at Ulf in a slightly different light, he felt that the fighting man he had grown to admire so quickly, was not quite as shrewd as he had first thought when he had originally met him in Hesthamar Utne several months ago.

Ulf was of course unaware of Olaf's thoughts, he simply got on with his life and kept himself busy buying other weapons and enjoying himself playing various games for money, drinking the evenings away and spending yet more money on women who never seemed to be in short supply in Kaupang. Indeed, there were many slaves, both men and women. There were also many children, some as young as five or six summers, who were forever arriving at and disappearing from the town. They were a sorry sight; some were destined for far off southern shores, to work in the purported blistering heat of the day. Others were purchased by jarls from Hordaland, Rogaland or other Norse areas. Much of the silver created by this trade in human misery found its way into the great trading centre of Kaupang from the far-east in the form of strange looking coins or small bars that had been struck with some stamp so as to verify their quality and pureness.

℘ ℘ ℘

The long summer faded and the days became autumnal. There was less much less daylight and proportionately less activity in the whole of the community. Nights in contrast began to lengthen; temperatures dropped. The land became strangely still, as if in anticipation of the grip of the winter that was sure to follow. Trading continued, but at a much reduced level. Animals that were not in the best condition were slaughtered and hung up over tree branches to drip their dark blood onto the soil. When the carcasses had more or less dried out, some were cut up and partially roasted over open fires before the meat was treated with salt to preserve it. Salt, of course was another of the prized commodities that had trickled into Kaupang from eastern areas for as long as anyone could remember, in exchange for all kinds of produce.

The *knarrs* had all been repaired and had been painstakingly re-calked. The process was a lengthy one, but one which was done with a systematic and almost loving devotion. The men, carrying out this work, in the late autumn of the year A.D. 785, knew that their efforts and attention to detail may save their and their fellow sailors lives at some later juncture. Not only did the men work on the *knarrs*, but they also worked on several *drakkars* that had arrived from somewhere in the north. One of these ships was in a very poor state. Its bow, where a fierce dragon's head may once well have peered, was splintered and for the most part missing. Water had forced its way between the planking and as the boat had dried out on the pebbly beach where it had been unceremoniously dragged, the planking had warped and some of the individual planks had forced themselves away from the timber frame of the boat itself. The mast was in good condition though and it lay inside the boat supported by the cross beams. Most of the decking, where the rowers would have sat had been removed to allow access to the lower timbers, some of which were clearly rotten. The boat had no holes for oars, but simply had pegs between which the oars had sat. These must have moved this way and that, as some unknown oarsman had pulled and returned the oar to its original position. All of the pegs been removed as had the sump plug, which had been thrown somewhat unceremoniously to the rear of the boat. The boat stank of rotting seaweed, fish and human excrement and to the untrained eye would have passed for nothing better then fire wood.

ÓþyrmiR and Ulf had purchased this particular *drakkar* from a merchant who had brought a *knarr* into the port, which had been laden with animal furs and a good consignment of dark and hard amber. The boat had not been used for some time and its previous owner had not even haggled over the price of what appeared to be a wreck. ÓþyrmiR had spotted the *drakkar* as soon as he had arrived and had found out who the owner of the boat was, its history, including where it had been made and more importantly whether it was for sale and the asking price. Very little silver changed hands and Olaf shook his head in disbelief when he heard about the purchase. Even Ingvar appeared to think that the vessel was beyond repair, but he thought the price was low, very low. He asked ÓþyrmiR why the boat was so cheap and the answer went some way to restoring his faith in the older man. It seemed that part of the deal was passage on the boat when it was repaired, for two of the owner's boys.

It took a long time for the boat to be brought back into working service. One of the reasons for this was that the men working on her had to split their time between this *drakkar*'s repair and the task of building another new ship, to the same specifications. Everything on the new boat was built to precisely match that of the older vessel. The dragon's head which had previously graced the bow of 'Ormr', had by the owner's stern instruction found its' way onto the older *drakkar*'s prow, whilst a similar but even more fierce looking figurehead had been placed on the new boat. ÓþyrmiR considered this *drakkar* a new toy and said enthusiastically that he would call it 'Ormr', whilst the brand new boat would go by the name of 'Mjollnir'. The faithful old *knarr* that had lost its name to the older of the two *drakkars* was simply to be called 'Hamar.'

ဆ ဆ ဆ

Winter passed slowly, so slowly that it seemed the sun would never regain any of her former strength. The nights became longer and longer and light what little there was of it struggled to gain a proper grip on each day in *Midgard*. It became cold; so cold that the sea in the fjord finally froze over and Kaupang became cut off once more from the outside world. The shoreline was first to succumb to the cold and soon became a long strip of gnarled ice. Eventually, several hundreds of yards of open wind blown sea flattened into a plane of sea ice. Then, slowly but inevitably the bay froze.

A few traders still managed to arrive at the port, but they were few in number and were for the most part from nearby areas, which could be readily reached by foot. In fact they came to the bustling town on long wooden skis and usually had teams of semi-wild slavering dogs, which howled like wolves long before they reached Kaupang, giving away their imminent arrival. It was said the dogs could smell the town from far away and it was this that prompted them to call out in expectation of food and rest. It was more than possible that the smells of Kaupang could drift for miles on a gentle breeze, as the whole place stank of human and animal filth, smoke from hundreds of small spluttering fires, rotting meat and vegetable matter, boiling tar, tanned leather and of course a multitude of different fish in various states of terminal decay.

Both Olaf and Ingvar had of course been put to work. ÓþyrmiR had told the young men that they had to earn their way and he shrugged his shoulders when Olaf had remonstrated with him. Both were to look after farm animals, cleaning them out, feeding them, tending them if they were ill, slaughtering them as required and carrying out any other jobs as deemed necessary by the owner of the animals. They were not to receive any silver or gold, their payment was in the form of free board and lodging.

The small hut they stayed in was just about adequate as a place to sleep. They had been given very little firewood and therefore spent much of the early evening when it was dark in the hut occupied by ÓþyrmiR. The other young men they shared the hut with were never to be seen in the evening. Appearing late at night, they were usually drunk and wholly unreasonable. There had as a consequence been several fights, but in the morning everything seemed to be forgotten and so it continued month after month into the depths of a harsh and unforgiving winter.

The helmsman as he was often called by the locals was quite content to see Ingvar and Olaf in his longhouse, because he deemed if he could see them, they would not be getting into scrapes. Here, the fire remained well fuelled for many hours into the evenings and the three of them played various board games whilst talking and occasionally singing. It was during these times of relaxation that ÓþyrmiR learnt how accomplished Olaf was in using his memory and in strategy. Ingvar simply couldn't compete and after a short time he would pretend to lose interest and either go to sleep in the corner on a bale of straw or wander off into the frozen night to join other young men and women of his own age who were like him attempting to fight off the boredom bequeathed by long dark evenings. There were many things to do of course, but as is the case so often with human nature, almost all of these necessary tasks carried little appeal. The interminable spinning of wool, the unending task of weaving new sail material, nalbanding new socks and mittens, all of these things had to be done. There was a variety of carving work and a whole host of other carpentry tasks to be completed as well.

Ingvar impressed Olaf by the way he fashioned a drinking cup from the trunk of an old gnarled piece of birch. He explained to Olaf how he had selected a 'clean' piece of wood and which tools he would need to use on it.

Olaf shook his head and picking up one of the more unusual wooden handled tools said he could not imagine using such strangely shaped pieces of iron.

'It's not the chisels that are that difficult to use, it's the entire procedure that is so demanding.' Ingvar continued, 'That's the important bit as well as patience of course. You must shape the wood, slowly but surely with these tools, using the ones with more delicate cutting edges as the bowl takes shape. Then when you have the cup or bowl exactly as you want it, you must spend several hours rubbing it down, to smooth its surface. When you're happy with it, you must then boil the thing for quite a time in a solution of brine, to draw any sap out. When you're happy this is done, you must tightly wrap the vessel in a rag, to allow it to dry very, very slowly. If you allow the wood to dry quickly, it will split. Oh and when I say slowly, I really mean slowly. Watch the phases of the moon, three times; *Nýi Niði, Nýi Niði, Nýi Niði* and then the bowl will be ready. I've heard it said that the moon's power somehow draws any moisture left out of the wood! I can't see it myself. I should imagine if power is needed then it comes from some witch or other, someone like Groa, who had the power to bring *Þorr* back from the dead.'

'Is there any blasted thing you don't know about?' Olaf enquired of his friend smiling.

'Lots, I don't know much for sure, but what I do know is this, the more I learn, the more I realise there is to learn my friend.' Ingvar's reply showed a deep humility, but even so it made Olaf feel a tad less than adequate. His response in turn also showed an appreciation of his shortcomings with regard his understanding of *Midgard*. Even Olaf it seemed had begun to realise that he had a lot to learn.

'Well, Ulf by that reckoning knows just about nothing and I am sad to say am guardian of less than nothing if that by *Loki* is possible!' Occasionally, Olaf and Ingvar came across Ulf. The great fighter's lifestyle was as different to Olaf and Ingvar's as it possibly could have been. For the most part he kept himself to himself in the daylight hours, but at night he appeared to come alive. He seemed to grow and change into a different person. He was quiet and reasonable during sun up, but as the light faded and the colours of day melted into shades of evening greyness, a dark side to his character became more and more apparent. As the winter entered its darkest times and frost and ice locked the land, Ulf's persona grew and he changed mysteriously into a being capable of great words and actions. He was often to be seen moving between his longhouse and various drinking houses, after darkness had fallen to enshroud the entire village with a veil of impenetrable blackness. At these times, he always dressed in a long swirling woollen cape, which hung right the way down to his well-worn leather boots. These just about covered his ankles and offered him a reasonable degree of protection from the dampness which seemed to pervade every aspect of the lives of Kaupang's residents. On his head, he simply wore a tight fitting skullcap, which exactly matched the colour of his footwear. His hair, which was a dark mousy brown, spilled out in all directions and was blown hither and thither as was the snow, by cold blasts of winter wind every time he ventured out of the longhouse he was staying in.

℆   ℆   ℆

Jól came and went. Children had, in the age old tradition, stuffed their socks with straw and hung them up in their longhouses for the great horse *Sleipnir*, on the eve of the winter festival. The morning brought with it wonder, for most of the straw was gone and all the children celebrated, happy in the knowledge that the magical eight-legged horse and its illustrious rider had not forgotten them at this most important of times. Parents enjoyed seeing their offspring's delight, before indulging heavily with wine or mead or ale or combinations thereof. It was one of the few times in the year when the entire community stopped their work and simply took it easy. For one and in some cases two days, people drank and ate to excess. All the careful planning to ensure food would last until the good weather returned was forgotten for that short period of jollity and unadulterated gluttony and sloth.

꙳   ꙳   ꙳

In time, warmer days duly arrived. The intensity of the daylight had increased and there was more time to do things while the sun moved across the sky at an apparently more leisurely pace. It grew warmer; plants were growing once more and suddenly animals, both wild and domesticated appeared to be everywhere. Ice no longer claimed dominance of the great bay and the sea beyond. Trading boats took advantage, beginning to arrive and leave Kaupang in increasingly greater numbers. The port, once again became the hub of a massive trading enterprise. Goods sometimes spent almost no time at all on the stone quays, before being swallowed into the hungry bellies of the ever present *knarr*s that lined up expectantly, sometimes three or four of them abreast, gently rocking in the tranquil water. 'Hamar' and three other *knarr*s, all owned by Ingvar's father had disappeared from Kaupang twelve days before. They were all bound for Hedeby first and then they were to venture on to Wollin and finally to the tiny Birka. Olaf had watched with Ingvar as they had disappeared. Both young men had been somewhat disappointed that their offer to go with the boats had been turned down. Both of them had been instructed to carry on with their jobs of unloading the boats as they arrived at the stone jetties or alternatively loading them before their departure. The time for working, producing various crops and looking after farm animals lay behind them. Olaf was so pleased to know that he had some gold of his own at last, with which he could not only start to pay his way in life, but also make decisions over what he chose to do. Confiding in Ingvar, he leant close and said.

'Ha, we can make a little and save a little. With luck, we will get other jobs from the traders. They always pay for information on this or that!'

'True enough, but remember they are the ones who make the real money. If they pay us one silver rod, then you can bet that they will make ten!'

'Better to have one silver bar, coin or rod than none at all', came Olaf's rather naïve reply.

After settling his board, he still had enough coin left over to pay for some of the luxuries in life he previously had not considered. He had obtained a pair of heavily knotted red mittens, almost exactly like the ones he had seen soon after he had arrived in Kaupang. Olaf had not only paid for them, but had been confident enough to considerably reduce the asking price by haggling furiously with the vendor. He was learning the ways of the world fast and was not to be conned in the way Ulf had been when he had obtained his sword.

⁋ ⁋ ⁋

I believe Snorri has come to like Olaf. I think he sees a little of the young man in himself. Well, why by all the gods not, I say? Tell me this, who has no desire to be clever, powerful and young? Are not these the things which we all so crave?

When I describe Olaf and his thoughts, I can see the tell tale signs; they kindle something of a twinkle in Snorri's young eyes. He seeks to know more things about Olaf; what he was truly like. Snorri told me he would like a helmet like the one Olaf tried on, but he like Olaf will never possess such a thing. My grandfather, the necromancer spoke at great length to me of such priceless helmets and confided that he had seen the final resting place of one of them in a dream. It made no sense to me at all. He said, 'In a boat in the ground, on the east coast of a country surrounded by sea.' That is all he would impart, he refused to give any further details. How I wish I could have understood fully what he meant. The thing about Saemundr is that he was and is an enigma; by the standards of mere mortals such as me and you, he is too far too complex a character for any of us to understand. Is he one of the gods? Are his words on the beginning of the world all his? Some think not! They strive to strip the great old man of his status, as a man of learning. They cannot accept him, because of the fabulous tales to which he is linked. It is as though these incredible and fascinating stories have too much power for their bellies; they for some reason discredit him. Just because his name is writ full on the title page of the most singularly important edda in this land of lands of ours means apparently nothing. Does not the title tell us anything at all, of the author? Well, 'Edda Sæmundar Hinns Froða,' does give to me just the smallest of clues. No, I jest, although I should not, for I am angry and feel that my grandfather should be acknowledged in his own right. Let the words attributed to him speak for him. Let those who doubt his scholarship step forward. But if any man or woman dares to, let them declare the name of the real scribe and if they cannot, then they should keep their over used mouths shut. That is my challenge! I am waiting. Let them speak up if they dare.

Snorri has also asked me several times about what became of Olaf at the end of this tale. I won't let on though, because I know that he will lose interest in the tale as all people who listen to tales would do if they were privy to their endings too soon.

He has confided in me that both trade and barter are not of much interest to him, but I have instructed him in quite a stern manner, that the realms of Norse peoples would not be as diverse and strong if it were not for the humble knarr and *its hard work. Some have said though, although I refute the idea, that the demise of the Frisians' boats at the hands of the Carolingians, not so many years before the time of Olaf, gave us Norse that little bit of extra help we needed. Their trading empire was well established, I grant you that, but we and I use the word we with pride, more than filled the space they left!*

Chapter 6

fíorþí mánuðr

Bírka
July, 786 A.D.

ÓþyrmiR half closed his weary eyes as 'Hamar' entered the most easterly of the two small natural harbours at Birka; Korshamn and Kugghamn. Unlike its nearby neighbour, the latter jutted quite a way inland and in so doing afforded a good degree of shelter from any inclement weather that happened to blow in off the sea. To the crew of all the boats, it had felt like a very long voyage, possibly because trading had not gone as well as all would have liked. Payment of course was inextricably linked to what was made on each merchant trip and this would have a bearing on whether their bellies and those of their families would be full in the long winter months ahead.

The prices their master had expected for the goods carried on this trip, had rarely been reached and ÓþyrmiR was for the first time in his life, staring at a loss making trip. If dealing in Birka was poor as well, he mused to himself, he would be unable to turn around his recent rather worrying trend of loss; he may have to sell one of the three *knarr*s, which now were tying up at the quay. What had made matters worse, far far worse, was the very recent, unnecessary and entirely avoidable loss of one of his beloved *knarr*s to the sea. He had lost the boat 'Hrokr', several of her crew and virtually all of her cargo within sight of the trading centre of Hedeby. This coastal town was an important trading community in the kingdom of Haithabu, ruled over by their monarch, Sigurd.

The boat had been fully loaded or rather overloaded with expensive and heavy goods and as the planking deep in its bilge had begun to leak, the two poor boys responsible for bailing such water had worked as furiously as they could, desperately refusing to give in, until their knuckles and knees had bled and it was clear that their battle for the boat was a lost cause. One boy had bailed, while the other lugged one of the two buckets they were using up on to the deck before throwing its contents over the side. When he returned, he had another bucket to empty and so on. The near freezing water in the hull had crept in slowly at first, making no noise and causing no great alarm to any of the veteran sea farers. However, it reached a critical level in no time at all and the waves around the boat seemed to suddenly grow in stature as if ready to pounce and in seconds they had breached the top strake and the boat was floundering. The boys, who had been bailing so fast, stopped without warning and simply remained at their station as though awaiting orders, which of course never came. To unwittingly speed up the influx of sea water into the *knarr*, four oar holes near to the stern of the boat hadn't been plugged, allowing many gallons of water to spurt through. So quickly did it all happen, that there was little time for panic.

The crew and passengers alike had been plunged into the *vatn*, dark and bitterly cold foaming water. Some of the men and women had shouted out, whilst others attempted to splash their way towards the remaining three *knarrs*. It was numbingly cold, with the waves striking shoulders and heads in the way hard unforgiving steel bludgeons mere human flesh. Some, arguably the lucky ones could not swim at all and in the difficult swell and freezing waters; they had simply disappeared from sight, to be consumed by the hungry sea in seconds. There was no respite.

Men and women of the other *knarrs*, were immediately aware of the difficulties being experienced by their sister boat and had turned around to help, as quickly as they possibly could, but little was to be accomplished by them. The strongest of the swimmers, five or six young men, from the sunken boat had within a minute or so somehow managed to clamber aboard the nearest of the other boats. They were all suffering badly from exposure to the cold, even though they must have been in the water for less than two minutes. A few pieces of buoyant cargo had conveniently floated up to the surviving boats, having been blown towards them by a sudden squall. These items were salvaged into one of the surviving *knarrs*, by two men wielding long ash poles, which had solid iron hooks firmly attached with nails of the same metal to their slightly tapered ends. All the other boat men, their women and everything else on board the hapless craft, were lost to the ever moving and greedy waters. Only a variety of flotsam and jetsam, which rode the swell, before being slowly dispersed across the sea, gave any indication that a boat had been lost. Iron and steel weaponry, including beautifully crafted damascened swords, some intricately decorated pieces of armour of two different coloured metals and several large, heavy and ornate wooden boxes which contained various precious stones set in silver and a diverse collection of gold jewellery had all sunk to the bottom of the sea in the blink of an eye.

'Hamar's owner and its helmsman was at that precise moment preoccupied with his own thoughts as the ropes made from birch bark were thrown from the boat to be tied up to the small quay. Birka was a very small port, one which didn't merit a trading stop under most circumstances, but to ÓþyrmiR it was important. He of course hailed from this tiny and remote place and had argued loud and long, usually in vain with the traders from Kaupang, Hedeby and Ribe, that one day it would be the most important of places to trade. 'Look', he would say to his fellow merchants, 'the whole place is surrounded by water and trees, what more do you need?' Also, he continued enthusiastically, 'It is placed in the centre of our world, the centre of everything. It is like the great tree itself, it connects different parts of the world and to travel anywhere, you have to pass through it. It is our *Yggdrasil*; it is the chosen place in *Midgard*, I tell you. From the north comes wonderful fur and all kinds of ivory and teeth, from the south there is the great Hedeby, from the west there is Kaupang and many other rich and distant lands and from the east, there are the great waterways. And waterways as we all know mean towns and wealth; they all need exploring and then exploiting. You wait, mark my words boys,' he would say to the men, 'by the end of our lives, little Birka on Björkö will be the place to make coin, both silver and gold. By the great serpent of the world, which forever crawls unseen on the ocean's floor, by *Jörmangandr* himself I speak the truth.'

ᴕᴐ ᴕᴐ ᴕᴐ

Now, the usually ebullient man cut the figure of a sorry and downcast wretch, he had not only lost a boat, a cargo, money, trade, but also some friends and relatives, all of whom were good crew. Some of those lost also had relatives in Birka, which meant that Óþy as he was known in the small port would have to deliver the news of their final demise himself. This prospect he didn't relish, because firstly he had never had to do such a thing before and secondly, because he was used to sharing a drink with these very people, his crew's people. They were his people; he knew that he would by informing them of their loved ones' loss, be ripping their meagre lives apart. The blame was as he knew only too well, his alone. 'Hrókr' ('Crow') was his boat; a boat that he had supervised loading before its terrible and untimely demise. At the time, he had appreciated it had been low, possibly dangerously so, in the water, but for some reason against his better judgement and instincts, he had refrained from ordering some of the goods to be taken off. Now, he would have to pay bereaved relatives what he could, but in his heart he knew it would never be enough. Perhaps, he thought, as though looking for some reason, the naming of the boat after a carrion bird, a bird which relished the flesh of the battle-dead was not such a good idea after all. Greedy birds they surely are, he thought.

Birka although small as a trading centre was always very busy, from early morning to the last light of day, all kind of goods were arriving and being exchanged; for the main part, silver. Silver was the universally accepted currency. Every single commodity you could possibly have wished for, whether it was a delicate silver arm ring or indeed a contract to build a fleet of *drakkar*, everything seemed to materialise magically within a day or so.

Everybody who came to Birka knew where to find what, or whom they wanted and the whole place was under the circumstances remarkably well organised and civilised with it. It was as different as it could have been from their last port of call, Wollin, where profit margins dictated a more aggressive form of barter or trade. In Wollin, boats were frequently seized with full cargoes. There were the constantly occurring and mysterious deaths of wealthy traders; the entire place as a consequence reeked of intrigue, dishonesty and fraud. You went to Wollin well-armed and with specific goals. The two most important of the latter were usually quick and hopefully profitable trade of a single commodity, followed by a rapid departure. To spend time idly in Wollin invited problems. The slave trade flourished here so well, that the whole population seemed in permanent flux. Merchants, slaves, travellers, all came and went. Only the older inhabitants and those who had been incapacitated in some way seemed to remain, to carry out the necessary, but lowly paid jobs that a trading community lives by.

ဢ ဢ ဢ

ÓþyrmiR spent a month or so in Birka. He managed to trade most of the goods he had acquired at Hedeby and Wollin for reasonable prices, meaning that his boats would return to Kaupang quite high in the water. Hvítkárr had been responsible for the most successful part of the trading enterprise and because of this he had been paid well and had been recruited to join the boats for the return journey. A tall man well into his twenties he was and the crew found him to be forever joking and making light of even the most difficult of situations. At first, he would spend quite considerable amounts of time exchanging ideas with the helmsman and it appeared that what he said had more than a little influence. One of his ideas was the one least liked by ÓþyrmiR. *He* had dared to suggest that one of the so highly prized boats were sold, to go some way to pay off the families of those lost in the sinking at sea. It was more than just an unpleasant idea, but in spite of his initial aversion to it, the 'Helmsman' as his crew often now called him followed Hvítkárr's suggestion, knowing it the right and proper thing to do. ÓþyrmiR not long after was to be seen kneeling in front of one of the older men from the village before uttering but a few words, *'Skip skaltu af mér Þiggja.'* (A ship you shall have from me)

It was late August and the days were beginning to draw in and the time had at last come for the return leg to Kaupang. Although there were only two boats in the company now, the crews of the original three boats had been reorganized to accommodate the loss. The boat which had sunk without trace had also supplied a few of the crew, those who had been good swimmers.

₨ ₨ ₨

Daylight and darkness balanced within one passage of the sun, meaning the warmth of the late summer was at last beginning to wane. Crops were once again being harvested and swollen grain and dusty dry hay was being brought by the cart load into barns. Threshing took place for many long hours each day. The sound of flailing sticks striking stone and tiny repetitive echoes filled the whole town, to mix with noise created by the hammer blows emanating from the many smithies. Some of the threshing actually took place inside some of the bigger barns. The side doors of these were deliberately left open to help induce a through draft, which could be used to help separate the grain from the chaff. These places were terribly dusty and the men and boys working here developed hacking coughs and reddened eyes, which they couldn't help pawing at pathetically.

The temporary housing area behind the more permanent structures was fully occupied with ingeniously turfed dwellings just like those in Kaupang, lending weight to the helmsman's prediction that Birka would one day be a major player in the Norsemen's game of trade. Blue and grey smoke billowed from roof holes of homes and from various smithies, to drift spiralling upwards into the pale blue sky. Early evenings were becoming slightly cooler and there were hints that frost and the chill of winter were not that distant. The boats were ready for departure and so were the men and women who would fill them.

ÓþyrmiR and Hvítkárr chose one early autumnal morning on which to depart. It was a slow and long winded process, getting ready for the open sea and a journey which would see the merchants back in Kaupang. The early morning sun shone on the two *knarr*s and bathed them in the pale golden light, which illuminated the several crew members on each *knarr* as they manhandled heavy and unwieldy oars in the still and ink-like water. The boats seemed reluctant to leave the tranquil bay of Korshamn and they appeared to make virtually no headway in the highly reflective, sparkling sea. It was as if out of respect for the nearby island of Adelsö that the boats took on a speed so slow that they hardly moved at all. Sails had been hoisted, but the wind was so light that the bows hardly nosed into the passive swell, giving them a lazy and almost lethargic appearance.

Only after the shrill cry of *'Miðra morgun'*, from a hooded woman on 'Hamar,' had broken the great quietness that shrouded the merchant ships, did wind of any reasonable strength get up. Fortunately, for the *knarr*s, the wind came directly from the west and consequently it drove the vessels albeit slowly at first, towards the widening channel that led to the open sea. By mid morning, the trading boats were moving speedily towards Helgö, another small trading centre, which had become the new focus of ÓþyrmiR's attention. He had decided to act on the advice of Hvítkárr and to call in at this port, to pick up various foodstuffs and drinks for the voyage. Although, it was in some ways like the nearby Birka, Helgö was slightly bigger and more cosmopolitan in nature. It also had the great advantage of being on the busier coastal route, which meant a brisk trade was always to be had by merchants and therefore fresh produce was usually more widely available. ÓþyrmiR used this opportunity to buy a whole range of produce for his crews, including fresh milk, whey, mead, beers and fruit wines of many types. He also purchased some of his own personal favourites, including several types of long lasting cheese, which he talked about with enormous enthusiasm.

'Ostr er góðr matr. Ek hefi hér ost góðan.' (Cheese is good food. Here I have some good cheese.)

Finally he parted with a small amount of silver in exchange for a variety of different types of long lasting breads. One particularly heavy type of these was almost inedible, being made from peas and pine bark; it was the one that presumably lasted the longest on the boats and ÓþyrmiR thought its taste and texture to be the reason that no one wanted to eat it. It was not only difficult to digest, but was also hard to prepare, due to the extended grinding or milling process the ingredients went through. The resultant bread was truly dark green in colour, exactly the same hue as *vringla*. It always seemed to contain teeth splitting granules of stone that for some reason inexplicably found their way between hard working and unsuspecting molars, which as a result tended to be flattened due to the effect of constantly being worn away. ÓþyrmiR was not a mean man, but years of trading, bartering and striking a hard bargain somehow pushed him, like a moth drawn in the direction of a candle, towards buying such cheap produce, even though it was for his beloved crew. Of course they knew him and his ways well and put up with his scrimping. He did after all provide them with work and coin, mostly silver at that and they, like most wily folk seized and to a certain extent created further opportunities that happened to arise or be made to occur. If there were things to pilfer, they took them and didn't pay anything to their master. ÓþyrmiR and his crew got on well; everybody knew exactly what was expected of them and what they could get away with. The indigestible bread was of course for the most part neglected when the men and womenfolk had other food to eat and more than occasionally, it was unceremoniously lobbed over the side of the *knarr's* top strake. This was done when their master was dealing with some issue that had been strategically brought to his attention with the result that he invariably failed to or at least pretended not to see or hear the splash as the offending loaf hit the surface of the water before sinking like a millstone to the seabed to disturb the Midgard serpent with an inedible morsel.

In Helgö, ÓþyrmiR recruited several more men, including Grúmr, SkarfR, Folkaðr, Guðbjörn, Fugl, Særða and Gagarr; they all joined the boats for the journey to Kaupang. The master seemed to be in the process of assembling a group of merchants for some new venture and would not let on to anyone what his exact plans were. The recent financial losses he had suffered were hard to bear, but there was no benefit in dwelling on the past. ÓþyrmiR looked up to the heavens and quietly spoke to himself.

'Vetrnætr will be upon us before long and the new trading year, if the gods allow it, will follow shortly afterwards.'

ᛒ   ᛒ   ᛒ

Kaupang was eventually reached once more by the boats. Some additional trading had taken place and to ÓþyrmiR's satisfaction further recruitment of crew been completed successfully. Paviken on Gotland, Eketorp on Óland and Lindholm Hóje in the realm that was covered with beech and oak; all were duly visited before the boats had finally tied up on the now familiar small stone quays of Kaupang. Olaf, Ingvar, ÓþyrmiR, Hvítkárr, Gnúpa and Ulf were all reunited once more. In addition, Fastaðr the weapon dealer had within a short space of time become close friends with ÓþyrmiR and his crew. Olaf didn't think this strange, because the master seemed to know inherently when to cultivate a friendship or finish one. It was almost beyond question.

Fallfest, Vetrnætr and *Jól* came and went. Kaupang like all bustling merchant towns became much quieter during the winter months. The amount of silver demanded for any commodity fell to its lowest point at this winter-time juncture. Buyers had little or no competition from rival bidders or purchasers and ÓþyrmiR unlike most other merchants seized upon all sorts of trading opportunities as a consequence. He was frequently accompanied by a group of men from his boats on such bargaining forays; these men were known to be formidable with weapons. The exchange of silver and gold and the barter of other items continued for weeks until the master appeared pleased with his stockpile of fighting implements and assorted protective clothing. Large numbers of axes, swords, shields and helmets were greased before finding their way into heavy leather sacks, for the ventures ahead. The days were not only shorter now, but the cold gripped the land in such a firm hold that it seemed to want to strangle the very life out of the earth.

Nothing grew on the land; it was both too cold and too dark for plants to flourish. There were fewer animals to care for, as many had been slaughtered. The meat from so many of the carcasses was preserved with salt, which was sparingly rubbed in, in the hope it would draw out any moisture and prevent the meat from becoming putrid. Kaupang's and indeed all of the villages and towns that were spread across the Norsemen's lands had their longhouses filled with the smell of death at this time. It was as if the people chose to live at this time in charnel houses. All of them were decorated with the various mortal remains of their many animals. Legs of fatty pork, dark red shanks of beef with blue veins perversely decorating their surfaces, the heads of sheep and goats, bloody and greasy intestines of many animals that defied identification, all hung from the roof trusses and beams. Slowly, these various pieces of meat were smoked into submission. It appeared that the fires alone had the single desire to try to prevent the lifeless flesh from infusing the roof, walls and floor with that unmistakable and rasping odour of death. Small streams of fat had made their way down the pieces of flesh to drip onto the floor or alternatively to crawl down the walls towards the earth at their base. As a result, large greasy patches decorated many of the panels, giving to most of the longhouses a feeling of decay, filth and squalor. Trotters from pigs, hooves from horses and feet from other animals lay in piles, balanced on crude wooden trays and indeed planks that were in turn balanced on roof beams.

Death had come as it did every year to Kaupang; it was as though it was an unspoken law, a law that decreed that Kaupang was given life back by death itself. Death provided the currency that enabled all the transactions of life to occur. Children played, men and women worked. Some of the older folk died as did some women in childbirth, a good number of babies lost their appetite and consequently soon their grip on life and disease continued to carry off the weak and frail, as it always had done. And all the time, detached from all the earthly goings on, the sun continued to traverse the sky, day after day after day, as it always had done so and soon the realm of *Midgard* was to ready itself for the return of life. The land once more was on the verge of waking up in the same way the great god *Óðinn* had returned from death, to be more intelligent, stronger and better prepared for the fray ahead.

ᔫ   ᔫ   ᔫ

Disablót, the Feast of Vali and the festival of *Ostara,* like the other festivals that had punctuated the year from the beginning of time came and went as they always had. Thus, as happened every year, the minor spirits had been celebrated, *Óðinn's* son had been celebrated and the goddess of fertility had now been celebrated as well. Winter had long since left and it was time for life to take over once more. Finally, on the day to celebrate the last day of *Óðinn* hanging from the great tree of *Yggdrasil,* the day when light and dark were balanced evenly, *ÓþyrmiR* had asked Ingvar and Olaf to call the men to his longhouse in the early evening, at '*miðr aptan*' he ordered. It seemed that a voyage was to be planned or already had been. Such a meeting Ingvar believed indicated that it was to be a trip that was out of the ordinary.

ᔫ   ᔫ   ᔫ

ÓþyrmiR alone stood in the middle of an uneven circle of both men and women, inside the longhouse. They sat either cross legged or had their legs drawn up to their bodies, so that knees at times could provide suitable resting places for chins. The speaker was an important man and he knew it. Being the *jarl* in the community, he was held in high regard by all the karls, many of whom were also merchants. He was even liked by the *Þræll*, the commoners, who could see him for good a man; by the way he treated all the other merchants and anyone he happened to have dealings with. Spreading his arms wide, he drew the attention of all within the longhouse.

The various conversations faded to nothingness, apart from one, which was clearly so interesting to both parties that nothing it seemed was capable of distracting either man. One of the participants, a rotund man with a balding head, appeared to be measuring some invisible thing with his outstretched hands, whilst giggling uncontrollably. He recovered somewhat and then spoke very loudly to his fellow conspirator, *'Hverr þeira segir þá öðrum'* (Each of them then says to another), before suddenly realising everyone else had ceased to talk. His embarrassment seemed acute as though he believed everyone present to have heard his entire tale. Apologising profusely, with a reddened face, he muttered something about talking about a fish. This seemed to make matters even worse for him, as virtually all present in the longhouse burst into explosive fits of mirth, spontaneously both stamping their feet and clapping their hands. ÓþyrmiR waited for the laughter and noise to subside before quietly beginning in the way of a confident and practised orator, 'This is a chance of a lifetime for all of us. We can make ourselves rich, that is, all of us so rich it is now beyond our sight or our wildest dreams to imagine. If we choose to take a little gamble, a gamble that in terms of the things we do every day, then that gamble is not really a gamble in the true sense. And we have the best boats by all the *Aenir;* we have boats that are so good they will make our passage easy. You will think we are taking our children sailing for the first time, when we pitch into the choppy waters, waters that eat other men's boats.'

'I smell bitter danger in all this soft talk and I smell risk and I smell the odour of poor second rate silver and that of gold that glistens and shines, but is too hard on the teeth. In short, I smell a voyage that will test us to the limits.' So spoke Ulf, but as he delivered these prophetic words of warning, he appeared for some reason to be smiling, which so utterly contradicted every single word leaving his lips, that his audience became spellbound, awaiting a reply.

'Yes, my friend, I cannot lie to you. You see through me, you are right and my words seem soft and by *Óðinn* they are soft. But are we not the same men, the ones who trade and the ones who fight? We trade hard and if we don't get what we want, we take it! Is Ulf worried by such detail?'

'Ulf is not worried by any detail at all, all Ulf wants to know, is where do we go and when do we go? Oh, and one other detail Ulf wants to know, is which *drakkar* does he command?'

'Ulf will command no boat on this trip, but he will be in charge of the landing parties, once they are ashore. Your ability to fight is not in question and your ability to lead men is second to none. You are no child, you fear nothing at all, nothing, not even the hafkitta from the deeps; your task demands other skills. I will organise trade and you will organise defence, if we need it. Your job is to equip yourself and the men in such a way that we get what we want, if we can't get it my way. Is that clear enough for you? I'm just going to sit and eat all the *síld, koli* and *lýðrr* I can get into my belly till we go on shore. Then this rosmhvalr,' he said slapping his stomach, 'that you see before you will spring to life and fill the ships with all kinds of things that will make us rich. Mark my words, we will be rich and there's no mistake.' ÓþyrmiR paused before continuing.

'We will make our way west, to a land where silver and gold are a plenty and the people are happy to see their coinage and wares taken away. Three ships is all we will take, for we trade. We will have two *knarr*, 'Hamar' and 'Mjollnir' and the one *drakkar* 'Ormr', just in case. We will see what the Christians have for us! They are, I have heard, generous to a fault.

The speaking seemed to go on forever. Olaf was beginning to lose interest in all of the arrangements, when ÓþyrmiR moved on to talking about the crews he intended to put in the different boats. Naturally, he commanded the lead boat 'Ormr', which had a comparatively large crew of men when compared with the *knarr*s and whose muscles provided its power, when the wind failed to blow into the voluminous sail.

'I will take with me on 'Ormr', Gedda my good brother, Ulfr whom we all know and Fastaðr my laughing Kaupang weapon dealer who drives a hard bargain.' With this comment he turned to catch Ulfr's eye. Ulfr failed to reciprocate, but spat instead to show disdain and then fixed his expression and merely pretended to not hear his friend's words. The ship's master thought he detected the merest hint of irritation from his friend, so he moved on quickly to avoid any further embarrassment for Ulf. 'Gnúpa, Hvítkárr, Leikfrøðr, Gjafvaldr, Skógi, Viðbjörn, Hónefr, Gríss, Grubbi, Spjall, Þórormr, Ofæti, Þiálfi, Rúnfastr and the young lad Fóthraðr, who will with two of his mates be in charge of all bailing on my dragon. The others already know who they are. There will be no room for women on the *drakkar*.'

Fóthraðr was to become good friends with Olaf in the full course of time, although neither young man had the slightest hint that they may do any more than acknowledge each other's presence.

The crews chosen by the master to look after his beloved *knarr*s were to cause a few raised eyebrows amongst those gathered there. ÓþyrmiR looked towards Ingvar and Olaf and beckoned with his left hand. 'Hamar' will be looked after by Ingvar, who will have Olaf to help him. On his *knarr* there will be the following, Gormr, Ketilbjörn, Heilfúss and his woman Alþrúðr, Þórbjörn, Sviðbalki, Ígull, Þórfastr and Magnhildr, HættingR and RagnalfR. Bailers will be Alþrúðrand and Heilfúss's whelps, Tubbi and their little one Hugi.'

'Mjollnir' will be skippered by my other brother Farþegn and he will have with him Grúmr, SkarfR, Folkaðr, Guðbjörn, Fugl, Særða and Gagarr with his adopted twins Geirhjálmr and Geirraðr as bailers.

₪ ₪ ₪

So that is the end of the first part of what I call 'The Saga of Olaf Bodvarsson' or should I say 'The Curse of the Drakkar'. Snorri hasn't castigated me too much and for that I am grateful. He says he thinks there should be a good deal more fighting and that there are too many names. He wonders how I can remember each and every one of them. I can't help but smile, because I remember them all too clearly. It is because they are family to me; the people who inhabit this tale all have their own lives. To them, each and every one of them, their life is singularly the most important one of all. Each one of these, however humble, could easily have a more than worthy saga devoted to it, if there were a scribe to take on the task. I have grown old and now I remember more people in each day I live, than the people I actually meet. In my mind I can still tread the high paths that wind through the mountains, ride all day and still have energy enough for a belly full of beer and a good woman. My body sadly would have me think differently though!

I have told Snorri that our lives are in their way like a walk along the many paths down one side of a fjord. They start at different points, occasionally they may cross, sometimes they may move parallel to one another, at other times they may diverge, but eventually they all end. It is up to us to make the most of our little journey and to learn about as few or as many of the other travellers as we find comfortable.

Part 2

Chapter 7

Portland, south Dorset coast of Britain

787 A.D.

Komí þeir sem koma vilja
Veri þeir sem vera vilja
Fari þeir sem fara vilja
mér og mínum að meínalausu.

Come those who want to come
Stay those who want to stay
Go those who want to go
Harmless to me and my own.

The Anglo Saxons had watched with only the slightest of interest as the Norsemen had jumped into the cold, choppy shallows from the solitary *drakkar* and the two slightly broader *knarr*s, to wade quickly, but somehow casually onto the beach. Since their boats had first beached, sometime after the sun had reached its greatest height in the sky, just a few hours had passed. Within this short space of time, the men and the few women, six to be precise, had already set up a makeshift camp.

They had taken whatever they desired from their new surroundings; from the small Portland community. Livestock, fresh vegetables, bread, cheese, and prepared drinks such as ale and mead had been systematically collected for the

Norse folks' use. Coins, not that there had been many, jewellery particularly anything that looked as if it might possibly be gold, weapons old and new of any type, even girls and young women for slave usage; all were taken without the slightest need for violence. The Norsemen hadn't threatened the local people into giving them their hard earned and valuable possessions; they had simply demanded them and accordingly received. Admittedly, there had been a small degree of menace, but for such an incursion it was surprising that there had not been more than the slightest rebuttal or half-hearted minor skirmish to demonstrate some Anglo Saxon 'backbone'. May be, it was the worry of reprisals and the possibility of greater numbers of Norse folk arriving from the sea that had extinguished any Anglo Saxon spirit or thoughts of standing up to the invaders.

Alternatively, it may just have been Anglo Saxon naivety at its worst. These unexpected circumstances were highly unusual, but they were not without precedent. Similar temporary trade camps had been established before near to this locality. However, the Norse folk were very fearsome in appearance and although small in number were heavily armed, with a range of high quality weaponry. Swords, spears, axes and bows, all were carried by the heathens in the same casual way that the Anglo Saxons handled their farming implements. Their demeanour suggested it was a part of their way of life, a life that seemed to enshrine the sword or axe as law.

Three whole days had passed and the Norsemen were becoming increasingly at home. They appeared to have become wholly unconcerned that their presence was beginning to cause considerable disturbance to the local peasants' way of life and more importantly it seemed, also to their masters. The heathens had simply laughed at the king's reeve, who had received his fateful summons from the King of Wessex the day before. The king had not been a well man for several years and it was perhaps his poor health that had contributed to the decision to send but a few of his men to the coast. If he had had the slightest notion of what was to happen, surely he would have sent a larger force to ensure the king's laws were observed and his taxes collected. Beorthric after all, assumed total power over his kingdom of Wessex. He also was more than aware that he had the military might and readily available assistance of the bretwalda, King Offa of Mercia. A marriage binding one of Offa's daughters to the Wessex monarch had sealed this pact of allegiance, yet utter and complete subservience in one astute political manoeuvre quite some time before.

The reeve, Alderman Wulfherd had duly ridden out and arrived as commanded, with the unexpected and rather unwholesome company of a certain Bishop Elstan and six or so lightly armed men of Beorthric's Wessex realm. The bishop's role was really rather unclear and it was unlikely that his utterly foul breath was to sweeten the proceedings in any way. Perhaps the king in his great wisdom thought that the holy presence of such a theological being would have some calming and civilising effect on the heathen, ungodly visitors. He could of course offer salvation to the Northmen as well, if the opportunity presented itself. It would provide these desperate souls with a wholesome and fulfilling alternative to their pagan and meaningless way of life. Elstan's words could offer them the opportunity of becoming men of God and his very breath would surely cast their many deities and spirits aside, reeling and nauseous.

Wulfherd had but little experience of any type of conflict apart from a disturbance created by a group of rough men at Hamton earlier in the same year. Thirty three pirates, of whom some, rumour in Dorset had it were Norse, had on that occasion been bloodily dispatched by the Alderman's considerable force of well equipped and trained men from Dorset. The men; some had called them pirates had come ashore and a little while later had been ambushed by the well organised Anglo Saxon force and been utterly annihilated. The combination of large amounts of drink in the pirates' bellies and a well hatched plan that had been executed precisely by the Alderman's force had given the outsiders absolutely no chance. Those who had fled desperately, some wounded, some reeling with both panic and drink from the initial conflict, had made their way noisily down a side alley in the small hamlet to apparent safety, before finding themselves cut off and heavily outnumbered. Their resistance was futile and they were summarily dispatched, with no heed given to their pleas and cries for mercy. It was over in a matter of minutes and before the rain had washed the paths and the central street of small Hamton clear of the blood that had been spilled, the weaponry and small amount of armour belonging to the dead had been rapidly dispersed amongst the Alderman's men. It was this action that had spawned the words that had spread and later implicated the Norse; some had said it was the Norse who hailed from the 'low countries', whatever that had meant. Two high quality pattern welded swords, a small number of well used round wooden shields painted red, but heavily chipped and scratched with central bosses of shiny metal and five dull pewter coloured helmets of various types implicated the 'men from the bays'. The helmets were unusual to the Anglo Saxon eye. Two were just about round, with slightly pointed tops, one had broad cheek protectors, another had a metal tongue that dropped down from a thick metal circlet to protect the wearer's nose and the last, well the last was quite simply an exquisite work of art. It had narrow slits for the eyes, highly ornate hinged cheek flaps and the entire thing was beautifully decorated with small emblems and even figures of different coloured metal. It was clearly not the helm of a common soldier, but possibly that belonging to a karl or possibly a king; but a king from overseas, where the workmanship and artistry of manufacture differed considerably from that possessed by local artisans.

That inconsequential victory, however, as with all victories, even those worthy of poems and songs, lay in the past and failed to exercise any vestige of power here. Now, somewhat nervously, Wulfherd found himself walking numb-legged with short and extremely precise steps into the makeshift camp. He came to collect a relatively small amount of tax; it was nothing more than just a token of respect and an acknowledgement to the resident rulers that they were in command. As was customary, first, he was to sweeten this not too unpleasant medicine with a genial offer. He was to invite these trades' people, all of whom were naturally assumed to be merchants, to the nearby castle of *Dornwaraceaster* for the purposes of trade and refreshment.

This had become a standard protocol automatically given to men of business or travellers who found themselves in this far flung realm, because the only possible reason for their presence was to trade or to exchange their wares and merchandise. The people of Portland and its immediate environs had increasingly used these now not so rare opportunities to marvel at and then haggle over the price of never seen before commodities and merchandise.

Strangely dressed and odd looking merchants and traders with unusual and outlandish hair styles, some with tattooed skin, hailing from many distant nations and kingdoms had for a number of years been appearing randomly over the many southern kingdoms of England, but also increasingly around the entire coastline of Britain. The local coastal and now inland communities were quick to have learned how to trade and barter for all manner of useful and sometimes bizarre commodities. The traders' expeditions had always been for the most part well planned, well disciplined, peaceful and were usually highly profitable. There had of course been some incidents where small misunderstandings had taken place, but these had always been quickly and efficiently sorted out by strong leaders representing both the trades and local peoples. Those causing any problems usually lost their goods and perhaps received a beating with staffs or worse.

Typically, lumps or bars of iron, tools for farming, weapons of unusual style and ringed metal armour were to be found in the boats of the traders. Also, delicate wooden spice or herb filled containers, exotic pickled foods and other strange delicacies which had been steeped in olive oil or brine and had been stored in what appeared to be glazed Roman Samian ware were being brought into all of the kingdoms of Britain. There were other things appearing at this time which had no obvious function other than being simply fantastic pieces of craftsmanship in their own right. Wonderful works of art; carvings of Norse and other heathen deities, scratched representations of heroic deeds or crude fertility symbols on bone and antler, runic spells and poems etched on wood and stone and rune stones themselves crafted from so many different types of stone, wood, amber, glass, antler, whalebone, teeth and porcelain; all these things had been loaded into the bellies of the hard working *knarr* in the Norse kingdoms and off again on the various beaches and shore lines of Britain. In addition, there were vast numbers of gaming-pieces for board games such as hnefatafl made from the same diverse materials as well as from cream coloured or white ivory, jade, horn, jet or increasingly from soapstone. Sets of a strange bat and ball game called knattleikr, with a wooden paddle for a bat and a surprisingly hard ball accompanied the other more sedentary games which tested and teased the mind. Drinking vessels of every conceivable shape, size and material, some even made from tough leather, accompanied every trading trip. There were nature's rarities and oddities; many, many walrus teeth, splendid twisted narwhals' tusks, whalebones of many shapes and sizes, pieces of amber, some small, some large as a fully grown man's clenched fist and trapped within their timeless clasp were frozen oddly shaped insects and even small frogs. Petrified within this honeyed glass, the tiny perfectly preserved animals seemed to be waiting for blessed release from one of nature's cruellest spells. There were lumps of obsidian as black as night, with concave serrated edges sharper than eagles' talons, unusual pink or clear transparent crystals, crystals that were like tiny fortresses of reflective silver or cloudy translucent ones that were supposed to tell you where the sun was, even when its fiery globe was hidden in dense clouds or thick fog. There were rocks of bizarre shape and colour; snakestones, thunderbolts, devil's toenails, fallen stars, leaf shapes in stone, wood that was in fact stone and huge stone tree roots. Glazed Roman pottery, shiny porcelain beads of exquisite design and colour, silver and copper wire, nuggets of gold, small dull silvery mirrors; all had arrived on Anglo Saxon beaches over the past decade or so in the hulls of more and more merchant ships.

Trades' people had traditionally been peaceful folk. They had learnt to develop an empathic understanding, an almost intuitive respect for local traditions and customs to the extent they often waited for the local king's or lord's summons before they had communicated in any way with their hosts. King Beorthric's reeve was a man of small, even diminutive frame and no one could ever have described him as being unreasonable or threatening in any way. He had always found it better to be polite, yet firm when collecting his king's taxes even with the full backing of the royal mandate. Yet now, in spite of the six armed fellows who stood with him and furnished with his king's decree, albeit scratched illegibly on a piece of foul smelling parchment, the visitors' response to this polite and reasonable man's request was to lie quite outside all his and his companions' worldly experience.

A hitherto unseen, large and full bearded axe wielding Norseman wearing a tight fitting black leather skull cap, assuming something of a leader's authority, emerged slowly from one of the crude temporary turf shelters that had been constructed in the early evening of the day of their arrival. His greasy rat tailed hair hung down limply on each side of his face to mix with his untidy straw coloured beard. He casually observed the reeve, nodding his head ever so slightly as though to imply that he had worked out the situation to his compete satisfaction. He let his plain metal helmet and his axe fall to the ground. Then rather disdainfully and without the slightest of apprehension, he adjusted the fetel holding up his woollen trousers before turning away to piss into the well trodden and flattened grass.

Other Norse folk had stopped whatever they were doing by now and became interested almost expectant; waiting for something to happen. They stood rather passively in small groups of three or four and talked quietly to one another in their mystical tongue. One of the older Norse men, who went by the name Gjafvaldr, a man of about thirty five years, whilst looking earnestly at his skull capped contemporary, confided simultaneously with Svana, his woman and said apprehensively,

'Sá þjófr er slíkr níðingr, at hann gefr góðum mönnum aldregi grið.' ('That thief is such a villain that he never spares good men.')

'Hann kallar sik menn.' ('He calls himself a man.') The woman replied with a resigned tone in her voice.

'Drottinn, vernda oss!' came his sullen answer. ('Lord protect us!')

'Drottinn hjálpar eigi.' she whispered almost silently. ('The lord will not help.')

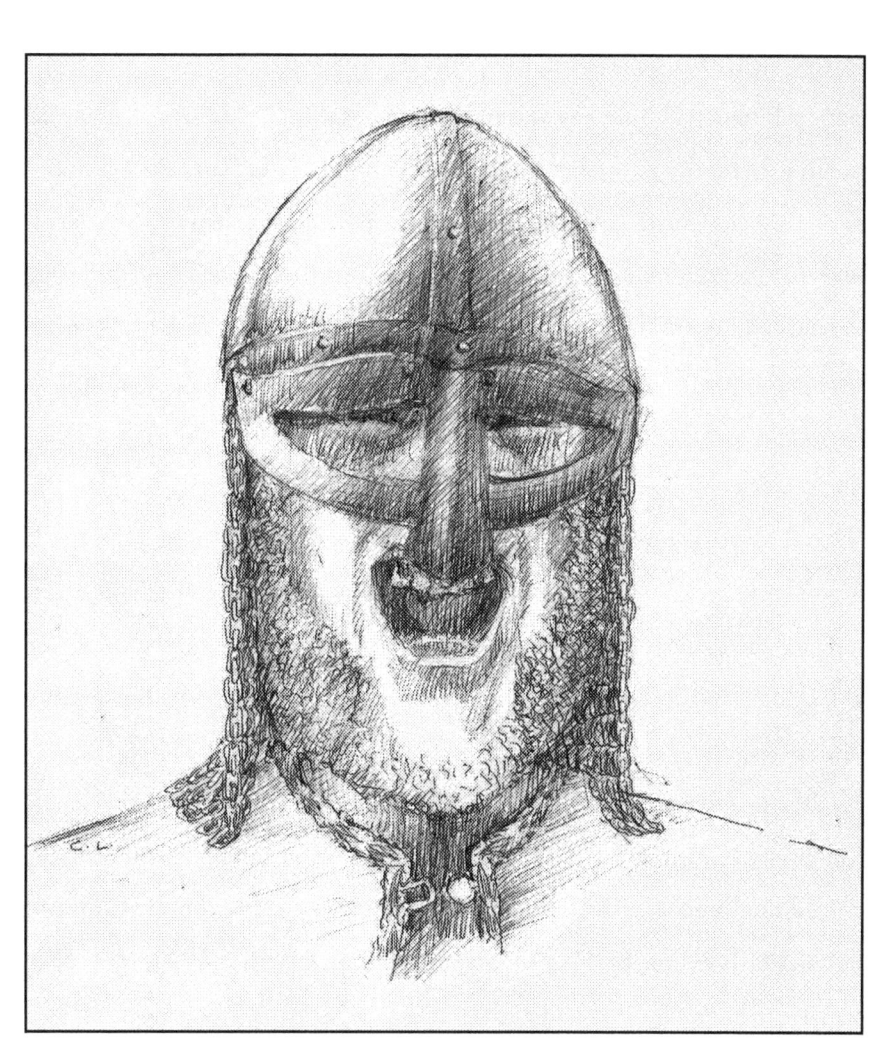

He was dressed in a dirty, long black woollen cape, which he had roughly pushed back over his shoulders, so that it came to hang from a heavy golden brooch of an exquisite and intricate design. His helmet had now been pulled onto his head and his axe was once more clasped tightly in his right hand. Advancing with menace; he purposefully he strode up to the waiting reeve and Bishop Elstan. Without any warning or provocation he pushed the alderman roughly in the chest not once, but a number of times. Bishop Elstan coughed nervously and made some polite if softly spoken comments to the Norse man and gestured pleadingly with his opened left hand, whilst his right hand nervously fingered the small dark wooden cross that hung around his neck. Each subsequent push by the heathen took on a greater magnitude, until his last shove from a fist that had not become clenched yet, was equivalent to that of a powerful punch from a man of a more average stature. This uncalled for and surprising contact possessed easily enough force to propel the Anglo Saxon man backwards with great rapidity. Simultaneously, the Norseman's long handled axe head's beak or *öxarhyrna* hooked itself around the reeve's left ankle and jerked forwards in a single motion, making him fall with a stifled scream.

The prized iron axe head, so efficient in incapacitating the startled Anglo Saxon had been manufactured in a hugely time consuming and technically demanding process. This involved the painstaking collection of many tiny nodules of bog iron by Norse farmers who armed with nothing more than sharp turf knives located and extracted their bounty. A full generation ago, some twenty five summers or so, pea sized pieces of relatively pure iron had been systematically removed from just below the top layer of peat in a remote unnamed coastal bog. Such a seemingly changeless watery place of heathers, sundews and other acid loving plants had been fed winter and summer alike for generations by small ever flowing streams. To feed these, higher up and considerably further inland, crystal clear springs continuously tumbled and leapt ever downwards from an elevated glacial source rich in dissolved iron compounds. This remote and wholly desolate region went by the name of Rogaland and it unknowingly gorged the sodden waterlogged and iron rich peat area. After the tedious collection stage, the small iron pellets had been heated at as high a temperature as could be achieved in a small charcoal fuelled stone clay-lined smelting furnace; then they had been left to cool. The resultant residue, a low grade spongy mass of iron had been subsequently reheated and hammered again and again by one of the greatest smiths ever to have lived in Ringerike, a small village north of the great trading centre of Kaupang He had been named Oddr and had literally beaten and pummelled the impurities and weaknesses from the stubborn hardening metal. The iron axe head which had after these processes slowly emerged from the tiny nodules of iron had then, been painstakingly sharpened, repeatedly polished and finally cunningly attached to a long gently curved hickory handle. Now, in something of a daily ritual its present keeper greased it lovingly with pig fat to keep any hint of rust at bay. It was accordingly immensely valuable. Oddr had long since become a draughrinn. Six years earlier, he had been mercilessly cut down and butchered by one of his own pattern welded swords. Today his wandering tormented and aggrieved spirit was surely in full approval of the way his axe had served its present master this day.

Alderman Wulfherd fell in a strange slow motion, his feet had jerked forwards and upwards into the air, but even so, he hit the churned ground hard enough to be winded from this unexpected collision. Searing pains ravaged the tendons and sinews of his damaged lower leg, which was already losing large amounts of his life's blood to the greedy grass and earth.

The Norseman had worked on this fighting technique many times in play as a youngster until he had perfected it with frightening precision. He now stood completely still, almost statuesque as he had done so many times before and after sparring sessions with his brothers and friends not too many years previously. On the side of a very long fjord on the western coast of Norway, in Hordaland, where his family had farmed for many generations the boy had grown to manhood, practising day after day with various wooden weapons, such as sword, axe, spear and sax, honing his fighting skills, waiting for the day he would need or rather choose to use them. That day had come so quickly and now that day itself seemed a long time ago.

The axe had not only tripped his victim, but had rendered him immobile in the blink of an eye. Such a disabling and cruel method of assault was usually saved for large scale organised conflicts, where linked shields offered a reasonable level of protection to the combatants' upper bodies. It was here in these violent circumstances that the axe's *öxarhyrna* could be used like a shepherd's crook, hooking and searching under the rims of the shields, to catch men's undefended legs and trip them with terrifying consequences.

In far less than a second, the reeve found himself blinking and squinting through stinging tears as he attempted to look up at and focus on the silhouette of his huge assailant. He sprawled on his back clumsily and writhed momentarily, his heels slipping hopelessly in the cloying mud, before lying still. He still protested; reasoning in the way educated men do when they are confronted with violent and irrational events over which they possess no immediate power. Without raising his voice, in immense pain, he continued to argue in this logical way, gesturing pathetically with one hand, reminiscent of a Roman senator in earnest debate, in the misplaced belief he would be able to placate the large man's brutally violent behaviour.

The six soldiers, if indeed they were real soldiers and the man of god, who had accompanied the tax collector, had not only lost interest in their work as protectors of the king's reeve, but had dispersed at the first sight of the large Norse figure. Indeed, now only two of them could be seen and they were disappearing hastily over a grassy bank some fifty or so paces away, without so much as a backward glance. One of the men had taken the helm from his head and after carrying it by his side for no more than three or four hurried steps, dropped it to the ground with an almost willing resignation. It rolled and bumped its way down the grass bank, to finally come to rest in the long grass. The Norse folk ignored the armed men disdainfully, apart from a boy of about twelve summers, who went to retrieve it as a prize or memento of his first trip abroad. Picking it up, he popped it onto his head and made his way back to the safety of the other Norse folk.

It was only when the long handled axe was used again, but this time to slice into his very being that the reeve had finally understood, the terms of payment he was to receive on his king's behalf. The axe blade passed effortlessly into a buckling and snapping rib cage before becoming momentarily stuck between vertebrae of the alderman's backbone. After yanking the bloodied lump of iron free from the unthreatening, small and still twitching body, Ulf grunted in contentment. A job well done he thought as he muttered to himself, *"Ek vegr þik"* (I kill you). Unthinking, he wiped the axe head on the grass before returning to and entering his temporary turfed hut to find in the dim light a small pot of foul smelling pig fat, with which he began to enthusiastically smear and thus coat the razor sharp edge of his axe.

ഗ ഗ ഗ

Yes, pig fat is extremely useful. You can even eat it, if you have nothing else. Snorri asked me today of Þingvellir. He wanted to know if any of his relatives attended the first gatherings in the year 930. I had to disappoint the boy and to make matters worse, I told him of Jorund the Priest and of his boy Ulfur. They are of course of my line and they would have gone for the fourteen days each year to the Lögberg, the great law rock. The speeches, the building of a country's constitution, they would have witnessed it all, from the very beginning. Everything decreed by the law speaker, the lögsögumaður, was quite literally the word of law. How the speaker was able to learn all the various laws and be able to recite them, one after another is quite remarkable. Of course, as I said to Snorri, the law speaker was in office for three full years, so in reality, he had only to learn a third part of the laws for each time he spoke to the national assembly. Snorri laughed and said in that case, each lögsögumaður would never have had to repeat himself. I castigated him for his irreverence at the time, but come to think of it, he was right!

   Also, as they didn't have any written laws or grágás then, the spoken word was good enough for one and all who attended by the shores of the greatest of lakes, Þingvallavatn. It was all so simple, the country was divided into four big parts called fjórðungar and each of those had nine chieftains or goðar. These men were powerful and it is said they carried out the rituals associated with the old gods; their office was after all called goðorð. Snorri likes the idea of being one of these chieftains, but I have upset him a little by suggesting that he is not important enough yet, as he would have no followers. Being a goði is unlike other posts, for it is a position of trust. There are no boundaries to be limited by, nothing but the limits which are created by the individual chieftain's abilities and persona. I told Snorri that if he doesn't like the local chieftain who goes to Alþing, then he can simply consider himself a supporter of a different goði.

Enough of our history though, the tale moves ever onwards and Snorri once more becomes impatient with me for my digressions. He cannot sit still and reprimands me, an old man, for my lack of concentration and occasional flights of fancy. He says that the name of my horse is so typical of my personality. He suggested a number of other names to me, but Gjalfr or 'Ormr' just don't seem right to me. Steed possibly, but Dragon, I ask you, what is the boy thinking of? The story, I must get back to the story. The light outside has faded so much that there is virtually nothing to see; I am forced to focus my mind. There are no distractions to catch my eye. Snorri can relax now and listen.

Chapter 8

Sumar, Annar mánuðr

Tjernagel
April A.D. 790

A full three summers had passed since Ulf had so mercilessly dispatched Alderman Wulfherd. Nothing of the least consequence had subsequently followed this act of heartless brutality, no reprisals of any description had occurred. It seemed that the Anglo Saxons were either quite prepared to accept the death of one of their kind, an alderman at that, or that the killing had simply not been reported quickly enough for any kind of retaliatory action to be taken. Communication of messages however important across a kingdom so vast as Wessex or Mercia involved a great many footsteps of a great many different men and a number of horse rides on various beasts. It was at best a demanding and laborious process; a process which totally relied upon all messengers completing their specific task well. One single failure in the message's chain and the entire modus operandi would fail.

Just three insignificant little boats had been pushed off into choppy cool waters that did their best to defend the south coast of Wessex. Only a few hours had passed since Ulf's axe work and the alderman's body had now stiffened into a contorted and unnatural shape; a shape fashioned by the unforgiving rigors of death. His hideously defiled blue grey and blotched body still lay where it had fallen, in a fairy ring of congealed brown blood that refused to disperse though drops of light rain had begun to fall.

'Hamar', 'Mjollnir' and 'Ormr' had moved stealthily eastwards, with the wind square behind them to help them on their way. The master had ordered an immediate departure, because he could imagine in his mind only to well, difficult problems forming on his horizon. All of his people would be in danger if they were to stay now, because a single one of his men had carried out a reckless and unnecessary killing. That man was Ulf and he was in no mood to compromise or take any blame. He shrugged his shoulders defiantly when questioned by one of the older men about his actions and all he would say about the incident was, 'My axe was getting rust upon its edge and needed some wood to cut. Now its blade has shown itself to be fair good enough to hew even the finest of Anglo Saxon timber.'

ÓþyrmiR sighed, because he knew his friend's mind well enough. He was, he mused too stubborn; on reflection, he concluded he always had been. There was no way his friend would be made to see reason; he would never be capable of realising that there existed a relationship between the cutting down of a mere Anglo Saxon and any delicate trading arrangements his master may have been attempting to negotiate. Ulf grunted loudly and spat on the floor. All he appeared to think about was the here and now and to be fair to him, that was probably why he had become such a reliable fighter and central figure in this trading mission, even if he had now prematurely terminated it. There was nothing for it now, but the drudgery of a slow voyage home. The master had fairly soon decided that six or seven hours at sea each day, hugging the unfamiliar coast line, would see the boats run ahead of any possible reprisals that might have been planned by the ruler of this green and pleasant rolling land. ÓþyrmiR believed the monarch to be someone called Offa, or at least that was what one of 'Hamar's' crew, Sviðbalki had told him. He also learned that this king was fortunately based rather a long way away. His affairs were conducted far from the sea, far in land with the result he would hear about this unfortunate little spot of trouble, only when it was much too late for him to do anything about it. Sviðbalki seemed more than well acquainted with the ways and customs of this strange land composed of a variety of small and larger rolling hills and gentle undulating pastures. He had knowingly told his master, 'that a puppet king called Beorthric was sitting on the local king's throne, but that he merely kept it warm for the real king, the one the Anglo Saxons called the *Bretwalda*; great King Offa.'

It transpired that over the past few years, Sviðbalki had travelled widely on a number of trading missions and had even taken a native wife from the shores of the land they were currently leaving. Hulda he had named her. She had been a small woman with braided flaxen blonde hair and her new name, as Hugi the bailer on 'Hamar' had put it, had 'befitted his bride', but alas she had fallen ill with a dreadful fever on her first and only voyage to Kaupang. Very shortly after the boats had been tied up, she was carried onto the land of the Norse, only to perish in some nearby long house.

Poor Sviðbalki never fully recovered his wits and even now, years later, he yearned for and spent his life returning time and again to her homeland in the vain hope of finding another in the image of his dear lost wife. At the time the poor man had commented that his loved one had never been capable of taking even a single step in the country of her husband. It was this impulsive drive that had made the poor man so reliable; it gave his now empty life a clear focus which dictated his need to survive. ÓþyrmiR knew of the man's heartache and he played on it and exploited it ruthlessly, apparently helping the poor man with his hopeless mission, but in reality using the man's expert knowledge of the local landscape, coastline and indeed the sea to great effect, for his own purposes. ÓþyrmiR's boats were never seemingly in danger of becoming lost here, for they were guided albeit unknowingly by one who felt a bond with this land like no other. 'Hamar' was often found leading the other boats around dangerous submersed rocks or sandbanks, or showing them the best and safest way into small bays or rivers. If Sviðbalki was unsure of which way to bring 'Hamar', he never showed it and when asked he would rather unnervingly reply that Hulda was guiding the prow through the waters and that there was no need to worry.

Twenty long days passed since the departure from Portland and now the boats lay beached, high and dry once more in Kaupang. Here the vessels were to stay for several weeks, before being subject to minor repairs. The men dispersed to their houses and families, happy in the knowledge that they were home, even if they had not made as much coin as they would all have liked. Ulf disappeared almost instantly he left the boats, as though in some kind of strange recognition that his actions had caused all those on the boats such unnecessary problems and the hardship that would invariably go with it. Ulf was not seen again by any of the crew for a long time.

ℰ ℰ ℰ

Three years is a long time to most men and women, but to those of a rather more tender age it invariably seems longer still. Olaf had changed in a variety of ways. His outward appearance had altered somewhat, but he still retained most of his youthful features. He had grown to become a tall and muscle bound man. In addition, he now possessed a short if unkempt, wispy, straw coloured beard. His mind had also changed and he had matured in some ways, but not in others; he was in some respects as innocent as the child, who had left Odda several years earlier. Fortunately for him though, he had made some good friends. Ingvar and his father had more than looked after him, when it was clear he was about to stray and these occurrences were hardly rare.

Kaupang like all places new to visitors had finally lost its initial appeal to both Olaf and Ingvar and they had as a consequence both moved, just a single year after returning from Portland, to a small coastal trading community in Hordaland which went by the name Tjernagel. ÓþyrmiR was usually to be seen here several times each year. In years gone by, the skipper had ventured even further north on his trading missions, to Sogn, but it had become a dangerous place to visit in more recent times.

Instead, Rogaland had as a result become slightly more attractive to merchants. The local king, Hjorleif Hjorsson the Fornicator, had inherited the throne from his father some ten summers earlier. Hjorleif single handed had changed the face of this small kingdom. Since the untimely demise of Hjor Jossurasson, his father, he had fashioned modifications that were not all for the good of his people. As his name indicated, his prime predilection was one for young women, but this did not distract him fully from his duties of leadership. He collected coin and bars of silver and gold from his people with almost too much enthusiasm and this had had the effect of stifling any interest traders or merchants may have had, because they knew that the hard pressed citizens of his land would in turn attempt to exact their losses from any traders who happened upon them. However, traders such as ÓþyrmiR have always possessed the required acumen to know where to peddle their wares. As a consequence Rogaland had been struck off many merchants' lists of current places where commercial enterprise could be carried out successfully, but not all.

The young men had also been subject to market forces; they had moved, albeit prompted partly by lack of money, but also because their work, which was now being carried out by younger men had simply become irksome to them and the coin was no longer deemed good enough by them. Younger boys and youths gratefully worked the long hours demanded by their masters for a miserly few slivers of silver. It was this that primarily irritated Olaf and Ingvar, but when coupled with the realisation that their money was being spent far more quickly than they were capable of earning, they had decided to call it a day at Kaupang. The traders as always seemed to continue to prosper as did ÓþyrmiR but it was he alone who made it clear that there would be more and exciting chances for the young men when he began his next foray out of the well known Norse waters. He had told them both to be patient and to wait for his boats. 'They'll be in your lives again before you know it. In the meantime I suggest you earn some coin, eat well and grow a bit more in your mind and body. Always be ready to sail though. Don't forget the ways of the oar and remember also to practise with axe and sword each and every day. The work you put in will be rewarded one day, never fortget that!'

Months passed lazily. When the days were at last beginning to lengthen once more and trading boats had begun to arrive and depart in greater numbers, a boat that was instantly recognisable to both young men had appeared in the small sheltered harbour of Tjernagel. 'Ormr' lay tied up to the small stone quay and beside her was what appeared to be a new and pristine *drakkar* by the name of 'Gjálfrmarr'. Ingvar had been the first to spot the boats, but had been surprised on two accounts, first to see the old 'dragon' in his new village and secondly to see the new boat, which seemed in many ways to eclipse the 'dragon'. Later that day, both Olaf and Ingvar were to learn that at least half of 'Ormr's old crew had been moved to the new boat, meaning that the master had had to recruit many new men to fill the spaces in both the old and new *drakkar*. The master had explained, not that he needed to of course, that by dividing his best oarsmen into the two boats would mean that the new men would learn how to crew both boats equally well. He would truly have sister dragon ships.

It was mid afternoon; both young men had been working on the restoration of a coastal trading boat, when Ingvar had made his pleasant and completely unexpected discovery. They had immediately downed their hammers, chisels and adzes, to race towards the boats in the way small children may have done, all of the time looking up, vainly trying to spot and recognise any of their crew members. It soon became apparent though that they must have tied up a good while earlier, for only the boys whose task was to bail had been left to look after the boats. None of these youths were known to Olaf or Ingvar. There they were, five of them in all, sitting carefree on the planking and eating what appeared to be a frugal lunch of rye bread and cheese. They also possessed a drink of some description. Periodically and somewhat erratically, this was being dispensed, from a bulbous animal skin into three shallow drinking bowls fashioned from what appeared to be a poor quality metal. The drink must have been a good though, for the boys squabbled and attempted to grab the skin and once one of them had possession of it, as one boy now had, he more than resented sharing it. 'Typical, selfish prick, reminds me of Ulf!' Olaf said to himself quietly. He did however greet them with a friendly wave of his hand and asked them rather more gruffly where their master was to be found. The largest of the boys, now in possession of the skin, took three or four huge gulps before replying in short out of breath bursts, that they had all gone ashore and were getting drunk in one of the longhouses 'over there'. He gestured vaguely with his free hand in the manner of a man who has had too much drink for his own good.

A short while later, the two young men were making their entrance, one after the other, into the darkness of a smoke filled longhouse. ÓþyrmiR by chance just so happened to be speaking and coincidentally had just mentioned his son and his friend and was now in the process of asking for news of their whereabouts. As he spoke, his back squarely faced the crude opening in the wall and thus he missed seeing the young men arrive. The stifled laughter of several of his crew members however brought their presence to his attention. Without turning around, rather dramatically he welcomed them by both by raising his left hand and pointing his fore finger to the rafters and simply saying, *'Vestu! Vestu!'* (Greetings! Greetings!) The men stamped their feet, hammered their fists on the tables and cheered in appreciation of their master's reading of the situation. They simply adored him. He knew exactly how to treat his men and they would do anything he demanded of them. The master then raised his drinking horn well above his shoulder for a few moments to indicate to all present that drinks were now to be paid for by his silver alone. A riotous cheer echoed around the long house, which made the boys back at the boats sit up and ask each other what may be happening.

ℂ ℂ ℂ

Three days had passed and the boats had now been made ready to leave. Olaf and Ingvar had said all their farewells. They left behind them a number of good friends; men with whom they had both worked on a regular basis and with whom they had at times become insensible with drink. They had as instructed, continued to practise their fighting skills with these young men, who all seemed to have been made in their image. Not all of their friends had been left behind though. Three young men named Jólgeirr, Snæbjörn and Smiðr had embarked with Ingvar and Olaf, along with two girls. Olaf had rather shyly introduced both to the master as his and Ingvar's women; they went he said by the names of Mardöll and Esja. The young men had been recruited by Ingvar on behalf of his father, due to their ability to work wood and above all to both fight, sail and of course pull on the oar. Their small coastal community reflected a typical Norse settlement. It was completely spread out, dispersed all along the shores of the fjord. There were too many young men and women for the land to keep.

Squabbles between the villages were becoming regular occurrences and the *jarls* of each tiny kingdom had to work harder and harder to resolve bitter disputes which flared up between families and friends. What land there was, was becoming far too sub-divided. Crop yields were down and always seemed to be dropping; they had quickly become inadequate. Problems simply mounted rapidly and like life, it always seemed to become more and more complex as time wore on. Old men and women shook their heads in sadness as they witnessed even the smallest fields being cut up to placate the demands of youngsters who insisted on their inheritance rights. It could have been the very community Olaf had left as a boy all those years before.

The few men and women who had willingly leapt aboard the waiting boats had done so because they felt they had run out of choices. Jólgeirr had not thought twice about leaving his family behind. He shook his head and resignedly said to Snæbjörn his cousin, 'What is there here for the likes of us? I'll tell you my friend, there is nothing, but rocks and stones. You and I, we have older brothers who want what is left of our father and grandfather's land. You can't live on rocks, only the spirits can do that!'

'At least we both have a little silver to start with, not like poor old Smiðr.' Snæbjörn's reply appeared to be an attempt to extract something positive from his own situation. He seemed to achieve this feat by deliberately analysing the plight of someone who he knew was worse off than he was.

'Smiðr will be all right, you'll see.' Jólgeirr although a practical and independent young man who had always been treated well by his kin, keenly felt the injustice heaped on Smiðr by his family. They had simply told him to go and find his own way. This rejection lay completely outside of the caring culture the other boys had grown so accustomed to and it possibly suggested that the way of the future was harsh. The poor lad had only seen fifteen summers or so and thus knew very little of the world and the way it worked. Jólgeirr had decided over the course of a few days that he would do anything he could to help the youth. He was after all not much older than the boy himself and by chance looked remarkably similar in many ways to his own younger brother with whom he had a great bond. Several days later, a small amount of Jólgeirr's silver mysteriously found its way into the small leather bag that hung from a leather cord around Smiðr's neck. The recipient thanked the gods again and again, whilst digging one thumb nail repeatedly into the small iron hammer that nudged the small silver filled *poki*. None of the boys ever mentioned giving or receiving the silver, but their kinship became stronger nevertheless. They worked as a team and looked after one another as blood brothers.

The other newcomers to the boats were birds, lots of different flapping and screeching birds. The young lads whose job had been to guard the boats on their arrival had been busy catching all manner of birds in well crafted wicker traps. Their prey was mainly birds which were happier away from the sea; there were twenty or so angry starlings, five or six rooks and three large grumpy ravens, with dagger-like beaks. The birds had been separated from each other in such a way so that each boat could carry a decent number of them. They had been housed in a number of quite spacious wicker baskets which were deposited near the back of the *knarrs*. Each bird was being carefully looked after by the boys. The 'winged ones' as Ingvar called them lacked for nothing; they had fresh water, meat, grain and even some pieces of fruit. Olaf as did all the crew, knew their presence was a sure sign that the master would be sailing in areas he was unfamiliar with. Exploration rather than trade seemed to be ÓþyrmiR's focus, clearly a high risk strategy, because if suitable land was not found, then the voyage would be a huge waste of silver and gold and of course it could end in tragedy for all of them.

Although their course appeared to be one of discovery, ÓþyrmiR as always remained unperturbed. It was in his nature, typical of his laid back character and it was this trait that inspired the men he commanded. If their master was looking relaxed and calm, then why should they worry. Their thoughts as a result turned to the provision of food and drink and also whether they would be warm and dry enough on the voyage.

ÓþyrmiR always equipped his boats well; he had insisted that there was plenty of dried food, enough fresh water and a large quantity of bread. These loaves were sealed in greased light weight sacking, in order to prevent them from drying out and going stale or at the very least to attempt to slow down the inevitable drying out process that would inevitably set in within days. He had spent a lot of good hard earned silver coin and he was as a result becoming impatient, because to fund an expedition of any sort was expensive and days spent in port were days were days lost. The weather had been good and at *ótta,* early on day after the festival of Ostara, the boats had slipped away into the sea without any due ceremony. 'Ormr,' 'Gjálfrmarr' and the three *knarr* kept in close formation, but instead of striking out due west or even south-west, they went due south, hugging the coast of Rogaland and then almost into Jaeren. ÁdiarfR, Aðalríkr and Ávarr wallowed in the water, flexing each time they rode a wave of any magnitude. It was as if they were alive, living and breathing in response to the rhythmic movements of the waves beneath them. The *knarr* had been well built and they had been loaded in such a way as to get the most out of each boat. The master had been particularly careful not to over burden any of them, remembering only too clearly the sinking of 'Hrokr' several years before. Each of the boats on this voyage had its own character and responded in subtly different ways to its helmsman's handling as well as to the waves and also to the dangerous forever changing currents.

Sviðbalki the expert navigator, was at the tiller at the back of the oldest of the *knarr*, Aðalríkr. This boat had worked the seas for some seven or eight summers and like all Norse boats had been rigorously maintained, any slight defects repaired with new rust resistant iron nails and copious quantities of tar. The other *knarr*s were nearly new and had, as was the accepted custom, been made out of new 'green' wood. The carpenters maintained that the new wood was easier to work with and that it bent more easily into the shapes they required. The other two *knarr*, Ávarr and ÁdiarfR were steered by Viðbjörn, who had previously crewed on 'Ormr' and the master's younger brother Farþegn respectively.

These men alone were aware of their master's plan. After sailing for two days in a southerly direction, all the boats entered the small port of Egersund, as far south of Rogaland as it was possible to get. The little coastal village lay, spread out along the shore, with dense woodland, hemming it in, in just the way an attacking army might have laid siege. The long houses; there were about thirty of them in all, appeared of ancient construction, with greying somewhat dishevelled thatched roofs. Approaching from the sea gave those in the boats the impression that there could be no arable land here to work whatsoever. This was in actual fact not true though, as a small amount of fertile ground did lie in a thin winding strip between the variously sized houses and the closely packed trees, all of which appeared about the same height. ÓþyrmiR was here not to trade, but to pick up three or four young men with their women and in three of their cases with children as well. They were to join the expedition. Hjorleif Hjorsson the Fornicator, the crew was to learn later, had made the arrangement with ÓþyrmiR on his last visit quite some time ago. It seemed that land and inheritance laws were such that even communities in Rogaland were beginning to lose young people who saw that their lives needed to be lived elsewhere.

All was not well in small Egersund. There were remarkably few people in sight when the boats had arrived and little interest was shown by those who happened to be present. The visitors it seemed meant little to the villagers. It was Farþegn who discovered the reason for the lack of people and the general apathy. Having spoken to an old man on the small stone quay, he turned to his fellow travellers, who were now in the process of climbing out of the *knarrs* and *drakkars*. When they had all assembled in an untidy group stretching the length of the quay, he addressed them in a quiet but firm tone.

'It seems that death has visited Egersund. Hjorleif Hjorsson, the' and here he paused, before continuing, 'well as I said, King Hjorleif has had the misfortune to have lost his latest wife, who as you know hails from here.'

'Well where are they all?' Snæbjörn asked, putting into words the thoughts of many present.

The old man, who had hardly moved, shuffled forward on well worn and cracked leather boots, straw clearly visible above his ankles and between the soul and cracked leather uppers. His dirty black woollen cloak flapped gently in the breeze as he spoke in rasping voice.

'They, as you put it, are not far from here. Up there! They are putting the body of my Queen Hælga in her final resting place, may the gods give her peace.' Without invitation he continued, 'The poor girl, my daughter's daughter, had been queen for no more than three moons and then she dies. Just like that! The king is not truly worthy of that high title, if things like this happen. He lost interest in his new queen far too soon. It ain't natural I'll tell ya'. He's now proving to his beloved people why he's called Hjorleif Hjorsson the Fornicator. I'd call him Hjorleif Hjorsson the shit, that's what I'd call him, but no one alas, listen to me! In fact, nobody has ever really listened to me! That's may be why they're standing up there looking down into that pit on that poor little thing. P'raps people should pay a bit of attention to what the likes of me and other like minded folk says.'

The master had for some reason quickly decided that attendance at the Queen's burial was a ceremony not to be missed. Looking towards Ingvar and Olaf, he shouted his orders. His boat commanders, his senior men, the men who operated the tillers and those who navigated were told to join him at the ceremony. He beckoned towards Ingvar and Olaf and said in a quiet voice, 'You must not miss this! A royal burial is a rare thing, not something you or I, may see again.' Turning to the old man he nodded as if in agreement with him and to show his respect. As he strode past him, he instinctively reached for the iron hammer that hung from a leather cord around his neck.

Hjorleif was nowhere to be seen of course. True, it was a very remote part of his kingdom, but a dead queen however young and lacking in silver, was still a dead queen. However, she was of no use to him now, no use whatsoever. Instead of attending her burial, he was in a leisurely fashion making his way slowly inland along a remote fjord, in search of any woman or girl who happened to catch his eye. It was possible his next 'catch' would become his next queen; Queen of Rogaland. As it was there were four current queens, but the king had for the most part lost interest in all of them. He considered time spent with his surviving wives to be onerous, so it was not surprising that he felt that any time to be spent with his recently expired queen to be nothing but a complete waste. After all, he was more than likely thinking that her relatives and friends will shed their tears on his behalf; more than enough tears for any girl. His absence would also prevent any unwelcome opportunity for the girls' relatives to tap him for any silver. No, they could find their own way in this little village from now on, he was far too busy looking to exact taxes and if by chance another queen was there for the taking, then so be it!

In complete contrast to the king's carefree demeanour, a small field in Egersund had become the focus of a great deal of grief. The girl, that was all she ever really had been to the king, was lying flat on her back with closed eyes. She had been put fully clothed in her finest garments into a neatly dug hole in the ground. Several paces away from the sharp end of this pit lay a variety of different shaped stones and boulders. They had been gathered some time earlier and left there, to be arranged neatly around an earthen pile which was to be thrown up to cover the girl's grave after the briefest of ceremonies. This pit had been very carefully dug, so as to exactly resemble the shape of a small boat, possibly an *Æring*; a boat that would carry her mortal remains away from *Midgard* for all time. She lay there, ever so peacefully, as though in a deep and well earned sleep, in her best little creased linen blouse and a neatly arranged woollen skirt and cape. Around her neck was a thin brown leather cord, on which was hung a tiny short handled iron hammer, the symbol of *Þórr* himself. This had been carefully positioned so that it just lay on the extreme edge of her white blouse, which now contrasted rather sadly with the bruised bluish and blackened skin of her thin and mottled neck.

As Olaf and his friend Ingvar approached with the master and several other of his men, they were at first keenly aware of how small the number of people in attendance was. A large man standing nearest to the recently dug grave now housing the dead girl raised his hand in muted greeting. It appeared that he had instantly recognised the master of 'Ormr' and with this, the briefest of salutations he continued almost carelessly with the death rites he was now administering. Olaf stared at the man in wonderment, for clearly he was someone who was as close to the gods as was possible to achieve this side of the rainbow bridge. The master whispered quietly to him that his name was Grímr and that those who knew him well called him called him Grímr the great. Even Olaf knew that Grímr was one of *Óðinn's;* the almighty great god's assumed names. Everything about him seemed somehow slightly different. He stood or rather balanced in an almost upright position, but achieved this stance only with the help of a dark crooked staff. His bleached white left hand spread out to claw the top of this support, making the vividly contrasting wooden shaft appear in spite of its colour to be a natural extension of his arm. On his head he wore a tight fitting shiny black leather skull cap, which had it seemed reluctantly allowed several plaited ropes of hair to escape from somewhere behind his large and protruding ears. His hair was greasy, oily dark, very dark; it hung limply down his back and gently swayed to and fro as if by its own choice. The man had no eyebrows to speak of, but possessed jet black eyes and as if to echo their severity, from his chin there descended a thin plaited beard which he had tucked casually into where his spotlessly clean white shirt was fastened at the neck. The rope like beard could not disguise what appeared to be markings on his neck that had been left by a real noose. This man it seemed had cheated death; he had swung from the sacred tree and lived. Olaf carefully studied this apparent reincarnation of the greatest of the gods, *Óðinn* and wondered if the man's breast would also bear the marks of the ritual sacrificial spear. The white almost shining iridescent cotton shirt he wore, surely hid the deadly flesh wound which Olaf had convinced himself must lie there. This god come to earth was clearly in charge of all matters relating to the spirits and the other gods. Olaf thought how could he not be?

Accompanying the wizard, for surely that was his role in life, was an ancient woman dressed in a dark blue woollen robe with matching hood. She was unknown to the master and as such demanded his complete respect. No one in their right mind would have crossed this woman, because her appearance suggested that she may well be a witch of some power, or even be *Loki* in a different shape or form. Her task appeared to be that of delivering solemn incantations, in the form of rune verses. These she chanted one after the other, whilst fiddling with a large bunch of teeth which she had threaded on a thin leather cord. As each rune was dispatched, her nimble fingers moved on with well rehearsed dexterity to the next well worn, rune engraved tooth.

Olaf and Ingvar knew that standard procedure at most burials dictated that a number of magical verses should be spoken, but a royal burial clearly demanded more. Groa for that was her name, worked her way through verses that celebrated the beginnings of the world through to its demise at Ragnarok. She rocked forwards and backwards as each line was sung in a high pitched and eerie staccato. *Seiðr* was the province of women and Grima knew this only too well. Her knowledge of the lore of runes and of *Galðr* was not to be doubted, it was a dangerous field, one principally the premise of woman and one he had as such deliberately shunned. At times such as these, it was important that things were done or at the very least seen to be done in the right way.

Óþyrmiʀ took a small delicately fashioned silver sickle from somewhere inside his cloak, leaned over the grave and with great and exaggerated care laid it next to the dead princess's feet. There were already two small scythes, a beautiful glass pearl, a small wooden box which had been carefully constructed with tiny iron nails and a rare ball of glass, which had been used by the girl in life to smooth washed clothes. The master noted that the girl was wearing a most elaborate bronze buckle, which gathered her cape close about her waist to emphasize her petite and now sadly somewhat pathetic figure.

'*Gjöf sér æ til gjalda.*' (A gift always looks for a return) The master looked at the girl kindly as he spoke the words in deliberate defiance of a king who cared so little for this, one of his queens. ÓþyrmiR knew that the king would be in his debt for giving the dead girl a gift of silver. Grímr his old friend would see to that. The small silver sickle would grow in the telling, to an object of exquisite beauty, encrusted with jewels from far off shores. Oh yes, he thought, the king will pay sooner or later, but he will pay! That was all that mattered.

Before throwing a handful of blackened soil onto the dead girl's body to symbolise the end of the death rites he had just administered, Grímr, the old necromancer simply said, 'Be gone! Cross the great bridge my child, do not be tempted to look back and above all do not return to us. Your time here is now past; you must leave for Asgard and there be a queen forever.' Then having cleared his throat, spat on the fresh earth before putting his fingers to his nose and venting both his nostrils, one after the other with explosive blasts. Wiping the palm of his hand on his mud splattered shirt, he turned to a small wiry man dressed in a filthy linen cape. The diminutive grave digger had been standing quietly at the back of the funeral entourage responded to his master's cry of, 'Axe!'

This small man, who had been leaning on a long handled axe, as though it were his staff, jumped to attention as though woken from a day time slumber. He soon came too though, and was in no time at all more than fully awake. In less than the blink of an eye he had leapt across the open grave, turned around and moved himself backwards with small steps away from the gaping hole. Then, without any warning, he raised the shaft of the long handled axe so that its iron blade was held high above his head, to be silhouetted black against the heavily clouded sky. In less than the time it had taken for Olaf to work out what he was about to do, he had completed his macabre task with a sickening efficiency.

The sharp cutting edge of the axe seared down from on high to swish past the earthen grave side and continue on its rapid way to the exposed left ankle of the girl. The bone splintered sickeningly and without giving his onlookers enough time to realise his intentions, the sharp blade had descended a second and third time, to crudely sever her blue bloodied foot from its spindly leg. Groa let out a shriek of high pitched but harsh laughter, before sniffing several times and then venting the contents of her mouth into the grave. The spindly man ignoring the witch's actions completely, leapt into the grave, with each of his feet landing on either side of the now desecrated corpse to retrieve the hideously smashed and detached foot. With an athletic leap he was suddenly out of the hole, with the bloody object grasped tightly in his left hand and his axe still in his right. Hurriedly, he rushed from the grave in the manner of a man beginning a task which would give to him the greatest of pleasure. Ingvar who had said nothing during the brief service, turned to Olaf and said, 'I think he's going to bury that thing elsewhere, so if she decides to come back and cause a nuisance of herself, she'll have difficulty getting about. He's stopping her from being a draughrinn!'

'He's not burying it you fool! He's getting rid of it for good. I expect he's been told to take it into the trees and leave it for the wolves or maybe he's going to burn it. The wolves'd enjoy some tender meat for a change though.' This purportedly knowing reply came from Sviðbalki, a man not known for entering into conversations that willingly. He spoke rather quietly as though in fear, or perhaps not to frighten any spirits away which may have been listening to his words. Sviðbalki had become more at ease and he seemed to relax now, possibly as he knew he was about to leave his homeland for the distant shores he so craved. His fellow sailors and most of his friends knew that this was at least partially due to his desire to go and find a replacement for his long lost Anglo Saxon wife. Amongst the other men there was a general feeling that he would never be successful in this quest though and sadly poor Sviðbalki himself was probably of the same opinion. He could dream even so; there was no legal decree against that. Every man had his dreams, but some choose their dreams more sensibly than others.

'As long as the sun shines and the world endures, I vow I shall seek for the one there must be, the one who exists in her likeness.' Sviðbalki spoke the words aloud, but to himself. Olaf not realising this, was on the point of asking the old sailor to repeat his profound words, before for some unknown reason, suddenly understanding that they had not been uttered for his young ears. Those utterances were for the savage wind alone, which without forethought duly carried them quickly away to who knows where.

ℰ ℰ ℰ

So you see, Olaf was lucky enough to witness a royal burial. Few of our kind ever have the chance of that. Mark my words well though. The influence and power of royalty usually has a great bearing on those who are closest to them. Snorri, must remember that a king as an ally is more than a good friend, but a monarch who is crossed can be more than a little dangerous. My paternal grandfather, the man with no shadow; he with the help of the three norns foresaw a crown, a skald and an untimely death. His wisdom and foresight came I am sure, from knowledge acquired at 'The Black School', which he attended so many years ago in the great city of Paris.

So, as I have said to Snorri, be warned! Be warned! I have no great love of kings as you know, for my mother's father; my other grandfather was none other than Norway's king, Magnus the Barefoot. Also, through my father's line you come directly to the first King of the Danes and of Jutland and to Óðinn of course! So you see, there is more to me than you might have thought. Although I'm a jarl, a preacher at times, I am also of regal stock, but in addition, I'm a pagan and here in Thule, I'm a republican. Like so much in life, I am a true contradiction. That's how I feel I should be and it is how I like to be!

Swelki

Sandey

Straumn

Paipey

Hedley

Vestrey

Roonsey

Siapinsey

Binsey

Hrossey

Hárey

ORKNEYINGA

Chapter 9

Sumar, Annar mánuðr

Orkneys
April, A.D. 790

The wind had been pushing the boats due west from *ótta*, at first light, until all light had just about disappeared and it was now truly *náthmál*. ÁdiarfR, Aðalríkr, 'Ávarr,' 'Gjálfrmarr' and of course 'Ormr' had encountered a few light rain squalls, but the weather could only ever have been described as good. Three times during the day birds had been released from each of the boats and on two of the three occasions, the ravens and starlings had flown off in the same direction as the boats' course. Understandably, it was impossible to rely entirely on the birds and the one bird that had flown off in what appeared to be a due northerly direction was ignored completely. 'That's off to the land of ice or even *Niflheim* if I'm not mistaken,' Ingvar confided in Esja. 'It'll need all of its feathers there all right,' he continued. She however, looked almost through him, thoroughly uninterested, as though he happened to be speaking in a strange tongue. Turning away from him in a manner that implied that she had tired of Olaf, she looked for and found her friend Mardöll. Esja giggled and then said something inaudible, whilst at the same time pointed towards Olaf, who was now sitting deep in thought somewhat resignedly near to the prow of the boat. He was looking out to sea, or more specifically at the distant slightly hazy horizon. Evening drew inexorably on.

The water was now as near to the blackness of the kingdom of *Hel* as it was possible for it to be in the land of *Midgard*; all around the boats it gurgled and made sucking, rasping noises as though speaking in some strange and watery tongue. Directly in front of the boats the very last of the light in the sky was now fading from first a salmon pink into then a dusky peach colour that in turn changed its hues ever so slowly but surely, until it became a matt and dull speckled grey. Indeed, the late evening was still just about managing to hold on to the last vestiges of light, when a voice broke the tranquillity of sea and sky.

'Ek segi goðin Þanginn.' (I see good brown seaweed) Smiðr shouted the words as loud as his voice would permit. He shouted it again in celebration and then again, for a third time as though for luck. At first there was no reply, as it seemed as though it was not only too dark to see anything through the stifling and all smothering night, but also too dark to hear any sound as well. Smiðr was not to be put off though. He had it seemed, for reasons known to just himself been prodding at the water for some time with an iron hook attached to the end of an ash shaft. It appeared that the passing waters had given up from their depths something of interest.

'Vikingarnir koma!' ('The Vikings are coming!') The reply when it arrived, came from Jólgeirr, but it was not quite nearly as loud or as clear, on that late evening as the phrase shouted by his friend moments before. It was however, a phrase that was to be heard many times over the next few years, but it was to be spoken far more often in tongues belonging to either Celtic folk, Picts, Anglo Saxons or Irish than it would be in the words of the Norse. And it would not often be spoken, but be shouted and screamed in terror and anger, not in the calm and relaxed way in which it had just been said.

Smiðr's excitement stemmed from nothing other than his

knowledge that such seaweed was to be found only in coastal waters; they were he assumed very near to land. His joy was such that he fidgeted distractedly with the smooth iron hammer hanging around his neck, whilst strutting hither and thither on the deck. Thinking about his lucky find, he said quietly, time and time again, 'I knew it. That unmistakable smell of land, that made me drop the iron hook and see what it would bring. It wasn't just chance, it couldn't have been luck; it was the sweet odour of life-giving land.'

His fortuitous discovery had led to all kinds of actions and activities on the five boats. Sails had been dropped and were now being furled rapidly. Oars were being hurriedly picked up by some men. Others leant out over the side of the boat and struggled to extract the bungs which had been rammed into the numerous oar holes on both sides of the boats. When these had been extracted, they were laid neatly in the centre of the boats, between the sea chests of the sailors, so they would not roll about and cause any accidents. Only the man at each tiller had not moved; he carried out his task in the knowledge that his line was of paramount importance. On 'Ormr' one man, it was impossible to make out who it was, had shinned up the mast to three times his own height. He had then shouted out in the same way as Smiðr. *Þat er hólm. Þar er sandr ok þat er hólm!*' ('It is an island and there is sand! There is sand, it is land!')

Sets of oars were now dipping rhythmically into the smooth pitch waters. The slightest of silhouettes against an almost obsidian jet black and heavily clouded sky gave away the presence of the boats as they moved in a nearly perfect symmetrical formation towards the land. The two *drakkar* were out in front; with exactly sixty manned oars in each, pulling in a precise almost hypnotic rhythm, not quickly, but powerfully even so. The pattern the boats made, if it had been possible to see them in the now invisible sea, remained the same, but with the faster boats simply pulling clear of the more sedate *knarr*. The two *drakkar* were out in front side by side, with the *knarr* dawdling behind them in single file. Both dragon boats were moving at a considerably quicker speed than that of walking pace, although the lack of any useful light prevented the keenest of eyes from detecting their rate of progress. Only eight oars powered the leading *knarr* ÁdiarfR, with two fewer oars being used on both Aðalríkr and Ávarr. These boats were not built for speed, but were far more at home in a heaving swell than the arrow like *drakkar*, which flexed on each wave and sped away towards their chosen targets.

Not even the master, with all of his experience had any real certainty about this landfall. Of course he had an idea that it was the land of the Picts, but there was no knowing for sure in this all enshrouding darkness. The men and women on the boats were exhausted from both the mental worry and the physical rigours, having spent a full day on the unpredictable and unforgiving sea. Now there was to be one final heavy pull on the oar to end the day. *'Einn, tveir, þrír,'* counted the lead man from each boat, *'Einn, tveir, þrír,'* he repeated to himself and to the other rowers, time and time again.

One or possibly two *víka sjóvar* would see the boats safe, if they could be beached in the near total darkness. The crews had removed the *drakkar's* dragon heads and the rudders on all of the boats had now been lifted to their highest position. Time seemed to stand still as the three *knarr* and two *drakkar* slowly pulled themselves towards the dry land that was hiding dangerously somewhere in front of them. All of the men pulling on the oars, whether sitting in the *drakkar* or standing in the *knarr* were repeating their strokes, whilst simultaneously calling on their gods. They had placed their lives in both the hands of the men at the back steering the boats and the men at the front acting as looking outs. They prayed that their gods would save them from the numbing icy waters and the sharp and wholly unforgiving teeth of the rocks. One or two of the younger rowers had failed to evict awful and dark thoughts brought to mind from childhood nightmares, especially blood curdling ones of hafkitta.

It was unmistakable; first the gentle crashing sound of small rolling waves pounding a shingle beach and then, not that far away, white foaming surf could just be made out, disappearing and then reappearing in the almost complete blackness of a moon free and heavily clouded night. Finally, the much needed reference point needed by the navigator in charge had suddenly presented itself as tamely and meekly as a new born lamb. There were to be no rocks to ambush them tonight it appeared, just a gently sloping and friendly beach. Gjálfrmarr was the first to ground, its keel running deep into the small pebbles and shingle, making a swishing and most pleasing sound as it did so. It was followed almost immediately by its sister boat, 'Ormr'. The two boats were no more than four oar lengths apart and were lying with two thirds of their length; their back ends still in the water. The crews had instantly removed their oars from their stations in the now total darkness had by feel alone stored them temporarily in the centre of the boats between the men's sea chests. Also, as though men bereft of sight from birth, they had amazingly somehow recovered the large plugs which were for plugging the gaping oar holes and inserted them without too many problems, in spite of the all enshrouding darkness. Only two or three of them in each boat had been understandably mislaid, which bearing in mind the difficult circumstances of the darkness and the rolling caused by the swishing surf was truly remarkable. At the same time it showed how well each man had been trained to know his particular piece of the boat.

The three *knarr* arrived, perhaps two hundred and fifty pulls of the oar after the *drakkar*, one after the other, about a hundred paces further down the beach, although they were not to know it and they were not quite so fortuitous with their landing place. It was decidedly steeper here and the waves that landed did so with a much greater power and venom. If they could have seen and thankfully they could not, the Norse seamen would have also appreciated how lucky they had been. Another fifty or so long strides would have seen the *knarr* encountering an almost insurmountable difficulty. A reef of hidden jagged rocks was busy cruelly tearing through the surf and if the boats had managed to negotiate their animosity, they surely would have been smashed to pieces on the sudden and shocking outcrop of vertical rocks that lurked behind, repelling the waves with an alarming force. There was no beach here, just rocks, deep water and the certainty of ship wreck and with it, no doubt a painful and violent death in the realm of *Jörmangandr*.

In the scrambled moments of the beached landing, there were men everywhere automatically fulfilling all sorts of strange tasks in the near pitch darkness; it seemed to fill the heads of all those present with a rare urgency. Some unseen men jumped into the shallows and then simply rested themselves against their side of the boat, trying desperately to keep the vessel stable in the ebbing and sucking waters. All sorts of cries were flashing past and over these men's heads, as they stood waiting for confirmation that their simple task was completed. Some of these men were not satisfied with simply holding the boats and were now encouraging their fellows to heave the hulk of the now empty ship up the beach to the safety of dry sand. Others still, obviously men with experience of the ways of handling larger boats were demanding wooden supports to be inserted slightly below the top strake to keep the vessel not only stable but upright. These men swore violently in the dark when they realised that such aids were not being carried by the boats. The master had always insisted that they were unnecessary and that his boats could and would do without being supported. 'I may drink from my horn many times, too many times some of you bastards say and I may start to roll like my boats, but never, never I say, have any of you lot, seen me need an arm to support me. I am like my boats, my boats are like me! The day I need help when I am rolling, you can take me out of commission and you can put me in the 'Ormr' and like the bastards I know you are, you can burn me! You'll have a good day all right and I'll know that you've treated me right as I make my way over the rainbow bridge on my grey steed of smoke. I hope he can move in the way of *Sleipnir*, with his full compliment of eight legs. By the gods, I'd love to see that, so I would. '

'It's all right for him, going on about things like that, but he doesn't have to unload goods from these bloody tubs, especially when they're half afloat in the water and bobbing up and down and moving from side to side like some bleeding half empty barrel that been dropped into a fast flowing river that keep changing its mind on direction.' Viðbjörn spoke his mind, but it mattered little, because nothing on these boats would change, it seemed impossible to him that it ever would, for he was not the master. ÓþyrmiR had heard others say exactly what he was complaining about a hundred times before, but as always he would smile benignly before saying that he would in due time think about it, but they all knew, in reality that he meant exactly the opposite. There would be no changes as long as he maintained his position as leader.

In the darkness confusion continued to reign aplenty. The landing had been for the most part successfully achieved, but other vital tasks also had to be completed. Men struggled with their sea chests, attempting to remove such things as their *húðfat* from them as well as one or two other items that were required to make their night's sleep a tad more comfortable. Each and every man, woman and child of them knew that it was going to be a difficult night, because their equipment, their weapons, their food and drink for the most part were still stashed safely on board. However, some more resourceful of their number had managed to remove a few skins filled with water, whilst others still had pushed several larger skins that were bloated to almost bursting point over the sides of the boats. Olaf found out later that night much to his delight that these contained a heady and rather full bodied beer. The sailors had carefully dropped these *'rosmhval'* as they jokingly nicknamed them into the swirling black waters and then carefully pulled them ashore behind them, attached to an ankle or wrist by a thin but strong piece of twine.

A voice in the darkness shouted with a considerable degree of urgency, *'Náthmál, miðn ætti, jafn nærri badu!'* (Night measure, mid-night, evenly near both!) It was pitch dark now, but thankfully some of the more practical sailors had managed to light several good sized fires which were now roaring on the beach. Each one was surrounded by standing figures, the near ones silhouetted black and those on the far side of the fires illuminated well by the light of their escaping flames. It appeared that some of these men were turning around every so often, as though in the vain attempt to dry salty and wet clothes. Woollen trousers and capes appeared to be particularly troublesome, stretching and flapping coldly against damp and chilled flesh.

Smiðr had found Olaf crouching close to one of these beacons, vainly looking out into the pitch black of night. The wind had fortunately been almost non existent, meaning that all of the fires had burned evenly and rather slowly at first. The two men now exchanged stories about how they had managed to get off their respective boats and ended up on this remote but fortunately dry beach. Their conversation, like most of the others taking place on the beach was focused on where they might possibly be. Most of the Norse folk were wholly unconcerned and seemed to be experiencing the unfurling episode completely in their stride. The bloated skins containing beer had been opened with considerable relish and some drinking vessels which had somehow miraculously appeared were being passed again and again amongst those who were now gathered round the fires. It was here that Olaf and his companion now huddled. There were too few bowls for all the men and only a single drinking horn to be had, so out of necessity, they were passed from one man to another with an increasing camaraderie. The man next in line for the horn or bowl would wait patiently, until he felt it necessary to prompt the slowing drinker to move the bowl onwards to him. That night Olaf learnt what it meant to sink happily into, a drink crazed oblivion. At first, he chatted happily with Smiðr, until he found the discourse of his fellow drinker repetitive and before he knew it, he was talking enthusiastically with other folk whom he recognized vaguely, but did not know at all well. So it was for what seemed to him to be a long time, until at last the grip of night was finally loosened and pale impudent fingers of light poked their way irreverently across the dark but just visible cloud striped pink sky to herald a new day.

The scene as the light improved was remarkable. The men and women who were awake stared in awe at the seascape. The beach stretched in front of them, with its almost burnt out fires pushing thin wisps of blue grey smoke up into the rapidly lightening sky. Relatives, friends and fellow sailors of those watching, littered the beach, lying in random formation in a multitude of well

worn cosy leather *húðfat*. The trusty boats lay high and dry in the foreground
of a peaceful scene whose backdrop comprised a number of small islands that
dotted the sea and emphasised its enormity. It seemed on that day long ago,
that the sea was truly never ending. Melancholy cries of sea birds were such
that those souls who were awake and alive to the world must have wondered
how those lying on the beach, huddled in their leather sacks could possibly
have slept on. The white whirling bodies of gulls, arctic terns, gannets and
large numbers of skuas seemed to fill the whole sky with both their graceful,
but energetic movement and their overbearing harsh shrill cries and calls.

The men in charge of the boats were all awake and busy, tending to their
craft with a small and apparently select number of helpers. The two *drakkar*
had between them two dozen or so men seeing to a number of different
jobs. ÓþyrmiR stood on the deck of his beloved 'Ormr' and barked precise
instructions to his men. He was moving his leathery hands in the air and
almost talking with great and emphatic gestures he made with them. Clearly,
the boats were not going to be staying here long, because nothing of any
description had been taken off them since first light. In fact slowly but
surely the waking men, women and children were climbing out of their bags,
stretching their arms and backs, before packing up their personal possessions
and moving them to one of the piles that were now growing by each of the
boats. The boat masters had seemingly impressed upon the crew to keep the
decks clear for the moment. They were otherwise engaged in activities such
as checking the caulking between the planking that covered the shells of their
craft. Now the boats were out of the water and dry, the opportunity lent
itself to such inspections. Other men were adjusting the stoppers in the oar
bung holes or looking for bungs that had disappeared in the previous night's
confusion. One man had been assigned to remove the sump plug of 'Ormr'

and another had been dispatched to the other slumbering boats to remind their particular masters to do the same with their vessels.

Sviðbalki had made his way over to 'Ormr' and was pointing towards the most easterly isle in sight. He then clambered on board and slapped ÓþyrmiR on the back with a great deal of enthusiasm. The two men were in high spirits and so they should have been bearing in mind their considerable good fortune. To have successfully managed to beach the five boats in total darkness without the loss of life or destroying any of the precious vessels was by anybody's standards no mean achievement. The gods had smiled on the Norse and it seemed their destinies had not been impaired at all by these strange islands' *landvættir*. The great navigator had in no time at all made his pronouncement. He was not certain, but declared anyway that they were possibly on the Orkneyinga; a group of islands ruled by proud men, but men who nevertheless paid homage to the Picts. ÓþyrmiR grunted approvingly, before saying that he didn't give a shit whom they paid homage to. They along with their Pictish masters would have some new lords before too long and it was to these new ones that homage would have to be paid from thereon.

As they concluded their brief conversation, one of 'Ormr's crew, a chubby man named Ofæti came up to the resting dragon and greeted the two men cheerily. Both then stopped to listen to what he had to say with a great intensity. The scout, for that was one of his roles, had been exploring, to see if he could find out anything that might have been of use to his masters and their navigators. Usually the rotund little man was busy preparing vegetables or meat, because his primary role on his boat was to cook for the men. Now, Ofæti assumed the much more important role of providing information that was to have a bearing on all those on that beach. Their immediate futures lay in his chubby hands as it were. These, incidentally constituted short stubby fingers that closely resembled the fat sausages he so liked to cook. Indeed, if anyone suggested such a resemblance as this to Ofæti, he would more than likely have laughed, finding such a comparison amusing. After all, the dish he most liked to provide the men with was also his favourite; great long sausages. These he boiled in a cauldron that also housed any root vegetables he had managed get his hands on. To him, these delicacies were no less than gifts from beyond the rainbow bridge itself, food of the gods of *Asgard*; they were to him great steaming and pungently aromatic cauldron snakes, no less.

'It is like this, my *jarl*. The boats and of course all of us are on a small uninhabited island. To the north, there are four or so craggy islands, of all different shapes. There are rocks also to the north, lying just below the water; I have seen the foam of the waves that dances over them. To the south and west, there is the greatest of the island group; a sheep covered island with many inlets and coves. There are one or two houses in sight; they look occupied, but are built a little way back from the coast, so it's impossible to say for sure. It is a wonder that last night we didn't ground on some of the sharp rocks that seem everywhere. North-west, there are several more islands of different shapes. The land on the islands looks good; some grass, some good soil and maybe some peat for burning. You could farm here if you had such a desire. The big drawback as I see it, is that there are no real trees to speak of. There are a few stunted gnarled old things that hide from the wind, but nothing of any importance. Boat building and repairs here would be nigh on impossible.' The scout had done more than well and he had provided his betters with all the information they needed for now. Ofæti made his way from the boat after the master had tossed him a small silver nugget that he had been toying with and warming in his hands as the little man delivered his words.

'So the Orkneys it is then. How could I have doubted you?' ÓþyrmiR teased his chief navigator and steersman, before continuing. 'The question is, where do we go from here? I have a mind to see what the large island is like. It may provide us with enough land to farm and give some of these poor souls we have brought with us their own patch. *Stýrimaðr, ver tekum Hringr.*' (Steersman, we take a round trip)

'Well, I'd suggest that we take just one of the *drakkar* and have a closer look.' Sviðbalki always imparted good ideas to his master and the latter knew it. There was power in both knowledge and experience and the skilled navigator seemingly had a good supply of both. His master nodded in agreement and signalled to a small group of men who had gathered at the back of the *drakkar* that they would be making a move as soon as the tide provided them with a bit of lift; his pedantic way of describing the refloating of his boat by the incoming water. These men shouted to others nearby what was to happen and without prompting of any sort, the crew had more or less assembled on the beach near to 'Ormr'. Ten or so men climbed into the grounded boat and handed down a good number of sea chests to those still on the shingle and sand. Every other oar bung plug was then removed and oars were then inserted into them from the inside. This looked strange, because instead of delicate blades pointing out of the ship, there were simply the blunt stubs of the oars. When the entire length of both sides of the boat had been transformed in this way, virtually all the crew took up positions on either side. Two men shoulder to shoulder grabbed each oar and with repeated shouts they were off. *'Einn, tveir, Þrir!'* (One, two three!) Each man lifted and at the same time pushed. The boat slipped across the smooth pebbles and sand with hardly a murmur. The dragon was powerful, but light and fleet of foot. It seemed to glide the short distance down the beach and back into the sea.

It was as if the vessel knew that it belonged to the sea and the sea to it. The master could not hide a broad grin across his face, for his men had needed no cajoling. They weren't prepared to wait for the tide, they were the Norse and they waited for nothing or no one.

The sea chests which had been removed prior to this feat of lifting were soon reinstalled on the deck in their rightful positions. The men on the other boats took little interest in these proceedings, but instead had taken to gathering driftwood to make further fires. A number of others had taken up positions at the most northerly and southerly points of the isle, so as to watch the other islands for any signs of life or more importantly any signs of opposition or hostility. The four men who had moved to the south end of the little island had been rewarded for their efforts, for they had spotted a fisherman in a small boat who appeared to be rowing parallel to the large island's shore. They had hidden by keeping low in the long grass that covered the sand dunes that protected this end of the isle from the waves of even the biggest storms. The men were in luck, because the small boat, no more than four paces in length, suddenly changed direction and made its way directly towards a small sandy beach that lay immediately to their right, no more than a Norse man's *hundrað* (one hundred and twenty) paces from them.

It seemed that his sudden diversion was due to the countless rocks and weeds that lay in great swathes near to the shoreline. He wasn't trying to avoid them, but instead actively sought them out. After beaching his little boat on a tiny patch of sand, as close as he could possibly get to the weed covered rocks, he leapt out before quickly looking all around, as if sensing hidden and prying eyes. The prow of his boat rested on the sand, whilst the blunt rear end floated gently, rocking up and down with the surge of each small wave. It was as though he felt the gaze of those who watched him.

However, instead of responding to such innate feelings of unease, he chose to blindly continue with each and every one of his usual routines, persuading himself not to be silly and to concentrate on what he was doing. Leaning into the boat, he pulled out a stout long wooden pole. Attached to one end of it was a strangely shaped net. It was not round, but instead shaped more like a bow; the pole being attached to it from where an arrow would have left the weapon of the same shape. Rúnfastr said quietly to his friend. *'Þat er háfr. Eysjarskeggi hefir háfr. Ek sé hann ok er garðr.'* (It's a shrimp net. The islander has a shrimp net. I see that he also has a fishery) A simple nod of the head was the only response he received, but Þórormr then narrowed his eyes and suddenly he was able to pick out the small poles that had been so carefully arranged so as to make two neatly converging rows. Both men knew this fishing method well as all men who had grown up in a coastal village would. Fish swimming into the larger funnel end would become distressed and when attempting to make their escape, a good number would become trapped in a net that lay at the other end. The boy, who must have been about fifteen summers, waded out until the water covered his knees and then dipped the net into the water. He used the flat end of his net to repeatedly stir up the sand. From his actions, the four hiding men knew that he was shrimping and that now he would be at his most vulnerable, because he was fully engrossed in catching his darting prey. Perhaps his plan was to retrieve the fish after he had caught enough shrimps for his supper. However, it was not to be.

It was all over within a few moments. The lad was being led away by Rúnfastr and one of his companions to meet the master and his new destiny. His boat was pulled up the beach and hidden and his fish, there were five or so good specimens were put in a small sack that Þórormr was carrying, for exactly such an occasion. The two Norse men were pleased, for they knew that they would be rewarded by their master. The two other men with them were not quite so lucky, as they were sent back by Rúnfastr to keep look out. He had earlier been put in charge of the scouting party by 'Ormr's navigator. No doubt he would have been cross if he had known that the two men left behind had taken it in turn to collect shrimps after he had gone. Whilst one filled the net, the other kept a fine look out. 'Look, there are three or four more; move the net more quickly or you'll lose them! Oh you're useless, let me have another go.'

The boy was clearly distressed and even wept a little. He didn't know who these strange men were and why they spoke in such strange voices. All he could manage was, 'Veddellemettis,' which only had the unfortunate effect of making the men laugh. Rúnfastr and Þórormr were only four or five summers older than the Orkney boy and they knew how he must have felt. They were not bad men, but they had been given a task to perform and they knew it had to be done well. If they failed in this, they would be in trouble. It was after all important not to upset the master, especially if they were in a strange place where hidden dangers may lurk in the way that *landvættir* always do.

Olaf and Ingvar hadn't moved when the two Norsemen and the young Orcadian they had captured came stumbling through the low dunes onto the beach. Olaf was suffering rather badly from a hangover and was somewhat unsuccessfully shielding his face from bright sunshine with a raised hand. His eyes were bloodshot, half closed and muscles in his eyebrows pulled them down as far as they would go, so as to repel the invasive rays of light that, uninvited sheared through his constricted pin-hole pupils causing him to draw back and wince. Ingvar and Olaf had just a short while earlier finished a brief discussion on the whereabouts of their respective families and for some reason the name Ulf had been mentioned. 'I've heard nothing of him for several summers, there's no mistake. I do sort of miss him though.' Olaf tended to think aloud at times and his thoughtful expression was mirrored almost perfectly by Ingvar, who replied, 'Yes, the old devil did make problems, but he was useful to have on your side and by *Óðinn*, could he use a sword. Remember that one he said was enchanted, you know the one he paid too much for.'

Rúnfastr was unaware of Olaf's condition and he was far from happy, because the master had departed in 'Ormr', meaning he was unlikely to receive even the tiniest scrap of silver from the two young men who had assumed leadership of the entire party. Both Rúnfastr and his friend Þórormr left shortly after their reappearance their apprehension confirmed; singularly unimpressed with the way things had turned out for them, they walked away dejected. In contrast, Olaf smiled to himself, because he could see how the men were feeling and knew that only several years before, he would possibly have been in their position and would undoubtedly have felt the same. Even so, he patted a small bag of silver under his linen shirt as though to reassure himself of its presence. He appreciated full well not having to part with any of his coin or precious metal on behalf of his *jarl*, Ingvar's father. The fact that the men had not even suggested a payment or made their feelings known to him or Ingvar also cheered him. Their demeanour had said it all; both Ingvar and he thought, they had appeared begrudgingly willing in their duties, but thank goodness they had also remained subservient. Looking sideways at he friend Ingvar, so that he would be unaware of his surreptitious glance, Olaf appreciated in that exact moment what his adopted family had done for him. It was this that perhaps warmed his heart a little and changed the way he was to treat the hapless prisoner. He felt surprisingly responsible for the boy and his well being.

Some of Norsemen had seen the arrival of the young stranger and were demanding that he be tied up and speared, to be hung from a tree to please the greatest of the gods. There aren't any big enough, Olaf thought to himself, what stupid bastards they are! The boy was beginning to look very frightened by now, due to the sudden appearance of a whole host of vicious looking weaponry and he also appeared to have at least understood the gist of what was being said. He glanced at Ingvar and Olaf for the least sign or vestige of help. Ingvar was completely oblivious to the boy's fear of the terrible plight he was seemingly about to suffer and instead appeared of the opinion that the men's violent suggestions were really rather splendid. It made complete sense to him as it did to the growing rabble. To make an offering to, or to bribe the gods was a recognised way of encouraging the great ones to look favourably on us mere mortals; it was a worthwhile ploy, particularly if you happened to be in the middle of goodness knows where and there just so happened to be a helpless victim on hand to sacrifice.

A long spear, its bog iron tip pointing skywards was rammed into the sand with enormous force to contradict the growing consensus. The ashen shaft remained upright in the sand even though the hand that had forced it so powerfully into the beach had left it, to raise instead another weapon, a long hickory-handled axe, high into the clear sea air. Such an overtly defiant gesture was not lost on anybody standing or sitting on the beach near to the boy. If anyone had wanted to take his life and there were some, then they would have to defeat the one recalcitrant man who now stood alone, between them and the boy. It was a moment of exquisite suspense; everything seemed to become suddenly silent, even the black headed gulls' incessant crying and baying abated, as though at the unheard request of the mischievous spirits who infest such remote and desolate islands.

In that brief hiatus, the dominance of a new force had come about. Ingvar hitherto had been an equal to Olaf; an equal whose position was more than assured due to the fact that his father was a *jarl*. Now, in an unplanned moment, the briefest of moments at that, he had seen his friend and adopted brother usurp him. Olaf had taken charge until the master and his boat returned. The boy's safety was assured, at least for the moment.

Olaf ordered the boy be taken to the other *drakkar*, Gjálfrmarr. With Ingvar and Jólgeirr, who no longer rowed in 'Ormr', he now intended to question the boy, without frightening him to death. First, he offered him a drink of beer from a skin that he withdrew from a hiding place under one of the boards that made up the deck. Veddellemettis accepted the drink, but with an apprehensive look; the look of someone who is taking care not to offend an over bearing host. He took little, but frequent sips from a dented and heavily tarnished silver drinking bowl that had been passed to him by Ingvar.

Pointing at his chest with the fore-finger of his shield hand, Olaf said very loudly to the prisoner whom he and the rest of his men now believed quite incorrectly to be a Pict, *'Ek kalla mik Olaf!'* (I am called Olaf) The response elicited was of no use at all to Olaf or anybody, for the boy babbled so quickly that all his words mingled into one seemingly endless guttural mass. At this moment, Spjall one of the men who had previously crewed on 'Ormr', but had because of his ability with the oar, been transferred to the new dragon ship spoke up. Spjall was a quiet man by nature, but even so he had a fearsome reputation for the powerful and accurate way he could throw hand axes. Being fairly short in stature, but with a heavily muscle bound upper body and arms, this was perhaps understandable. It seemed this skill however, was not all this quiet man had to offer. Olaf, Jólgeirr and Ingvar hadn't noticed their comrade's presence at first, but were now grateful for his timely intervention. He spoke with considerable insight, fore-thought and wisdom. 'I think the boy is no Pict, look at his arms, there are no tattoos. He looks to be a local, he's from these islands and if I'm not mistaken,' at this point he paused, pulled a contorted face indicating possibly some degree of indigestion or bowel problem, before continuing, 'he probably speaks the tongue of the Celts or some other language. It's possible he may even know a few Pictish words learnt from his true masters from over the seas.' At this point he pointed his axe throwing hand in a southerly direction, which gave Olaf an uneasy feeling. He had heard of the Picts, but wasn't too sure whether they would present him or his companions with any problems now or at some time in the future.

'And you speak Pictish?' Ingvar asked him incredulously.

'No, but some of our words are, I believe similar to theirs. I've heard it said that if you were able to write down our words in their script, then some of 'em could be understood.' Spjall's suggestion sounded intriguing to the master's son, but he wasn't to be convinced that easily.

'I can't believe they can understand our language written down, if they can't understand it spoken.' He replied dismissively.

Spjall was unperturbed nevertheless. He asked Ingvar and Olaf to get the boy on to the beach, suggesting they would be able to question him rather more effectively there. Shrugging his shoulders, Olaf agreed, because he simply had no better idea of what to do. In a short time the Spjall's ruse became clearer. He walked backwards and forwards for a little while, before kneeling at a point on the beach which was still dark and damp from the receding tide. Here the sand was flat and quite receptive to the scratchings of a finger or short stick. It presented the Norseman with a ready made parchment, with which he could communicate. With nothing more than his finger and a modicum of intelligence, he was to attempt to solve exactly where they were and where they might go. At first, he drew the little island they were sitting on as best he could and then to show exactly what he was doing, he embellished its edges with a few little squiggles to represent waves. He pretended as though to continue, before stopping without warning and opening his hands in a gesture that showed he was not too sure how to complete his makeshift map. Veddellemettis immediately comprehended what was required of him and at the same time probably realised this was one way to please his captors and ensure he lived a little longer. From inside his dirty linen shirt, he pulled a small stick which had been sharpened at one end. With nothing more than this he produced a remarkably accurate representation of the group of islands that they now found themselves on.

When he had finished, Spjall grunted approvingly, before roughly slapping him on the back and nodded his head up and down enthusiastically. Like Olaf, he too considered it good to know that there were a considerable number of islands, which could be explored with the idea of seeing whether they were suitable for settlement in mind. However, Spjall had not quite finished, he clearly had another idea. Drawing a crude picture of a longhouse in the sand, he once again showed the palms of his hands to the clouds in expectation. Once more, the young Orcadian was able to ascertain what was needed of him. He proceeded to put a series of neat dots in the sand, which Olaf assumed showed the position of the communities on the islands. The island group was it seemed not surprisingly dominated by one large island, on which the boy also drew a number of horses. It looked to have the greatest number of houses, which from the crude drawing were well spread out, but even so there was settlement of some sort on at least five of the other smaller isles.

Spjall had not quite finished. Pausing briefly to think, he then nodded to himself, whilst at the same time putting his tongue between his lips to give the impression that he was indeed searching for something in his mind. 'I know, I'll draw a runic word in the sand to see if he understands. I'll put down the word *fiskr* (fish), that's one word he surely should know. If he doesn't know that, then he won't know anything!' With that Spjall carefully drew five symbols in the damp sand.

ᚠᛁᛋᚲᛦ

The boy shrugged his shoulders and held out his hands indicating that the lines carved into the sand had no meaning to him whatsoever. 'Well, it was a long shot; I suppose I'd have to write the word in his language if he has any chance of understanding. Let me see, I know a few of their symbols, just give me a minute.' Spjall scratched the back of his head before rather affectedly holding the bridge of his nose between forefinger and thumb. He stayed frozen in this pose for no longer than a few moments, before making a series of markings in the sand of a quite different type. The last set of lines he drew at a slant and they cut right through the middle line he had drawn.

The boy clearly recognised the symbols, as Oghams used by his and other peoples, but failed to put the various devices together to make the word *fiskr* (fish) Spjall rubbed his nose before standing up and destroying the lines in the sand with his feet. I don't like making those markings, it doesn't seem right.' With that, the master of both runes and apparently Ogham as well, had finished his failed language experiment.

'I know what I'd have us do, but we'll have too wait and see what your father thinks when he returns.' Olaf spoke quietly to Invar and then thanked Spjall for his more than useful intervention. Just as he was about to take his leave, the muscular Norseman said to Olaf that there was something else he should know. There was a strange stone in the sand dune away to the north of the beach they were currently on. He said that it had been carved and bore a number of symbols, which may hold magical properties. 'I'd take the boy if I were you and get him to have a look at it. He may be able to draw a picture of what it is.' With these words Spjall trudged his way up to the top of the beach. Olaf watched his every step, before observing him slump clumsily to his knees in the sand, before lying down and rolling over. He lay there, flat on his back with his legs drawn up and with his left arm shielding his face from the bright sky, as if to induce sleep.

In a short time Olaf, Ingvar and Veddellemettis found themselves looking at an upright slab of grey stone. It had a series of unintelligible Ogham markings scratched into its surface, but in addition to these there were stylised, almost abstract carvings of boars and deer and a number of other strange symbols. These were 'V' and 'N' shaped and had been cut in such a way as to cross the animal representations without what Olaf considered to have any logical thought or apparent reason. Ingvar said he believed it to be just a grave marking, but he was not sure if it be known. 'Look at the way the corners have been carefully smoothed to be round and the way the dead man's name is written across the stone. The carving is neat, but the stone must be old; see the way the small orange and light green plants have crept into the cracks of all of the lines that make up the letters. Also, the grass is very long here. Notice that, rather strangely, there is not the remotest hint of any mound. This man must have been important having commanded such a stone. The question is why was he just dumped in a hole in the ground? This stone in time will crack and crumble and then there'll be nothing left to show where the old bugger lies.'

'I doubt it's a grave my friend for that very reason. It may be just a marking stone to warn us and others like us that we shouldn't be here. I've heard of them before and I like the idea. I think one day when I have my own longhouse I'll put them around my land to warn people and *landvættir* to keep away.' Olaf's reply was well considered and seemed to make good sense to Ingvar who grudgingly nodded and indicated to his friend that he may be right. Just after this exchange Veddellemettis pointed to the beach, then to the stone and then out to the small island lying immediately in front of them. Olaf glanced at the nervous looking boy and considered that he was genuinely trying to help them and of course help himself at the same time. He beckoned to the boy indicating they return to the sand to see if his theory was right. In no time at all, Veddellemettis had with the little stick he for reasons known to him alone carried, drawn a small picture of the stone in the course grains of the yellow and damp sand. When he had finished, he drew a circle around his representation and within the confines of this, he fashioned a crude representation of a figure. Having completed this, he attempted to replicate his drawing next to the original one. Olaf burst into a fit of laughter and clapped his friend Ingvar on the back with a heavy palm. 'That seems to show I am right, my friend. Well, what do you think?'

'So it would seem, but I'm sure they may have other uses as well,' came Ingvar's slow, pensive and somewhat irritated reply.

       ℰℭ   ℰℭ   ℰℭ

Dawn came clear and ruby. The small tent-like shelters or booths that had been hastily erected high up on the beach now cast their long shadows in the watery golden sunlight that slanted across the beach virtually parallel to the ground. Each footprint or slight depression in the sand became hugely exaggerated and left the beach looking as pock marked as the face of Niði, the waned moon that was in spite of the encroaching light still riding defiantly high in the sky.

From the greenery which smothered the sandy hillocks above the beach the voice of a solitary look-out rang out. Olaf couldn't help but jump as he heard the shout, even though he was by now fully awake. In fact, he had been awake for some time, having slept fitfully through the night, under the twinkling stars in his *húðfat*. Mardöll, his woman had lost any interest she had had in him by now and she was currently sleeping with another young crewman of Gjálfrmarr instead. He was not the first or second man she had turned to after leaving Olaf and at first Ingvar's friend resented her for this. Although he tried to mask his feelings from those around him, he had never the less spent a considerable time wallowing in a kind of self-pity at first, but in due course proceeded to hide his irritation by immersing himself in the organisation of the boats and in other practical matters, such as arranging for fresh water to be obtained and ensuring that catching and cooking of fish continued unabated. By coincidence, Mardöll's female friend Esja had now also spurned Ingvar as well, but in contrast to Olaf, he at least seemed quite disinterested or even pleased by this development. Esja had not taken to another man, but had instead kept herself to herself and for safety's sake had made friends with a few other young girls who had no current partners. As a result, she was being sneered at and teased by the younger boys who quickly realised that they could not have her for themselves. They shouted hurtfully after her, 'Kvinna, kvinna, kvinna! Þu ert eigi gladan brúðr! Þu heitir ok hest *reiðan svartan!'* (Lesbian, lesbian, lesbian! You'll never be a happy bride! You angry black horse!)

The boys who now teased the indignant girl were ignored staunchly by Olaf, who had stood up to see if the dragon ship happened to have appeared. The shrill cry from the sharp grass covered dunes had indeed heralded the return of the master himself on his esteemed boat. Without prompting of any kind, the men and the few women on the sand began to busy themselves with all sorts of tasks that hitherto had not commanded their interest or attention in the slightest. The return of their leader provided impetus enough to galvanise each and every single one of them; from the relatively few important men left in charge to the more numerous small and carefree boys whose main duty was to bail unstintingly on the boats as they rode the dark icy waters. Huts made from the remains of worn out sails were rapidly dismantled. Sand was either kicked or heaped by hand onto fires. Drift wood that had been gathered the previous day had been bundled and tied neatly. Bags which had been so recently slept in were now tightly rolled or had instead been stuffed with a diverse array of personal possessions, to be transported back onto their owner's particular boat.

'Ormr' neared the beach, but its master clearly had no intention of landing. Instead, Guðbjörn who was near to the prow shouted with cupped hands to those on the sand. He waved with both hands and then pointed in an easterly direction. The message was clear enough to those who sat or stood on the fine yellow sand; ÓþyrmiR had found something he liked the look of and there was little time to lose. The dragon wallowed uneasily for a few moments in the shallow water in the way a dog waiting to be taken on a walk pulls one way and then moves back, always looking to its master for approval before making a final decisive move. Olaf now made his way down the steeply sloping beach and with him he brought the local boy. They both left deep elongated footprints as their heels dug into and slipped in the welcoming sand. Óþyrmiʀ waved an arm lazily from the back of the boat indicating that he was not concerned in the slightest about any matters on the islands, at least for the present and then clapped both his hands together. He didn't wait though; without hesitation he shouted something to his steersman. To those on the beach his words were completely inaudible and within moments the great boat was spinning about its central point before moving off slowly in a southerly direction. Olaf sensed his friend's presence by his side and turning towards him said to Ingvar, 'Your father has formulated a plan and it's clear he's in a quite a hurry. We'd better get all the boats and folk ready to follow him, before he disappears. Also, we'd better pick up the boy's *snekkja*, which I believe is hidden somewhere around the headland. Go and get Rúnfastr and his friend, what's his name, Þórormr that's it and confirm exactly where it is.'

Both men were delighted to be remembered by Olaf as their hopes of a reward of silver had been raised once more. 'Óþyrmiʀ will see to a payment if he thinks fit,' was all Olaf would say to the men after telling them to find the little craft they had hidden. The tide had only moved up the beach a matter of about the height of two men, before the dragon ship and the *knarr*s were all in the water once more and moving as one in a tight formation southwards. As they passed the protruding headland, the boats swung out to begin in a due westerly direction, with the sails of the *knarr*s at once billowing as they filled with an obliging if weak wind. The *drakkar* had no sail set, but for once relied upon the massed ranks of Norsemen who rowed precisely and with a stroke that seemed to coincide with every breath each man took. The boat seemed to take life; to move effortlessly in the water as though a beast at ease in its watery realm. The blades of the long oars dipped rhythmically in the ever moving swell, to catch and reflect beams of sunlight every so often and when this happened, the light that bounced away would instantly close eyes and knit foreheads of any who so happened to be admiring the passage of the *drakkar* in full flight.

But for the briefest of stops to collect the small *snekkja* belonging to the young Orcadian Veddellemettis, there were no interruptions. The little narrow beamed craft had been securely attached to the back of the large *drakkar* with a rope Olaf called a '*bræða.*' The four boats now moved relentlessly in a north-westerly direction between the island they had briefly stayed on and what appeared to be the largest of the islands. Olaf remembered the crude sand map that the young boy had drawn and tried to predict where the 'Ormr' would be when they found her. It was not as easy as he would have liked it, because their passage was complicated by a small island with two large islands lying off its eastern side, which lay directly in their way.

Having rounded this they were forced to move in single file between another larger island and the biggest island that now lay off to their left. The waters here were clearly rich in fish; at least twenty or so cormorants were bobbing up and down on the surface, before periodically lunging forwards to dive below the water's surface. They would reappear quite some time later about a *drakkar's* length from where they had disappeared, before cocking back their heads to apparently swallow whatever fish they had managed to catch. Again, directly in front of them were more guano covered rocks and an odd shaped triangular island that lay in what should have been the deepest part of the sound. Quick moving waters here indicated a strong pull of the tide, which caused no alarm for the *drakkar*, but ensured some delicate manoeuvring on the part of the *knarr*. As soon as the pull of the current or *rás* had been negotiated, the boats popped out of the confines of the comparatively sheltered waters into the darker water of the open sea.

Moving due west now and with the wind once more behind them they made good time in the powerful swell that lifted and fell rhythmically. Occasionally a seal with a grey speckled colouring would pop its head above the surface of the water to look at the boat with baleful and inquisitive eyes. Then when all hope of seeing 'Ormr' seemed to have left them, there she was, to their left beached, sail down, on a small island opposite to and no more than a hundred strides from another similar looking beach belonging to the largest island of the archipelago.

'That is so typical of ÓþyrmiR. Your father, he doesn't miss a single trick. He has it would seem found the perfect place on these islands from which we can restore our supplies, defend ourselves and plan our course of action. If he so chooses we can settle here, or we could launch off again into the waves, to see where we might wish to end up.' Olaf spoke his words with a great deal of affection and admiration.

Undorneykt had arrived and all the boats were once again together, high and dry, lying side by side on the soft sandy beach of the little island that was to offer them a good degree of shelter. The tide had fallen to its lowest point and the main island could quite easily be reached by foot. In fact, several heavily armed men had been sent across the shallow stretch of knee deep water to act as lookouts and at the same time guard the rest of the Norse folk who had arrived under the protection of their leader ÓþyrmiR. All of the men carried spears and several also had long handled axes hanging from their waistbands. In addition, they carried with them their brightly painted round shields, which had until now been stashed below the decks of the boats. The master had decreed that they be stored this way in order to prevent them being lost overboard in the event of a storm. ÓþyrmiR could see no advantage in displaying the expensive round devices along the side of the ship unless they were to fend off the arrows or spears of attackers. In battle of course he argued that they could be easily and quickly put into place. If kept in such a position under normal circumstances however, they would hinder the oarsmen, increase their chance of loss significantly as well as ageing prematurely with the constant exposure to brine and sunlight. Now their function was to bring to the attention of the local inhabitants, the power and wealth of the Norse.

As soon as the other *drakkar* had grounded on the soft welcoming sand of the tiny island, Olaf and Ingvar made their way with the young Orcadian to the *jarl*. ÓþyrmiR observed the boy with a contrived indifference, whilst listening intently to his son, who recounted in quite exact detail how Olaf had stood up to the rabble who to a man had wished to sacrifice their newly acquired captive. Nothing appeared to be stirring within the mind of the Norse leader, until at last he broke his silence to first congratulate his adopted son and then instruct the steersman of Aðalríkr, Sviðbalki to fetch some silver from a bag he had closeted away in a chest on the *knarr*. The leader asked for the two men who had captured the boy to be brought to him and when they duly arrived, he rewarded Rúnfastr and Þórormr for their efforts after all.

In an act clearly designed to attract the attention of everyone present, the master held up a large and heavy nugget of sparkling silver. He began throwing the uneven ball of precious metal up into the air, again and again, to repeatedly catch it in his welcoming soft leather gloves. It was as though he was playing some sort of mind game with a young child, whilst at the same time appearing to crave the attention of all who looked on. Three, four, five times, the precious metal rose and fell, before it suddenly disappeared from sight and from his gloves, as if either by some unexplained magic or more likely by some deft sleight of hand. The enchanted crowd gasped as one, first to wonder what had become of the precious silver and secondly, if it be known, to hope beyond hope that they may become the silver's new guardian. The master dismissively turned his attention from the crowd and towards the frightened young captive instead. He held out one of his gloved hands as though in a welcoming and friendly gesture. The boy anxiously reciprocated, to mirror the actions of the older man, holding out his hand to shake the other's, in an attempt to please. Suddenly, without any warning a smile burst forth onto his previously worried countenance; a smile of joy and at the same time one of relief. Raising his spear hand high, he held above his head the piece of silver in celebration. Rather incredibly, the shining nugget appeared to have grown in size. Perhaps it was some hidden magic, or may be the boy's hand was simply much smaller than that of the gloves of the master. '*Tveir eyrir brannt silfr,*' (an ounce of pure silver) the disappointed voice of a young woman broke the hitherto spell of the silence. Olaf span around, in instant recognition of the owner of the voice, to whom the softly spoken words belonged. There before him, but with eyes keenly averted from his and instead transfixed on the shining metal stood Mardöll.

'Silver, is that it? Is that all?' Olaf sneered at the girl in disbelief. He half expected a reply, but wasn't really surprised or disappointed when none came. As he moved away from both the boy and the enraptured Mardöll, he became acutely aware of his master's glances; he felt he was being surveyed keenly. The master mariner approached Olaf with purposeful strides, indicating to Olaf some need for urgency.

'Olaf, you have done well,' he began, 'you saved the boy's life. That is good, because some of us will be settling here for good and to kill a native on our first day here would not do. It would not do at all.'

'Well, *Foðurbróðir,* if I dare to be so bold as to call you that, I don't share your feelings. I have lost out, there's no mistake.'

'My son, my adopted son, you can call me by that name, of course you can. You must know that to lose is sometimes to win. To let go that which is no good is better than hanging on to that which has little or no value. You have played the 'King's table', you know of the need to sacrifice gaming pieces at times. Yes, that young boy has the silver and now he has that girl, but she is better off without you and you without her. The boy lives, when he might not, he thinks he is happy! Soon, he will have a wife, a giggling and silly girl, but a girl who nevertheless may save many Orcadian souls and a fair few Norse men. She is but nothing. She will soon willingly to take the lad and by lying on her back and pleasing him, she will bring together two sets of people. She little realises what power she wields; if she had just half a brain in her empty head and she took a little time to use it, she'd want more than a nugget of silver today! Think of her grubby bed chamber as the place where the unofficial treaty will be marked by her on behalf of all of us, the Norse and those who have given up their lands to us.

Heed my words, you will not be staying here Olaf, but a fair few of us will. This is now Norse land your feet stand on, but there is still more to do in the world out there. I will speak with these islanders before too long, but I will wait for them to search us out and see if they welcome us, or seek to thrust a spear into our bellies. A marriage between our folk and theirs could well see a peaceful glorious victory. Imagine that for a victory; a battle without need to chip the edge of an axe or scratch the surface of a sword or shield.'

'It doesn't sound too much like a victory to me. It sounds to me, if you'll excuse me being so bold, that you've finally gone soft in the head.' Olaf spoke from the bottom of his heart.

'Sometimes, victories are more about winning than the way you win.' The master's final words were delivered with clarity and power, but Olaf was not wholly convinced. The game was up as far as this mission would go, he thought to himself. The master had to all intensive purposes hung up his war axe and become an island farmer. *'Jarl ÓþyrmiR, Eysjarskeggi Orkneyinga,'* (Earl ÓþyrmiR, inhabitant of the islands of Orkney) Olaf spoke these simple words quietly to himself, almost in disbelief.

ᔥ   ᔥ   ᔥ

The master was, as he always seemed to be, correct. The islanders and their horses did eventually come out and greet the Norsemen. They did so with more than a little trepidation at first, but not, it must be said wholly unwillingly. The boy returned to his family home with his bride, Mardöll and in time they raised a large family. All their children bore Norse names; names to reflect the glory of the Norse and their great gods. Further to this, *Mardöll's* children also bore her name and not their father's. There were three sons; Þjóðgeirr Mardöllsson, Bröndólfr Mardöllsson, Smiðkell Mardöllsson and three daughters; Geirlaug Mardöllsdottir, Hallgríma Mardöllsdottir and Brynhildr Mardöllsdottir.

ᔥ   ᔥ   ᔥ

So you can see that in just one short generation the Orcadian names had begun to disappear. This one family unknowingly indicated how things were to be on these islands. Even the dogs and the horses bore names that were not out of place in the fjords that lay so far away.

Byrgisey or the Brough of Birsay was the name of this tiny island with gentle pastures that sloped gradually to the sea and it was in time to become the centre of a large and important Norse settlement. It was an isle covered in lush springy grass and it was built of land that climbed gently but steadily towards the sheer cliffs at the most westward end. These were densely populated by a massive colony of sea parrots. They hopped about clumsily on rocky ledges, before flapping their wings and taking off to the sky, before diving into the sea in search of plentiful sand eels, their favourite food.

I heard from my grandfather that another Pictish marking stone, one with three soldiers carrying spears and square shields had been found on the island. On it there appeared to be a massive swimming beast which almost defied description. 'An animal of huge proportions, from I believe distant lands to the south,' was the only description to be offered and it came from Ingvar, who had studied it for a considerable time, before shaking his head in utter disbelief. The stone was left in its original position on the stern instruction of the master, because he said it gave a degree of hope to the local Orcadians and a timely reminder to the Norse that they were still and would remain in this, a foreign land for many years to come. What my father's father would have made of that wondrous beast I can't imagine. He knew about many such things, but always for reasons known to him alone, became silent when questioned on this particular matter. No matter, for the beast is like the stone, it is but a mere distraction to this tale. Snorri is getting used to my frequent asides, but he has yet to show the slightest enthusiasm for them. He would rather hurry to the conclusion in the way most young folk always seem to want everything straight away. Gone are days when hours given to study and the patience needed to go with it were attributes that were seen as normal. To practise a skill to improve the artistry with which it is done was the only tried and tested way. Now, now, now, that is all I ever hear today! We would all do well, especially the young and those of an impatient nature or disposition to remember the three norns. What has passed shaped the present and now, the present duly passes to shape what is to be!

ଔ ଔ ଔ

Before some of the boats finally left this small cluster of islands, Olaf had spoken with many native Orcadians and a considerable number of Picti who had settled there and who had a reasonable understanding of the Norse tongue. Brude, Drosten, Itharnan, Peanfahel and Uirolec, all petty chieftains were summoned by the master and from them Olaf and his fellow Norse men learned of another distant group of islands to the north. They had made their counsel, when it became clear to them that some of their fellow islanders would be dispossessed of their lands. Their Norse master was as was his way, straight with them right from the outset. Acquisition of land was his first priority, but he wished even so for a peaceful settlement in the islands if that was at all possible. Drosten, an *Orkneysjarskeggi*, was the unofficial leader of the small band. He spoke eloquently to the Norse folk and made a good case for his fellow people. He began by describing in great detail the beginning of the world and the great gods of his Celtic people. There were too many to remember for those who listened. Olaf however, sat spellbound with his mouth half open as he heard about Brigit, the 'High One', In Dagda, also called Eochaidh Oll-athair, the all-father, who controlled druidic magic, Morrigan, Badb and Nemain, war goddesses, Lug the skilled and Goubniu, the great smith who always took the first drink at feasts. He described the terrible Cath Maige Tuired, a huge battle between the people of the goddess Danu, who overcame the Formoiri, a race of hideous evil beasts, with their more advanced magical skills.

The master, Olaf, Ingvar and many others listened patiently to these tales and smiled as and when they perceived was necessary and then looked serious or sad or surprised when such other expressions were similarly demanded. All of the tales related to the struggle between the powers of goodness and darkness. The irony of being recounted such deep moral stories was not lost on the master and on a good number of the others present. Drosten went on to describe Ogma, the champion of the gods; sun-faced controller of the martial powers of Mag Tuired, the god who invented their strange Ogham script. When the island leader finally finished speaking, his place was taken by an older man, Brude the father of Veddellemettis.

Olaf thought Brude to be playing an interesting game of wagering, because he described the wonders of what he called the 'beautiful islands to the north' and how they would make a much better settlement area for the Norse. He said they were virtually unpopulated save for a few sheep rearing monks who chose to live their wretched lives all alone. The fishing there was good, the land bountiful and the sun shone brighter in the sky, so help him Brigit. He swore all these things on his son's life. Olaf was more than a little confused by his strange speech and quite perplexed when he referred to his boy as Fedelmid.

'I thought his son to be Veddellemettis, who is this other boy Fedelmid?' Olaf's brusque question was directed at Drosten, who replied without the slightest hesitation, indicating he possessed not only a clear knowledge of his friend's personal history, but something else besides.

'The two are one and the same, for he is called Fedelmid by his father, because that is his name in Irish. The boy's line is from the great isle ruled over by Donnchadh, the son of Domhnall, son of Murchadh. Their king has already minded his throne for a lifetime they say.'

The master really had no interest in the acquisition of such knowledge and was instead musing deeply on the talk of other islands. He was truly delighted; yet more and more land for the Norse to explore, even if it was not going to be done by him personally. His son would be all right now though, he thought, smiling to himself contentedly.

One of the little isles and indeed a good sized house was taken by the master in due time, to became his permanent home. The isle he had chosen was large enough to support him and his woman and indeed her family, for she was of the islands herself. It lay just to the north of the main island and in time became known as Rousay. His wife, a wild and strong individual came to be known as Ótama; ÓþyrmiR had refused to accept her Celtic name and thought a Norse one would suit her better, mainly because he simply refused to tolerate the thought of shouting a Celtic name, which he confided he found difficulty pronouncing, at all times of the day and night. His friends laughed at and understood his choice of name for her, for it simply meant untamed. Although the master was at least forty summers when he stepped onto these isles for the first time, he still bore her two children. The eldest was called Þengill, but alas like many very young offspring, he died when little older than one month. A second son she bore him several years later, but he only troubled *Midgard* until aged some fourteen years, dying little more than a week after the master himself had passed away. Ótama had found their deaths, which had been so very close together almost impossible to accept. She duly spent a huge amount of the family's silver fortune on the funeral feast and burials. Two huge holes were dug and into each of these was placed a good sized boat. One was a very old *drakkar* and the other a *knarr*. Her husband, she had insisted would lie in the ancient dragon boat and her young son in the trading vessel. Both were similarly attired; dressed for battle, armed with sword, axe and shield, but into the grave also went their tools for working the land. The master began his life in the Norse heartland and ended it on the little island of Rousay in the Orkneys. He had been a warrior, a merchant and a farmer. He had left *Midgard* in the desperate hope of crossing the rainbow bridge in a boat, a much loved boat named 'Ormr', to travel to Asgard and that was the way he would have wished it.

$$\mathit{SO} \quad \mathit{SO} \quad \mathit{SO}$$

Within the cycle of just one moon; *Nýi* had become *Niði*, great changes had taken place on the little island of Byrgisey. Some of the local houses had been taken over by the Norse and there were scratchings in the turf to show where a number of family houses were to be constructed. Within a short space of time, there would be long halls with central hearths, built in such a way as too point in the direction of the prevailing winds. The main building materials were on hand, they were to be the very earth on which the buildings would stand and the stones that conveniently lay all about in copious quantities. In addition, there was a need of course for a supply of wood that would in time be used to form the beams and trusses of the roofs. This commodity would out of necessity have to be brought in to the islands because of course there were no real trees to speak of. Some gigantic rib bones from whales, had been found high up on one remote beach and had served in the place of wooden rafters in some of the smaller houses or huts, but these were not too plentiful.

Before the end of the month, in fact on its very last day, several boats were being pushed out into the water for another voyage of discovery. The great *drakkar* 'Ormr' and 'Ávarr' the trading vessel or *knarr*, were however unmoved. ÓþyrmiR's last words to Olaf were of warning. 'I have heard said that north of these islands the great sea-mill *Swelki* is lying in wait for whoever may chance upon it, grinding and grinding until the end of the world. It is turned by the twin ogres *Grotti-Fenni* and *Grotti-Menni*, who now have come to resent their never ending task. In the treacherous waters, if it is meant to be, you will find this great churning maelstrom. It is so very dangerous, for it could swallow your ships whole and then grind them and you to nothingness. It is I believe vast.'

'Where can it be found?' Olaf's reply showed a degree of interest, but at the same time it lacked any real concern or conviction. The master sensing this paused a little before continuing.

'North, that is all I know. The mill was originally used to make good things, but the twins were put into slavery and this made 'em both spiteful and change its use. Now, all it does, is turn out salt and more salt and the water in the seas pour through the grind-stone's centre hole to create this unwelcome demon for sailors.'

'I'll take my chances with this watery devil. I'll wager it's nothing more than a bit of swell. Anyway, there's nothing any of us can do when it comes to fate. You and I, as Norse folk know that what will happen, will happen if it is meant to. We have but little power to change the way of things. If I am meant to die fighting in a battle or even a drunken brawl, then there's nothing I can do to prevent it. I will raise my sword in the best way I can, in the hope of preserving the name I carry with me and in the great hope that I may cross the rainbow bridge to *Asgard*.'

'You, Olaf can do as you like my friend. For me, I believe that I will make that momentous journey one day, but only after I have changed things for the better!'

'There's nothing that proves I or you will make any such journey. We must protect our names, the names given to us by our fathers and hope beyond hope that we are chosen by the *Valkyrja* to go. Not everyone can or will go, so by *Þórr's* great hammer, I ask for help.' Olaf spoke no more now, he was slightly depressed having almost convinced himself that the hallowed halls he so desperately craved, were nothing more than the feeble dreams of weak men, the type who bore tears in their eyes when they thought of their own death. He contemplated the most sanctimonious of all men he knew, the Christians; they were the worst he thought, they made pompous and holy assertions all the time! They would smile parsimoniously as though to deliberately indicate to anybody present that they knew more or were simply better than anyone else. What utter bastards! By *Óðinn* and all the gods, how he would like to dispatch them and hurry them back to their maker, if they so believed the muddle headed crap they spouted. *Óðinn* had hung on the great and wondrous tree after receiving his mortal spear wound and had confounded death by returning to life, of this there was no doubt. The men of Christ maintained their god had done the same in so many words. Why couldn't they have been more imaginative and created something of their own. By all that was sacred, why couldn't the Christians and all those others who craved new religions come up with a new idea? All they did was copy. They made him wretch. What was more, he knew their religion was slowly but surely creeping across the land in the way that plague blights entire communities and eventually countries. What an obnoxious prospect, he thought.

The boats lay grounded on the sand above the high tide line; for all of the world looking rather melancholy, but even so appearing sublimely oblivious to the departure of so many men. All of the women were staying on the islands, they were needed for a host of different tasks, the singularly most important of which was child bearing. The Orkney Islands were now the property of the *Gaill* as some of the native islanders had called them and most surprisingly no blood had been shed. Hrossey, the largest of the islands acquired its name, because of its abundance of horses, whilst another island with a great and precipitous stack of rock sticking out of the savage sea just to the east of it now went by the name of Hoy, which of course meant high in their tongue.

ℬ   ℬ   ℬ

As this tale unfolds its secrets, there is bound to be at least some resentment created in the mind of the man or woman who listens to it. Snorri is singularly unimpressed with the lack conflict and peaceful settlement of Orkney and he has told me in no uncertain terms. He curls his top lip to show his displeasure. He would change the way it was and allow Olaf to fight for each pace of every single island at the top of Bretland. Alas, disappointment reigns supreme in his mind on this occasion, but the tale has some way to meander yet, so I may regain some credibility in his eyes a little while later.

Young minds boast a keen cutting edge even if they lack subtlety or possess aforethought. My young listener wholeheartedly agrees with his hero and is happy to call on the old gods when he feels he needs them, or to curse, which happens rather more frequently. Yes, the strong feelings I am imbued with, regarding my beliefs, still apparently linger on in a watered down way somehow in the youngsters of today. My tacit agreement with Olaf is full and proper, but I would add to his acrimonious and vitriolic diatribe that even the Mithraists, who themselves came before the Christians had copied our great Óðinn. He wouldn't have known this of course. They were, I have heard tell, rather more like us than those who replaced them; they sacrificed as we do, but the bull and copious quantities of its blood was their focus. They also like us tended to use the spoken word for their agreements, their ceremonies, their rules and their laws. They, were however more mystical in many of their ways than us and they tended to hide themselves away from the common people. Theirs was predominantly a warriors' cult, whereby ours is so much more!

As for the Celts, what can I say? Their beliefs look quite like our own. Ogma, their sun-faced controller reminds me so much of our great god, the alfather in Saemundur's poem <u>Sólarljóð</u>. Yes, the alfather, my grandfather told me he had even heard it told that the Christians, from the lands of the Anglo Saxon had *prayed to him. At the time of Olaf, they used to begin one of their most important prayers in their old language, 'Fæder ure þu þe eart on heofonum.'*

Snorri is as I have already reported to you, young and his mind is easily changed; he is vulnerable and is in many ways impressionable. Living in a land where the Christian cross has taken over and now is master, means that he must and it hurts me to say so, comply if he is to survive and flourish. He will have to consign the great and worthy gods of yesteryear and our language to history and embrace the one god! If he acts thus, who knows what opportunities may be presented to him. Conversely, if he deems this path unattractive, his star will undoubtedly fade in the way our spoken traditions are slowly but surely eroded and dimmed by the advent of the church's written Latin words

Chapter 10

Sumar, þriþi mánuðr

Hjaltland

May, A.D. 790

Olaf had taken charge of all the men who were leaving the islands. They rowed on either Olaf's *drakkar*, Gjálfrmarr or crewed on one of the two *knarr* ÁdiarfR or Aðalríkr. Farþegn, the master's brother remained as ever in charge of the trading boat ÁdiarfR, whilst Sviðbalki continued as chief steersman on Aðalríkr. Their course was nearly, but not quite due north; north, but slightly eastwards. The powerful *drakkar* was not fully manned now, having something like a third of its oars stashed in the middle of the boat. No man was to be seen sitting at every third station or so; the oar holes here had been plugged to prevent any sea water entering the boat unnecessarily. The extra space had of course been used up, as it always seemed to be on each and every voyage, with a multitude of supposedly essential items. Land birds in cages seemed to be virtually everywhere. There were skins full of water, skins bloated with beer, some odd shaped porcelain containers with wine, obtained from the local Orcadian populace and various dried meats in baskets that had been stashed as neatly as possible below the removable deck of the *drakkar*, or at either the front or rear of the two *knarrs*. On the *knarr*, these and other perishable goods were carefully stored under a waterproof sheet that had been rigged up to appear like a tent, built to survive a severe storm. In addition, a large number of different kinds of rye and mixed grain loaves of bread had been meticulously wrapped in greasy sack cloth to keep them fresh. These had been stored in large wicker baskets and had been placed under the tent like structures. Furthermore, a good quantity of very hard cheeses in a dirty brown wax rind, as well as some softer cheeses that would clearly not keep as long as the others were stashed somewhere below the deck.

There had been no great ceremony to wave the boats out of the *rás* between little Rousay and what the Norsemen had quickly come to call the mainland or more to the point their mainland. Those who had decided to stay in an attempt to establish a new life here were extremely reluctant to acknowledge those who were leaving them and their little isles. It was as if they hadn't fully made their minds up and may have possibly wanted to return homewards as well. They couldn't really help themselves at this time. It was quite unintentional that they looked the other way, unlike the black headed gulls which took more than a passing interest. They cried harshly and hovered in the breeze without the slightest movement of wing to lift them. They veered this way and that in a random and erratic aerial dance. Behind these kite like birds, on the sloping gentle sands five or six oystercatchers darted this way and that looking for dainty morsels to eat. Occasionally, they would cry out in their unthreatening and unmistakable manner; peep-peep, peep-peep, with their long, bright orange beaks wagging in the same way an irritated finger might admonish a misdemeanour of some sort.

Olaf had noticed the dearth of well wishers, but obviously there was nothing he could do about it. He merely shrugged his shoulders and as an after thought whispered to himself, 'Miserable bastards, that's what they are, all of them.' Ingvar was with him and rather nervously burst into laughter when he heard Olaf's critical comment, perhaps because for the first time in his life he was now finally adrift of his father and more to the point, his father's influence. The master knew full well that his son would be looking for a farewell gesture and for that reason he kept well out of sight, preferring to take a long and not particularly suitable knife to a piece of drift wood he had picked up earlier that day. As he scraped and scratched away at the wood he thought deeply of his son and for the very first time in his life he felt a deep regret that perhaps he would not see him again. This pang hurt him to the core and in spite of all the years of fighting, hardness and toil, he felt the beginnings of a tear well from his left eye. Blinking several times, he pushed the knife hard into the wood and turned the blade to form a neat little hole that rather well mimicked the beady eye of a puffin. By the time the toy like bird had been crudely fashioned to vaguely approximate its real life counterpart, the boats containing both his son, adopted son and a host of other Norse folk had disappeared from sight. All three craft had rounded the headland before making for the deep and dark waters of the open sea. A great school of grey and blue speckled porpoises swam across the bows of the *drakkar* that led the way as though in recognition of their departure. Each effortlessly flew through the water; every so often breaking through its surface to create short lived magical arcs and curves in the air before re-entering the welcoming waves, to reappear several moments later to recreate the magical scene. '*Godan marsvínana,*' (Beautiful porpoises) Olaf's spoke quietly to himself as he marvelled at the beauty of the creatures which wove their elusive watery patterns; patterns that were never to be exactly repeated.

On the *drakkar*, Olaf had assumed complete command. His friend Ingvar seemed to be at ease, even pleased with the arrangements. Like all second in commands he always seemed to have less time to think about things than his friend who was now leader. However, he didn't grumble, for that was not in his nature and if truth be known, he liked to keep himself busy. Ingvar had on a number of occasions confided in Olaf that busy hands have but little time for mischief. He now shouted loudly to Olaf who was at the back of the boat.

'We need to fit a new '*rakki*' on the mast as the old one has cracked and is in danger of splitting. It'll last for a month or so in good weather, but if we hit a storm it'll break when we can least afford it. It's best we change it now, whilst the wind shows us it can be kind. As it is, that crack in the metal, it's rubbing and at times getting stuck in the wood of the mast and catching and fraying the ropes. Those ropes are too good to be ruined, I've a number of other uses for them, before they fray, come on we'd best get stuck in now.'

'Well get those three lazy bastards, Geirraðr, Fugl and Guðbjörn to help you,' came the new master's reply.

'Stæðingr, get the stæðingr ready to store the sail, as the sail and all the ropes are coming off the mast. They'll need to, if we're to replace the rakki. It'll be tricky enough for us at sea as it is.' Ingvar knew precisely what needed to be done. His immediate concern though, was to get the valuable sail off and out of the way, because he knew that by doing so he would reduce the risk of it getting damaged. The stæðingr he referred to was just an enormous canvas bag, which had been carefully crafted so it would accommodate the sail perfectly, but only if it had been rolled neatly and without unnecessary overlaps, which irritatingly somehow always seemed to appear from nowhere. Ingvar had already decided that if he was forced to change the rakki, then he would also renew the strengr or ropes and even the *staglína*, the special chain that was firmly attached to the anchor. The crew naturally grumbled at the apparently unnecessary extra work, but they knew it would have to be done, now that the order had been issued.

Guðbjörn was expert when it came to ropes, he had acquired a wealth of experience on 'Mjollnir' and so it was up to him to take overall responsibility for the removal of all the old strengr and their replacement. He had all of the ones that were carefully removed meticulously coiled up and knotted in a special way, quite loosely, for some later use. Fugl an old friend of his, who also happened to have crewed on the same old long ship, had in the mean time found a replacement *rakki* which had been stored somewhere within their current boat. He now held it somewhat proudly with both hands. The inordinate and seemingly unnecessary amounts of grease that it had been coated with to protect it from the damp atmosphere in the boat's hull, covered his large calloused hands. In fact, he had on his own volition returned to where he was accustomed to row to use some of the excess grease to lubricate where his oar and some of his peers' oars customarily lay.

The weather was being kind to the men carrying out the repair; in fact it was because of its clemency that the work had been attempted in the first place. Olaf would never have dreamed of trying to facilitate a repair of this kind, even though it was not so difficult a job, in anything but near perfect conditions.

Geirraðr's task was a simple, but an important one; he had been instructed to shin up the mast, remove the old but working rakki at the top, place the brand new iron ring over the top of the mast and then let it slide down before finally replacing the top *rakki* into its original position. To achieve this particular task required an ability to climb like a spider; the climber needed tremendous strength in hands, arms and legs, plus a head that would allow the body to work at some height without hindrance. Geirraðr had no real problems completing his part of the job, apart from the short delay caused while he attached a short rope or strengr to the top *rakki*. Whilst he struggled momentarily at the zenith of his climb, two thick set men prised the old and damaged *rakki* from its position at the base of the mast, with a large bar of dark and well greased iron. He called down to them in delight and relief as he finished his task. One of the men at the foot of the mast shouted what sounded like some kind of encouragement up to him.

'You've grown up son, since you bailed on that old dragon.'

'Shit, that's going back, who's that down there who knows me? Dare I come down?' The now retired bailer shouted back.

'Just an old man, who should have known better than to get back on a boat that shouldn't need repairing,' came the riposte from the squat deck hand.

'What's your name friend?' Geirraðr began his descent as he spoke his words between breaths.

'Særða, that's my name,' said the man looking up, whilst half closing his eyes and blinking.

'You've shrunk, but you've developed a sense of wit my friend. On the 'Hammer' you were a right miserable bastard, by *Fenrir's* breath you were and there's no mistake!'

'Yes may be that was true, but you've grown more than a bit and I think now I'll let you be. I don't have time to be as miserable now, let alone pick fights with youngsters. I'm far too busy these days for that kind of thing. You young 'uns don't know the half of what you're doing most of the time and I'm left to pick up the pieces. You can just about scratch your arse, but even then you have to be told to.' The old man had clearly mellowed and laughed in mock despair as he delivered his condemnation of the present day's youth. He didn't dare let on, but he was actually an uncle to the boy. He thought fleetingly that he may help him out in the future if he were to stumble into trouble, because the look of him didn't repulse him, but that was as far as he would go. 'If the little bugger knows I'm his uncle, by *Óðinn*, he'll be coming running to me if he can't get something. Let him look after himself,

I'll let him be. If he's a man and he's lucky with it, he'll manage,' he mused to himself.

૬૦   ૬૦   ૬૦

The old, broken but shiny *rakki* hung disconsolately from a small hook that appeared to have no obvious function right at the front of the boat, just under where the dragon head was attached to the prow. Olaf had placed it there himself rather thoughtfully and said that he had a job for it.

Even his best friend and fellow sailor had not worked out what Olaf planned. The new master had become a little less predictable and short tempered of late and Ingvar put this down to the fact that he still longed for his lost 'mermaid'. The boats made good progress north eastwards and the general feeling on board was that everything was going well. As evening drew on, Ingvar looked up as if to consult the sky before observing, '*Miðr aptan.*' (Mid-evening) Olaf grimaced for he knew that a night on the open sea was not the best possible option and that time it seemed had conspired against them. A short time before, the boys who had been below deck, bailing had been told to come on deck and take a rest and if they so desired to look for the first stars which would make themselves visible. Olaf had for some reason put aside his melancholia and fallen into a happier mood now and put up a prize to the first man or boy who could spot the appearance of the very first star. He jested light heartedly that if it was he, then he would have a sliver of silver from everyone on his boat. The bailers took his words more than seriously and protested loudly before being cuffed rather heavily on their ears by Ingvar, who also told them to stop making such a noise or they would become food for the monsters that dwelled in the deep. The light decreased little by little. Slowly but surely the stars appeared one by one; a few, the travelling stars shone without blinking, but most emerged magically to twinkle with their own delicate beauty.

A shrill voice rang out a few moments later and the prize had been claimed. It was not one of the bailers, but a young lad who really should have embarked on Orkney, but had decided at the last minute he could not. Gagarr was his name, he also had been on the 'Hammer' as a child bailer, but now as a young man he still lacked nearly all of the skills he needed to make his own way in life. Olaf tossed him a small silver coin and looking at the youth said, 'You've the eyes of a hawk, do you have its mind as well?'

'I've the eyes of a hawk. I've really got the eyes of a hawk, have I?' I don't know if I've got the mind of a hawk though,' came the boy's reply. Olaf sighed loudly, whistled and averted his own eyes skywards.

'By *Óðinn*'s sacred tree, this boy'll need all the money he can get, for he'll get little for any work he performs I'll wager. No wonder his parents sent him off, poor bastards, they must have been driven to distraction; they were probably grateful to get rid of the little devil to some far off parts where there'll never have to see or hear of him again. The Orkneys can do without another mouth to feed, especially the likes of him. I'll wager that he'll have no line in the future and thank *Óðinn* for that. Wherever he goes or stays he'll remain a burden all right. Like shit on your shoe, you can't seem to get rid of it!'

Olaf's musings were cut short. Farþegn on ÁdiarfR had shouted something to his longship and several men at the front were waving back in acknowledgement. One of these now took it upon himself to make his way down the full length of the vessel where Olaf sat with the tiller. Spjall leant on the top strake with one hand and with the other he gestured generously.

'It would appear that we have land in sight, just where that Orcadian said it would be. Most helpful, most helpful that young man has been and no mistake!'

Olaf nodded, but with a little less enthusiasm than his crew might have expected. Sullenly pointing towards the landmass, he mumbled to himself, 'It's like the thin coating of scum that forms on the surface of the water in the wash tubs; it appears as if by magic there, each and every *Laugardagr.*' Then brightening in an instant he spoke much more loudly to his crew.

'Hold the course steady now and see if we can have a little look at this jumble of rocks they call islands, without us all getting too excited.' It was all Olaf their new master could muster.

'I thought we'd be doing a bit more than just looking,' Ingvar replied sullenly.

'Sometimes looking is preferable than doing, especially when we have too few men. Also, some of them are, as I'm sure you'd agree a little less than bright. Shiny, they're certainly not, I should say dull and about as useful as *bleikt silfr* with it.' Olaf had slowly become more pragmatic and worldly wise as responsibility took its inevitable toll. He now possessed what could only be described as more than the slightest veneer of cynicism. Ingvar had noticed this new character trait in his peer and now considered it for a little while. He came to the conclusion after just a few moments, that for some inexplicable reason it seemed to arrive in the hearts of all men unannounced and was he considered usually an unwelcome guest. It appeared to act as a balance against the more positive advantages that were also brought by greater maturity. Disconsolately, he surmised you couldn't expect the one without the other. 'What a pity,' he said to himself, grimacing in such a way that a casual observer would have deemed him to be smiling, but not so much as smiling happily, but rather more ruefully. In truth, however the smile was in fact a grimace; it was elicited for yet another reason altogether, a degree of irritation caused by a lower bowel problem he had been carrying for more than a little while.

'Well I don't mind taking a closer look, because I wouldn't mind looking first, before deciding where I'd like to set up house.' Ingvar was still positive despite his friend's apparent pessimism.

'Look, listen and learn! That's all I'd suggest you do for the present, because you'll not be getting your boots wet today my friend. We have other journeys to embark on and this one's not for us. It would be worth a fair bit of good silver I'll wager, but that'll be it for now as far as you and I are concerned.' Olaf's riposte hit home with the subtlety of the great iron hammer that belonged to *Óðinn*'s warrior son.

'So what'll you have us do now, the light is closing in, we've got land in our sights and we're tired, by the goats that pull *Þórr*'s chariot we are tired.' Ingvar spoke not just from his heart, but for the men on board as well, but he might as well have spoken for the dead, who swept past the ship with the wailing wind.

'Make some noise, that's all I ask of you for the present. Get out that drum; the one the Celts have a name for, though I can't bring it to mind. I've noticed it stored below deck. Give it a hitting it won't forget. I want the folk on shore to hear us and see us and for them to come out. I don't want them to forget us!' Olaf had made up his mind and he wasn't going to change it now.

Sure enough, the tightly skinned drum that had somehow found its way onto the longship from Donnchadh's land; the far away Ireland was beaten and beaten until it shouted out as though screaming in terror at some unseen beast.

The locals, at least twenty or so of them with their hounds and their short horses did indeed come out to see what all the fuss was about. They seemed to be most perplexed as to the arrival of the large and strange ships in the late evening. The magnificent *drakkar*, the likes of which no Hjaltlander had ever seen, approached the beach in a majestic silence. The people on the rough shingle appeared to be neither frightened nor apprehensive in any way; why should they have been? As it turned out on this occasion they had no cause to be anyway. The great glow of a cloudless sunset ensured just enough light to see the beach and the people on it. They appeared to the Norse on their boats to be a disparate group of individuals. There were men with long but thin greasy tails of sandy coloured hair that either blew around their faces randomly or which had been tied in small pig tails. Also, four religious men could be seen, severely tonsured, wearing cassocks of dark brown colour. One of them raised his hand in a peaceful gesture and shouted out something that could not be fully made out by the men on the *drakkar*. Whatever he said was carried away by the wind apart from two words which sounded like '*sonn*' and '*dafek*'. A number of young girls danced wildly on the upper sandy beach and two or three boys of five or six summers threw stones into the waves ignoring the boats as though they were of no consequence. One small and grubby boy shouted for joy as his flat stone skimmed off the surface of the level and friendly sea to bounce time and again before colliding gently with the vessel's clinkered hull. His shout died instantly in his throat as he saw the stone sink without trace into the dark shallow water. A long legged black and brown dog, presumably belonging to him, bounded in loping strides into and out of the water, before barking aggressively at him and shaking its shaggy coat wildly. Droplets of water flew from its fur to cover two naked little girls who had made their way down the beach and were now standing close by. They shrieked in surprise and giggled uncontrollably as they ran away, completely oblivious to the menace of the nearby dragon riding the swell.

Olaf granted himself a brief smile, before striding purposefully to the front of the ship and announcing to all on the boat and all on the beach that these islands belonged to him and his people. Sviðbalki began waving from the back of his *knarr* Aðalríkr and it he also seemed to have something to say. Cupping his hands, he shouted to Olaf who was something like two *drakkar* lengths from him. 'They speak some form of Pictish from what I can gather, but it is a strange type. It seems to be a mixed language, one that has changed because of where these people come from and where they now are. They have been cut off from the rest of their kingdom for quite a while. The two words I heard him say were, '*sonn*' and '*dafek*' or *dabhach* as I've heard it before in Gaelic. They mean, I think they mean, grain kiln and bucket, but I'm not all that sure. Whatever that priest said meant precious little to me, but he didn't seem as though he wanted to take us on with his cassock and crosier at any rate. May be he was offering us some grain, or may be he was saying they didn't have anything for us.'

The little boy who had skimmed the stone laughed irreverently before being cuffed heavily and somewhat unnecessarily on the ear by another grubby looking child who at most must have been only several summers or so older than he was. Olaf was done. The boats were not to land after all and the Hjaltland Islanders were to keep their lonely group of rocks for the moment. Before the ship finally reversed out from the beach backwards, but with a precision that is only achieved with a great deal of practice and application and of course with the help of thirty or so oars, Olaf leaned forward and retrieved something from a hook at the front of his vessel. With a great swing of his sword arm and loud belly grunt he let go of the object that span and whistled away from him at a great speed. It did not reach any great height, but move quickly it certainly did. In less than the blink of an eye it had sliced into the wet sand of the beach and embedded itself there as though it had become a living part of the islands; it lay there half submersed in shining sand resembling the crown of a king who had just fallen to be deposed in battle. Olaf grunted quietly once more and with a dismissive hand gesture bade these rocks which seemed to have been thrown by some giant's hand far into the raging seas farewell. 'Worms, that's what it is, they're eating my guts for sure,' he said to himself. 'Bloody bastard worms, they don't half itch, by *Óðinn* and all the gods; I'll scratch my arse bloody if they don't stop! Fetch me some mead now, I have need for a drink!' These remote islands and their people belonged to the Norse peoples now, but they did not yet know it, although in due time they soon would.

ℬ   ℬ   ℬ

Snorri, this island of Thule, our rough jewel in the coldest of seas was taken slowly but surely by the Norse some hundred years after the settlement of the Hjaltland Islands. Those times were much harder than they are today; we have it far easier and for that we should be grateful. Hrafn Valgardursson my illustrious forebear was the first in my family to settle here. I have him to thank!

It's hard for us to imagine Olaf's path in life being so difficult. It made him tough though and that in times of discovery and warfare is a good thing if you are a leader. Remember back to an earlier part of this tale, to the time Olaf was just a boy, playing the game of Hnefatafl with his mother's friend. Little did he know then, that such practice would help his thinking and the leadership decisions he would have to make in the future in the real world.

So, Snorri has learnt that this is the end of this evening's telling and it is a good point to stop, because three long years pass before the tale is taken up again. In that time all the people living within this saga are breathing, eating and drinking and generally getting older. Beards and hair lengthen, clothes are worn out, children come of age and Hel carries off those she wants. Sails are woven, beer and mead is brewed and thankfully drunk, cattle are fattened, slaughtered and eaten, the festival of Disablót comes and before we know it, it is midwinter and Jól is here again.

Such is the way of the world. I have asked, no implored Snorri to remember these things and then one day a long time off in the future, he may understand a little more and hopefully be just that tiny bit wiser. Olaf would have known about the three Norns from a young age. They are as we all know the maidens who live beneath the roots of the great world-tree; Urdi, Vedandi and Skuld being their names. Snorri, also knows that they are the guardians of the past, the present and the future, but he must also make room for other newer ideas. Saemundur, my grandfather used to say to me, 'Vedandi is only Urdi of Skuld' or to confuse me, 'Vedandi is only Skuld of Urdi. He is, was and always will be right!

Chapter 11

Sumar, áttanðí fíorþí mánudír

Lindisfarne
June 8th 793 AD

"And they came to the church of Lindisfarne, laid everything waste with grievous plundering, trampled the holy places with polluted feet, dug up the altars and seized all the treasures of the holy church. They killed some of the brothers; some they took away with them in fetters; many they drove out, naked and loaded with insults; and some they drowned in the sea."

Simeon of Durham

Brothers Egbert, Alcuin, Oda, Agilbert, Coelfrith, Ealdred, Wilfred, and Cathwulf, all of them with similarly tonsured hair, were shortly to make their way to a small and plain refectory for a rather poor and somewhat meagre midday meal of fish soup accompanied with hard, stale bread, but alas with no conversation.

After finishing eating, as was customary, the brothers were to return for their fifth of eight visits that day to St. Cuthbert's Church for their afternoon prayers. The men, all of whom were from St. Aidan's Monastery wore identical clothing; plain brown, itchy woollen cassocks. They had spent their last few holy hours in a variety of different pursuits.

Brother Cathwulf, one of the youngest monks was near to the great concentration of breeding birds, whose vast and noisy colonies spread along the entire length the northern shore of Holy Island. He was busying himself, trying to complete a diverse collection of seemingly unrelated objects, which his master, who happened to be the most important artist as well as head scribe of the isle had demanded the young monk find. He had taken his task most seriously and consequently toiled hard for the most part.

As a result of his dedication to duty, he had found and placed in the plainly woven basket of reed he had been provided with, several young woad plants, some folium and some generous handfuls of two or three differently coloured lichens. These Brother Cathwulf knew, were to be used in the production of a glorious and heavenly range of purple, crimson and blue inks. He also had collected orpiment for yellow and acquired a good pile of bleached sea shells and some smashed gulls' eggs for grinding up to make a white paint like ink. Brother Cathwulf had also done something a little out of character; he had acted on his own initiative, completely without instruction, collecting more than a good handful of sea spinach, which he was going to drop off at the kitchens. This tiny act of independence had made him feel contented and of some value. He had been far busier on this particular day than he had been for quite a considerable while.

A delicate trace of smoke, the merest smudge of grey in the cavernous and celestial blue sky, back over the monastery, gave away the secret of a meagre fire Brother Cathwulf had also started much earlier that day. He had carefully prepared and duly lit some dried grass and a few twigs. These finally burned strongly enough to catch alight some dampish squat blocks of peat. These he had carefully cut by hand and stacked a number of months before. This small slow burning fire was to provide his task master with the sticky sooty ash he sought for the manufacture of a particular brand of indelible black ink. A delicate and rather diminutive bowl of toasted lead lay forlornly amongst the now dying embers and hot ashes, having been heated by the same fire. These materials had been meticulously placed here to produce several subtly toned yellow and red inks. Sometime before making this fire and considerably earlier that day, back in his cell, at first light, Brother Cathwulf had begun his day with another exact task for the creation of yet more ink. He had suspended several thin copper strips he had been given over a bowl of rather pungent and acidic smelling vinegar. He had put all of this equipment carefully to one side in his tiny cell where he slept, to prevent it being knocked over allowing it to remain there, he hoped, undisturbed for several weeks. The copper strips were to provide a range of beautiful translucent shimmering green inks from the resultant magical verdures, which he hoped would begin to slowly appear, if his God so willed it onto the dull brown metal. All in all he had done well this day and he knew it. He was for once completely at one with his world and was also feeling quite pleased, almost smug with his achievements. His work would be appreciated in the scriptorium.

All his fellow brothers and indeed many of the nuns as well as all the other men and women folk of the community had at some time collected these things, because of course they comprised part of the essential ingredients the numerous resident artists needed for the illuminated scripts that were painstakingly being produced here on God's island. These scripts were delicate, detailed and utterly beautiful, but above all they were massively time consuming. Each one, created lovingly by the chosen artist was an '*opus dei*'; a work for God. Dawn till dusk, of each and every single day, year on year, winter or summer alike, the work went on regardless of anything without respite. For six or may be seven years or in some cases more; the vellum parchments would be attended to until they were finally finished. If during the lengthy production process, the artist happened to be gifted with visions, then so much the better, for it showed he had been touched and was moving just that little bit closer to God himself. 'You'll never be blessed with such sights, you're not wise enough.' The present bishop had few words for Cathwulf and those he had were never very encouraging. Cathwulf listened, understood and inwardly digested the words, whether they were mildly disparaging or vitriolic in contempt. Either way, he dismissed them from his head rather too quickly for his master's liking. Also, he rarely confided in his fellow brothers or his god for that matter, preferring to take solace from the natural beauty of his surroundings and it had been noticed. His memory was excellent, but remarkable at the same time, because it had the unerring ability to forget hurtful comments as well as the meaningless and trivial things that between them constituted the majority of the duties of which his life was composed.

Cathwulf like all his fellow brothers knew that the devotion and tradition to the production of these exquisite manuscripts had started some seventy years before, when Eadfrith, the then Bishop of Lindisfarne or Inis Metcaut, 'The Isle of Winds' as it had earlier been known, had begun his great and most holy of works. He had as the whole community knew full well, been inspired in turn by Cuthbert, an even earlier Lindisfarne Bishop who had been in charge of their close knit community from the years of our lord 634 to 687. Cuthbert had become a legendary figure in his own lifetime and was now remembered and revered as both a *loeknir* or plague healer and as a hermit.

Bishop Cuthbert of Lindisfarne as he had become, had been an inspiration to the lives of many, both during and well after his lifetime. He had chosen the eremitical way of life in order to find God and had gone to live on nearby Farne Isle, which as all the wide eyed Christians knew was full of evil spirits.

Here, surprisingly he had managed to prosper mentally, living in extremely inhospitable conditions, before finally being recalled to Holy Isle itself. There, he still managed to live the reclusive life he craved, but also succeeded in fulfilling the helping role the local monastic community desired and he deemed so important. He achieved this by having a small and insignificant hut built outside of the monastery and village, thus allowing him to live independently, but also enabling him to fulfil the cenobitic way of life he had so deliberately chosen. Cuthbert quite unknowingly had created a huge following for himself and after his death he was ultimately elevated into the realms of sainthood. He had almost single handed made Lindisfarne not only a place of pilgrimage, but the most holy place in all of his country. Christians claimed that many years after his death that his body having been dug up on at least three separate occasions was incredibly and miraculously found to be uncorrupted, showing that he was truly chosen by God.

Followers of Cuthbert had duly poured into Lindisfarne in huge numbers after his death and in awe of the great man had bought the locally made rosary beads to help them with their prayers and of course to commemorate their hero. These in time had become known as 'Cuddy beads' and their manufacture was now a small thriving industry. The Bishop of Lindisfarne surprisingly did nothing to play down rumours of miracles and some of the heathen cynics believed the whole venture to be nothing more than a money-making yarn, created to fleece the unthinking and believing Christians out of their hard earned coinage. Cuthbert's dried out and much disturbed mortal remains now lay in his church just below and to the side of the main altar.

It was perhaps not that surprising that from him the inspiration had thus come to Eadfrith who went on to create the fantastic Lindisfarne Gospels. These he had lovingly fashioned, working without respite every day for many,

many years. Eadfrith's astonishing work on completion was taken to and beautifully bound by Bishop Eathiwold. Afterwards, to preserve the weighty tome for posterity, it was then put into an incredibly intricate and strong metalwork binding, by the anchorite Billfrith. The current bishop thought in the way of any crafty and cunning master; he used the length of time spent of these documents to form a yardstick for sufferance and abeyance. He considered that any project that required any less than six years dedicated toil was as he used to say, 'simply laughable'.

80   80   80

Brothers Oda and Agilbert were in contrast helping to prepare the refectory for the arrival of their fellow monks. As was usual, for this basic meal they simply put out the required number of wooden bowls and spoons for each of their fellow brothers on a number of long functional tables in the plain and damp, white-washed rectangular hall. Small, high up windows allowed just enough light to invade the room and allow the men to see their food to eat it. Brother Wilfred often grumbled and joked to his rather more serious contemporaries that it would have been better to have eaten it with no light at all, thereby improving its appearance. This sarcastic comment never elicited a response of any description from his peers, but this did not stop the young man from pointedly repeating the phrase every so often to his fellow monks. He chose to do so for his own mirth and sanity and to a certain degree to see if anyone, just anyone might acknowledge that he kept repeating himself. But they never did.

Brother Wilfred liked to think and daydream and play with words, compose short poems and create riddles. He enjoyed drawing buildings and people with charcoal or painting wildlife, he was particularly keen on sketching the sea birds which fascinated him with their incredible diversity.

Sea parrots, shags, cormorants, gannets, petrels, guillemots, oystercatchers and many others were all beautifully represented on scraps of parchment that were surplus to the requirements of the working artists. In fact, Wilfred would do anything at all that he thought would help to keep his mind active. He was as a consequence a singularly resourceful person. The routine so rigidly adhered to by his fellow monks was not at all to the liking of this slightly unorthodox monk. It had landed him in trouble on several occasions with the Bishop, who thought him 'an idler' and 'a waste of good time', but there was little that appeared could be done to castigate him, other than increasing his workload on the farm, or giving him other necessary, heavy and tiring labouring jobs around the monastery. In fact, due to one quite recent indiscretion, he was at this very moment shovelling out straw and animal waste from the pig sty with a poorly constructed clumsy wooden spade. Brother Wilfred was being more than philosophical about this somewhat dirty task and in fact was humming to himself as if he found it to be one of life's more pleasant activities. He was tired, sweaty, filthy, extremely smelly, but for once he was reasonably content with his lot. He had spent a few seconds examining the way the blade was attached to the shaft of his shovel and decided that a wooden pin driven hard into a pre-drilled hole would prevent the whole thing from bowing every time he lifted a heavy load of waste and straw. He wasn't to know it, but his present circumstances were to turn out to be an important turning point in his life.

Brothers Coelfrith, Alcuin and Egbert had been busy in the fields weeding and generally tending to the crops being grown. There never seemed to be enough hours in the day to look after the different vegetables being grown. Obtaining fresh water for watering crops and for drinking had been quite a problem earlier in the year a number of times. Unexpected and unseasonably heavy rains had come and gone intermittently; now there was not enough rain for the crops again, to make them grow well on this barren part of the windy Northumbrian coast.

Talk on the mainland had been of dragons, demons and fire, storms and pestilence. The year had been one of the worst in living memory, poor germination of seed caused by too little rain at first, followed by then too much. Hailstorms had damaged soft fruit crops such as gooseberry and plum and it seemed that even the apple was not to be spared from the attentions of the elements. There had also been problems with the bees and this did not augur well for honey production and the resultant mead that was so craved by the monks and in truth almost all others. More important still, plague had returned earlier in the year and made huge numbers of men, women and children desperately ill, with great numbers perishing after dreadfully drawn out and lengthy periods of appalling sickness. Most of those falling ill developed terrible swellings in their armpit and groin areas. It was the most appalling of symptoms and one considered by those far enough away from it, to be god's way of dealing with the wicked. The superstitious and godly had as always in such times claimed it was God's wrath. The bishop himself had been heard frequently to mumble with greatly furrowed brow, 'It serves us right for being sinners, evil doers and folk who make pacts with the devil! What right have we to defile the land given to us by our gentle and tender Lord?' Perhaps, on this occasion the bishop and his god fearing tribe were right.

The diminutive bell in the tower started to ring unexpectedly, jarring the entire monastic community into life. Such an unexpected occurrence was in itself no indication that anything was amiss or indeed that action of any description was required by the men comprising this tiny remote Christian enclave. This, the only bell of any size which was capable of producing a sound that could be heard from more than two hundred paces meant a number of things to the monks and nuns. First, it was possible that a boat may have been in some distress and needed help, or secondly that travellers on the causeway should hurry up to avoid being inundated by the incoming tide or thirdly as on this occasion that the monastery was to receive a visit from unexpected guests. The bell also had one further function, that of a signal to indicate things were not as they should be. On this June afternoon, it happened that the bell had been rung for the third reason.

The monks who had been working inside various buildings made their way slowly and unhurriedly outside to see what was happening and if there was anything that they could do to help. Nothing seemed awry and after several minutes it was generally accepted that the bell had been rung for an unknown reason. Brother Ealdred grumbled to himself that this sort of thing would never have happened in the old days. He disliked any changes in his routines especially if it meant that he had to start thinking or act on his own initiative and be forced to do something out of the usual. He stood just outside the building that housed the scriptorium and library, with his right hand levelled above his eyes to shade them from the brightness of the sky. His brow was wrinkled, his eyes screwed up and his top lip pulled up at one end making him resemble some brute of a dog that may have been about to snarl at some invisible intruder.

Brother Ealdred was not the oldest monk in the community, but his old fashioned ways, slightly irritating repetitive habits, unfortunate body odour and at times a sarcasm that was more bitter and acidic than the smell he emitted, gave him the demeanour of someone many years his senior. Monks a full decade older than him, Brothers Agilbert and Oda looked to Brother Ealdred for guidance in how to appear serene and at the same time holy, whilst at the same time doing very little. Brother Ealdred had perfected the

art of becoming invisible or at least impossible to find when there were tasks
that needed to be completed. Instead, he would be in either the vegetable
garden just about to start some important weeding or thinning out or he
would possibly be reading or even or on the point of beginning cleaning in
the library, depending on the weather conditions and more importantly his
inclinations.

℘ ℘ ℘

The silhouette of the Farne Isles to the north, against a cooling blue sky
had become visible to all of the Norsemen in both the *drakkars* and *knarrs*.
The presence of even such a tiny landmass had been signalled to the lead
drakkar or dragon ship quite some time ago by the wheeling and diving sea
birds. Their white bodies appeared to be being blown over the blue canvas
of the heavens like the foam and spray that was being forced from the prows
of the fifteen or so ships. Just over half of these were *drakkars* and now they
made their way determinedly towards the coast of Lindisfarne Isle. High
water was perhaps but half an hour away and the waves seemed to wallow
without real power or venom. In contrast, the wind had changed direction
and at the same time increased in strength within the past few minutes, to
blow directly at the ships from behind. It pushed the small fleet at a steady,
but unremarkable rate towards their destination, which happened to be the
unsuspecting St. Cuthbert's Church on the Holy Isle itself. Ropes tightened
and creaked, straining to hang on to the now billowing sails, which were all
aligned so neatly, to point in the same direction. The sail of each vessel was
brimming, filled with a forceful wind that continued to gradually grow and
sweep over the back of the vessels and leap forward over the prows towards
the fast approaching island of Lindisfarne, the 'Holy Isle'. The outer Farne
Isles were sleeping off to the east and aroused not the slightest interest in

the crews other than as points of reference for navigational purposes. Fluffy white and grey clouds which had appeared quite some time ago were currently riding across sky northwards, as if wishing to outrun the boats and escape for reasons known to them alone.

To the west, of the boats were the inner Farne isles, unfriendly craggy rocks, which jutted out of a grey and passive sea in a variety of random and unexpected formations. Several of these, all liberally coated with white guano had cormorants or shags perched on their highest points. Several of the former, the slightly larger of the two species held their wings outstretched, perfectly still, as though to bring attention to themselves. The wind, which had previously rasped and tugged at the longships and *knarrs* quickly died away to leave the vessels momentarily to drift serenely on the swell in the sound between the two sets of islands. It was at this timely hiatus, that the order was issued for large leather bags to be pulled from below the removable decking. Inside these voluminous sacks were numerous different types of helmets, swords, saxes, daggers and axes. The men squabbled amongst themselves for a short while until all had claimed some suitable weaponry and a helmet that might fit their heads with the addition of a little padding if needed.

It was going to take rather more than a few minutes before the flotilla could slide onto the beaches, one boat after another. The helmsman called for the rowers to take their positions in both the *drakkars* and the sturdier trading boats. There was some grumbling amongst the men, but the thought of the prize soon to be theirs was enough to make those on the *drakkars* bend their backs and their long oars in a well practised and wholly synchronised unison. Those on the *knarrs* rowed whilst standing, a slightly more difficult process and one that didn't really exploit the strength of the men fully. As a result, the *knarrs* usually only used the rowers when the boats were very close to the shore line. One of the masters of a lead *drakkar*, a tight black skull cap hugging his greasy scalp, reassured his team of rowers that it would be much less than one *víka sjóvar* before they would be grounding. And he was right.

The keels of the boats made a sweeping, crunching noise as the first oak keel pushed hard into the coarse sand. All of the Norse folk, save two at most, from each boat, leapt out from the sides of the *drakkars* and *knarrs*, to splash their way noisily up and onto the beach. All of those moving up into the sand dunes were fully equipped, ready for anything that a fight or battle might require of them.

ဢ   ဢ   ဢ

The air moments before, had been gently tousled and teased by a light and friendly wind, but had quickly succumbed to a dreadful cacophony of sound and confusion. The rhythmic thumping of angry axes on a nearby solid oak door, the screaming and shouting of panic stricken voices, the crackling of burning buildings, the splintering of wood, the jarring noise of the cracked and yet defiant bell still ringing; all of these sounds merged together to create a maelstrom of noise; the desperate sound of destruction in all its guises.

Within just a few minutes the heavy wooden door was broken and now lay discarded, slightly to one side of the church's entrance, its heavy iron hinges remarkably twisted and at the same time hideously distorted out of shape. St. Cuthbert's Church was not only open to the wild of the elements, but also to that of the Norse.

Once inside the dusty stone edifice, Olaf who with his trusty axe had more than anyone helped to destroy the door, stood still momentarily. He gaped in wonderment at the contents of the silent and peaceful the church, the likes of which he and his kind had never seen before. Bright beams of light penetrated the small windows to illuminate the interior of the building, to pick out vividly contrasting silver and gold artefacts. These, in turn sent out a myriad of smaller beams, which reflected and danced happily off their shiny surfaces in all directions, to pick out flecks of dust in the still air.

Even to his heathen eyes, the church's interior proved to be a revelation. Initially, it was the sweet and vaguely sickly smell of incense that struck him. He briefly froze, to breathe in several lung fulls of air through his nostrils and wondered if this was the odour of the one god. His indecision and stillness was but fleeting, as his eyes now drank in the interior and its extraordinary furnishings. There was an overpowering richness and obviously significant value to seemingly every single item crammed within the 'architectural cross' that constituted St. Cuthbert's Church. All of these divine creations had been so lovingly and meticulously crafted to standards so high that their place in the holy church on The Holy Isle could not be questioned, even by a Norse man who came to take them away by force.

Shaking himself out of this unexpected state of mind, he took two or three paces forward and smiled before whistling to himself quietly. The fabulous display of riches quickly began to register deeply within him. Thoughts of indescribable wealth and what that would mean to his lifestyle when he returned home took over. Money and gold to buy strong male slaves to work his land and possibly rebuild or extend his home, to collect wood for the harsh winters, to provide him with his own fighting band, to grow food and harvest it, to tend his newly acquired animals. There would be female slaves to spin wool, weave, make his clothes, build, light and maintain fires, cook and then he chuckled to himself, to look after his every need. There would be better food, better weapons, possibly a linked mail hauberk for him, more gaming, in fact more of anything he desired. It was going to be a very good day, the first of many, he thought, saying to himself through clenched teeth,

'Þórr á hamar góðan.' (Thor has a good hammer)

The church was packed with every conceivable object of consummate artistry, craftsmanship and glorious artifice. In the timeless interior of this god's house were sumptuously ornate golden crucifixes with the most incredible detail. There were 'chip-carved' crosses with a mysterious glittering sheen; an effect created by the artist hammering thousand upon thousands of tiny pyramid shaped punctures into the surface of the precious metal. Golden and silver candle holders and candelabra sat everywhere, embellished with garnet, amber and amethyst. In addition, many crosiers and innumerable silver pyxes which had been decorated with stunning cloisonné work seemed to jostle one another, cheek by jowl. Here the craftsman or artist had built up tiny cells on the surface of the silver and somehow inserted miniscule garnets to create a magical sparkling and shimmering surface.

There were ciboria and various heavy and solid golden chests of many different sizes, containing stacks and stacks of intricate illuminated manuscripts bound up by tangles of red ribbons and similarly coloured wax seals. Some caskets were filled with necklaces or ear rings, pendants, buckles, amulets, brooches, bracelets, precious stones, semi-precious stones, small bars and nuggets of gold, gold and silver coins, small golden crosses and crucifixes and highly coloured decorative millefioriglass rosary beads. These had been finely made with different coloured glass rods, which when very hot had been fused together and twisted. The resultant amalgam had then been cut into small sections which were then rolled into small spheres, to produce transparent beads with delicate lined patterns threaded within them. Some of the chests were constructed out of solid plates of gold, others were delicately engraved and others still were the result of extraordinary filigree work. The craftsmanship of the men who had created these masterpieces was of the highest order possible. It must have taken the artisans weeks or months to perfect the delicate art of twisting such fine strands of gold wire into the intricate patterns they so craved. These tiny works of immense labour were then laced or fused together to produce the surfaces of these chests. They were essentially composed of spun gold, nothing less. Dozens of carved ivory, bone or ebony reliquaries lined the side walls of the church. There were many beautifully designed and woven tapestries of every conceivable style, colouring, design and size, hanging from the side walls and from the back wall of the church. There were also dozens upon dozens of other newly made as well as many ancient tapestries carefully rolled up, lying in neat triangular piles near to the rear of the church. It was as though they had been carefully stored for all of time, for the invaders to use or discard as they deemed fit.

Olaf's mind absorbed everything he saw. He took little heed however of the five monks who were kneeling in penitence by the altar at the front of the church. It was as though there was nothing occurring that day that could be of any possible concern to them. The large Norse man smiled to himself because he saw the majority of the wealth here in this Christian house, as now being his; he would do with it as he chose. The treasure trove that lay unguarded in this church must he reasoned have been put there for some reason. The church it seemed had over many years become a massive repository for these untold riches that had been bequeathed by the pious and wicked for the repose of their blackened and blighted souls. The simple Norse man from Odda had learned much about the Christian idea of salvation and forgiveness of sins on his many journeys; he also had his friend Ingvar to thank for a lot of this worldly knowledge. In addition, he even had some first hand experience of these 'men of god' before, having come across a group of extremely ardent followers of Christ; believers who had even prayed though he had not wished it for his wicked, eternally damned and blighted heathen soul. Their way of thinking was odd, in fact downright bizarre to his heathen mind which now raced unerringly to its inevitable and blasphemous conclusion. 'Why were there so many vile and ungodly Christians pacing to and fro in *Midgard*, the world of men, who seemingly filled it with their lies and their sordid filth of every description? How could they think it at all possible that they could pay or rather bribe their way into the hallowed kingdom of their God? Was their little dirty payment of gold or silver going to be enough for their eternal happiness? His gods were easier to understand. In contrast to the man on the cross, his gods, all of them by *Óðinn's* runes, knew so much better and so did he. Money and gold and refined works were the playthings of men. It was not meant to be and could never have been meant that gods themselves were to stockpile wealth in their dusty, damp, cold houses that they called churches. Why in the name of the one god's son Christ was it possible for any worshipped one to crave gold?'

Drawing his plated sword whilst at the same time issuing a hideous blood curdling scream, he began to run towards the altar, where the five brothers knelt and prayed. In just seconds he had hacked hard down on the tonsured skull of the largest monk in the middle, a monk whom he had not known or even met eyes with in life. Brother Oda slumped heavily to the stone floor, his hugely damaged grey brain and copious amounts of his holy blood, like a rich communion wine were spilling from his neatly split skull. Brothers Ealdred and Egbert soon joined the hapless Oda on their heavenly voyage. Ealdred received the same sword; the sword which belonged to Olaf in the back, whilst Egbert was dispatched from behind with a jabbing stab of a sax, executed by a blonde lad of about fourteen summers, who had crept into the church unseen, shortly after Olaf's entrance. He shouted in great joy, almost ecstasy as he witnessed the hapless monk fall clumsily to the unforgiving hard cold floor. Whilst looking at Olaf for approval, he gasped earnestly, 'I can fight like you, a true Norseman!'

'It takes more than cutting down a Christian worm from behind to be that. You will have to learn to use that sax properly for a start. It is a slashing weapon and you should not thrust or stab with it. If you stab like that little boy, you'll break the blade off or may be even get it stuck in some awkward bastard's ribs. While the ungrateful sod's choking his last, he'll sting you with his *bryntröll* or *brynklunr*', came Olaf's ungrateful reply.

'I can fight!' the boy hesitated, 'I can learn, I'm good at learning,' the eager youth continued, apparently ignoring the rebuttals of his erstwhile master.

'Fóthraðr, that's your name isn't it? Take these two monks we've spared outside and give them to Bodvarr, he'll know what to do with men of Christ, he has a good way, you'll learn something from him,' replied Olaf ignoring the youngster's attempts at conversation.

The monks passively obeyed the signals of the now sullen boy with a dignified resignation that irked the youngster, for he wished to see some pain or at least a degree of anguish. Once outside, Bodvarr, a small bald man who seemed to be know the monks would be duly arriving, raised his axe above his head and pointed with his other hand at the rope about one of the monk's cassocks. Brother Coelfrith appeared to understand what Bodvarr had meant and calmly whispered something to his fellow monk, Brother Alcuin. At the same time he began taking off his sandals which he put neatly together and to one side followed by his cassock, which he folded very carefully. Once both monks had removed their clothes and were fully naked, Bodvarr shouted harshly to the young Fóthraðr.

'These two dirty men of god are going for a bathe; like the others, they are to be baptised by the waves of their god. Let them meet him and see if he has a miracle or two for them. Me, I really don't want to see their fat white bodies again.'

So it was that the young Fóthraðr marched the two startled and naked monks to the water's edge. Here, he indicated with the spear he now grasped in his right hand that they were to enter the cold waters of the sea; the sea that had delivered the men of the North to this remote place. The monks obliged without protests of any description and in a short space of time their pale bodies were floating face down in the surf, being pushed one moment out to sea and the next back towards the shoreline, along with some fifty or so others who had received the same fate. The drowned bodies of both the men and women became fish and gull food over the next few weeks and after that only a few bones bore testimony to their existence at all.

Olaf was still grumbling, but he had not wasted any time at all. He had sent for some of his warriors and they were now busy carrying off any items perceived of worth they could from the inside of the church to the waiting *knarrs*. The tapestries were for the most part ignored apart from being used to wrap up some of the larger objects or alternatively were used to cradle lots of the smaller things, whilst they were being carried out.

The men in charge of the boats seemed pleasantly surprised and chattered noisily to one another when seeing the quantity of riches being loaded in the hungry expectant keels. It was hard work getting the heavier chests and reliquaries into the *knarrs*, because of the high sides of the boats. Each object had to be first carried to the boat, which by now, was lying clear of the water and then be simply lifted by three or four men upwards, before being lowered onto the middle deck. It was a task that required nothing but brute strength. There was of course plenty of this at hand and the work progressed speedily.

Once the goods had arrived on the boat, the men who had stayed with their vessels moved the objects about with well practised ease. Some objects were taken to the front and some to the back, to balance and distribute their weight evenly. This was a satisfactory arrangement, because the more valuable pieces could be put under a semi-waterproof cover to protect them from the worst of the elements in a sea crossing. They were safe from rain, but above the bilges in the boats, meaning they would not be damaged by the water that ever seeped into these boats of burden. Indeed, the amount of water that entered the boats was such that they were permanently being bailed by the children in the boats, who took it in turns to use a wooden bailing tool to keep the vessels floating. Fully laden, this task took on even greater importance, as the boats lay deeper in the water and therefore were more liable to waves coming over the sides and swamping them. At present, the boats were high and dry and the masters of the vessels were taking advantage of this by removing their sump plugs to allow any water within the boats an opportunity to drain away.

Back in the church, Olaf was indignant, having damaged the head of his spear. He had rammed it hard between two floor stones and used it as a lever in an effort to find out if there was anything valuable buried beneath the altar. He had been told by his friend Bodvarr, who seemed to know much relating to the men of the cross worth knowing, that the Christians were prone to hide things of value. Bodvarr had mysteriously said to him earlier in the day to look for old bones that were stored carefully in precious boxes. He had said no more and when Olaf demanded what possible value dead men's bones could be, his friend had replied, 'More than the draugrinn you're insisting on creating!' Olaf had for some reason rather liked this answer and thus had probed no more.

The altar itself had already been brutally smashed to pieces and large lumps of white alabaster looking marble lay strewn about the end of the church. Olaf hadn't realised it, but in the storm of violence he had unleashed upon the church, he had disturbed the venerated and most holy bones of the great St. Cuthbert. A few of his finger or were they his toe bones now lay hidden amongst the white rock debris that littered the dark stone floor. Perhaps St. Cuthbert even now was playing a trick on Olaf, who didn't realise these odd fragments of his mortal remains could still be held hostage.

⧼ ⧼ ⧼

Outside the church there was a gathering of some fifteen monks and about the same number of nuns who had been spared from the spear or blade. Brother Cathwulf and Wilfred were amongst them. Cathwulf spoke to the forlorn looking group, principally addressing Wilfred whom he knew best. 'It seems they have killed all of the older men and women, but allowed us, the younger ones to live.'

'The question I feel I must, but hate to ask is why?' Wilfred replied.

'We'll find out soon enough my brother, make no mistake. Our community is, it seems lost.'

At that moment, the large figure of a young Norse man appeared from the church. In one of his hands he carried a spear, but used it more as a staff on which to lean. He surveyed the motley band with a quizzical eye, but without the slightest hint of emotion. He shouted something to a blonde boy who had emerged from the church just moments after he had. His words seemed harsh to Cathwulf for the boy pulled the kind of face very young children do when castigated for some misdemeanour. He left at a run shouting as he did so a name, or so Brother Cathwulf believed, the name Ingvar.

Not a word was exchanged between any of the monks whose total subservience suggested that they expected the worst. The nuns in complete contrast huddled together and held onto one another, most of them crying despairingly as they realised that their torment had not yet started. All the while Olaf looked at the men and women of God dispassionately, as though they were nothing more than cattle. Only a few moments had passed before another young Norse man arrived, but to Cathwulf and his peers it seemed as though time stood still. Cathwulf assumed that this man was Ingvar and his theory was proven correct instantly, when the man carrying the spear spoke once more in a tongue he could not begin to understand.

'Ingvar, take these people to the boats. They are the lucky ones for they will see a better way of life.'

'It won't seem lucky to them now, my friend,' came Ingvar's reply.

'Well they are lucky, because we could've butchered them all. Remember Ingvar, these few will not be having a better way of life, but they will be seeing it, that's all. And they will see it from very close quarters, because they are no longer men and women of their God, but are slaves. I grant you that we have put them in a very good position to think and one where they may think prayer is a must, but they are in a better position for work and more work. They will be working all right and their work will make the life of us heathens as they like to call us, a better one. They will be crying out to their man, the one they say was nailed to a tree to save them. Well they'll find out soon enough if he has that power. All the time they pray, they will be working for us, both night and day, for men descended from the greatest god of all *Óðinn*. Such a power has he, that after hanging from the great tree for a full magical nine days and nights, he came back to life having defied death. We are of him. We alone have the great knowledge of the runes thanks to his suffering.' When Olaf had finished his impromptu speech, Ingvar clapped his hands together in mock appreciation.

'Be careful wise man. Your words are sharp. Remember you cannot have sharp weapons and sharp words. The two don't mix. If you spend too much of your time thinking, you will have no time left to whet that stone of yours.'

Olaf understood and appreciated Ingvar's comment although he feigned as though he did not. He resisted any temptation of a verbal riposte, because he knew that Ingvar was a much better wordsmith than him. He knew also that his blade was as keen as it could be and that Ingvar's words were little more than a jibe directed back at himself really. Ingvar was far deeper and much more scheming than he often let on. Olaf had on many occasions listened quietly in admiration as his friend had played with words to produce not just clever ideas, but words worthy of a recognised skald.

'Hvat veldr yðvarri ógleði.' ('What causes your sadness?') Ingvar said quietly looking at one of the young nuns, whose tears now ran quietly down her face. He thought the girl most attractive and considered that he may keep her for himself, as a slave.

She failed to reply, but instead cast her eyes downwards indicating to him her enormous suffering and shame. Ingvar now spoke once more, but his tone was harsher. He addressed a number of Norse men who were not involved in taking treasures to the boats and who had finished their task of drowning the other older monks, nuns and other Anglo Saxons who happened to be living on the Holy Isle.

'Move these folk to the boats. Mix up the men with the women, but put that one on Gjálfrmarr, I'll take care of her.'

Olaf nodded approvingly, before striding away with a spring in his step. 'Put Wilfred and Cathwulf in with her; put them in that *drakkar* as well.'

'Why them?' Ingvar enquired of his friend.

'They may not have the looks of your Christian girl, but they have something else, something that may be of greater value still.' Olaf appeared to be scheming already. The fires of the buildings were still wrapping themselves greedily around their end walls and sending showers of sparks and thick black smoke across the now ruined settlement.

'That one smells of pig shit, what d'ya see in him by *Loki's* teeth?'

'You'll see in good time; a man who smells of shit, is a man who is not afraid to work!' came the large Norse man's reply.

$$\text{\textsreversedornament} \quad \text{\textsreversedornament} \quad \text{\textsreversedornament}$$

Wilfred had been truly saddened by the demise of so many of his fellow monks and also that of his community, but even so, he was not feeling sorry for himself. In truth, he considered what had happened to him and to his fellow survivors of the raid to be a kind of blessed release. He quickly convinced himself that the terrible end of his community and all of the deaths of his fellow brothers and sisters had from his perspective been wholly unavoidable. It was a situation not of his own making and therefore he should make the most of it, he argued with himself that he should in a perverse way welcome it, for it gave to him a new beginning of sorts. The rigours of prayer, the rigidly timetabled lifestyle that he was so used to, all had been swept away so quickly and so decisively that he felt guiltily and at the same time blasphemously, as though he had been reborn. Extraordinarily, he was feeling quite relieved at the thought of doing something new with his life at long last. He dared not confide the outrageous and blasphemous contents of his mind with Cathwulf or indeed with the weeping nun. She sat at a strange angle, almost slumped, opposite him towards the rear of the strange Norse ship. Cathwulf was completely unlike his peer Wilfred, who now sat close by. He was more concerned or if it be known rather interested with the way of life of his captors. He cast his eyes over the ship, within which he was sitting and marvelled at the diverse craft works that had been so skilfully carried out in its manufacture. He ran his hand along the top strake and whistled quietly to himself in appreciation. The way the mast was fixed in such a practical manner in the boat, the exquisite and perfect carving of the dragon head, the clever arrangement of the benches, the exactly identical oar holes with their plugs, the incredible variation in the kinds of ropes, everything that he saw, his mind drank in and made him shake his head in disbelief and at the same time smile in a great appreciation. The young nun in contrast sat and cried, not taking in anything of her surroundings. She sobbed endlessly, before finally looking to the two monks, for solace of some description, but instead was amazed and immediately disgusted to see that both had apparently become for some reason quite content with their new lot. The men for they were men now, had put down their hoods and with it had seemed to have thrown away the mental shackles that came with their ordination into the brotherhood of God. They were still monks for sure, but monks who soon would be living and breathing the life of pagan heathens, after all these were the ways of their new masters.

The boats had put to sea not long after the wide eyed captives had clambered aboard. Sister Cecily had stopped crying, but the ruddy circles about her eyes had become if anything more noticeable as her complexion had changed from a healthy looking pink to a decidedly bilious greenish hue. She no longer cared about her fellow sisters and brothers who bobbed up and down in the water off the beach, but simply wretched the last of the contents of her stomach over the side of the *drakkar*. She wished for death more than anything she had ever craved and hoped desperately for solace in the arms of her one lord and maker. Strength and any resolve that existed in her small frame, at that moment seemingly fled. Her slight body slipped slowly down the side of the ship, to rest finally in a dishevelled heap on the deck's planking. Her head remained at what appeared to be an uncomfortable angle, somewhat incongruously propped up by one of the crew's rune covered sea chests.

'Help me my God. Help me by Christ's blood!' The sound her quiet voice made was as lost in this lonely seascape as the foundations of her Christian life. Ingvar watched her from afar for some time, whilst pretending not to take the slightest of interest in her. When it seemed that the dark brown haired and olive skinned nymph could void her stomach no longer, he approached her and offered her a drink of fresh water from a skin. His first clumsy words meant nothing to the helpless nun, who simply groaned and shivered as though with a fever. *'Heil Nótt ok nipt! Heil! Vit teljum okkr Norðmenn. Ek heiti Ingvar. Hann heitir Olaf.'* ('Hello Night and her sister! Hello! We are men of the Norse Kingdom. I am named Ingvar. He is called Olaf.')

The monks in contrast took a great of interest in this generous hospitality, for they had become desperately thirsty by now. Both were dry-throated from the fact they had not partaken of any liquid for many hours and also for the reason that they were both incredibly nervous of their captors. The girl however refused the skin's quenching water, preferring instead to lie motionless with her eyes transfixed on the knots and whirls in the grain on the boards above the keel. In contrast, the men readily beckoned to Ingvar, pointing at their mouths and shaking their heads to show what they needed most. Neither of the captives suffered from the motion of the sea and Ingvar was pleased at this, as he knew that he would soon be putting them to work on an oar. He poured out about three mouthfuls of water into a dented and dull metal bowl which he had just pulled from a deep pocket and then in turn the men drank. Ingvar addressed them when both had finished drinking, firstly pointing to himself and saying, 'Ingvar'. The men understood and without hesitation offered their names and that of the nun willingly. So it was that the Norseman learnt they were called Cathwulf, Wilfred and the girl Cecily, although for his own reasons he only really wished to find out that the name belonging to the girl.

The coast had faded to the merest hazy violet line on the horizon when Cecily at last came to, having recovered just enough to take a small dry mouthed drink and nibble unenthusiastically on some stale desiccated bread, which Ingvar had provided. She took care not to look around or show an interest in anything happening on the boat, preferring to keep her hood up and her eyes firmly averted downwards. Cathwulf took more than a passing interest in her and offered her a little advice; suggesting she stick to him over the coming days. Cecily failed to respond to his, as he thought, more than generous offer. At this point Wilfred also took a sudden interest in the girl but in contrast suggested she showed friendship towards the Norseman who seemed to be keen on her. This second and wholly unexpected idea appeared to be as unappealing to Cecily as the first. She began to cry once more, prompting a pensive looking Wilfred to consider what he had learnt in the monastery, on the subject of temptation. The girl was he thought, in spite of his religious upbringing and of course his current attire, just a trifle to be fought over, he supposed. Crossing himself, he considered that if this was so, then he would like to consider himself as one of the combatants. As he mused over this most unlikely proposition, his mood became suddenly morose, for the realisation rapidly dawned upon him that he would never be in a position to fight for any woman; he was nothing more than a lowly slave on a Norse ship travelling relentlessly to God knows where.

Ingvar as though sensing the man's deeper and possibly darker thoughts moved him and his fellow Anglo Saxon to oars nearer to the stern of the boat as if to deliberately scupper any hopes either man may have had in wooing the girl or even of gaining her confidence. Unlike them, he sat with her for a while and drank in her company in the way a man with a raging and unquenchable thirst dispatches horn after horn of fine ale. After a little while she noticed his quietness, but being wholly naïve in such matters remained for the moment at least sweetly oblivious of his desire for her. 'She'll know soon enough,' he thought before moving away from her and discussing the optimum course of the flotilla with Olaf.

৯১ ৯১ ৯১

By the time the boats reached Kaupang, still nearly fully laden with the treasures acquired at Lindisfarne, a change had come over the crews of the boats. Olaf looked across from where he was sitting near the rear of the *drakkar* and said to Ingvar and the girl who only some twenty or so days before had been a nun on a small and comparatively insignificant Anglo Saxon island, *'Tuttugandi ok áttandi, FiorÞi mánuðr.'* (Twenty eighth of June) Ingvar looked up at his friend and without speaking nodded. His demeanour like the other men had changed quite considerably during this trip and it was a change that Olaf was not sure he liked.

The crew and the new slaves had worked hard during the voyage back to the great trading centre. Other ports had of course been visited, but not so much as to trade, but more to sell off some of the stranger goods cradled in the boats' holds in exchange for gold or silver or any other useful commodity that may have been on offer. These stop offs were enjoyed for the most part by the free men on board the boats, but they also helped to shorten the individual spells of time spent at sea and also provided those on the boats with an opportunity to obtain fresh water and food. It was not such a good time for the slaves however, as they were given all the difficult and time consuming tasks, which the free men considered well below their station. For those who suffered with sickness of the sea, it was a not so much a relief as a blessing, to stand on firm ground without the horizon swaying this way and that. Brief respite though it was, it made all the difference to the souls whose stomachs it seemed were not designed for a mariner's way of life. These men and women enjoyed the simple pleasure of feeling well again on firm and dry land before the next instalment of debilitating illness had them in its grip.

Only the girl who had captured Ingvar's eye was spared from the onerous duties of slavedom; her role instead, was to accompany Ingvar into the various communities they visited and simply to socialise with him. Olaf sneered disdainfully at his friend who was finishing a piece of rough rye bread and an over cooked lýðrr, as he felt he had lost his drinking companion for the moment. *'Þú ert kveldúlf!'* Olaf sneered once more, knowing how to needle Ingvar. ('You are an evening wolf!')

'Well, that may be true,' came the reply, 'but at least I am beginning to have a better understanding of the many and varied Christian ways. They are not all bad, the ways of their Lord, I can tell you. The Christians also learn much better than you would expect and they know full well what's good for them.' He replied with a knowing wink followed by a smile, which he had considerable difficulty concealing.

'And you know what's good for you do you? I doubt it my friend, I think you'll find that what tends to be good for any of us has if it be known an unpleasant taste. Be warned, keep your eyes open and let your head rule your body. Don't let your heart or your prick do your choosing!' Olaf was suddenly laughing with his fellow Norse plunderer. Times were not hard and even the weather appeared to be smiling on the whole of the Norse world.

Ingvar conceded under his breath. 'I don't know much about anything, but I know something when it's good!' As an after thought he said to Olaf,

'Ek em sadr.' (I am full / satisfied)

The girl's appreciation of the world was in stark contrast to that of her new companions. At first, she tried resolutely to hang on to the last vestiges of her religion, but knew in her own heart that she was damned to burn in hell for the rest of time. What appalled her more than the heathen religion and its meaningless gods was her own reaction to the young Norseman who had taken her for his own. Initially, she had cried for long periods. At first, she had done so, for herself, because she knew that in the eyes of Christ she had been defiled. To add insult to this heart felt wound, her hurt had been inflicted by a man; a heathen who despised her God and all he stood for. Later, she had sobbed heartily, because this godless man, who knew nothing of the ways of her Lord, had become someone whom she had actually grown to like. Tormented and sickened by her feelings, she had suddenly capitulated, surrendering her previous way of life in everything but her name. The prayers, the robes, the crucifix, the fear, the hardship and most of all the guilt were swept away as though by a raging flood, to be replaced by a life that pivoted on nothing but a steely will to survive in an inhospitable world. Cecily was the slave of Ingvar and for that she had grown grateful. The brothers who also had been taken from the island had witnessed her rapid and disastrous fall from grace and when they had time they prayed with clasping hands on bended and bruised knee. They called to their god for the repose of the blighted and wholly diseased soul that continued to inhabit her mortal being. She was as good as dead in their eyes and of course their lord's; she lived a life of hell on earth. Her death, Cathwulf, the younger of the brothers sneered jealously, 'would be a blessed release for her from the heathen nightmare of degradation she had suffered; although he noticed she appeared to take this suffering somewhat lightly.' Wilfred was more forgiving than his fellow brother; he wished he could take her away to a lonely isle. Here, he could farm land with her and if at all possible rescue something of her being. He would do this on behalf of their god of course, not for his own gain. He fantasised that he would struggle to repair the great wrong doing of the Norse and save her. Somehow, he considered he might find a way to do some good, even if that good helped no one here. May be, just may be he could help a community like the one he had been so violently ripped away from.

Ingvar spat and said, as if attempting to impress the girl that the men were just boys and that they would have to work their passage to make their way in life. The former nun, who was known just by her name Cecily now, unwittingly shuffled herself closer to the young Norse man. *'Hví foerir þú þik til mín?'* (Why do you move closer to me?) Cecily looked at Ingvar and although not understanding his words realised in that exact moment she had lost her battle with him. She now looked to him for safety, comfort and redress in a hostile and unforgiving savage world. She had in that instant lost her Christian way, to become one of the many despised and loathed heathens. Cecily was now one of the people whom she had heard so much about and whom her fellow sisters had shaken their heads in sorrow at. They wailed their prayers in disbelief at how wicked their actions were and asked for forgiveness for their fly blown souls.

℘ ℘ ℘

So it seems that the Christians despised our ways and we despised theirs. I have heard told that we are universally hated for our ways and for our despoiling of the churches of the one god. Remember though, that the spread of the Christian word is not based upon peace and peace alone. The Norse way of life is much older than that of those who follow the cross. Incompatible, that is what they are; it is hard to imagine them existing side by side. They contradict one another completely; the Norse way represents small and well defined communities and jarldoms, whilst Christianity embodies a sprawling and large, so large as to be almost beyond imagination, state. It is headed by their god's single representative on earth. Add to this the French Christian people's desire to expand their frontiers and you have the most dangerous of mixtures.

The great French king, Karle the Greate took his ideas on Christianity to the world without a second thought. Be warned I say; a convert to anything is always going to be the most dangerous of beasts; that is, for what it's worth what I think. The fervour, the zeal, the expectation of revelation, it all builds in such a way as to push previously sane and reliable individuals to most unpleasant and unwelcome actions. Oh yes, the French king, or at least his displeasure with our heathen Saxon brothers was well demonstrated by his actions. In just one day alone, he forcibly had some four and a half thousand non-Christian Saxons baptised, in order their blighted and wretched souls could find salvation. Then in a charitable Christian act he had all their heads cut off! Such brutality is hard to understand. It is little wonder that our forbears thought to fight back against the barbaric Christians and the land seeking French. The kingdom of the Danes was the one most at risk, as it was at not just at a border between the two lands, but between two wholly divergent ways of thinking. Learn well Snorri, learn from all such intolerance!

Vemundur, my ancestor, must have taken a part at least in the telling of this tale and no doubt he will have contributed many ideas and feelings of his own as well. Snorri doesn't appear to take any notice of my asides and clues regarding my ancestors, but he will or should I say might be a little surprised when he learns that Vemundur was actually on the boats I have described for him. Well, come now! All the details and the plans, they simply couldn't have come from anywhere could they, I ask you?

Chapter 12

Sumar, fiorþi mánuðr

Orkney

June A.D. 794

Wilfred and Cathwulf had been enjoying sitting in the sunshine and the sea breeze and for a change doing very little. Their rowing duties had for reasons neither of them could possibly have guessed been curtailed and their food and water rations had been increased. Both men were no longer that different in appearance from their Norse masters, apart from the fact both were in possession of a slightly darker complexion. They no longer had their hair cut in the customary manner expected of their monastic background and both now had unkempt long hair and bushy beards. In fact not one singular vestige of their religious background had at least from looking at them, survived. Wilfred had at least tried to cling to the beliefs that he had been immersed in year on year and said his prayers and prayed for forgiveness in any spare moment he was able to create. Cathwulf had terrible problems attempting to reconcile his soul, his very being with this new and wholly unexpected way of life. Even so, he had to grudgingly abandon anything to do with the way of his blessed Christ. At least, he had done so for the moment.

The boats, all seven of them were moving across a wide and inviting open sea, a sea that ebbed to and fro in a playful manner. Olaf stood at the back of his beloved *drakkar* and was for some unexplained reason looking rather pensive. He stood there, his legs swaying to counteract the rocking of the longboat in such a way as to leave his upper body apparently motionless.

The world around him moved, but his stance was firm as though challenging the very fabric of *Midgard*. His expression had changed though, slowly but surely to one indicating a degree of worry. He felt unhappy, because although he was fulfilling his destiny, travelling to a foreign land to plunder valuable and precious things, he felt quite alone. His great friend Ingvar had, he believed, settled down with a wife, his first; a simple Norse girl, but for the life of him, Olaf couldn't even remember her name. He considered to himself, it was either Droplaug or Jangerð, he mused. He remembered seeing her pretty face though, just once, it was small and round with petite rosy lips and had a small perfectly shaped nose. The girl also had large and rather questioning innocent looking blue eyes. She had looked less than happy at the betrothal ceremony and for good reason. The nun, as Olaf had always called her, had made absolutely sure of that. Sister Cecily as she had once been called had made this poor young girl, who must have been only several summers younger than her fully aware of her now well established role. The girl who had brought a reasonable haul of silver and gold, with her as part of pact of wedlock could surprisingly not match the slave from Inis Metcaut in all of the other ways deemed necessary by such a union.

Since their homecoming the previous year, things had not gone the way Olaf had expected at all. Ingvar's sudden betrothal to this girl from a half decent family in Hordaland had been something of a surprise to most who knew him. His woman had quickly become with child, but this strangely had seemed to cheer the moody slave girl, who so recently had been a mere chattel of the young man. Not much before that, he remembered she had been a lowly nun in the convent of the Lindifarena Eg. Now, the slave girl took her chance and once more caught the eye of Ingvar, who just several summers before had been such a revelation to Olaf. The slightly older man shook his head, scratched a well-hidden louse or two in his beard, farted loudly and thought to himself how Ingvar his friend had changed. 'By *Óðinn's* sacred tree the poor man had lost his way,' he said to himself rather forlornly. All he's interested in these days is that pretty little woman who has all but taken over his jarldom. What a thing to happen! Olaf shook his head once more and with that resolved not to waste his time thinking about the nun who was sleeping with his friend and causing considerable upset and grief to his diminutive and now heavily pregnant wife.

On his *drakkar*, in contrast there was a good crew of hard working honest Norsemen who would make their intentions more than well known to the monastery of his choice. To be fair, all of the boats carried experienced and hardened sailors who could pull an oar for several víka sjóvar if necessary. There were four *drakkar* and three *knarr* in the flotilla that made its way slowly but defiantly towards the coastline of the Picts and Anglo Saxon kingdoms in the land called by many Bretland. Olaf, for he was now in complete charge of this grand operation had decided to call in on his great friend's father abode in the new islands he had acquired for himself and of course for his people the year before.

Olaf took Cathwulf to the back of the *drakkar* and pointed to a few scribbles for that was all they really were on a piece of well-worn vellum parchment which he had extracted from a small leather *poki* or bag. Cathwulf understood what the Norse leader wanted and because of his comparatively good education and background appreciated and understood the details on the map showing the coast of eastern Bretland. There, clearly marked on the curling brownish leaf was a large dot, more of a blot really of a brownish red ink representing none other than his very own despoiled isle; the once holy and undefiled Lindisfarne. At various other positions on the map were a series of dark brown blobs, all marked with small crosses. These

Cathwulf recognised instantly were the locations of a good number of other monasteries, priories, convents and abbeys. The map was really quite detailed and Cathwulf's inquisitive mind drew his eyes up to the top of parchment, to an area of sea and what appeared to be a distinct group of isles, which seemed to have been cast out from the Pictish mainland by some unseen giant's hand. Being quick of mind, he immediately realised this group of islands had to be those which the boats now neared. The map he considered was really quite exquisite, with a variety of fabulous and fierce looking sea beasts decorating its outer edges. There were also small areas of sea, where a number of little waves had been neatly drawn, presumably to show the whereabouts of various dangerous currents, tides, maelstroms or just where heavy seas were most likely. Cathwulf's mind froze for an instant, because he suddenly realised that the map was more than just familiar, he was sure had seen this very parchment before.

Thinking hard, he glanced once more at the worn vellum with much renewed interest and suddenly he had it! The last time his eyes had danced across the outline of this coast, was four or maybe five long summers before, when he had by chance come across one of the older brothers in the library, who at that time had happened to be studying it. Cathwulf's mind cleared now, because he for some reason remembered he had been sent to the library fetch Brother Agilbert for some duty or task which he couldn't presently bring to mind. Agilbert had stretched the vellum out flat on a low wooden desk. He had prevented the ancient skin from curling up along its length by weighting down the reluctant corners with a variety of curious objects that he had close at hand. One corner was trapped by a pot of black ink, another by a smooth stone which the monk for some inexplicable reason carried with him, the third by a small highly decorated ivory box and the last with a plain wooden crucifix still attached to a thin and shiny cord of leather, which Agilbert had clearly just slipped off his neck for this very purpose. Cathwulf felt the pain of his monastery's demise once more, as he realised that the parchment was the product of one of his fellow brothers' labour. Unwittingly, their community's thirst for knowledge and the irresistible desire to record each and every aspect of it was now to be the undoing of the very people the struggle for these facts had been made for.

Olaf was oblivious to Cathwulf's interest in the strange beasts or indeed in the representation of the coastline and simply pressed the former monk into giving him the information he so craved. Speaking slowly at first and most reasonably in his deep voice, Olaf asked Cathwulf about the positions of various monasteries and then with eyes shining, whether they had great treasures to speak of.

A rapid change in Olaf's demeanour came about. It was so obvious to Cathwulf, because it had appeared in the way a dark stormy evening arrives after a long bright day. To the bearded monk, the change was manifested by nothing more than the sudden appreciation of the Norseman's shallow desire for more gold and silver, which he had been able to read on his Norse owner's face as though it were there transcribed in legible runes. The concept of grasping indescribable wealth had begun to form and weave the beginnings of an idea within Olaf's mind. He asked the slave whether the isle he had originated from would have new treasures in place by now or, pointing at the map, whether he should try this one or that one. Olaf reminded the slave of a spoilt child who couldn't make his mind up when offered two toys of a similar type. So it was that Cathwulf suggested to in the hope of manipulating the Norse leader that a small monastery, one of a twin would be more than an excellent prospect. At first, he suggested both of their names, Wearmouth and Gyrwe, but then he fell quiet and indicated that Gyrwe was not a good idea really. He added that they were in fact much less than half a day's walk from each other. The smaller of the two, he confided was also on a river, but one that lay a little further to the north. 'It may not hold much of any consequence really and it is quite a way in land. Your big boats may have a few problems getting in and out.' Olaf listened to him with interest, but now deliberately played down any enthusiasm that he may have had due to this mixed news.

After this short and somewhat tense conversation, the great ships from Hordaland and Birka came to rest on the sandy beach of little Byrgisey, protected from the rough seas by the bar of sand that at low water connected the small isle with the largest isle of the group. Olaf first made his way to see his great friend's father, whom he knew lived on the small island of Byrgisey. Time it seemed had stood still here, but its invisible ravages had taken their terrible toll on the old master. ÓþyrmiR had aged quite visibly; his face was heavily lined now, his hair thinner and nearly all white and his fingers appeared almost clawed by some ailment that attacked his joints. His mind was alert though and he was clearly saddened by the fact that his son had chosen not to raid the territories to the south and in so doing manage to visit him en route. 'But then I should know better,' he said to himself, 'never expect or try to guess what will happen in life. In the merest blink of an eye a boy becomes a man,' he mused 'and then he thinks for himself and does things his own way and that is that. There is no going back and that by the gods in Asgard is how it should be. The dead after all do not return to blight our lives, so why should the strong and young visit those who grow old and weak.'

Olaf left the old man and then made his way across the broad sandy isthmus to the main island in order to seek out the Irish boy and his woman Mardöll. Their small dwelling was easy enough to find, but very quickly he became disillusioned. The boy had grown surly and seemingly didn't appreciate the freedom he had been granted at all. Not a single word of any kind did he offer to Olaf; simply turning his back indifferently on the Norseman he walked slowly away, towards the shoreline. The girl, who had once been his, was clearly heavily pregnant; she had become rather more than portly and when smiling, which she did frequently possible out of worry or nerves, she unwittingly showed that most of her upper teeth had gone. What teeth remained appeared darkened and diseased in some way; they were almost greenish grey in colour. The poor thing, he thought, was dirty and what was more she barely recognised him. Olaf stood quite still in front of her, in his finest Norse garments. The delicate twill of his cape and the gold pin that fastened it caught her gaze briefly, but she looked no further; her eyes had dimmed and the lids covering them drooped heavily, as if to hide a secret from which emanated some terrible guilt. Olaf in that instant shared the same feelings of his friend's father and inexplicably found himself thinking of the old man. He felt an unexpected close affinity to the master of old. For some reason, as he surveyed the girl, he felt as though betrayed; although, he wasn't too sure whom or what he could blame. In his heart, he appreciated that the melancholia that had overtaken his being came from nowhere but within. It was just a part of life and one of its occasional nasty little tricks. Never return, he commanded himself, I should have known not to. Never return, never, especially to a place that holds any fond memories at all and never by *Loki Laufeyjarson's* lies return to a woman.

With this last thought still in his mind, he turned his attention to the purpose of the trip. 'Never return,' he repeated out loud to himself. 'Never return!'

His thoughts returned to his earlier discussion with the monk and his ideas, which now seemed to have reasonable foundations. But then he may be hiding something from me, he mused. Speaking to himself in barely a whisper he said, 'He looked as though he knew the coast well and could probably find the places he talked about with little difficulty.' Well, he further reasoned to himself, if he says that his isle will have no silver or gold then that may be true, but how can he be sure about the other places, which he may never have even been to. He must have heard or know something about them, but then perhaps he is keeping that to himself. He picked out the one called 'Wear' or whatever it was and the other one called Gyrwe, but he seemed less than keen on Gyrwe for some reason. Perhaps his god is still pulling his strings. Maybe he is trying to keep my greedy heathen fingers from the gold on his altar. I wonder just which option I should choose. Perhaps I should sack both in the same day or just pick off the one with the most gold and silver. I don't normally share my plans with my crew, but this time I'll tell them we'll sail for the place called 'Wear' or whatever its called and maybe we will go there or more likely we'll have a look at the other twin. I'd like to see the reaction of the Celt, especially his face when he hears my plans, I have a feeling he may be up to no good.

Cathwulf feigned complete indifference to the supposed plans, but some time later he did speak at considerable length to Wilfred and some of the other slaves who also happened to have been taken from his sacred isle the year before. A great deal of scowling and finger wagging took place and this did not escape the young Norse boy's attention; a boy who had been sent by Olaf to watch the reaction of the slaves to his purported plans.

೮ఎ   ೮ఎ   ೮ఎ

One whole month was spent on The Orkney Isles; the moon had turned full cycle before Olaf decided that the time had come for the real business of their trip. Naturally, the *knarr*s had been restocked well with an impressive quantity of food and drink, as well as a variety of other commodities. The biggest cargo that had been carried by all of the boats was wood. There were several large tree trunks that had been secured down the middle of the *knarrs*, some smaller pieces of wood that must have been cut from branches, as well as large quantities of planking. Olaf remembered what his friend Ingvar had said to him years before, concerning the transportation of wood. It made him smile just thinking of the irony. 'First, what is the point of carrying wood in a boat when it floats? Second, why cut it up to make planks, when it takes up so much more space when it's been split? Third, why not cut down trees when you get to where you're going?' Ingvar's words seemed to make a lot of sense, but they didn't take into account that Orkney was an almost treeless group of islands. Olaf's boats had delivered a good quantity of wood for beams and trusses in the construction of roofs. There was little else here to build from, he thought.

One other important change that had taken place was the way the crews of the boats had changed. Some men and their womenfolk and children left the boats to join those who had already settled on the isles. They took with them as many possessions as it was possible to carry and a fair share of the timber stashed away on the boats. In contrast, one or two families had given up their land on the islands and decided to return, preferably to their native homeland; having made it known they wished to travel with the flotilla. If the original Norse kingdom was out of the question, they were content with travelling to wherever the boats happened to be going.

All of the comings and goings were monitored by Olaf's appointed leaders. It was at this time that he missed his friend Ingvar most, because the men who had replaced him were simply not up to the task. Some of them were quite well known to him, having sailed with him on earlier trips, but his memory had dimmed with all the changes that had happened to him in the last few years or so. Geirhjálmr on Olaf's orders was scratching away at a stick, trying to make some kind of list of people who were to travel. Spjall and Særða were similarly engaged, but they were taking note of what was taken off the boats and by whom, for as Olaf had said, 'We're here to help, but we're also here to help ourselves as well.

During the time spent on this small cluster of islands, there had been ample opportunity for all of the Norse men and their slaves to relax as far as possible and to prepare themselves for the events that lay ahead. The moon had waxed and waned, the birds had made nests, crops were growing and everything appeared as normal as it could be in what had been until recently a foreign land in the realm of *Midgard*.

Both the longboats and the *knarrs* had been hauled out of the sea and they now lay rather lazily high up on smooth and rounded stones, which had been worn by the relentless pounding of icy waves over the millennia. Naturally, this meant that the boats could be repaired and any work that needed to be done could be carried out. All sump plugs had accordingly been stored somewhere near to the prows of each boat. The ornate dragon head from Olaf's boat had been taken off and stored in a nearby longhouse. Viðbjörn and his family who lived there were proud to have been chosen to look after such a prestigious artefact. He was unaware that the real reason was that Olaf had been told that the man who resided there was the most accomplished of carpenters or workers of wood who was to be found in the entire islands. Nothing had been said to Viðbjörn about possible repairs to the dragon, but he had taken the hint when he had been given several small bars of silver and a number of golden coins by one of Olaf's men. The chubby man had worked hard and long to restore the snarling head to its original glory.

Viðbjörn had firstly cut out any sections of wood that appeared to have become rotten. He had used a bog iron lump hammer to strike the wooden handle of curiously shaped chisel. Then he had crudely filled the resultant holes with small pieces of timber he had obtained from a store of wood in the *knarr* that lay right next to the dragon ship 'Gjálfrmarr.' When he was happy that the new wood had been securely glued into place, he began his work with a variety of differently shaped chisels. These he had sharpened with a piece of stone that he had possessed for many years; more years than he chose to remember. The tiny crystals in the stone shone out and the carpenter told his youngest son once more, that they were tiny stars which were no longer needed by the gods. *Óðinn* has let them slip to earth and it is the heat within them that allows us to put an edge on the iron we have pulled from the gods' marshy ground. Who was to say that the master craftsman was wrong? His skill was unsurpassed and the dragon's head soon looked as though it had been completed for the first time and not been the result of his remarkably quick restoration project.

During the time the boats lay on the beach, the tides came in and went out again, relentlessly time and again as they always had done. Olaf took to visiting some of his old friends who had settled on the islands and at the same time explore the main island of Hrossey. He was accompanied by two men from the crew of his *drakkar*, *Spjall* and *Særða*. They were astonished to find a great ring of stones and a massive ditch that Spjall suggested must have been erected when the world was very young and the sun shone all the brighter. Most of the stones were three times the height of a man, one height in width, but only slightly thicker than one hand's breadth. The men gaped in awe and wondered at the effort required to construct such a thing. 'Why in *Óðinn's* name did they, whoever they were, build this thing?' Spjall asked looking up and gaping in wonderment at one of the largest megaliths. One of the stones, a small one comparatively speaking suffered at his hand, for the young Norse man using a dagger of damascened iron, scratched into its surface a series of spiky runes. He told Olaf that he wouldn't be coming back to the islands again if he could help it, but that he liked to leave something of himself behind, to show people who came here in the future that he had already beaten them to it. Olaf spat at the stone and mumbled something about them being cursed and told him that it was the stupidest way of using a blade he had ever seen. Særða looked quite worried and urged his companions to leave the place suggesting that it was not a good idea to meddle in the affairs of the 'older peoples', let alone upset them.

Not far from the impressive earthwork and its stones was a great grassy knoll or mound, which stood out in the landscape and provided the men with a good vantage point from which they were able to view a good part of the island. 'I wonder if a king lies inside here,' Olaf grimaced as he spoke and then maintaining his pained expression continued. 'They say that's the locals, that the 'older people' buried their important folk in these, with all of their gold and silver. Imagine what might be under our feet now. There was more gold in those days and the sun shone longer in the sky, for it was younger and had more strength.'

'Well I'm not digging this pile of shit up for anyone, not even you Olaf!' Spjall was unsure of what the mound was for and at heart was more than a little anxious about meddling with the affairs of bygone folks or with upsetting their spirits.

'It would do well for us to leave it and them alone and go. It is not good even to speak of it.' The nervousness of young Særða had not left him and his apparent reticence galled Olaf, who rammed the iron head of his spear hard down into the welcoming earth.

'They're all dead and gone as we will be soon in the great scheme of things. *Óðinn* and his fellow gods are looking after us, we sacrifice to them, and we keep them sweet! Don't worry about some old bugger who left years ago, he won't cause our gods any trouble and if he did, do you think he's be a match for our *Loki*? He's little chance of being a draughrinn round here, look, there so few trees we'd all see the perishing thing, before he ever got close enough to scare any of us.'

'Well even so, I think it best we leave and try not to offend the dead even if they're long since cold and whether they follow our gods or not.' *Særða* spoke these words rather disconsolately as he trudged off the mound, as he realised that later that day he would probably be riled by his fellow crew for being scared of the dead. He thought to himself, as he always did that it was better to be on the safe side and that he could live through the jibes of his friends. Perhaps Olaf should have listened to him for once and considered caution as a possible option.

胫 胫 胫

Wilfred awoke to the harsh scream of sea birds that whirled in the sky relentlessly. He had not slept well, but at least he had managed to fall into a series of light slumbers. Penetrating cold and rain, coupled with nightmarish dreams and an increasing gnawing hunger had all played their part in making this night on the coast as uncomfortable as it was possible to imagine. It had been four days since he had made a break for it and now he was somewhere on the east coast of northern Pictland. He knew that as an escaped slave, he would if recaptured by the Norse, be put to death in the most hideous of ways imaginable. The escape itself had been quite unremarkable really. His fellow monks, at least those who used to be at the monastery of Lindisfarne with him and several other native men from the Orkneys had put together some provisions for him and managed to arrange for a boat to take him south to the top of Pictland. The man who took him across the great heaving band of water did so late into the evening of a clear summer's day. Wilfred had not been missed by his masters until after the noon of the following day.

Back on the islands of Orkney, repercussions were quickly felt by Wilfred's fellow slaves, as reprisals being meted out by the Norse folk were severe. Olaf had questioned Cathwulf concerning the departure of Wilfred and assured him that he would be joining his one and only god if his answers were less than satisfactory. Olaf wanted to know just two things. First, who had helped effect his escape and second exactly where was he planning to go. Cathwulf knew of course that he was in a far greater and more immediate danger than Wilfred, whom he now presumed was wandering in a southerly direction somewhere in the wilds of the northern Pictish realms. Cathwulf had practised his response many, many times, but it still sounded rather hollow even to him. His single toned reply went thus. 'I consider that Wilfred is making his way to the Isle of Iona, a sister island and monastery to the great Lindisfarne, which you,' here he paused, 'er already know. It lies somewhere to the south west I believe and is crammed with gold and silver and the bones of many saints. It is I have been told remote, but even so it is the centre of all that is holy in the kingdom of men on God's earth. It is in waters between the lands of the Picts and all the Irish Kingdoms.' The latter part of his answer was added as a sort of verbal padding to make the earlier less believable part of his speech have a degree more credibility.

Olaf was not happy at all. Being in complete charge of all the boats and all of their crews was tiring work. He didn't like the thought that one of the slaves, one of his slaves had made a break, a successful one at that for freedom. Also, he was at a near total loss as to where the man may have gone.

It hadn't taken a huge amount of questioning to ascertain that Wilfred had been helped off the isles by someone with at least a fair knowledge of the isles' coastline and more importantly a boat. Olaf enlisted the help of Ingvar's father, who knew nearly everything there was to know about the islands and its inhabitants. ÓþyrmiR shook his head and sighed before confiding in Olaf that there were a great number of men with small boats that were used for fishing and others still who had larger boats that were used for the delivery of goods and merchandise. It could he reasoned have been virtually anyone on the islands, that is anyone who had a reason to resent the Norsemen's incursion into the previously undisturbed Orcadian world. 'They are not bad people you know, all they wish to do is to go on with their lives without disturbance. They fish, they fish, they look after their folk and they resent outsiders. Who can blame them for that?'

Nothing of course could be proven, but Olaf had his suspicions that the young man who had been offered and subsequently taken his woman all that time ago, was the culprit. 'Veddellemettis, that's whose behind this, you mark my words. I don't suppose we'll ever know for sure, but I'd put a *knarr* full of silver on it, that he's behind this.' Olaf spoke to himself grimly. He found quite some difficulty hiding his irritation, which was finally sated by a number of vicious beatings which were mercilessly meted out on the slaves. Those selected, were all men who had been taken from the monastery of Lindisfarne the previous year and all had quietly resigned themselves to their fate, whatever that may have been. It seemed that they almost hoped for a savage beating or worse in preference to being cruelly sacrificed in the name of some pagan god.

Veddellemettis had been sought out and was asked many a question about his whereabouts the night before. At first he feigned complete ignorance, shrugging his shoulders repeatedly and blowing out his cheeks and making a number of tutting noises. This had the effect of initially irritating and then annoying Spjall and the other Norse men who had been given the task of obtaining information on the uncalled for departure of Wilfred. This surly man clearly knew something and he was not letting on. He would though, even if it took more than a little time and energy.

Spjall had quickly become exasperated, because he was not used to the niceties of such work. He also for once resented his master Olaf, at this time, because rather than taking responsibility for extracting information from the young Orcadian, he had taken himself off with a young girl named Eilíf. To make matters even worse Spjall had fancied his chances with the girl, but Olaf had made it clear that as leader he would exercise his rights and dominance. Spjall felt aggrieved and now just wanted to get the questioning over with. He looked into the young Irishman's eyes, before asking him, 'How much did he give you?' Spjall worked on the simple premise that the boy was guilty unless he could prove otherwise.

Veddellemettis was not helping himself at all. He looked down and mumbled something to himself about having not done anything wrong. Finally, when all hope of a confession seemed gone, he admitted that he had taken some man with a beard to the mainland in the early hours of the morning. 'I took his coin and thought nothing of it, what have I done wrong? How was I to know he was a slave, he looked like and spoke like you. All I do is fish and try to earn a little silver or gold in any way I can.'

'The man you took is one of my master's slaves and you knew it.' Spjall's reply was brief and it heralded a terrible thrashing. The Irish lad fell silent, knowing full well that he had put not just his own life at risk, but also those of his family. He was beaten bloody about the head by three young Norse men wielding thick ash sticks. The very same three had meted out the beatings to the slaves earlier and they had been ruthlessly efficient in their work. Veddellemettis in time made a full recovery apart from his teeth, which were damaged terribly in the assault. What teeth he had left caused him intermittent pain and over the next few years, they too, diminished in number due to bouts of gum disease induced by painful infections. Of the slaves who had been beaten, two had died; one immediately of appalling internal injuries, the other being not quite so lucky, taking a full three weeks to slip out of the world of men. He had been blinded in both of his eyes and had at the same time lost the ability to speak. One generous local family had allowed him to crawl under a lice-ridden blanket in their longhouse, but it was to no avail. He shivered uncontrollably for days and foamed at the mouth. Eventually he ate nothing of the food offered him and took no water.

Ꝙ Ꝙ Ꝙ

The boats were once again in the water and making their way due south towards the top of Pictland. Time spent on the Orkneys had been pleasant for most of the men. There had been some time to relax, time to meet old friends and time to make decisions. Olaf knew some of his men would stay, but similarly understood that some men who had decided to settle the previous year would have changed their minds and would be travelling away with him. It was the only way. He preferred to have men on board who were there because they wanted to be. Only the slaves had absolutely no say in their destiny, they simply went where their masters' decided.

Olaf stood at the prow of his *drakkar* and pointed vaguely at the nearing headland, all the while he stood transfixed, thinking of the girl he had left behind on the islands. The great dragon headed boat was lifted rhythmically by the waves, skimming across the great living sea with consummate ease. Its keel or kjölr cut into and through the water like a savage predatory beast clawing into the flesh of some helpless prey. All of the craft; the *drakkar* and the *knarr*s sped onwards with scant regard for anything but the prize that awaited them. The dragon's head of 'Gjálfrmarr' leered menacingly out over the seascape which had became so calm, it was as though it had bowed in complete subservience to the overpowering presence of such an awesome force. The slightly smaller *drakkar* and the *knarr* followed behind the lead ship and for all the world looked as if they were being pulled along by magical and invisible ropes that kept them moving at a fearful pace and in tight formation.

Only six boats left the shores of Orkney that summer. One of the older *knarr*s that had been taking on rather too much water for the boat's young bailers to keep up with had been plundered for spare parts. Those parts of the boat that were too rotten for alternative uses were left to dry and eventually used as fire wood. Before the boats had been pulled down the beaches, several carpenters had already dismembered the prone craft to little more than a skeletal hulk. What was left, the heavier timbers were mostly destined to be part of the roof frames and trusses of several longhouses already under construction. Olaf surveyed the whole scene, but remained singularly uninterested and happily unconcerned. Instead, he preferred to concentrate more on the immediate future. As if needing to share his thoughts with someone, he began, 'We'll have room enough for the treasures that await us.' For some unknown reason he felt obliged to reassure his crew. 'They say the kindly priests are stacking up their precious goods for us, so that we won't have to waste time bundling them up, before carting them away.'

℘   ℘   ℘

The dark comes earlier each day now. As with this tale there is a feeling of expectancy, it is as though something magical hangs in the air. It is invisible, but it is there all right. Outside the cold of winter has taken its grip and the landscape is covered with a thick layer of white snow. The distant steep sided black mountains rear up in defiance of the all covering blanket of ice. They alone remain untouched by the purity of the skies' messengers.

Our new year has come and gone and now we wait for the festival of Jól. The darkness is all embracing and the cold, by Óðinn's breath, the cold is too much for an old man like me! The stars stand out from the blackness and it is as though a path of them girdles the whole of the night sky. The moving lights of green and bluish red also dance in recognition of some heroic deed; why else would they move hither and thither in such a way?

The fire helps now of course, but the thick smoke as always makes my eyes run and smart and I have developed a cough that comes from the centre of my being. Why is it, that the young don't notice the effects of the cold or of the wind? Snorri only puts on his nalbanded mitts when the wind and snow between them have the power to suck the heat of life from the body.

No matter; the story lives on in spite of the cold. The longhouse is warmer today though, probably because over half of it is now home to animals and to my horse, Sleipnir. Snorri managed to round up most of my sheep in the gloom. They are a nuisance to me though. They call to one another through the night, incessantly. They smell of dampness, rot and shit! I suppose they do at least contribute to a little warmth and for that we should be grateful.

The tale must continue now, for Snorri is sat down and whilst he massages some blood and warmth back into his toes he would like his mind distracted from his own hardships.

Chapter 13

Sumar, Miðsumarblót, fyrstr ok tuttuganoi, beyannir

Gyrwe Monastery
21st June, Beltane, 794 A.D.

'A furore Normannorum libera nos, Domine'
"From the fury of the Northmen deliver us, O Lord."

Gyrwe monastery was small. It rested quietly on the banks of a slow flowing and ebbing river that swept serenely passed it in the way its waters had done for more generations than anyone cared to remember. The buildings were not particularly attractive, but were out of necessitude highly functional. There was the main squat rectangular church, with a number of other buildings arranged apparently randomly around it. These disparate constructions and their relationship to the central building, gave most visitors strong initial impressions and feelings. The importance ascribed to this house of God was paramount. Everything had been constructed to revolve about this central building, not just in a physical sense, but also in the daily rituals that occurred again and again and again. The masses, the services and various other goings on in the church meant that the local community of monks appeared to be forever arriving at or leaving its hushed and hallowed enclave. It had been this way for more than two hundred years and now to the settled residents no other way of being could be imagined. God had placed the church at the centre of the little community in the same way he had placed Man at the centre of his creation. All of the monks knew this and were comforted by the infallible truth of their knowledge and logic.

Five monks, all but one of them elderly had spent several hours hurrying in and out of the main church. Each had been particularly careful when he entered the building, as the bright sunlight outside induced in all of them a temporary blindness. The inside of this damp and cool stone edifice was now very dark and it was this that forced the men to slow down for fear of walking into unseen objects. The last member of this small group of men was wearing a conspicuously new set of robes and stiff leather sandals and he walked with just the slightest limp. His hair looked as though it had been cut short very recently. In fact, but one hour previous, he had been sitting patiently in one of the few outbuildings, while a fellow monk had carefully removed a neat circle of hair from the top of his head. He had also lost his rough shaggy beard and bathed in warm water for the first time in many days. Now, he was barely recognisable as the man who had shuffled sore footed into their grounds the day before.

He had been treated rather well on arrival; in fact much better than he had half expected. A selection of cheeses and bread and even a brown glass bottle containing a rather fine wine had been placed at his disposal. Most unusually, the abbot himself had put aside a number of urgent commitments including his prayers and made time to see this man. The abbot was a middle-aged man with a large stomach and an expression that seemed to impart to visitors to the small abbey a smug contentment that was mixed with a liberal portion of thinly veiled self-importance. Disconcertingly, his lips regularly curled into a smile that could easily have been either one of sarcasm or that of simple enjoyment. To the monks and other residents at Gyrwe monastery this dilemma had become an established and generally unwelcome problem. The abbot's violent mood swings veered him from sudden rushes of enthusiasm for projects and occasional moments of congratulation for his staff to swingeing attacks of melancholia which were accompanied by the associated and uncalled for bouts of criticism to all those below him in rank, in other words all others in the monastery.

Sitting quietly and enjoying his change in his circumstances, the stranger sat in a small building almost on the river front. Periodically, he pulled off lumps of coarse bread from a small round brown loaf. His fingers moved quickly and carefully with a practised dexterity and precision. First he would push one of these rough pieces into his mouth and then without thinking pick up the delicate silver goblet he had been provided with, before pouring in two or three generous gulps of the full-bodied ruby red wine, to crudely mix with the mush of bread which his dried out tongue had been so unsuccessfully trying to manipulate. Between these greedy mouthfuls he absentmindedly picked off pieces of grain that were half embedded in the thick and chewy crust and flicked them with the forefinger of his right hand across the room. He had not spoken for some time, but now smiled to himself, whilst musing that things had taken a decidedly good turn for the better. Heaven and the blessed angels of the Lord would surely be waiting for him when the time came for him to leave his monastic life for the very last time, he thought.

The abbot coughed loudly as he entered the small stone room as though to announce his entrance, as well as to clear his throat of phlegm. He spat the contents of his mouth against the left hand whitewashed wall of the room; a great green gobbet of spittle exploded on its uneven surface. What little of it remained behind adhered stubbornly to the mildewed stonework, before crawling slowly downwards towards the straw covered floor. Wilfred looked up and belched instinctively as if to acknowledge the importance of the cough and the resultant disgusting release of acidic saliva. He failed to recognise the abbot of course, because the latter had decided to question the visitor, in the plain robes of a novice monk thereby reducing any possible risk of intimidation. Instead of employing his usual aggressive approach, he pulled up a crudely fashioned stool and asked if he could join the guest for a 'frugal bite.' Wilfred nodded instantly. He was completely and blissfully innocent as to the importance of his visitor. 'Well, my friend your feet are blistered and your skin shows me that you have been travelling for many a day.' The abbot was in a singularly good mood, but as his contemporaries knew only too well, it couldn't possibly last. He had just sent the young boy who had been assigned to clean his room and to tend to his needs in every conceivable manner away. The boy had left bruised, bleeding and crying having received a sound beating from the abbot. He called after him as he staggered away, 'You are a vile and wicked child for tempting me into performing such unchristian and unnatural acts.' Smiling, he now turned his full attention to the haggard man who had arrived without a warning of any type. A verbal assault followed; a tirade of questions that built one upon the other in the way water creeps up the banks of a swollen river. 'Why have you come here? And where have you come from? What do you want from us? You can see that we are but a small community with little enough for others who may chance upon us.'

The abbot perspired heavily even when undertaking the lightest of physical actions and he was now dripping wet through with sweat. Wilfred couldn't understand why the monk who stank of rancid body odour and who was quizzing him now spoke so clearly and with such apparent intelligence, when he was seemingly just a lowly monk. Shrugging his shoulders he did his best to supply the information this inquisitive if rather obnoxious man desired, for he had no real reason not to. Very shortly after their discussion had begun, two other monks who were clearly rather senior in status, joined them and it was to these men that Wilfred offered a much more profound respect. The other man, whom he had treated as an equal, said little now and instead preferred to listen. Wilfred suggested somewhat dismissively that he leave now, but the man simply smiled serenely and said that it was better if he stayed and listened.

'I hail from the Holy Isle itself, the great and wondrous Lindisfarena eg. I have returned to these lands after being taken as a slave by the vile and heathen men of the north. They sacked our wonderful piece of heaven and in doing so, drowned a good number of our monks and our sisters. They took a fair number of us overseas to their lands, to work their fields for them and to build their barns and tend their cattle. But I am by the grace of God back to warn you of their terrible plans.' Wilfred paused, before continuing. 'Less than one full moon ago, I managed to escape with the help of an Irish lad; Fedelmid was his name. He took me off the islands to the north of Pictland and landed me safely on the top most shore of this great land.'

'But how could you escape the clutches of these Norse men so easily?' The leaner of the two men who had just arrived asked him, with furrowed brow

'Well', Wilfred began, 'it was late evening and because my fellow slaves had given me all of the silver they had come by, I was able to bribe this Irish lad with a little silver, to take me in his small boat. In truth, I think he may have taken me even if I hadn't been able to pay him. He seemed to have little regard for his rulers, even though his woman was one of theirs.'

'So what about this fantastic tale of yours; I have heard rumour of it already. Oh and may I say to you my hungry fellow, that you also haven't explained how you made your way through the wilds of Pictland to find our sanctuary. You may begin when you are ready.' The same monk, who had spoken before, continued the questioning. His last question was delivered however in a more light-hearted manner on account of Wilfred becoming wholly engrossed in the loaf of bread in front of him.'

It suddenly dawned upon Wilfred that his mission to save the monastery may possibly have failed, for the reason that no one appeared to believe anything of what he had to say. This monk, how dare he, he thought, looked as though he doubted the detailed circumstances he had so carefully described of his desperate departure from the isle of Lindisfarne and to add insult, he didn't even seem to believe anything of the tale of his sudden reappearance. Wilfred said nothing for quite some time as the enormity of the situation washed over him. In spite of this, he still felt that he must push on with his story and try to impress on these sceptical monks the dire position they were now in. He really had nothing to lose after all.

'I am grateful for your more than generous hospitality. I am indeed indebted to your entire community. But I am really here to warn you I say, not I humbly beseech to threaten you. I say to you, that I will go no where; I will not leave this blessed land. I swear to you that I will not leave here until you can see the truth of my words for yourselves. Please, please for the sake of each and every one of you and your blessed abbot, please take heed of what I say to you. It matters not how I came here, but why I come to warn you. If you must know I managed to pay the owner of a small Pictish trading vessel with what silver I had left, for a good passage south. But this doesn't matter. I feel you doubt my words of warning and prefer to question whether I have an ulterior motive. You can by all means hear the entire story regarding my journey here, but that I promise you should wait, until your great and holy abbot himself realises the mortal danger you are all in and the terrible possibility of the ruin of this beautiful and sacred place.

The *Finn-Gaill*; that is the name the Irish have for these men.' At this point, Wilfred paused unexpectedly as though to draw breath, before continuing. 'I have lived amongst them for a year or so. I have worked for them and I look for forgiveness for my blighted soul, for perhaps I should have done away with myself. I have seen their ungodly ways and the disregard these filth have for our sweet and unblemished God. Many of my fellow brothers and sisters' mortal remains lie hidden in the sand under the cold waters off poor defiled Lindisfarena eg. It is this and many other wicked and vile deeds besides, which have brought me here, to you. I cannot pretend that I am not frightened, for if they take me again, I will be fish food or I will hang from one of their sacred trees after they have had their sport with my wretched body. God, our one and only god thanks be to Christ for his suffering, has kept me safe through all the temptations and vile practices I have had the misfortune to see and forgive my sins, been made to participate in. I will surely burn forever in the fires of hell unless our Lord sees fit to forgive this weak and feeble sinner you see before you. Each and every night I am tormented by the visions of hell on Earth I have seen perpetrated by the men of Hordaland. Sleep and rest are not things that come lightly to me now as they used. I fear I will never be at peace in this world thanks to the heathen swine.

The men of the north, the Norse, the 'white foreigners' or whatever other accursed name you wish to call them by, have come to this, our land and at this very moment they are travelling here in their dragon ships, to your precious monastery, your Eden, with more than an evil and unspeakable intent. They will come; oh they will come all right, although I know not when. And when they do, by all Christ's saints in heaven and all those forgiven of their sins, they will defile and destroy all that is good. Please, please, for the sake of you all, please listen to me and be more than ready for these devils vented from the very bowels of Hell. Their terrible and bloody assault will undoubtedly be launched soon. It will be swift, it will be very bloody and it will be done in the name of gold and greed, for would you believe it, they care not for their own gods, whom they think look after them in their battles and in matters of lust. They would prefer to sacrifice a sickly animal or slave to cheer their gods and feed the carrion crows. Hanged men, women and beasts dangle from the branches of a chosen tree, to be picked clean by vile creatures that have a taste for such flesh. Such despicable and heinous beasts grow fat on the swollen, rotting flesh and sinew of both people and wild things. Horses, I have seen full grown horses hanging next to living and dead pigs and there besides are rotting men and their womenfolk hanging, weighing down the branches of these trees of death. The rank and bitter stench of death in its many forms and terrible nauseous decay fills the nostrils and chokes and blocks the throat. All you can do, as a God fearing man of Christ is to vent your stomach again and again. It makes me wretch even thinking of what they do in the name of their king god by the name of *Óðinn*. I can smell the putrid odour now and it sickens and permeates every ounce of my poor cursed soul. By all the sinners in Christendom it truly will be the end of God's mission here if the Norse scum arrive unopposed to take what they will.'

Abbot Ethelbald was a troubled man. He had only recently arrived from Wearmouth. As little as two days ago with some twenty monks as company and for protection; he had walked through the vegetable gardens and into the small church to take prayers before attending to any other trivial matter that may have been put his way. He had in truth been looking for a period of several weeks in which he proposed to do very little apart from pray, eat and cause hardship and distress to the boys sent to the monastery, whilst at the same time he meant to enjoy himself. He considered his elevated position in the church to be his 'right', almost god given; it was something he believed he had worked hard for. A privileged post it was all right, but he felt he had toiled hard for many a year to get to where he was today. The good food, the comfortable accommodation, the high quality clothes he normally wore, all bore testimony to his importance and to his considerable endeavour.

This extremely awkward situation was the very last thing he had expected or even dreamed of and naturally it was the last thing he would have wanted. He knew immediately that he would have to start sorting out this difficult problem without employing any of the usual delays he customarily used, to slow matters down and this pained him grievously. It was more than likely related to the day the sky had blackened to night at the death of summer the previous year Abbot Ethelbald thought. He had heard many times about the sack of *Lindisfarena Eg* and knew that something terrible would surely follow the unpredicted and terrible disappearance of the sun on the twenty sixth day of August. It may have been nearly ten months since that event, but the day of retribution was now apparently upon them all.

A deep sigh and frown to match transformed his forehead into a number of deep furrows to betray the deep anxiety he now felt. If this stranger was telling the truth and by God's infinite wisdom, there was no real reason to doubt him he thought, then the greatest crisis in the history of this, his community had arrived. Something had to be done by him and it had, he thought be done quickly.

$\wp$ $\wp$ $\wp$

After Wilfred had finished his meal, he walked with four monks to the small church. The abbot had decreed that the visitor and those who accompanied him were to take all objects of any possible importance to a safe place within the boundaries of the monastery's grounds. He had allowed the eldest of the monks to decide where such a place might exist and simply told them, 'to get on with it.' In the mean time, he had arranged a brief meeting with the more senior of the monks at Gyrwe, as Ethelbald called it, to decide on their most sensible course of action.

Little over an hour later, plans were in place that might have made Olaf, if he had been aware of them change his course of action. The small stone church had been stripped completely of anything that had the slightest value. Even the decorated altar cloth had been carefully folded up and stored in a long wooden box in a nearby farmhouse. The few tapestries that had adorned the back of the church had been unhooked, rolled up and stored atop the rafters of a small dwelling on the banks of the nearby river. Gold objects; there was a considerable quantity of these, were packed into three ancient oak chests of different sizes. These were then loaded onto a cart pulled by a large dappled white horse, with a long shaggy mane that had been neatly and expertly plaited. Four older monks, the same ones who had been working with Wilfred, walked away with the beast in the direction of nearby woodland. The abbot had also instructed them to go quickly into the largest of several close-by copses and to bury the treasures without any due ceremony. He had ordered two of these men to dig and two to keep an eye out for anyone who might be interested in such a valuable burial. The cart was important in an operation of this type, because all of the earth removed from the newly dug holes had to be carefully taken away from the digging site to prevent the slightest of tell tale clues being left.

The monks were all skilled farmers and used their digging tools with great aplomb. In just a short time three holes of varying size had been sunk into the soft and welcoming earth. The green and lush moss and grey and yellow lichen covered sticks that had carpeted the ground for so long had been meticulously put to one side by the brown cassocked men. The earth, almost the same colour as the monks' garments weighed down the small cart so that its wooden wheels creaked and groaned to suggest that it may have been complaining at such heavy work. The tallest of the monks threw the stick he had been using to measure out the distances between the holes, high onto the cart as it left the sun speckled glade. He then used his strong and claw like fingers to lift up and grasp the first of the small chests, before lowering it with some reverence into its designated hole. The procedure was repeated twice more, before a small quantity of earth was put back onto the top each of the boxes, so that the holes were filled perfectly in line with the ground. At this point the other monk, who had been designated to dig, rearranged the shaggy moss and twigs and sticks that had been put to one side, back to where they had been before they had been disturbed just a short time earlier. When this had been done to his satisfaction, it was almost impossible to tell where any of the chests had been buried. The tall monk and his companion nodded to one another and they happened to smile simultaneously, before the shorter of the men spoke. 'Just remember that oak tree, the one with the split trunk. It is from there that we take all our measurements. Six paces to the east. It's easy to bring to mind brother; think of the Prologue from the Rule of St. Benedict. Verses one to three, or should I say one, two and three! '

'I'll remember all right. At least I will if I'm still alive. Burials like these are a serious business. Gold of this quantity could dare I say it, pay for any rebuilding works that may need doing.'

'I know that only too well. The abbot has never had reason to hide our treasures before. It must be that there is a terrible enemy nearby who has some great power if not intelligence or subterfuge.'

'That is not a matter on which we may or should speculate Brother Godric.'

'Aye, you are right, we must turn all our attentions to prayer and perhaps then our Lord will protect us from whoever or whatever comes this way Brother Eadric.'

Eadric nodded, he had heard rumours and he didn't like any of them. These had included amongst others, sightings in the locality of great and terrible flying beasts, of fire breathing dragons, there were tales of dark and cruel men in longships and even whispers of burning monasteries. The worried monk flinched nervously before tugging at the plain wooden crucifix that dangled around his neck from a greasy leather cord. 'We are being punished, I tell you for our sins Brother Godric. Our pure Lord can see each and every of our evil and selfish ways and he'll surely burn us all in the raging fires of all consuming hell. He can have no possible use for us, the weak and self centred brethren that make up little Gyrwe community. Some say the abbot himself is the cause Brother Godric, but that idea must stay between us my friend. This could be the end of the world if the harbingers and omens be true. We had better pray my Brother, for our desperate and blighted souls may soon be weighed by our beautiful and wondrous maker.'

'The abbot's is a law unto himself! We must do as he says, obey all of the monastery's regula and pray for his soul all right. I'm not going to judge a man who is better than the likes of us, even though our Lord may frown upon some, in fact quite a few of his ways. If I behaved in the way he does, then I'd expect to fry in the fires of hell's kitchen. He tells us of the great and worthy Cassiodorus who founded two monasteries and makes us read his 'Commentary on the Psalms,' although he himself seems to take his life in other directions he chooses for himself. He also, the Lord forgive me, tells us of our own and beloved St. Benedict Biscop who founded our twin monasteries in much the same way as our Roman friend and how he looked to take the best practices from the best monasteries he knew. How things seem to have changed, even though our current abbot wouldn't see this! Our Abbot tells us on one hand that 'the eating of the flesh of quadrupeds shall be abstained from and that a hemina of wine in enough for each and every man', but still partakes of flesh and more than his measure of wine. It is one rule for one and one for another. I fear I must stop my words now, for I have sinned terribly. Prayer for forgiveness for the utterance of such words against my master is my immediate penance in the sight of God.'

℘ ℘ ℘

Ethelbald, the appointed abbot of Gyrwe stood on the river muddy bank and whistled quietly to himself. He felt alone, truly alone. The small waves made by a boat little bigger than a coracle, had just reached the edge of the bank close to where he stood. The tonsured man paddling away furiously in the water was wholly oblivious to the eyes of the heavily perspiring thinker who looked down upon him. The paddler deftly moved his delicate and light craft into the middle of the river and then paused as though in triumph, to let the lazy current carry him away downstream to his business whatever that may have been. Abbot Ethelbald watched him disappear around the gentle bend in the waterway with a fixed expression; he hardly blinked. At the precise moment the unknown man became no longer visible to the watching abbot, a change came about in the thinking of the supposed 'learned' and robed man on the bank. Ethelbald shouted out as though struck by one of his

Lord's fire bolts. He shuddered and took one step back, with a blinding rage engulfing him. He screamed some scrambled and garbled words at the chapel and other monastic buildings, before striding purposefully in their direction. As he did so he lost one of his leather sandals, the retaining leather strap had snapped at his sudden and wholly unexpected movement. He strode into the small chapel leaving muddy foot and sandal prints on the pounded tile floor behind him.

Brothers Eadric and Godric had arrived back at Gyrwe church of St. Paul before the abbot and thus had unwittingly beaten him to his immediate destination. Both monks now knelt, shoulder to shoulder at the front of the tiny stone church before the now plain and completely bare altar. For just the briefest of moments the abbot froze as if to question the rationale behind the two men's sudden apparent enthusiasm for prayer. Quickly overcoming this initial scepticism, he remembered his own urgent reasons for prayer and as a result he clumsily pushed both men apart to kneel somewhat unceremoniously and in a somewhat less than dignified manner between them. Eadric winced instinctively, wrinkling up his nose and then pulling away from the sweaty and greasy skinned man, who emitted an odour so terrible that it may well have been the breath of death issuing from Hell itself. Godric also moved away, but instead of gagging at the man's stomach churning stench, instead sniffed at the air suspiciously, with a great deal of care. He felt a compulsion, drawn by the disgusting smell in the way a moth is drawn unerringly towards a spluttering and dancing candle. He simply could not help himself at all as he sampled the rancid body odour in disbelief. The man, he concluded was disgusting in every conceivable way. The abbot was he considered not just a hypocrite, but a filthy and disgusting individual; a putrid man who adopted the ways of the devil himself and seemingly he emanated an odour so vile as surely to be in league with him.

Godric could not hear the words of prayer whispered by his utterly loathsome master, such was the hold of the disgusting, revolting and all pervading smell. Eadric in contrast had stood up and was making his way hurriedly towards the heavy wooden door, before turning around and speaking. 'I will summon them all Abbot, all the trader merchants, the ciepemenn, I will get them here for you. Godric quick, come and help. Why in Christ's name don't you move man?'

Godric shook his head, before leaping up as though breaking free from a spell to rush to join his fellow brother before asking, 'What shall we do Brother? What in God's name shall we do?'

'I suggest we do as the venerable abbot bids, weren't you listening to his words, his words of wisdom?'

'In truth Brother Eadric I was trying to listen to our Lord and not the servant sent in his place to Gyrwe.'

'Well, I heard a voice, but alas it was not that of the Lord Almighty, but that of a mere man; our esteemed abbot. Even so, it was a clear voice and you and I have to move quickly if we are not to be lashed by the unforgiving tongue that issues so many orders. You my friend and I are to make known the threat of the Norse men. We are to do this not just here at our monastery, but also in the nearby villages and we are bound to get a message to our fellow brothers in our twin monastery of Wearmouth. Oh, and we are to take Brother Wilfred with us to help us as we recruit.' Eadric's reply could not have been any clearer to Godric, who responded gloomily.

'So it has come to this. We are to raise an army to fight off the filthy heathen swine, who will be arriving in their dragon headed boats. By sweet Jesus himself, I cannot believe I took up the cassock and cenobitic way of life to swing a blade to protect both myself and my or should I say our church.'

'You won't be able to protect St. Paul's by yourself my friend. You, Brother Godric and I are not trained in the use of weapons. We are men who live by ora and labora; prayer and work, that is all we know. We are going to need an army of men, a sizeable army that is both well equipped and skilled in wielding spear, sword or axe. We'll need that and nothing less against the heathen Norse.' After completing his brief and somewhat depressing response Eadric placed his hand on a heavily carved stone set into the wall near the solid oak door. 'This stone was placed here, see the carvings, on the 23rd April in the fifteenth year of King Egfrith, that being the fourth year in the abbacy of Coelfrith. That is over a hundred years before our own Ethelbald my fellow Brother and in all that time there has never been a threat such as this.'

'Brother Eadric I am frightened and you feel no doubt the way I do.' Pointing at the delicate stained glass, he murmured quietly, 'Look at those coloured glass windows, the likes of which surely exist elsewhere, but by Christ and his angels, I'll never see them for they surely only decorate the great and mighty churches of Rome.'

જી   જી   જી

Olaf had lost count of the number of days that had passed since the boats had rowed away from tiny Byrgisey. He had soon become weary of the Pictish coastline which passed ever so slowly on the right hand side of his flotilla. For most of the time, he mused idly about which monastery he should visit first. 'The twins seem to be the best course.' He had reluctantly confided his half made up mind with Spjall due to the fact there was no one else on board he felt he could share any sensible thoughts with. The reply from his fellow Norse man was little more than a grunt even so. His thoughts lay else where, or more accurately on the gold he was to plunder, to make up for the huge losses he had so recently incurred whilst gambling on the island of Hrossey.

'The twins are some distance apart.' Olaf's mind was trying to fashion a plan which would enable him to surprise both monasteries. He didn't want the one he raided second knowing about its sister's demise though. 'The map is good, for all I can say, but distance is another thing. Cathwulf couldn't give me an accurate idea on distance or time, but I'd have to say that by boat it'd be about two *víka sjóvar*. On foot may be half a day's march between the two. Also, it could be wet under foot and that'd surely slow us down.'

'May be, just may be I'll go for the little one and see what prizes it holds. If they turn out to be half decent, then it would be more than a tad churlish to refuse those offered by the bigger and greedier one. Or may be I'll do it the other way round. The monks in either, it doesn't matter which, will be more than inviting I'm sure, as long as that blasted slave hasn't warned them of our coming. He's probably run to that island monastery though, to save what precious there is left of it. If he went to Gyrwe or Wearmouth though and convinced them of our approach, then they'll have buried everything. Devious and impudent squirrels they are! Just like Ratatosk, running back and forth and creating mischief.'

'Why is it that these men of Christ feel the need to stock so much worldly treasure in their little churches, tell me that my *jarl*.' Spjall's question slightly surprised Olaf, who for a moment was reminded of his great friend Ingvar, who was of course many, many a world away. Before replying, he paused whilst considering whether he would ever see that youthful face again. His well considered response was really to Ingvar and not Spjall, but the Norse man standing in front of him was clearly unaware of this. 'It is the way of men. We are all different and we all have just a little time to make some kind of mark on *Midgard* or whatever we choose to call it. We, my friend spend our gold on our boats, cattle, slaves, food and drink, women, gambling and weapons of course. We have a great need for it and silver of course, because we desire many things. These men of the god of Christ, they store the gold and other treasures they have been given, in their wood or stone churches. It comes, as far as I can make out, from both good men who have nothing to give and from bad men who have much gold and little regard for what their church really stands for. Most of the men in this country have very little to eat and most of what they have they must give away to their church. The rich also give, but it is just a bribe to pay for their 'sins' as they call them. Silver and gold by all account can prise open the door to their heaven it seems.'

'I'm not sure I follow what you say *Jarl*, but I have a need for gold and I see no reason for treasures the likes of which you have described to me to stay in old and damp churches gathering dust. Let the monks do their praying. They are more than welcome to it, whilst we can spend their precious and bright metals.' Spjall's rejoinder cheered Olaf up as it fitted in well with his own thoughts on life.

'Yes, Spjall you are right, we must see what the little sister has for us to spend. By my reckoning in two days we should be loading our boats with their holy treasures. Remember, gold and silver is good, but the little boxes that hold bits of bone or hair are worth plundering. My old friend Ingvar assured me that these things contain parts of their blessed saints. They will pay large amounts of gold for such things, Ingvar assured me. Don't ask me why, because by *Óðinn's* steed, it seems bloody stupid to me!'

Spjall shrugged his shoulders, but failed to reply. He knew better than to question the large man about why the dusty bones were so valuable, but instead thought an unspeakable reply. 'What utter rubbish! I can't believe that even the Christ men value such things. Is Olaf soft in the head or is he trying to play some kind of trick on me? Don't these men fear and curse *draughrinn?*'

'Look Spjall, can you make out those islands; off yonder?' Olaf asked, seemingly in a good humour again, interrupting the young man's line of thought.

'Why isn't that the island we visited last year? I can't remember its name, but we certainly filled the boats with strong slaves and gold, very good gold.' Spjall had identified Lindisfarne correctly, although he had for some inexplicable reason forgotten its name. 'Why don't we make a detour and see if they have restocked the church; it was full, remember?'

'No my friend, we won't be visiting that one for some while. May be we will if things go awry with the two beautiful sisters, but I can't see it.' In truth Olaf had already decided which monastery was to receive his greedy crews. He knew and he was making sure that no one else did so for the moment.

℁   ℁   ℁

Wilfred had been walking for what seemed to be a long time. He had stopped three times with Brother Eadric and Brother Godric for prayers and it was this that made him realise that the sister monastery was more than merely a short stroll away. Wilfred ceased his walking, to stand quite still on an open stretch of the green way they were following. His leather sandals were now quite wet from the splashes of dew that bedecked the long blades of grass, turning the tanned hide to a much darker shade of brown. Brothers Eadric and Godric also became motionless, sensing that Wilfred had either heard or seen something untoward in the tranquil landscape. Eadric asked in a worried and whispered tone. 'What is it my brother? What's the matter?'

'By Christ and all his blessed saints, that heathen swine is more than clever. He is clever all right. Sainted Jesus what have I done? I think he must be in league with the devil and all his deceitful and evil beasts.' Wilfred's strange, loud and unexpected reply worried Godric greatly, who by the tortured expression on the stranger's face could see that he was for some reason genuinely fearful. Godric therefore asked him earnestly, 'Brother, what is it you have done? Tell me for we may be able to put this wrong right.'

'It is what we are doing now that is the problem. Don't you see? The heathen bastard Olaf told me his plans, but why did he? He may have been bluffing. He suggested, no he said that he would raid Jarrow and possibly Wearmouth, but he didn't say for sure. Knowing the way his mind works, he's probably on his way to mop up what's left of the blessed Holy Isle of Lindisfarne. I'm so stupid, he's outwitted me and knowing him he may even have allowed me to escape as well.' Wilfred's reply was beginning to make some kind of sense to the two brothers, whose job it had recently become to recruit an army to defend a monastery. The question though was, which monastery of the two, should the monks begin to defend. Godric gasped and looked down before speaking in a terrible monotone.

'You are telling me that if we take all our brothers away from the larger monastery, from the church of St. Peter's to defend St. Paul's, then we may be opening the treasure house of Wearmouth to the heathen swine. Wilfred, are you saying that this Norse leader, Olaf you say, may be going for the bigger sister as you call it!'

'That's exactly what I'm saying. We can't win can we, if the heathens come to Gyrwe second, they will already have sacked Wearmouth. It doesn't matter if we foil their attempts to spoil Gyrwe, the damage will have been done and they will come back when it suits them!'

'Wilfred, you have good reason to cower, for the abbot would have you done away with if he knew your thoughts. For your sake, thank Christ he does not. You and Brother Eadric and I had better pray as we have never prayed before. We must hope that your suspicions are simply wrong, for we can do little to alter the Norse man's plans. What he thinks is a mystery to us, but it will soon be solved one way or the other. There is nothing for us to do but to attempt to amass as powerful a force as possible and take it south to our own little and helpless Gyrwe. There's an end to it! If we are wrong, then we as monks of one monastery will pay a heavy price in gold and silver and the abbot I suppose will make sure that we three will pay in other ways as well. From where I'm standing the difference between our Christ and his religion and the heathen swine's idols and beliefs appear now to be less and less.'

Eadric scowled before adding that things were never usually as bleak as first thought. He decided however not to share his thoughts concerning the mustering of the army and how when assembled it should be deployed, because he could see that his fellow brothers were not in the mood for any of his creativity however clever and cunning it may have appeared to be.

Wearmouth was much, much larger than little Gyrwe. It was surrounded by well tended fields which were growing all kinds of vegetables in almost straight lines. Wilfred marvelled at the texture of the soil and its apparent fertility. All of the plants were strong and lush green, commanding their own designated patch of fertile earth unopposed. Weeds simply had no chance in this rigidly maintained and rigorously run garden. It needed a lot of men to tend and a lot of men it certainly had. Wilfred could see that if there was any possibility of raising an army to fight the heathen scum, then it was here in these vegetable plots that their seemingly impossible mission just may be accomplished. The abbot was of course already in Gyrwe or Donemouth and it was not to him, but to his deputy they now went. Having spent some time drinking water from a skin they had been given whilst sheltering from the sun in the shade of St. Peter's, they now waited for the next most senior monk, the prior. Their wait was in however vain. Brother Wilfred soon became impatient and showed his annoyance by shouting out loudly. Brother Godric put a finger to his lips to hush him, before suggesting they recruited their army without entering into any time consuming consultation here, because none was really necessary. Eadric was not fully convinced, but after waiting for what seemed a very long time he reluctantly agreed to this proposition.

The three men decided to split up, the idea being that two would work their way through the beautifully manicured vegetable gardens, whilst one would enter the church to find men who would be willing to take part in their unenviable quest. It was not very long before the message concerning the imminent Norse raid had reached all parts of the monastic estate. Empowered by the abbot's decree, recruitment was in reality extremely easy. Most of the monks saw their march to Gyrwe as a matter of course. They didn't like it of course, but most felt they were finally putting into practice a practical aspect of their prayers. They, the monks knew that their serenity here was soon to be shattered, but if it had to be, then let it be broken in such a way as to allow their God to heal any damage that might be perpetrated. One older portly brother rallied to the cry enthusiastically, shouting at the top of his voice that the heathens should not be allowed under any circumstances to desecrate either of their beautiful churches and indeed any of God's buildings or property. His high pitched voice echoed off the sides of the stone church almost as though their god was adding impetus to his rallying cry.

By early evening and with the sun shining with a lovely golden hue, the hurriedly gathered army was nearing a completion of sorts. Various and disparate forms of men, with their odd assortment of agricultural weaponry cast long shadows on the only area of untended pasture within Wearmouth monastery. Some three hundred or so brethren were assembled there in their brown cassocks, waiting for the singular instruction to begin the march of several hours to Gyrwe. After waiting for just a short while, they set off en masse, without any orders or prompting of any description. Irritation had it seemed, built to such a level that the group moved off with what appeared to be an innate sense. Brothers Godric and Eadric had held back from addressing to the assembled group and issuing the 'off', because they were aware that at least a further fifty or so brothers were still out in the fields and should have been joining the impromptu army before much more time elapsed. As it was the brothers didn't march, they merely walked quite casually as though out on a late evening stroll. Brothers Godric, Eadric and Wilfred were trudging slightly more quickly. Soon they found themselves at the head of the spread out line of hastily armed monks. As they passed each of the small groups of brothers which constituted the living and moving line, they offered words of praise, encouragement and thanks. Surprisingly, extremely little was offered in return, just the odd nod of the head or merest grunt of acknowledgement. The monks were wary; they were preoccupied, having just two things on their minds. First, they knew that passing between the two monasteries was not just a simple journey for them. They were aware that immediately after they arrived at their destination they would have to lie prostrate on the floor of the oratory and as the abbot himself had instructed, 'ask for the prayers of all for any faults that may have overtaken them on their journey such as sight or hearing of an evil thing or of chatter.' Secondly, they also knew that instead of opening their hearts and minds to their beloved God, they would be hiding in wait for the Norse men, before trying to send each and every one of them to the fires and cauldrons of hell.

∞ ∞ ∞

After the boats had pulled their way laboriously out of the open sea and into the wide and gaping mouth of the river that Olaf knew to be called the Tyne, their sails were taken down. Olaf had particularly enjoyed their passage past the Farne isles and of course Lindisfarne for two reasons. First, he smiled as he imagined the horror of the monks if they happened to be looking out to sea and secondly the thought of amassing greater wealth gave him a warm feeling inside. He thought to himself, how good it was to be doing something he enjoyed and something that was so worthwhile. After all, the men of Christ were becoming more and more powerful, or at least so he had been told when he was on Hrossey and in his opinion and in the opinion of many of his folk, they needed their vast wealth to be cut. Their type would become dangerous in time if not checked, he thought. Slowing them down a little now, was no bad idea and the gold and silver that could be had off them would be most useful.

All of the men on board seemed to take heart and acquire extra strength, possibly for the reason they were not far from their destination and they knew it. They were now pulling on their oars with gusto, willing their boats onwards, beneath a friendly pale blue sky. Distant and completely inoffensive white clouds that hung almost motionless over a far southern horizon appeared to be receding ever so slightly, at a rate that could hardly be measured by the human eye. The perfect sapphire dome high above them looked however, to be threatened by an uninvited change of weather that had been brewing darkly and unseen somewhere to the north in the land of the Picts. A thin and well defined line of dark clouds just above the horizon could be made out and it was clear that this weather front was beginning to move towards them with increasing speed. To seasoned travellers' eyes this meant a coming of wind and rain. All of those rowing on the boats had noticed that a change in the weather was afoot, but this was just something else that had to be kept in mind. Olaf as the leader of the Norse group narrowed his eyes and thought that at least if the clouds brought a storm with them, then it would be better if it broke whilst the boats were in the more sheltered and protected enclave provided by the high tidal banks of the river they had just entered. It might also help with the raid as the monks would be more likely to be inside and therefore unaware of their approach. The dragon prow of his *drakkar* could be seen, he knew, by people working in the fields from quite a way off as it made its way along the inland waterway.

Small waves of brown water of the lazy swollen river slapped heavily against the sides of the six boats that now made their way rather more slowly up river. The tide had clearly just changed and was now going out, with the result that the men were having to pull very hard on the oars just to keep the boats still, in the sucking and swirling waters. Olaf watched the near grassy bank slide ever so slowly past the oar holes. Oars moved backwards and forwards with a rhythm so natural that it appeared to mimic the motion of the swans' wings that were suddenly beating frantically overhead before disappearing as quickly as they had appeared behind a cluster of trees not too distant on the northern bank.

'When will we arrive at the monastery?' Spjall quizzed Olaf who unusually for him stood near to the front of his *drakkar*, with his black leather skull cap dangling from his hand. The other *drakkar* and *knarr* were now in a single line that snaked this way and that through the tidal waters of the river. One of the *knarr* had been roped to the rear of the last *drakkar* as it had been shipping water and was becoming slower and more difficult to handle. The two boys who worked as bailers had been working hard, but were making little impression.

'*Undorneykt, undorneykt,*' (Afternoon, afternoon) Olaf's reply seemed detached from the question he had been asked a few seconds before. Spjall however, smiled contentedly at the answer, as he was looking forward to the forthcoming activities at the monastery that afternoon.

Olaf was suddenly struck by his own words and then with the realisation that the time for plunder was very near. Accordingly, he ordered all his boats to the northern bank, where they tied up to allow the men to have one final briefing prior to mayhem that was bound to follow. Olaf was a realist and he knew from past experience that things never go exactly to plan. It was, he thought, as though the gods enjoyed meddling in the affairs of men and changed the ways that things happened to make them more interesting. Always expect the unexpected; that was one of Olaf's maxims. He cast his mind back through the years to when he played the game of hnefetafl with Hjaumlaug, his mother's great friend. The great game of strategy had taught him much about conflict and the range of seemingly endless permutations that might arise during any armed engagement.

The boats took but a little time to deck out for battle; with the shields of all the men being tied to the sides of the boats. Such an arrangement was prudent, as it meant that these circles of wood could help prevent any arrows or even spears of any defenders striking the rowers as they would approach the rough timber quays. In addition, by putting them in such a position, they would then be easily accessible to the Norse men as they leapt out of their boats to begin their gruesome work.

Weapons were sharpened and greased lovingly by their owners, who tended to use favourite or particular stones for this purpose. Huge numbers of throwing axes, mattocks, spears, swords, saxes and other strange shaped blades glinted in the hurrying, passing pockets of sunlight. Each and every owner closely inspected cutting edges to ensure that they were still fit for their purpose. Tightly fitting skull caps of both metal and leather were pulled on, as well as other pieces of protective clothing. Out of the numerous *húðfat* that had seemingly magically appeared from below the decks of the boats were quite a few bearskins, the possession of which confirmed that their owners were the elite fighters; the renowned berserkers. Olaf nodded his head towards his men in recognition of the fact that a good proportion of them were simply the best at their trade; a trade that could be measured in the vast amount of blood and carnage they had managed to and certainly would spill.

Mead and strong ale was being drunk by many of the Norse, including some of their women, whilst others still also hungrily ate mouthfuls of dried mushrooms of several sizes and types. These were to increase the vision and skill of these men as fighters and also to fend off any possible fear that may arise in them. All of these men were berserkers; some with bearskins of greatly different condition upon which they now sat. Others simply lay on the grass, stripped to the waist, whilst they waited for the powerful hallucinogens to take effect. The other Norse and their women made sure they were well away from these men as their reputation as fighters and womanisers was second to none. Some men were having their skins decorated with dark bluish tattoos or paints of the same hue, which swirled up their arms. Within the delicate inky patterns some had a number of runes inserted. These spelt out the name of their woman, whilst others had the name of the monastery they were to sack on their forearms. So it was that Olaf ended up having ᚵᚢᛦᚢᛁ inscribed on his non fighting arm. He looked at the runes suspiciously and said quietly to himself, 'Gyrwe, let's hope Gyrwe will be remembered.'

It was inevitable that several fights would break out and they did; these were over petty things such as where the next mouthful of mead was to come from or due to profanities and coarse personal insults. More serious clashes also took place, these were drug and alcohol fuelled; reasons being one man's desire for another's woman and even long standing feuds that only were remembered at such times. It was a worrying time for Olaf; he was more than aware that he would have to get the men back on their boats once more and into Gyrwe monastery, before more blood was wasted by his own men. Three men had died, two more were mortally wounded and a further half dozen of the *Þræll* were either injured or so badly affected by the drugs they had ingested that they would be of no use in the attack.

Olaf shouted out loudly, to summon and rally his men. To help achieve this he had decided to take personal responsibility for a *blot,* to bind the men together before the frenzied assault. He summarily dispatched a young bleating lamb that had been taken from pasture to the north of the river, with his long handled axe. Holding the animal by its neck in one hand he juggled with his axe so that he held the ash shaft almost next to the blade itself. He struck the struggling and writhing tiny wool covered body just the once. Instantly, blood from the small and now still beast dripped slowly from the black blade to mingle unceremoniously with the blood of two of the men who had also been mercilessly relieved of their life by the axe's master. He had just moments before resolved two of the fiercely contested disputes between his men himself. Blood; there was a lot of it, dripped onto the long river bank grass, before Olaf shouted dry throated to his men to get back on to their boats. 'We are all here together, we are the Norse and now by the gods, we row! We attack, we burn, we plunder, we kill, we take and then and only then do we leave. Listen to me men. You will all do well to listen!'

Olaf raised his axe high above his head and when he had the full attention of his warriors he began.

'I know of the eleventh magic rune:
When I lead trusted comrades in arms to fight,
I can chant its words behind my shield,
And unwounded they will go to battle,
Unwounded they will come from battle,
Untouched by any blade wherever they may be!

I know of the thirteenth magic rune:
If I throw a bowl of water over a warrior,
He shall not fall in the cruellest of battles,
Nor sink beneath the sword.'

The *Prœll* began to cheer wildly, almost hysterically and without thought of any kind jumped into the boats enthused by their master's simple words. They pulled wildly at their oars and for once it was in an unsynchronised fashion, sometimes banging blades together and sometimes ineffectually splashing the surface of the disturbed water. In normal circumstances they would have waited for the master of their boat to call the order for rowing to begin and then and only then would they all have began to pull at the same time. Usually, the boat would have been carefully manoeuvred into a position where the signal could be given for combined and concerted rowing. Olaf realised the problem immediately and signalled to the men in charge of each of the boats, to have them untied as quickly as possible, so they could drift clear of the bank. These men knew better than to become inebriated, as their lives and all of their fellow men's depended on their abilities at the helm. In addition, Olaf had forbid them from indulging in drink before an assault and this decree was more than enough of a deterrent for each man. It was not a wise thing to do to cross or disobey the master.

The men were still pulling on the oars and remained unaware of the steersmen's problems; they simply pulled and pulled with innate well rehearsed action. Some of the steersman cursed the mass of unthinking men on their boats and shouted all sorts of profanities at them; unthinkable words and names. This didn't matter at all to the *Þræll* of course, as they were so full of mind expanding and at the same time numbing substances that they simply continued to pull wildly, oblivious of everything outside of their immediate being. They sweated, they pulled, they swore, they spat, but above all, they cried to their gods for inspiration and strength in the battle. They knew of course that if they were meant to die here, then they would do so. Their concern was to fight bravely and if they were to die, to be remembered for their valour. All any man could ask for was that his name lived on after he had gone. *Loki, Óðinn* and *Þórr's* name could be heard every few moments as the men steadied their own minds and reminded their gods of their fervent and unbreakable allegiance.

ℰℴ   ℰℴ   ℰℴ

Snorri refuses to sleep or at least tells me that he cannot and demands the end of the tale. He insists on knowing how the Norse conduct themselves in this conflict. He wants to know if the brothers of God will have his help. In short, he insists I carry on into the small hours with my tale. He would know now, if Olaf has the devil himself on his heels, but he, like you my friend, must be patient. Wait and you'll see all in but a little while!

Chapter 14

Sumar, Miðsumarblót, tuttugu ok þriði, heyannir

Gyrwe Monastery
23rd June, Beltane, 794 A.D.

"Listen carefully, my son, to the Master's instructions, and attend to them with the ear of your heart. This is advice from a father who loves you; welcome it, and faithfully put it into practice. The labour of obedience will bring you back to him from whom you had drifted through the sloth of disobedience. This message of mine is for all, and armed with the strong and noble weapons of obedience to do battle for the true king, Christ the Lord."

(Rule of St. Benedict, Prologue, verses 1-3)

In all, about three hundred and fifty monks were hiding in various places inside and around the monastic community of Gyrwe. All of the brothers; oblates, novices and monks carried weapons of different description. In addition, quite a number of men not directly attached to the monastery, but who worked the land nearby had also taken up arms. Some, just a few of their number, had ancient swords that had been handed down to them by their forbears. Others still, gripped the smooth wooden handles of their axes. These had been soundly attached to curved darkened blades that had keen and silvery edges. Such sharpness was due to the frequent attention given to these tools by their masters, who used them almost daily on willow and other trees that punctuated the banks of the Wear and Done.

Abbot Ethelbald had taken himself south with Prior Eanfrith and four other of his senior monks. Wilfred in contrast, was lying in the long and wet grass under a low thorny hedge at the very side of one of the pasture fields, which adjoined the river. He was not just thinking of the abbot, but cursing his soul; musing to himself that the abbot had gone to preserve himself, whilst the likes of him had to unquestioningly put their bodies on the line for the church of St. Paul. Wilfred was not at all happy. He felt the burning injustice of it penetrating into his being and at the same time realised the complete hopelessness of the present situation. The Norse, he concluded were more than a match for the combined strength of his brothers and now the time was nearly upon them.

Ethelbald had coincidentally concluded the same and thus because of his position had been able to make his rapid retreat with his small, but carefully selected entourage. A scout had returned not long before, to confirm his worst suspicions and tell him of the six ships that were making their way up the river towards little Gyrwe. 'South is good, for the Norse are coming from the east and may be, just may be some of them will come from the north as well. I would not care to entertain such a host; the heathen filth have no business with me or should I say us. Abbot Higbald of Lindisfarne, bless him, he has given me all the inspiration for preservation I need. We, brothers of our most holy church in Christendom, St. Paul's must keep our minds pure and be ready to aid our fellow brothers after the Norse have departed.' The prior a man of about the same age as the abbot raised an eyebrow at his superior's suggestion, seeing his feeble excuse for what it really was. His subterfuge did nothing to hide the miserable cowardice that dwelled in his scheming and selfish soul. Eanfrith felt his skin prickle and a deep dull churning pain in his stomach. At the same time his mouth became strangely dry in the way it always did when he was nervous or when he had to carry out one of his frequent penitences before the abbot. He asked in a hoarse voice.

'Are you sure that our Lord would wish for us to take this course, my abbot?'

At first, the abbot appeared not to have heard this question, but then turned his twisted face towards his junior before replying in the quietest of whispers. His voice was almost inaudible, but stench of his breath was such that it very nearly matched his malice. 'Brother, if you would like to return to the church of our dearest saint, then you should go. Yes, I can see your soul is troubled my son. It would be good, I think, for you to follow your calling and also for our monastery. Join our brave brethren I say, yes, that is it, I command you to lead them to a magnificent and glorious victory over the Northmen. Go now, I say, do as you must!' The abbot's response was such that his immediate deputy, the prior had little choice but to carefully retrace his footsteps back through the meadows to the peaceful small church that had reputedly been built by masons from Gaul.

On his way back he felt almost relieved; he walked with a slight spring in his step and was oblivious to the light rain that now fell, but noticed instead the thousands of bright yellow buttercups that shone out almost defiantly in the grass. It felt to him as though a heavy and unwieldy burden had been lifted from his shoulders and he considered light heartedly that he would no longer have to be in the company of the vile man who purportedly carried out God's will for little Gyrwe's monastic community. He pondered the possibility he would meet his death at the hand of some heathen swine, but at least he knew he would not die a coward in the eyes of his pure God; his belief would, he knew, carry him through.

Wilfred was the first monk at Gyrwe to notice the prior making his way up the greenway that led northwards and back to the monastery. He instinctively called out to the man, because for that moment he didn't see a prior or indeed any church dignitary, but just a smiling seemingly happy man hurrying towards the place of where his soul wanted to be; his beloved church. Wilfred had no reason to ask why he had returned, but instead crossed himself and thanked God for this little sign; a sign that showed that there may be hope after all. Surely, Wilfred thought, trying so hard to convince himself, God would not make the prior return, just to let him be slaughtered in front of his fine glass windowed stone church.

'Ora et labora.' The prior's first words to Wilfred washed over him and once more emphasised the purity of the man's thoughts and his actions. Prayer and work were of course the bedrock of the entire Benedictine community. Wilfred smiled instinctively for the sound of those little words gave him both comfort and at the same time reinforced his beliefs. God would help them, he knew, he just knew he would. Just after the words had been spoken, a large crow which happened to be flying past, harshly called out twice as though to mock the prior's beliefs.

'The abbot has sent me back, to lead us to victory!' Prior Eanfrith's dry throated statement rushed over Wilfred and left him cold. God had played no part in the brave man's return, it was it seemed just another cruel twist of fate; Wilfred felt utterly bereft. This good man's return was simply the result of an order hatched from the blackened bile of their leader. Wilfred instinctively reached for the smooth leather bottle he had been given earlier that day. It contained a good two hemina of wine. Passing it unthinkingly to Eanfrith, he listened with baited breath. In hushed tones, the prior whispered, that only through the greatest of suffering would come enlightenment and only through hardship could true humility be found. Even so, he took several large draughts of the strong liquid that ran down to temporarily burn his throat. Stopping drinking, he choked, coughed and spluttered, before meeting Wilfred's gaze, with tears welling in his eyes.

'Apologies prior, but this wine is too bold and not at all good for quenching a thirst.' Wilfred's concern amused the prior, who shook uncontrollably whilst laughing loudly.

'Thank you, Brother, both for your thoughts and for your drink. The wine is truly excellent. It is as good as any I have ever tasted. In other happier circumstances and better weather, I think I would like to sit under that willow tree, that one over there and idly drink a hemina and then possibly another. Naturally, I would invite you my fellow Brother to join me, so we could discuss the way of the world, the lives of the saints and all that is good and even ponder some of that which is bad.'

'I would like that my Prior. But then our Lord would surely consider it sloth and idleness. Would he not?' Wilfred's answer betrayed the fact he felt slightly bemused by such a suggestion.

'Well he may think that, or he may not. Perhaps he would be too busy worrying about the soul of our dearest abbot, who is at this moment probably doing exactly what I suggested to you that we may do. We may think about sloth and idleness, but he, our dear and beloved and blessed leader actually indulges in such things. You and I should pray for the repose of his soul, for I consider that a lot of prayer will be needed if he is to enter into the kingdom of our Lord.'

'Are you suggesting?' Wilfred began, but his question was never completed, for the reason that from the corner of his eye, he could see something sliding smoothly, ever so smoothly into his line of sight. 'There over there,' he began again, 'it is the first of the boats, look, and see how big they really are.'

The prior who had been sitting with his back to the river that was still swollen from the tide, slowly turned the upper part of his body in order to see the arrival of the first *drakkar* and *knarr* that surely brought with them the curse of the Norse.

'Well this is it and there's no mistake.' The prior seemed relieved that what was to happen, would soon unfold.

℘℘℘℘℘℘

On 'Gjálfrmarr,' the very first of the *drakkar* to arrive, Olaf had shouted to some of the men to stop pulling on their oars. Those sitting on the side of the *drakkar* nearest to the bank simply allowed the blades of their oars to hang limply in the water, whilst those on the other side had lifted their oars clear of the water and pulled them as upright as they could manage. The momentum of the boat coupled with the drag of the oars ensured that the vessel began to swing around in the water on an invisible pivot, to end up perfectly alongside the small wooden jetty that had been carefully built to protrude into the tidal river's shallow and muddy waters. Olaf had practised this manoeuvre so many times over the years that it came as naturally to him as swinging his long handled axe. He had very rarely experienced any problems with either of these actions; they were as natural to him as the drawing of breath.

It was the master himself who was the first to leap onto the somewhat crudely built wooden structure. Olaf was fully armed for battle. His head was covered in a tightly fitting leather skull cap and his upper body covered in a snug fitting leather jerkin. His recently tattooed left arm was smarting and still felt to him as though his skin had been either scorched by fire or scalded by boiling water. He had tried to relieve the area of irritation; the patch of ink-needled and tortured flesh, by spitting into one of his large hands and rubbing the bubbly liquid into the smarting area. When he had finished doing this, with his left hand, he picked up his round wooden shield by the thick leather strap attached to its back. In his right hand, he casually held his long handled axe. The wooden shaft and bog iron head seemed a natural extension of his arm. It moved and swung in such a harmony with his arm and body to suggest that Olaf had spent most of his life attached to the weapon. It was a part of him.

He stood on the rickety old jetty in the light of a fading summer's afternoon, which was now threatened with the approach of a storm. Something dawned on him. In that briefest of moments, his mind travelled back to the panic of Lindisfarne a whole year before. That day had been warm with a good breeze and the arrival of their ships had caused such a reaction that the contrast with today could not have been more vivid. Now, there was no harsh bell sounding, there were no monks to be seen. Also, there were no labourers tending to the small monastery's fields, in actual fact no people any description were to be seen going about their daily tasks. To the Norse, the only visible and audible sign of life were a large grey long coated hound that bounded playfully up and down the river bank whilst barking loudly at the boats and a group of five or six geese. These were moving slowly in a direction away from the dog that seemed to have disturbed and annoyed them. The dishevelled and hungry looking beast seemed genuinely pleased to see the men in their boats. Olaf in contrast, was somewhat rather less enthusiastic about the dog's presence, considering it to be just another unneeded irritation. '*Loki*, I'll wager. That beast is here to warn us or trick us.'

Spjall hesitated before replying to his master. 'It's just not right. Where are they all? They should be swarming all over the place like ants whose nest has been disturbed.'

'Ants, that's right. Perhaps our little ants are hiding underground somewhere. Or more likely they've scattered themselves far and wide into the countryside. Whatever they've done, they've done it because they have been warned. Chances are that all the gold and silver of that little church of theirs over there has gone with them into nothingness.' Olaf's tone of voice barely concealed the irritation he was feeling. 'It'll have been that blasted slave who escaped us, from Orkney. It'll be his doing, I'll wager. He has somehow made his way here; his wretched body driven all this way by some picture that is lodged in his head; an image of his lord nailed to the tree. Why in *Óðinn's* name should he do it? Why should he care so much? There's nothing in it for him, but certain death, if he chances to come upon us again.'

'He can't have got here or sent a message all this way surely?' Spjall tried to reassure his master. 'If he has, then he's not interested in anything for himself as you already know master. All the monks own nothing. They have no interest in worldly possessions. I've heard they have only one change of clothes. That's all they're allowed.'

'Spjall, all you say is true. However, the time for learned debate on the ways of the brown cassocked monks lies elsewhere. We must see what the church has to offer us and then we'll burn the lot. If it burns here, we'll burn it.' Olaf's irritation had now grown into a rage; a blinding rage that was so red that it distorted or eradicated any logical thoughts that may have been trying to form in his mind.

'Some monk or other I heard about had three gold coins of his own which he kept year after year hidden in his little cell. The story goes that just before he died, he confessed all to one of his brothers. His sin was considered so great that the poor devil's gold was thrown into the shit pit along with his body.'

'Shut up about the bloody monks will you. I'll put them all in their pissing shit pit when I catch the bastards.' Olaf now shouted to the men to ready themselves to fight. 'Men we may not be able to see the blasted enemy, the scum are hiding somewhere, but I can smell them, each and every one of them. Have your shields and weapons to hand. It'll not be long before we are cutting them down like a copse of weedy saplings that needs thinning. Remember just this; only spare the young strong ones and any women worth saving.'

Olaf and some forty of his men ran slowly down the short jetty and onto the small stones that had been spread out on the earthen bank to prevent the area becoming a muddy and difficult mess to cross, when it rained. The big dog now ran away yelping as though having being summoned by a distant master's inaudible whistle. The gaggle of geese, in contrast, made their way towards the heavily armoured Norse and began spitting and hooting, to make a terrible commotion. At that exact moment, the first of many large and heavy raindrops began to splatter on the planking on the wooden jetty, leaving large dark blood-like stains.

The weather was turning quite stormy and it was turning rather quickly. The sky had changed from being a sullen pewter colour moments before to become so dark that it seemed the sun had become temporarily eclipsed by some unseen and vast force that was more powerful than nature itself. The black and grey clouds seemed to tumble over one another in a violent frenzy, indicating the arrival of strong powerful and erratic winds. Out of habit, Olaf sniffed the air so as to drink in the slightly bitter smell of the advancing rain. He had always enjoyed its distinctive smell, likening it, to the amusement of his close friends, with the odour of bog iron or fresh blood. Now however, the mind of the leader of the Norse raiding party was otherwise occupied.

The waves in the river were growing, the wind was beginning to pull on the boats rather erratically and rain was now beginning to lash down, to soak and seemingly damn everything in little Gyrwe. This is not going to be the way things are meant to be, Olaf thought, scratching at a hidden louse in his beard, before cursing terribly to himself, 'This way men! Come on, for *Óðinn's* sake get a move on, let's make this slaughter as quick as possible. Boys, hear me, we don't want our weapons out in the rain too long. Let's kill some of those pasty faced Christians! To their church! First, we go to their church.' With that rallying cry of encouragement he started running towards the stone building that was the heart of the small monastic community, unwittingly dispersing several of the noisy and angry geese as he did so.

He couldn't run that quickly due to the combined weight of his protective clothing and that of his assorted array of weaponry. This included a short handled axe, a desperately sharp sax, a pattern welded sword and his solid long handled axe; his favourite and most trusty weapon. In spite of his words of enthusiasm, he cursed to himself; nothing here seemed right and he knew it. Gripping his faithful old axe in his right hand, he loped towards the church swearing vile and meaningless curses as he went.

The men on the other boats were oblivious to their master's chagrin and were still either floating aimlessly about on the river or were slowly moving their boats to line up with 'Gjálfrmarr.' Now that Olaf was no longer on his *drakkar*, there seemed to be no one capable of assuming any leadership or at the very least anyone who could possibly manage to get the boats sorted out and tied up. There was a complete lack of urgency and clearly no plan had been shared with the men. Time drifted and passed interminably with the *Þræll* making no or very little progress. These men were completely unaware of the movement of the group that had already assembled on the bank.

Olaf's band of men was some fifty paces from the church and it progressed as a tight group; most of the men were snarling and shouting riotously in their drunken state. Weapons had already been drawn and some of the men, those fuelled with drink and drugs now held sharpened iron blades above their heads in a frantic and fevered blood lust. The fervent anticipation of glory soon to be won drove them blindly onwards.

ℰꙄ   ℰꙄ   ℰꙄ

Inside the small church nothing moved save a small brown mouse that scurried to and fro in search of any meagre morsel it may find. As it moved about, in those exact moments, the sunlight which was penetrating strongly through the small stained glass windows, shone brightly on its tiny little body, giving to its fur unearthly or possibly heavenly colours. One second it took on a yellow hue, the next crimson the next a deep purple colour and then suddenly it was yellow again. The tiny body moved rather more hesitantly now over the dark ruddy coloured tiled floor as if concerned or in the very least, it behaved nervously for some reason. Suddenly it stopped moving altogether, before shooting off at great speed to disappear under some wooden benching at the back of the small rectangular building. The beams of light that had so briefly penetrated the sanctuary of the church suddenly dimmed; to dissipate so wholly and rapidly that the interior of the building plunged into a great and foreboding darkness.

Only seconds later, two large and calloused hands lifted the heavy rope-like cast iron ring that adorned the great oak door of the church. They twisted the circlet of heavy metal violently this way and that in a vain attempt to unite the assembled heathens on the outside with the peace and tranquillity of the inside; the house of the Christian god. Olaf swore violently and blasphemed his profanities terribly against the one god whom it seemed had decided not to allow him to carry off any of his gold this time. 'Bastards, they're up to something and there's no mistake.' The mouse at that very moment forced itself through a small opening in the masonry at the base of the wall and in the blink of an eye was making its way through the closely cropped grass at the rear of the church of St. Paul. Several sandals moved; their owners unwittingly altering the mouse's route of escape.

The monks, there were at least sixty of them here were huddled up against the far wall of the church, somewhat sheltered from the rain that was falling. They had been in their chosen hiding position for quite some time and had witnessed the rapid deterioration of the weather. Whispers had passed between the brothers of the Benedictine Order that their lord was passing judgement on the godless men of the north. 'He' was showing his displeasure by fashioning a storm, a storm that would preoccupy the heathens and keep their thoughts away from any ambush that may have been laid for them. The brief and unexpected beam of light that had moments before penetrated the swirling clouds, to illuminate the church, had suddenly been extinguished returning the church to its previous dull grey hue.

A bright flash of lightning, momentarily light up the church and its surroundings once more, to be followed almost instantly by an ear splitting crack of thunder, which ripped and rolled across the river valley. At this precise moment, several of the Norse men were running around to the back of the church to check if there was another entrance and also if there were any stray monks to be felled. The startled helmeted few were met by a wall of brown cassocked men who were each and every one of them variously armed. Before any cry of warning could be issued from any of the few Norse, pitchforks and staves held by the brothers at the front had met the surprised men with a force that could scarcely have been imagined. Once the startled men had been knocked to the ground, they stood absolutely no chance, as thick and unforgiving ends of stout sticks bludgeoned into them, splitting lips, smashing noses and teeth and breaking skulls. Rather perversely, the brethren seemed to enjoy exacting this punishment, one which their all-forgiving god so demanded.

Brother Wilfred and Prior Eanfrith had seen nothing of the first melee and were instead thinking what exactly they should do. From their vantage spot near to the river bank they could see the first wisps of smoke that were; they understood the hallmarks of any Norse raid. The outhouses were being set on fire; to see if that would provoke a response from the apparently deserted community. Spjall with about twenty men had smashed his way into a number of dwellings some hundred or so paces from the church and on finding them empty had decided to torch them. The wind was getting up, but even so the rain was doing its level best to disrupt the fire raising proceedings. Spjall felt miserable as he looked at the rather plain little shacks that passed as houses. They couldn't have been very comfortable to live in he thought and they certainly didn't burn at all well. The roofs of three were now alight, but the heavy drops of rain that now fell, dampened the lively dancing of the flames. The straw and rafters smouldered, to produce voluminous quantities of blue and brownish smoke that was pushed away from them by a rapid and chilling wind. It may have been the middle of summer, but it felt more like a late autumnal day in Hordaland.

Just about all of the Norse men, apart from those whose duties involved looking after the boats were ashore now. Some were clearly in a wild and frantic frenzy and they made their way this way and that calling out to invisible spirits and cursing anyone or thing that that came into their line of vision. A number of conflicts had broken out between some of the confused and more intoxicated Norse, who simply wished to draw their blades and fight. They didn't care who they fought as long as they would be allowed to wield their axes or swords. Several berserkers were also making their way for some inexplicable reason along the river bank in exactly the opposite direction to the church.

Wilfred had spotted them and knew instantly that his and the prior's hiding place was soon to be discovered by one of these terribly confused men. Instinctively he whispered, but then realising the noise of the growing storm, shouted several desperate words of warning to the prior. The reaction from Prior Eanfrith was not in the slightest what Wilfred had expected. Instead of crawling away on his hands and knees in the way the abbot surely would have done, he stood up defiantly in full view of the approaching men. The Norse soldiers however, were so engrossed in the search for hidden monks and were at the same time so intoxicated, that they failed to see the calm and serenely still figure of a man, who stood barely fifteen paces ahead of them. Wilfred knew instinctively exactly what he had to do and without prompting rapidly crawled away under the hedge to signal to five or six of his fellow monks as he went. His simple unspoken plan seemed fortunately to make complete sense to the monks. They had seen their prior stand up and they knew that this act of bravery was one that may just help them all.

It all happened so quickly that Wilfred later found it difficult to recount what exactly had gone on. The first of the two berserkers, wearing a bearskin around his body had stopped, completely taken aback by the effrontery of this monk who seemed to have appeared from nowhere. A long handled axe was raised high above the huge bearded man's head. Shouting abuse, the drug crazed Norse man staggered towards Prior Eanfrith with the clear intention of severing his head from his shoulders with one mighty blow. The other berserker was several paces behind him; he was bare-chested and armed with just a *sax* and a small round black shield; he looked on in glee. His expression was fixed into a most wickedly smile or death like grimace. Before the axe had a chance to be buried in the neck of the prior, a blade had cut its way through the tendon at the back of the leading Norse man's ankle. He felt no pain or appeared not to have done, but instead tried to carry on rushing towards his target. He limped and trailed blood and only when a second more damaging blow smote his other leg, did he turn to see the cassocks of the monks who were now upon him. The rain of blows on his body soon incapacitated him, but did little to stop the violent assault of his comrade. Six monks armed with staves, pitch forks and axes of their own, made little impression on the man whose strength seemed beyond imagination.

As the monks surrounded the snarling Norse creature, he turned and turned flailing his desperately sharp sax blade at them. One stave punched its way into his ribs, but bounced off him as though his body were immune to such crude weaponry. Only when the same stave end finally rammed hard into the back of his head, was any advantage seized upon by the monks. Momentarily, the blow appeared to have awoken the man living inside the body of the wild berserker; his eyes widened and rolled back in their sockets.

The monks couldn't help but pull back, in awe at the strength and resilience of their pugnacious prey. A pitch fork had now plunged into the Norse man's right leg, perforating the lightly tanned skin and lodging itself deep inside the twitching muscle. Instinctively throwing his shield at the monk whose fork had injured him, the berserker desperately grabbed at the rusty prong that was buried in his leg. He stared wild-eyed at his assailants and at the same time carelessly pulled the offending shaft of brownish metal straight out of his own flesh, in a brutal uncaring and unthinkingly violent act. Blood poured and pulsed out of the gaping scarlet wound to run eagerly down his still twitching leg and onwards to cover his knee. He still felt no pain and moved more or less as though his leg had received no wound of such a serious nature. Grinding his teeth together defiantly he advanced on the monk who had lunged at him with the fork, determined to despatch him from this world. The sax in his bloodied hand moved this way and that in high and well formed curves; it seemed to slice through the very fabric of the air itself.

The Norse man's back, due to his advances was now wholly unprotected and it was here that the three monks behind him now concentrated their combined efforts. A welter of hammer blows struck him repeatedly, but still apparently took little toll. His advances were such that the blade of his sax was now running with the blood of two other Benedictine brothers. The handle by which he held his chosen weapon was so wet and slippery with dark congealing blood that he was having quite some difficulty holding on to it, let alone gripping it for the purposes of fighting. One of the monks whom he had seconds earlier met for the first time was now lying face upwards in the grass with his eyes still wide open. He no longer drew breath however, but gazed unseeingly up as his fellow brother received the same blessing of the Norseman's blade across the back of his neck. A fountain of blood arched over the sword arm of the berserker who was now in the throws of a terrible and unsustainable blood lust. More and more blows cascaded down on his leather skull capped head and on his upper body. The Norse man's will to carry on fighting and causing death seemed to Wilfred to be utterly inexhaustible, but as with life there comes a time when things change; a change that lasts forever. Minutes passed and the fracas continued wildly, until suddenly and with no warning, the Norse man stopped wielding his blade. The monks carried on smashing him with their sticks for several seconds before they too stopped, with the sudden realisation that he was no longer fighting back in any way.

He dropped his bloodied *sax* and without warning gripped desperately at his chest with both his hands. Opening his mouth wide as though to shout, he drank in what was to be his last breath. His furrow browed gape showed that many of his teeth were gone. Before exhaling noisily whilst at the same time trying to shout out one last defiant cry, he spat out several yellowed teeth; teeth that he himself had so recently broken off, whilst gritting them powerfully together in the terrible throws of battle. Dropping to his knees heavily, but with no mortal wound apparently upon his contorted and twitching body, he slipped out of *Midgard* to follow his fellow berserker across the rainbow bridge of *Bifrost* and into some remote hall in *Asgard* in just the way a drunken man may fall and drift from consciousness into a heavy and dark slumber. He would now continue to practise his fighting in readiness for *Ragnarok*.

ဢ ဢ ဢ

Prior Eanfrith's reaction to this small victory seemed out of all proportion. He clenched his fists and admonished the heinous devils who had come to his abbey. Wilfred had seen this sort of reaction before, but it had been in the Norse homelands. Bloodlust was not at all what he expected to see in a man of God. As these thoughts passed through his mind, he was momentarily distracted by a noise that was coming from somewhere near to the church itself. It seemed to Wilfred that a large number of his brown cassocked brethren had suddenly appeared from nowhere and were now meeting the Norse folk who had made their way uninvited to St. Paul's'. There were cries, shouts and finally the clash of metal on metal and metal on wood. Swords Wilfred noted seemed to make a less resonant, slightly more high-pitched sound than that of the axes that thudded dully on impact.

Olaf was for the first time in his life truly surprised by the massive onslaught that came to greet his men. His weapons were to hand of course, but he really wasn't expecting to be using them quite so soon. Even so, he didn't shirk from the wall of Benedictine souls that came to wipe out the sons of *Óðinn*. Instead, he rallied his men with a deep shout to attempt to bring them to their senses. It worked to some extent, but at least half a dozen of so of his group were so confused by the various mushrooms they had ingested that a solidly formed wall of defence was not remotely possible. These crazed men created unwelcome gaps in the skjaldborg or line of shields that had instinctively been raised to prevent immediate death. In just seconds, the improvised army of monks was upon them, raining down blows from diverse instruments of conflict. Surprisingly, the unreceptive Norse men who had prevented the tight wall formation were in themselves quite a deterrent that even Olaf as leader could not have guessed at. They happened to be quite apart from one another and their detached and horrible screams and shouts seemed to wholly unnerve the younger of the monks. Three of these men had thrown their shields at the enemy preferring to do battle with weapon; axe in all of their cases and with no defence. One had even pulled off the bearskin he was wearing to fight in nothing other than his grubby short woollen trousers. Cursing profanely and uttering as many insults as his befuddled mind would allow, he advanced on the cassocked brethren wielding his axe in great swinging semi-circles in the air.

'Keep it tight men! Keep it tight, as tight as you can!' Olaf's voice was nearly lost in the tumult of raucous percussive sound. Clearly, the monks were not used to such conflict and once the shouted Norse order had been responded to, the tonsured men were rapidly pushed back. At least a score of men had fallen already, the majority of whom had been wearing wooden crucifixes. Even so, numbers were still heavily on the side of the men of St. Paul. The Norse who lay on the ground were dead, wounded or simply stupefied with drink or hallucinogens. Olaf watched incredulously as a retreating monk smashed the skull of one of his comrades with a metal tipped staff. The Norse man who appeared to bear no external wounds jerked at the blow, to reveal he was possibly a victim of his own making. The master would never know though, as the man could no longer answer for himself.

Whilst this singular act of violence was committed, the hasty retreat of the monks actually stopped. Incredibly they were on the advance again, propped up by greater numbers who seemed to be streaming into the fight from unseen hidden areas. Blowing heavily now, Olaf called out to Spjall, whom he had seen with about a score of men. They were beyond the monks, fighting on slightly higher land away towards some burning dwellings. The monks would see a true slaughter now, he thought as he raised his axe again and again. He had more than a little time to parry the blows aimed at him, for he fought so skilfully and with such speed and aggression that the comparatively poorly trained brothers could hardly get close enough to him to deliver blows of any merit. Those strokes that did succeed in getting near to him were usually fended off skilfully with the side of the shaft of his axe. The hooks of his axe now dripped with the purest blood of the Benedictine Order. Spjall, cried out in acknowledgement to his friend and master, but sadly his words were lost to the noise of the storm that was still growing. Rain was lashing down now. The monks' cassocks were absorbing the rain water and the fabric was starting to hang limply off their emaciated bodies, accentuating their thin frames; most brothers clearly had just about enough to eat to carry on with their godly pursuits. The Norse were also being affected by the relentless downpour, leather skull caps darkened and slipped, as did the leather shoes that covered the feet of these men. Both sides blinked as rain splashed into their eyes, both gripped their weapons with renewed vigour and both suffered losses.

The men with Spjall; Olaf could make out two of them, Guðbjörn and Geirhjálmr had just released their throwing spears, aided by the *snærisspjót* that they all carried. The accuracy and power achieved by the men who were running was devastating. Spears tore through the air and landed unerringly, penetrating the thin wool of the monks' cassocks, their skin and deep into their flesh. Men were falling and dying in larger numbers by now and the scene looked as though the Norse would have their day after all. This day however, looked to have been singled out and blighted by the gods; the rain continued to fall with increasing intensity and no sign of brighter conditions beckoned.

The divided ranks of Norse combatants had very nearly fought their way back together to become a single combined force once more. Indeed, the men who had taken their time to get off the boats were now streaming up the creaking wooden quay in large numbers, to join in with the desperate fighting. The Norse group was swelling and becoming larger all the time and it seemed as though they were at the same time becoming better organised in spite of the atrocious weather conditions that would normally have precluded the start of any such conflict. Perhaps the effects of the strong drinks they had consumed and the mind bending toadstools and mushrooms they had consumed were beginning to wear off.

Looking across once more to see the whereabouts of Spjall, the master noticed to his considerable dismay another great cohort of monks rushing to join the fray. This new contingent was arriving not from the direction of the church, but was approaching from along the upstream river bank. 'That's clever, very clever,' Olaf cried aloud to his men, who couldn't in the circumstances work out exactly what he meant. 'That's exactly where I'd have hidden them, so when we arrived, they were well out of the way and out of sight! It is as though the commander of the monks' has played the 'king's board' and understood the power of a diversion. We'll show him though.'

Smoke and there was a lot of it about was now being driven by the rain laden wind right across the scene of conflict. The dwellings that had been set on fire were not burning at all well, but were producing copious quantities of cough inducing blue and black smoke that arrived in great swirling eddies. For a split second Olaf caught a glimpse of Spjall raising his axe, but the blow he was mustering was never dealt, as he was caught full in the throat by a pitch fork. The monk who had delivered the lunge to perpetrate Spjall's terrible injury stepped back almost amazed at what he had achieved against the armoured might of this Norse fighter. Blood spewed from a gaping wound at the side of Spjall's neck and in less than the blink of an eye he was falling forwards with his eyes turned back in their sockets, leaving them to appear even from where Olaf stood, completely white. He still seemed to grip his axe defiantly though, but it was all over for him as he slumped heavily in the thick mud that cloyed under foot. It was not just Spjall who had fallen; others around him were being cut down in increasing numbers. Geirhjálmr had lost his balance and whilst on hands and knees had been hacked to death by three monks carrying axes that were more used to the felling and chopping of wood, in the surrounding orchards.

'Back to the boats! Back to the boats!' It was not Olaf's order, but another man, Folkaðr, who seemed to believe that his master had lost not only his touch, but his ability to command. The Norse soldiers were being beaten and it appeared now they knew it. Olaf continued to fight though, as if this prospect was still an impossibility; a living nightmare. He had heard the rallying cry issued by Folkaðr and even he had responded to it, realising immediately that the unexpected shock of what was happening had temporarily nullified any decisive battle acumen he possessed. He spoke to himself again, but this time it was in disparaging tones. 'You've lost it. You've hesitated and you've been out thought, by a group of bastard monks, who haven't a decent weapon between them. Olaf Bodvarsson you have let your men and your folk down! May all the gods of *Asgard* be merciful on you!'

It wasn't quite over yet though. There were still some seventy or so Norse fighters, who were determinedly pushing their way back towards the wooden quays which they had so recently left. These men were the finest wielders of weapons and now they had a clear focus; they fought their way out or they died, there and then.

'Get those shields together and push!' Olaf's deep voice rang out and at the same time gave renewed hope to the men, who had been confused by the order issued by Folkaðr just seconds earlier. They responded with a will and force that could only have been granted by the greatest god of them all; *Óðinn*. The men at the rear turned to face their foe, whilst those at the front pushed on and attacked the massed ranks of monks, who stood between them and their salvation. The Norse fighters were now completely surrounded by a huge number of God's men. Where they had come from of course was a complete mystery to the men who were now fighting for their lives. They couldn't have possibly guessed that the information delivered to the monastery by Wilfred and the subsequent mustering of the monks had brought about this terrible rout.

The brightly coloured circular shields were tightly locked together, forming an almost impenetrable wall of shiny wet wood. Olaf shouted again, 'No gaps in the *skjaldborg*, keep the shield wall tight!' Those men locked in at the front, gripped their shields furtively, whilst at the same time they managed to muster the energy from somewhere to hack down over the top of the metallic rims of these, with their heavy long handled axes. The men directly behind them held their spears at shoulder height and every few seconds thrust these vigorously at the monks, between the heads of their own men. This fighting technique made it virtually impossible for the Benedictine brethren to injure or kill any of their Norse adversaries.

Holding firm and relentlessly surging forwards, the round iron helmed men made their way inexorably towards the boats and their craved salvation. The quay was reached and it was here the Norse nightmare worsened. It was clear that smoke was appearing from behind the Benedictine brethren on the quay, meaning that some or possibly all the boats had been put to the torch. The Norse men spear-heading the charge at the front, were forced to change their formation in order to gain access to the slippery wooden boards that constituted the structure that jutted out into the river. Only three men were able to stand shoulder to shoulder as each plank was grimly fought for and won. Several men lost their footing and slipped over the sides of the quay to land heavily on its edge, before being swallowed by the heaving swollen river.

The boats or at least what was left of them were now simply a dozen or so good strides away, when all of a sudden the last twenty monks between them and freedom chose to leave the conflict en masse. The tonsured men at the back, nearest to the *drakkars* and *knarrs* were the first to throw their makeshift weapons into the quickly moving current followed immediately by their own bodies. As they were not encumbered by weighty armour, the men in the water shouted to one another and allowed themselves to be carried downstream, presumably to a point where they could crawl out at what they considered to be a safe distance from the Norse. The remaining monks did likewise and suddenly the quay was empty of all save the surviving Norse, of whom there must have been just thirty or so.

Olaf jumped into the nearest boat; his own *drakkar* and knew instantly that it was lying rather low in the water. He cursed at the realisation that the last fleeing monks must have removed at least one of the sump plugs of his beloved dragon ship. As his men poured into the boat, he shouted to the man who was just jumping over the top strake to remove a plug from 'Aðalríkr' the nearest *knarr* and to be quick about it. 'It could be worse, the dragon could be on fire and then we'd all be on our way to Valhalla sooner than we'd like.' He spoke the words loudly but calmly showing to his men some of the qualities of a leader they had come to expect from him. The men rallied realising that he was not beaten by the situation, at least not yet. The other dragon ship lay on the outside of the *knarr*s and was burning as fiercely as the *knarr* 'ÁdiarfR,' next to it. The middle *knarr* of the three was still high in the water and free of fire. They had to be quick, if they were to make their way back to their Norse homeland.

Straight away, Gagarr did as he was ordered and in seconds had the replacement plug taken from the *knarr* next to the dragon ship and inserted before much more water had the chance to pour in. It seemed that the monks had in the final few seconds of their occupancy of the boats tried to scuttle them in the river as they lay next to the wooden quay. The bailing buckets fortunately were still there and Gagarr had had the common sense to bring with him two more from the trading vessel Olaf had clearly decided to abandon. The *bræða* or rope holding them to the quay was swiftly cut by Olaf with several hacking chops from the blade of his heavy axe and finally they were adrift. Some of the surviving men and a few women clambered across the dragon ship into the now stricken *knarr*, to make their way to the next *knarr*, the sturdy boat 'Avarr,' that was tied up to it. Of the boats that had made it to little Gyrwe, only two it seemed would be leaving with at least some of their crews. There were still many oars on the boats, in spite of the fact that a number of them had been thrown over board by the monks before they had finally given up their possession of the vessels. 'Gjálfrmarr' and 'Avarr' had barely enough crew to move effectively by use of the oar in the water. The boys and young men who had been left in charge of the boats were either missing or their bloodied bodies lay slumped in the bellies of their beloved vessels. The *drakkar* had a greater number of men, but four of these, due to the excessive amount of water taken on board, were given entirely to bailing and not rowing. Their task was not made any the easier, by the relentless rain that continued to fall and seep between the deck boards adding to the unwanted water already in the sump.

Gagarr had returned to 'Avarr' and now shouted something to Olaf, who had taken up his position at the rear of the dragon ship and could clearly see the young man, standing on the *knarr*, pulling on a long oar. He briefly stopped to wave and then pointed frantically back to the quay from where moments earlier they had made their escape. Olaf glanced over his shoulder and back at the receding quay; for now he had the ship more or less where he wanted it, in the middle of the river, with his back to and moving away from cursed Gyrwe. At first, because of the driving rain and also because he was concentrating so hard on the passage away from this terrible place, he could make out from the corner of his eye just a dark and apparently unthreatening shape on the very end of the quay. Gagarr's clear concern however made him crane his neck further and realise instantly that again the monks and other labourers associated with the monastery had planned their counter attack most cunningly. The initial shape had been of little interest to him, but now it did, because it was in fact a group of some twenty archers, who now fired off their arrows as quickly as they could at the departing boats. The dragon ship was little more than a single length away from the quay and moving very slowly as the first of many poorly aimed arrows began bouncing off the wooden planking that made up the sides of the boat. For every three or four of these feeble efforts, there was in contrast an arrow that came fast and true, to bury its iron head into the soft wood or unprotected flesh of an oarsman. The men were rowing as hard as they could and unlike Olaf could clearly see the blur of the flying wooden shafts and in response they instinctively let go of their oars to reach for their shields. These they attached as quickly and as best as they could to the sides of the boat between the oar holes. The shields of course afforded the men a degree of protection as they formed a series of semi-circles above the top strake behind which the rower could take limited shelter.

As the men struggled to complete this task, Olaf lifted an unclaimed heavily scratched black shield from the deck of the boat and slung it over his shoulders to protect his back as he desperately tried to steer 'Gjálfrmarr' to safety. The steering blade was raised up to a fairly high position, allowing the boat to be manoeuvred in shallow water, but even so the dragon responded poorly to the master's touch. He knew that for several minutes at least the ship would be in danger from the stinging arrows fired from the quay and from several other men who had taken up their positions on the muddy bank of the river nearby. 'Avarr' had done surprisingly well compared with the *drakkar*; the *knarr* had somehow managed to become free from the other doomed *knarr* and had slipped almost effortlessly into the safer reaches of deeper water in the middle of the river. It was now a good stone's throw from the *drakkar*, when Olaf realised why their passage was so sluggish. The four bailers although working as fast as it was possible to clear the water in the bottom of the boat were making no impression on the water level. Instead, one of them stood up and threw down his bailing bucket to show his utter despair and to the rowers the hopelessness of the situation. Olaf snarled at the man to keep bailing, but then stood up and shouted as loudly as he could to the *knarr* that seemed to be pulling away from the stricken *drakkar*. 'Bastard monks, they've holed her.' The rowers nearest to Olaf understood the implication immediately. The *drakkar* had, whilst the men were up at the church fighting, been damaged irreparably. One of the monks must have removed a portion of the light weight decking and clambered underneath, to hammer a hole in the planking near to the keel. The removal of the sump plug was clearly a clever ruse to make the Norse believe that the boat was seaworthy when it was not and therefore encourage them to use it for their departure. 'Gjálfrmarr' was doomed and all men and women on the boat knew it.

ဢ   ဢ   ဢ

Brothers Eadric and Godric stood soaking wet through on the river bank to look across at the burning Norse ships; the wallowing dragon ship and the small trading boat. Brother Eadric slapped his companion on the back completely oblivious to the rain that on most other days would have driven him indoors. 'Our Brother Wilfred from the Holy Isle itself may have lived the life of a Norse man, but he is clearly one of our finest Christian brothers, for his actions have saved our community. True, the church is partially burnt and many cells in the dormitory have been ruined, but we have survived a terrible onslaught of the Norse.' His words were almost blown away and lost in the wind that now tore across the river towards them. It brought with it heavy clouds of blue and black smoke from the burning boats. These scurried past and around them making them blink and cough as they did so. Brother Godric sagely nodded his head in agreement and instead of replying to his fellow brother's comment, waved his arms to attract the attention of the men below them, down on the quay. Then he pointed downstream beyond the burning boats; towards the bank. Intuitively, the men appeared to have understood and immediately they began running from the quay to make life if that was possible even more unpleasant for the failed raiders.

'Did you see our prior?' Brother Godric asked his fellow brother.

'Yes, he was away over there, with Brother Wilfred I believe,' Eadric replied, gesturing vaguely with his left hand. Brother Godric turned to view the smoking church with piles of dead and dying monks and Norse men before it, to murmur.

'He'll surely be pleased that the monastery and all its treasures are still safe.'

'Yes, the Abbot himself will no doubt heap praise upon all those who defended his blessed church in his absence.' Eadric felt little for the leader of tiny Gyrwe.

'Brother Eadric, it looks as though your work in that ship is having its effect. It is clearly taking on water and soon all the fighting heathens will be receiving a baptism of sorts after all.'

'Yes and our mighty God alone has seen fit to provide them with a storm with which to remember their raid. The smaller boat, can you see, it looks as though it is going to try to reach the one with a dragon's head. I wonder if they'll make it.'

ℰ   ℰ   ℰ

Gagarr had heard his master's shout for help and had as before responded with great speed. He had ordered the rowers on the *knarr* to push their oars, to hold the boat as still as possible in the surging waters. The *drakkar* had continued to drift downstream in the water with the aid of the men who continued to row in spite of the water that now was beginning to seep through the decking and wet their leather clad straw filled shoes. The bailers had stopped bucketing water out of the vessel minutes before and they too now rowed with any strength they had left. It was terribly sapping work compounded by appalling weather conditions; all the men felt utterly miserable and exhausted. Some men called on *Þórr* in this their darkest hour and it seemed as though he answered as a great bolt of lightning tore down and smote a tree on the south side of the riverbank. The flash was followed by a deafening crash of thunder. One large branch of the struck tree was cleanly blown off by the impact, to fall into the long wet grass. A small puff blue of smoke appeared briefly from its resting place before being dispersed by the relentless and unforgiving wind.

Guðbjörn who was nearest to the front of the sinking *drakkar* threw a rope across to the waiting *knarr*. It was caught neatly by a man leaning out over the side. He then pulled in the slack and with his feet against the top strake he heaved with all his might. Slowly but surely the two boats crept closer together until they met with a bump in the choppy waters. At the moment the two boats touched, water surged into the *drakkar*. The men at the back of the *drakkar*, furthest from the *knarr* leapt up and tried to splash their way towards the safety of the sturdier trading vessel. Olaf shouted to them to be still, but it was of no use. In just seconds, the water level climbed to a point where it was clearly going to flood through the oar holes. Men who had been rowing at the front leapt from the *drakkar* into the water to reach out for the helping hands of those on the *knarr*. At least six men managed to pull themselves on board. Those in the middle of the *drakkar* and those at the back were struggling to leave the vessel and were trying in the briefest of moments to decide whether they could salvage their weaponry as they did so. Some of the men had abandoned any idea of making it to the *knarr*, for the reason they could not swim. These men shouted and tried to make their way along the top strake, holding onto it with clenched knuckles and clawing whitened fingers. Some dozen or so men at the back of the *drakkar* stood on the top strake and plunged off one by one into the swirling brown waters to attempt to make it to the nearest riverbank.

'Cut the *bræða* for all the gods' sake!' Olaf could see that the weight of his sinking *drakkar* was going to pull the *knarr* down with it. From his position at the back of the sinking 'Gjálfrmarr,' he saw the rope tighten and the rear of the Avarr lunge downwards. 'Cut it now! Cut it now, you fools!'

Guðbjörn who had made it across to the *knarr* acted on his master's instruction. He still had his sax at his side and with this he cut through the creaking tightened rope in several sawing motions. As the rope separated, its ends whipped back in their parting, to seemingly propel the *knarr* away from the *drakkar* that instantly became swamped with a great in pouring of water. The dragon's head, which had not been removed during the raid plunged downwards and momentarily disappeared beneath the water. The ship had been lost and men who had any ambition of reaching the safety of the *knarr* realised this last hope had now gone. Those men who could not swim disappeared under the waves to reappear seconds later as did the dragon's head and almost instantly disappear again. The weight of swords and axes pulled any men that still clung to them downwards. Olaf had leapt at the last possible moment from the raised prow at the back of the *drakkar* into the unseasonably cold water. As the bow had rushed downwards, the rear of the boat had pushed up and as it reached its greatest height he had thrown himself as far as he could towards the muddy river bank.

The water engulfed him completely and he felt himself sinking deep into its welcoming embrace. With his long handled axe in one hand and his sword in the other he kicked again and again as hard as he could, up towards the surface. Into his confused and befuddled mind there suddenly came a clear vision of beauty itself. Olaf blinked and blinked again, because before his eyes almost within an arm's reach of him floated a vision of inordinate beauty. 'By *Óðinn's* trickery,' he thought, 'she must be the great *Lofnheiðr* herself.' The perfection of the girl's deep, rich brown hair and her matching eyes forced Olaf to stare at her in complete disbelief. He still felt the water pressing coldly around him but he felt compelled to gaze at the vision granted him and for the briefest of moments he felt as though he were suspended between two worlds. He lived for those few moments apart from his world, where he had grown to be a leader and breathed lung fulls of air. A great feeling, a sudden and deep urge drove him to reach out towards the shimmering image of feminine splendour. His arms uncontrollably stretched forward and as he did so the wondrous form disappeared quite as quickly as it had materialised. Even in that shortest span of time, Olaf knew in his mind that the beautiful woman was forever unattainable and in a violent reaction to this unpleasant and defeatist thought, he kicked out. It seemed to him in this brief and truly desperate moment that he would not make it, but when all hope appeared lost and his lungs felt as though they were going to burst, his head finally broke the surface of the water to allow him to take in a huge draught of life giving air. He felt as though he had returned from a journey that had taken him almost across the great bridge of *Bifrost*. Instantly, he ascertained the direction of the bank, but as he did so he sank beneath the unfriendly waters once more. He pushed off again, more resolutely than before. Every three or four powerful kicks of his legs brought him back to the surface again and again, allowing him to breathe or rather gasp in the much needed air. The bank was just yards away now. Its muddy shiny steepness almost beckoned to him, welcoming him back to the land of the men with the cross.

Gagarr looking back at the swirling waters behind the *knarr* swallowed nervously in the knowledge that Guðbjörn's brave action had almost certainly doomed their master and all the others on the *drakkar*. 'Pull men, we've got to pull or we'll be back in the hands of the men of Christ as well. Let's make our way out to sea and find out if our gods will allow us home after this terrible defeat! I'd rather face a storm than all those men with their crosses.'

The bog iron axe head sank deep into the bank's mud and allowed Olaf to pull his body up and out of the water. He lay there on his side for a second or two regaining his breath from his efforts, whilst at the same time wondering what was to become of him. He had somehow managed to swim ashore with his axe and sword and that at least gave him some feeling of security. Of the other men who had attempted the same course of action, four it seemed had successfully reached the bank. The others were not to be seen and Olaf realised that *Hel* had summoned them and clearly wished them for herself.

Avarr moved slowly downstream; the crew's faces were turned back to see what was to become of their master and of their friends. 'There's Olaf, he's made it!' The high pitched voice of one of the rowers seemed to hold out some kind of hope for their master.

Olaf had pulled himself upright and now dripping and bedraggled he climbed the steep river bank, until he stood on its top. Quietly and speaking just to himself he uttered, *'Þessa skiptis munu vit iðrask siðar.'* (We will regret this later) Raising both his sword and axe above his head, he called on his gods and he called on his enemy. *Þórr, Óðinn, Hel* and *Loki*; all were summoned by the man who simply refused to surrender to the men in brown. Of the four other Norse men who had made it the river bank, fortune had treated them quite differently. One man had nearly drowned and he now lay face down choking and vomiting into the mud. Another had somehow become injured and now bled profusely from an upper body wound; he still held his sword, but his pale complexion and unsteady stance showed that he would pose little threat in any forthcoming combat. The remaining two men could not have been more different, one was young and thin and armed with just a *scrimasax*, whilst the other who could easily have been his father was thick set and armed with a pattern welded damascened sword. Olaf called to his three comrades who were standing to join him in one last defiant stand. 'We'll take a good number of them; let's show them how a man fights.'

The monks, there were about twenty of them, who had left the quay had almost reached Olaf and his three fellow Norse, when something quite unexpected and extraordinary happened. The little church which had been reluctant to burn was now issuing a loud, clear and quite beautiful sound. Someone for whatever reason had begun to ring the church bell and Olaf's mind was transported back to Lindisfarne the previous year where similar chaotic scenes had engulfed a similar day. Olaf couldn't help consider that the bell here was much better than the one he had heard before; its sound was almost musical, so different, a far cry from the irritating monotonous clanking of the one from Lindisfarne.

Suddenly the brethren appeared unsure of what they should do. Six or seven of them simply turned around, dropped any weapons they were carrying and ran as fast as they could towards the stone building as if summoned by their God himself. The remainder who had been making their way with as much haste as possible towards the Norse slowed right down almost to a complete standstill. The monks at the front glanced sideways at each other and spoke in whispered voices. Those at the back glanced over their shoulders at their retreating brothers, who were clearly distancing themselves from any possible dangers. It seemed that the ringing of the bell had somehow infused doubt where there had been none and apprehension where boldness had previously reigned.

As a natural leader, Olaf had sensed this change of heart instinctively and now rallied the Norse men by his side. 'Take them now and let's see if *Óðinn* and *Loki* will allow us a little more time in the land of men. I for one am not ready to leave *Midgard*! I wish not to meet *Hel* yet.' With these words he leapt forward to bring his axe head firmly down on the bald pate of the foremost monk. The splitting of the skull made a terrible cracking noise, but even before he had time to prise the head of the axe out of the monk's brains, Olaf had slashed sideways wildly with his sword. The blade cut across the cassocked chest of one brother and ripped into the face of the man standing next to him. In the blink of an eye Olaf had killed one and incapacitated two of the band of monks who now stood before them. As his sword flashed, the damascened blade of the older Norse man and the scrimasax of the younger man also began to weave their spells. With well practised swirling cuts the Norse blades cut into and drove back the group of men who had until seconds before been the rampant pursuers.

The group of monks had shrunk in number and it was clear their effectiveness as a body of fighting men had diminished. Olaf shouted again and again, goading them to take him, but they could not. The young lad was not so lucky and received an appalling blow from the end of a staff and fell to the ground to lie motionless to join the wounded Norse man who also now lay prone. Olaf and his thick-set counterpart however, still stood and fought to the end; an end that was quick in the coming. Olaf had sheathed his bloody sword and now both of his hands gripped the long shaft of his axe, which swung to and fro in a macabre dance of death. The swordsman's work was equally effective and in moments the combined lack of desire to join their 'maker' ensured that the remaining Benedictine brethren, of whom there were five, retreated. In fact, they did not so much as retreat, but turn around and run for it. So it was that Olaf and Særða won a famous battle.

Olaf, however was not thinking about the glorious victory he and his companion had achieved; instead his mind focused on the immediate situation which now presented itself. He ordered Særða to get off the river bank and out of sight, after congratulating him by slapping him on the back and telling him he was one of the best if not the best. They both slid down the bank and into the mud to where the body of the drowned Norse man lay. Olaf explained his plan as briefly as he could to Særða and then with the greatest respect spoke directly to the dead body, *'Ek vil skipta við þik vápnum.'* (I want to exchange weapons with you) He then tapped his own head lightly with the fingers of his left hand, as though to steady himself. After doing this he then slowly took off his leather skull cap, followed by his intricately decorated belt, his beautiful sword and even his trusty axe, which had not left his side for many, many a year. Whilst he was doing this, his companion stripped the drowned man of his weapons and outer clothes. This was an unpleasant and difficult task as the poor man's clothes were wet and muddy. With the help of Særða, the dead man was soon dressed in Olaf's much finer garments and Olaf had suddenly become just another man of the *Þræll*.

'They'll be back shortly and they'll be back in numbers! We need to get as far away as possible if we're to have any chance. When they return and find the body of a leader and all of his fine weapons, they may well give up the chase, because common men, even of the Norse variety, I'd imagine command but little interest. The only problem is the sacrifice I'm making regarding my sword and my axe. It pains me to leave either, but I'll just have to make do with this miserly scrimasax for the moment.' Olaf clearly had not given up thoughts of escape and his desire to survive pushed him ever and relentlessly onwards.

'Which way should we take?' Særða, asked as the two men readied to leave the desolate and muddy riverbank and the grey, but finely dressed corpse.

'There's only one way and that is towards the sea,' came Olaf's brief rejoinder. As he spoke he threw the newly acquired scrimasax to the ground, so that its deadly point stuck into the welcoming earth, leaving the handle vibrating back and forth. He picked up his trusty axe almost lovingly. 'We'll not be parted after all, I'm not leaving you!'

As luck would have had it, 'Avarr,' the *knarr* that had left the doomed dragon ship had made very poor progress down the river. In addition, the men on the *knarr* were aware that the conditions at sea were not good, as the weather still raged and railed against them. For the entire time since landing at little Gyrwe, it had been blustery and it had rained; how it had rained. The men on the *knarr* had been busy attempting to put up a canopy to keep the rain off what little and precious cargo they had left. Once they were as happy as they could possibly have been with their boat, they attempted to make a break for it and push off into the great and angry sea that boiled beyond the end of the river they now bobbed up and down in.

Olaf repeated his earlier explanation to Særða as the two men loped along the muddy edge of the river hidden from the monastery by the bank, that he wished 'them' to think the leader was dead, because that would surely take the sting out of any possible pursuit. His repetition showed his anxiety. 'Two Norse soldiers can be picked up later, after they've put out their fires. After all, this weather will prevent any possible escape and there are no more boats here capable of crossing the great sea.' Olaf reasoned out loud. 'We, my friend must get ourselves to the *knarr* before it leaves us for good. We must make haste and we must make a little luck for ourselves, or at least ask *Loki* to side with us for awhile.' Olaf was getting desperate as he knew that the departure of the Avarr meant almost certain death to himself and his worthy companion.

Almost two thousand Norse paces downstream of the drowned man, who now lay dressed as the master, Olaf and Særða were granted their piece of luck, although Olaf didn't consider it small at the time. Whether his request had been granted and it was the work of *Loki* the trickster or mere chance, it is hard to say. Hauled up clear of the water and lying upturned to prevent it filling with rain water, there was an *Æring*, or at least something very similar to it. To Olaf, at least that is what it was and with the help of Særða, it was very soon in the water, with both men pulling hard on the oars that had been concealed beneath it. The small boat moved surprisingly quickly in the choppy river water and after rowing, with the knowledge that their lives depended on it, for what seemed a long time, they slowly turned a long and gradual bend to glimpse the back of 'Avarr' in the widening river mouth.

The terrible weather ensured that the *knarr* still had its sail down and it was this alone that gave any hope to the two men who pursued it. Glimpsing over their shoulders periodically, they pulled and pulled on their oars in a desperate attempt to first be seen and second reach its relative sanctuary. Fortunately for the rowers, the men on the *knarr* were as vigilant as it was possible to be and their extraordinary efforts were soon noticed by none other than Gagarr. At first Gagarr couldn't work out which Norse men rowed the little boat, possibly due to Olaf's change of clothes. Guðbjörn responded to his slightly delayed shout, by ordering the men to keep Avarr as still as possible in the water, by pulling firmly against the current.

Olaf and Særða managed to reach the *knarr* in several minutes and their joy was immense and their exhaustion almost complete. The men's reunion however meant so much to all on board; it was as if there had been a signal from the gods themselves that all was not lost. Gagarr thanked both *Njord*, the god of the sea and also *Balder*, *Óðinn*'s son, whom all on board knew as the good god. Olaf thanked both *Óðinn* and *Þórr*, but no one present thanked *Tyr*, the god who granted victories in battle. All of the surviving Norse men were smarting not from their defeat, but from their utter rout and humiliation at the hands of a group of ill armed and poorly trained Benedictine monks. Their terrible loss, however appalling it had been, would not be known about or spoken of back in the distant homelands if the small boat Avarr were to flounder on its way back though.

The master lay on the wet boards of the deck, motionless. His eyes closed in spite of the rain, the heaving of the boat in the swirling waters and the accompanying spray that leapt over the top strake to soak everything again and again. Olaf wasn't asleep though; his mind had focused on the series of unfortunate events that had so quickly unfurled as to bring about the near total destruction of his flotilla as well as the deaths of so many of his men. He played through each and every tragic scene that constituted this failed expedition, knowing full well that there was nothing at all he could do now to make amends for the catalogue of mistakes that had been made. He realised that to change the course of history was impossible and that it was simply as it was meant to be.

Gagarr ignored the apparently sleeping figure and aided by two other men lifted with some difficulty the pale and wan bodies of the two Norse boys, who had been bailers and who had been left to mind the *knarr*s and *drakkar*. They placed them with sombre ceremony and with not a little reverence inside the small boat that Olaf and Særða had so recently arrived in. When this slightly tricky and unpleasant task had been accomplished, another body, this time that of a man, was also added with considerably greater difficulty to the small boat's already grisly cargo. As soon as the three bodies were in the vessel, it was cut free without any words being spoken, to be carried away from the surviving *knarr* on the heaving swell. Some of the men rubbed the small iron hammers that hung about their necks and at the same time they bade their deceased companions a farewell glance, nothing more.

Olaf suddenly opened his eyes wide and simultaneously stood up on the deck of the rolling vessel. He gazed with one hand above his eyes towards the river's mouth, which now lay quite close. His other hand instinctively rubbed the smarting and inflamed tattoo that decorated his upper arm, unnecessarily reminding him of the monastic community that had driven him and his fellow Norse warriors out of its enclaves.

No other boats had dared take to the waters in such terrible conditions. Waves, wind and strong currents made any pursuit impossible or at the very least madness. Smoke from the burning buildings had recently ceased and from where the boat currently lurched in the boiling seas, the greenery of the trees and the steep shingle beach looked positively inviting. The Norse men and the few women on the boat couldn't see a single person either on the rain lashed river banks or on the soaked shore line. This did little to tempt any of them to return though; they had had enough of Gyrwe and its Christians.

Olaf looked out to the surging sea and raised one hand high above his head. The noise of the wind and waves carried the words he spoke away. No one on the boat heard what he had said and no one cared. The waves which buffeted the boat broke into great gashes of white foam that were lifted and fell in the powerful swell. Olaf wondered if he would see Hordaland ever again.

കൗ   കൗ   കൗ

So you and Snorri can see, that like all sagas and stories of any note, they never really finish. They are merely the beginning of something else, possibly something far more important. One final detail that has managed to arouse Snorri's mind and imagination is the fact that Olaf the man, the great leader never really existed under the name we have come to know him by! Yes, that's right; I the story teller have the power to change his life in some fundamental way, just like that, when you now feel you have got to know him but a little. He does however not cease to exist, but appears in the vellum leaves under another's name, a real name and a name that belonged to a real man.

Well, where does that leave this man, who is central to this tale? I really shouldn't be so cruel as to disappoint young Snorri by saying that this is merely a tale made up to pass the long evenings after all. So, I will finish by saying that I cannot deny the real man himself after all I have recounted! He lived, loved, fought and died and he was of my father's blood line; a full ellifu (eleven) generations back. He went, as I hinted a little earlier under the name of Vemundur Thorolfursson; he was the son of Thorolfur Vaganefsson and he was born in the year 760.

Notes

All of the major historical events described in the tale are as accurate as was possible for me to obtain from various research sources. Reference books, vast numbers of internet sites, visits to museums and various places mentioned in the book constitute the background to this work.

Most of the characters are fictitious, but some are real. The list of names at the front shows gender, a brief description of character, literal meaning of Norse name and occasionally dates. An asterisk denotes that this character is recorded historically in some way. The family trees of both Snorri and of Jon are as accurate as was possible to determine. Some names are spelt differently at various points in the text, to reflect changes in location. Spelling was as haphazard in the late eighth century as it can be today!

The names of the longships or drakkar are placed within inverted commas, whereas the names of mythological boats are in Italics. This method was implemented to try to avoid confusion.

I have used the term Norse more frequently than Viking, as it essentially means Northmen. The terms are interchangeable really; Viking meaning men of the bays. Also the long ships are at times referred to as longships as well as *drakkar*. I have used *drakkar* as singular as well as plural at times. The same goes for *knarr*.

The use of Old Norse in the text was only made possible by extremely useful internet sites, particularly useful ones being: **Old Norse** for beginners and **Old Norse** etexts. Both are well worth a look.

Dates are as accurate as was possible to ascertain. Some dates are confirmed by The Anglo-Saxon Chronicle. Occasionally, I have moved events within times of the year to make them more feasible.

All other information on runes, festivals, dates, number systems, time telling, the pronunciation guide and Oghams were gleaned from sites too numerous to mention here. The most rudimentary search of the internet will provide a multitude of data and facts. It is up to the individual researcher to decide which are accurate and worth exploring.

Within the body of the story are many references to specific items, such as weaponry of all types, boats, religious beliefs, various ceremonies, burials and magic. Some information relating to these can be traced to the Codex Regius.

Some archaeological sites have been referred to in the text. These do not at present have accurate dates ascribed to them and therefore have been fitted in where most appropriate. The burial at Egersund is a good example. The grave goods described were all found with the body, which was believed to be from an important family from this approximate date.

The eclipse referred to by Gyrwe's abbot actually occurred on 26th August 793. The path of the eclipse was directly above Jarrow. Data for this was obtained on the website: sunearth.gsfc.nasa.gov/eclipse/eclipse.htnl

The burial mound on Orkney is Maes Howe, the stone circle is the Ring of Brodgar and the strange rune covered stone referred to, stand to this day on mainland Orkney or Hrossey. Each of these would have been well known to the Norse.

The maps of the Norse World and the Orkneys and illustrations of Oddi and Óðinn's ravens were sketched by me. The drawings of Olaf wearing the ornate helmet and of Ulf were kindly drawn by Charles Liley.

Extended Genealogy of
Jon Loftsson of Oddi

Sceaf

V

Bedwig

V

Hwala

V

Hathra

V

Itermon

V

Heremod

V

Sceldwa

V

Beaw

V

Teatwa

V

Geata

V

Godwulf (80: Asgard)

V

Flocwald (100: Asgard)

V

Finn (130: Asgard)

V

Freothalaf (160-?: Asgard)

V

Frithuwald (190) + Beltsa

V

Óðinn (215-?: Asgard) + Frigg (219-?)   brother Skadi

V

Skjold King of the Danes (237)

V

Friedleif (259)

V

Frodi (281)

V

Friedleif (303)

V

Haver (325)

V

Frodi (347)

V

Vermund (369)

V

Olaf (391)

V

Dan (412-?)

V

Frodi (433-?: Denmark) + ?

V

Friedlief (456-?: Denmark) + ?

V

Frodi (479-?: Denmark) + ?

V

Halfdan (503-?: Denmark) + Sigris

V

Hroarsson (526-?: Denmark) + Ogne

V

Valdar (547-:Denmark) + Hildis

V

Harald (568-?: Jutland) + Hildir (Hildis, Hervor) Heidreksdattir (572-?)

V

Halfdan (Snjalli) (590-650: King – Jutland) + Moalda (Digri)
Kinriksdattir (594-?)

V

Ivar (Vidfame) (612-647: King Denmark) + Gauthild (Gyrithe)
Alfsdatter (614-

V

Hraerekur (Slongvangbaugur) 640- ?:King Denmark) + Auour
(Djupauoga)

V

Ivarsdottir (640-?)

V

Haraldur (Hilditonn) (690-776: Denmark, King of)

V

Thrandur (Gamli) (700)

V

Thorolfur (Vaganef) (730)

V

Vemundur (Orolokarr) (760)

V

Aevarr Vemundsson (785-?) + Thora

V

Valgardur Aevarsson (815-?)

V

Hrafn (Heimski) (845)

V

Jorund the Priest (878)

V

Ulfur 'Augothi' (914-?: Iceland) brother Valgurd the Guileful

V

Svartur (949-?) Helga Thorsgeirsdottir Bodvar + Viking Karisa Kolbein
the Young

V

Lodmund (985-1060) + Thorgerda Sigfusdottir

V

Sigfuss (1020-1076) +   Thoreya Eyjolfsdottir

V

<u>**Saemundur the Learned**</u> (1056-1133)   sisters Elín and Halla

V

Loftur frodi (1085-1163) + Gudrun Kolbeinsdottir

Brothers: Eyjolfur, Lodmund

Sister: Thorey

V

Þora Magnusdottir + **Jon** (1124-1197)

Other wives: <u>Aesa Thorgeirsdottir</u>

(a) <u>Ragnheidur Thorhallsdottir</u>

<u>(son **Thorsteinn**: 1159)</u>

V

Gunnar*(1189)*

V

Sigmundur (1212)

(b) Halldora Skegg Brandsdottir

V

Saemundur I Odda (1154-1222) + Ingveld Ingridadottir

(sister   Solveig)

V

Sveinbjorn (1238)

V

Magnus (agnar)

Andresson (1220-1268)

V

Andres (1180-1268)

V

Oddur Alason (1180-1234:Iceland) + Steinnun Hrafnsdotti

V

Hrafn (1222-1289) + Thoruridur Sturludottir (1228-1288)

V

Jon (1266)

V

Svein (1280)

V

Jon (1330) + Thorgerdur

V

Finnbogi (1365-1441) + Arnfridur Torfadottir

Snorri Sturlason genealogy – all Iceland

Jorundr (975-?) + Hallveig Oddsdottir (980-?)

V

Snorri (1015-?) + Asny Storladottir (1025-?)

V

Gils (1060-?) + Thordis Gudlaugsdottir (1064-?)

V

Thordur (1095-1149) + Vigdis Svertingsdottir (1098-?)

V

Sturli (1115-1183) + Gudny Bodvarrsdottir (1120-1221)

V

Snorri (1179-1241) Stadarholl, Iceland + Herdis Bersadottir,
                    (a) Thuridur Hallsdottir, Hallveig Ormsdottir,
                    Gudrun Hreinsdottir, Oddny Sturlason.

V

Oraekja Snorrason + Arnbjorg Arnsdottir

A Guide to Pronunciation of Old Norse

In general, Old Norse follows Continental pronunciation rules

Vowels:

- **a** *as the "a" in hand*   *galðr -* **ga***lthrer*
- **á** *as the "a" in rather*   *Álfablót -* **ar***lvablott*
- **e** *as the "ee" in street*   *drenkr - dr****ee***ngrer*
- **é** *as the "ea" in wear*   *vé -* **fea***r*
- **æ** *as the "ou" in shout*   *bræða - br****ow***tha*
- **i** *as the "ie" in thief*   *fiskr - v****ee***skrer*
- **o** *as the "o" in blow*   *ostr -* **o***strer*
- **ó** *as the "o" in hot*   *drótt - dr****o***tt*
- **u** *as in French roux*   *Austur - owst****oo***r*
- **ú** *as the "oo" in droop*   *brúðr - br****oo***threr*
- **ö** *as the "o" in not*   *bryntröll - brintr****o***ll*
- **au** *as the "o" in how*   *aurar -* **ow***rar*

Consonants:

Double consonants *followed by a vowel are pronounced double, hence the KK in drakkar is pronounced as in bookkeeping.*

When final or followed by another consonant in the same syllable, double consonants are pronounced long, being more than a single consonant yet not the repitition of the full double one.

D, T, N *and* ***L*** *are all pronounced with the point of the tongue against the teeth* *(as in French and German) not with the tongue against the gums as in English.*

HL *voiceless L*

HN *voiceless N*

L *is pronouced normally when standing next to D, N, L or R or when following an unaccented vowel, but the L is trilled somewhat in any other position where it is not voiceless.*

NG *or* **NK** *is pronounced like bangle or blink*

F *in the initial position, or when followed by a voiceless consonant, is voiceless, as in English fat. Otherwise F is pronounced like an English V. Voiced F followed by N was nasalized, so that jafn often was spelled and pronounced jamn*

V *was usually pronounced as an F, but HV was a voiceless V or KV.*

P *was pronounced as in English except when followed by S or T, here it becomes an F as in soft.*

R *is always rolled as in Scottish dialects. Final R (such as in dvergr) was not pronounced. A voiceless R is always spelled HR.*

S *was always voiceless, as in English last*

Þ *or* **þ** *the rune thorn is the voiced "th" sound of thorn*

Đ *or* **ð** *the rune edth is the unvoiced "th" sound of there*

Z *is pronounced as TS*

J *is pronounced as "y" in "yellow"*

G *in the initial position or in NG or when doubled is a voiced velar plosive (a hard G), like the "g" in English got. If NG or GG occurred before S or T, the G became unvoiced to K (thus "eggs" would be pronounced ekks and "sings" as sikks)*

G *in the middle or end of a word is a voiced velar fricative (a soft G), almost a "j" sound as the "g" in the English reign -- unless the G was follwed by S or T, when it becomes the hard CH of Scottish broch (thus drengskapr would be pronounced drenkkapre)*

Younger Futhork

Younger Futhork or "Normal Runes" evolved very slowly into the Elder Futhark over a great many years finally stabilising by about 800 A.D., the beginning of the Viking Age. It constituted the main alphabet in Norway, Sweden and Denmark throughout the Viking Age, finally being replaced by the Latin alphabet by about 1200 due to the conversion of most of Scandinavia to Christianity.

Three variations of the alphabet developed in Denmark, Sweden and Norway:

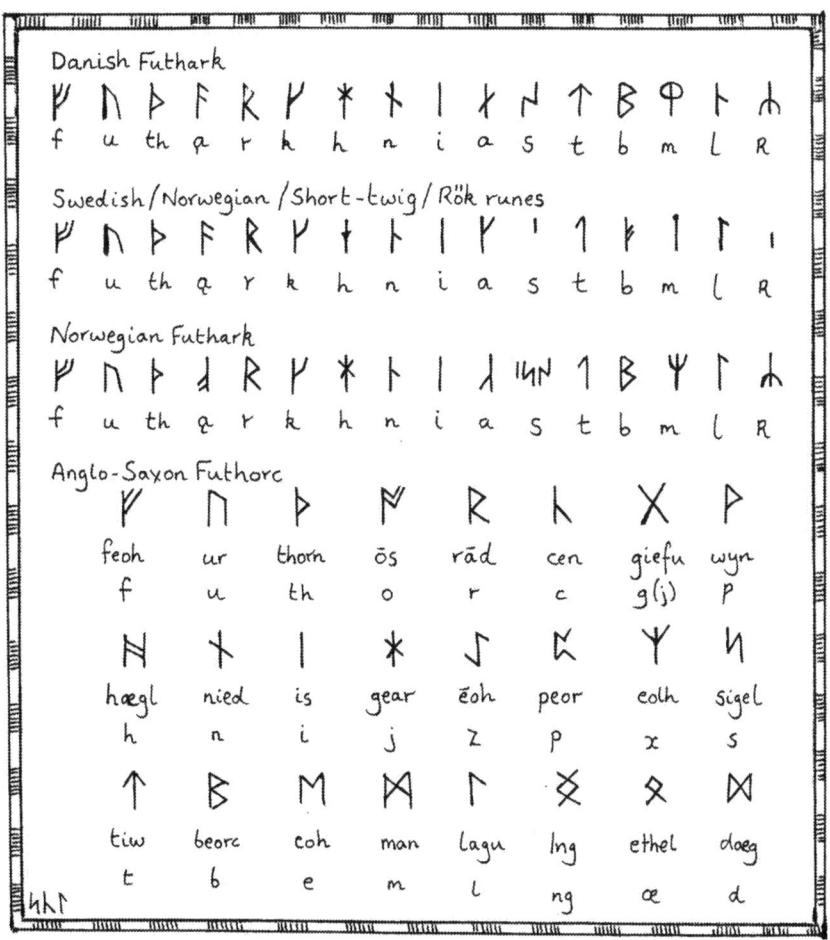

Norse Words

Aenir	Gods of war
Æring	small narrow boat, narrow enough for each rower to man two oars
Álfar	elves
Álfablót	sacrifice to the elves
Asgard	home of the Gods, divided into twelve realms
Áttæring	eight-oared æring
Aurar	plural of ounce
Austur	east
Bifrost	rainbow-bridge giving access to Asgard (through death)
Bleikt silfr	debased silver – usually less than 90%
Blót	sacrifice (usually to gods or spirits)
Bræða	rope (nautical)
Brannt silfr	burned silver – pure silver
Brúðr	bride, young married woman
Brunhild	leader of the Valkyrja
Brynklungr	sword (rare type)
Bryntröll	sword (rare type)
Dísir	female spirits - control fertility & nature's crops for men – they visit the new-born
Dammr	water reserve
Drakkar	Long ship
Draughrinn	a wandering cursed spirit
Drenkr	member of a ship' crew
Drengskapr	honour
Drótt	lord

Dróttinn	lord's warband
Dvergar	dwarves
Ey	island
Eyrir	ounce (equivalent to 27g)
Eysjarskeggi	inhabitant of an island
Færing	two-man Æring
Fenrir	Wolf – son of Loki (At Ragnarok he devours Óðinn)
Fiskr	fish
Fjörbaugsgarður	outlawry – banishment for three years, property kept
Flikki	bacon rasher
Flói	bay, marsh
Fylgjur	guardian spirit, often in the form of an animal – seeing your own is a sign of imminent death
Fjðurbróðir	uncle
Gaflak	javelin
Galðr	spells often sung
Garðr	fishery made with two rows of poles with net at end
Gjálfrmarr	steed of the sea
Gjallarhorn	Mimir's drinking horn sounded at onset of Ragnarok
Glíma	Norse wrestling
Grima	One of Óðinn's disguises (an old hooded man)
Grotti-Fenni	One of Swelki's millers
Grotti-Menni	One of Swelki's millers
Gungnir	Óðinn's spear
Hafkitta	fantastic & immense creature that lures children – lives at the bottom of the sea
Háfr	shrimp net
Hangerock	apron-skirt
Hlaut	blood from a sacrifice

Hamar	*hammer*
Hamingja	*spirit or soul*
Heimangerð	*bride dowry (paid to groom by bride's father)*
Hel	*Goddess of the dead (daughter of Loki and giantess Angebotha)*
Himinioðurr	*rim of heaven, horizon, sky*
Hófr	*spider crab*
Hnefatafl	*Norse board game (The King's table)*
Hringr	*ring, round trip*
Hrogn	*fish eggs*
Humarr	*lobster*
Húðfat	*leather sleep sack used on boats*
Huginn	*'Thought' – raven of Óðinn*
Hnefatafl	*board game – 'king's board or game'*
Írskr	*Irish*
Jarl	*noble class of Norse man*
Jörmangandr	*the world serpent – lives in the ocean surrounding Midgard*
Jötnar	*giants*
Jötenheim	*the land of giants to the east of Midgard*
Karl	*middle class of Norse man*
Kjölr	*keel*
Koli	*hake*
Knarr	*merchant boat*
Knattleikr	*bat and ball game*
Kriki	*little bay*
Kveldúlfr	*evening wolf (look for love affairs – hunting like a wolf)*
Kvinna	*bad life woman - lesbian*

Landvættir	*land spirits that live in rocks – control prosperity of the land*
Læknir	*healer*
Loki Laufeyjarson	*Loki the trickster – mythical being (Liar, shape shifter)*
Leikmót	*games meeting*
Lýðrr	*Pollock*
Marsvín	*porpoise*
Mastr	*mast*
Midgard	*the gods' place for men*
Midgard serpent	*serpent - Jörmangandr*
Mimir	*god who owns spring of wisdom and drinking horn: Gjallarhorn. Head cut off by Óðinn, who gave up an eye to drink from spring of wisdom. Head preserved by herbs and used by Óðinn for consultation*
Mjollnir	*Þórr's hammer*
Mogr	*young man*
Mork	*mark of silver (equivalent to 8 ounces - átta aurar)*
Mundr	*price of a bride (paid to bride's father)*
Muninn	*'Memory' – raven of Óðinn*
Niflheim	*realm of cold & darkness & of the dead (Hel) into which Hel was thrown*
Nýi	*New-moon (troll name)*
Niði	Waned moon (troll name)
Norns	*3 fates (maidens) who live beneath the roots of the world-tree; Urdi (past), Vedandi (present) & Skuld (future)*
Óðinn	*King of the Gods (Odin)*

Öndvegi	high seat – most honourable place to sit in longhouse
Öndvegissúlur	high-seat pillars
Öxarhyrna	beak of axe head
Ormr	dragon
Ostr	cheese
Papi	Irish monk
Poki	bag
Ragnarök	the end of the world
Rakki	collar which is put around the mast to diminish a yard friction (Naut)
Rálik	rope which reenforces the sail edges (Naut)
Rás	strong current in a channel
Ratatosk	squirrel who runs up the trunk of Yggdrasil to carry insults
Rosmhvalr	walrus
Sax	short sword
Scramasax	type of sax
Seiðr	sorcery, witchcraft; practised by völva or seiðkona and Óðinn
Seiðkona	witch who practises seiðr
Sexærings	three man æring
Síld	herring / pilchard
Silfr	silver
Snekkja	boat that is easy to steer
Skjaldborg	shieldwall
Sköfuleikr	scraper game – extremely violent, with high level of mortality
Skóggangur	full outlawry – banishment, not to be fed or housed, property taken

Skyr	*curds*
Sleipnir	*Óðinn's horse*
Snærisspjót	*throwing strings for a spear*
Stæðingr	*canvas that wraps up sail or covers the boat*
Staglína	*chain bound to anchor*
Strengr	*rope (nautical)*
Stýrimaðr	*steersman*
Súðþakiðr	*roofed with overlapping boards*
Suður	*south*
Svelgr	*sea-mill*
Swelki	*name of maelstrom north of the Orkney Isles*
Tún	*hay field*
Tiald	*tent pitched on the deck of a boat*
Þang	*long brown seaweed found on rocky shores*
Þilja	*upper deck*
Þing	*local legal assembly*
Þollr	*mast or other wooden post about which element pivots*
Þorp	*Village in a forest clearing*
Þórr	*Norse God (Thor) eldest son of Óðinn*
Þjófr	*thief*
Þræll	*lower class of Norse man (including slaves & bondsmen)*
Umgjorð	*scabbard*
Ulfhedinn	*wolf-coats – beserkers wearing wolf skins*
Ulfhednar	*wolfskin worn by beserkers*
Urð	*heap of stones fallen from a hill side*

Víka sjóvar	*a 1000 strokes of the oar (standard time for rowing, usually not exceeded) – n.b. a Norse thousand = 1,200*
Valhöll	*gathering place of fallen warriors – a palace in Asgard*
Valkyrja	*female warrior who chooses who falls in battle and takes their souls to Valhöll*
Vanir	*Gods of peace, harvest & fertility*
Vatn	*rough water*
Vik	*fjord or bay*
Vikingr	*Pirate / bay dweller from Norse homelands*
Vatni ausinn	*sprinkling of water on the baby's head in naming ceremony*
Vé	*a holy place where no bood may be spilled*
Völva	*seeress who may practise seiðr*
Vringla	*type of seaweed*
Yggdrasil	*sacred mythological ash tree*

Norn words (gaelic / pictish – hjaltland - Shetland)

Sonn	*grain kiln*
Dafek	*bucket*

Irish terms

Dubh-Gaill	*black foreigners – term for (Danish) Vikings*
Finn-Gaill	*white foreigners – term for (Norwegian) Vikings*

Gaill	*Gentiles or foreigners – term for Vikings*
Grád Fhéne	*commoner's dwellings*
Lochlann	*lakemen – term for Vikings*
Normanni	*north-men – term for Vikings*

Pictish script — Oghams

The vertical strokes should join up and cross the central line – M, G, NG, Z & R are written at a slant

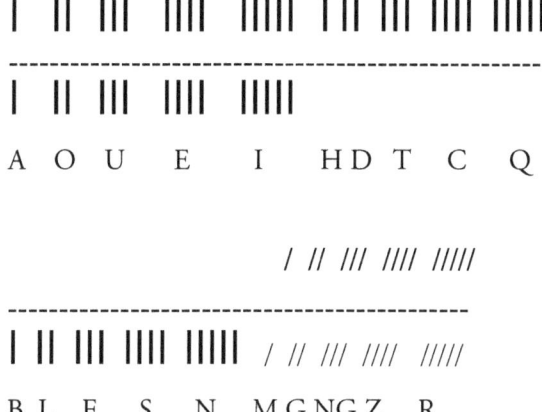

A	O	U	E	I	H D	T	C	Q	

B	L	F	S	N	M G NG Z	R			

One theory suggests that some Ogham script can be deciphered if translated into Old Norse. This suggests that some picts spoke some Old Norse or were at least able to understand it and translate it for their own use.

Norse Calendar
Days of the Week:

Sunnundagr	Sunday
Mánagr	Monday
Tysdagr	Tuesday
Ódinsdagr	Wednesday
Þórdagr	Thursday
Frjdagr	Friday
Laugardagr	Saturday – washing day

Norse Festivals:

Name	Modern date	Details
Disablót	1st Feb	to Disir (minor spirits & deities) AS - Imbolc
Feast of Vali	14th Feb	Óðinn's son
Ostara	21st March	Goddess of sun & fertility Spring Equinox
Last night of Óðinn hanging	30th April	May Eve
Midsumarblót	21st June	Midsummer AS - Beltane
Fallfest	23rd Sept'	Harvest Autumnal equinox AS - Lugnasad
Vetrnætr	31st Oct	Winter Nights, Norse New Year AS - Samhain's Eve

Name	Modern date	Details
Jól / Yule	21st Dec	Wild hunt at greatest - Straw filled socks for Sleipnir (Óðinn's horse) AS = Anglo Saxon

Months & Festivals:

The Norse year was divided into two halves, the 'misseri'. These were sumar (summer) and vetr (winter)

Misseri – Sumar

Months

1st month
    -i fyrsti mánuðr
    Gauk mánuðr- cuckoo month
    Saðtið – seed time

2nd month
    annar mánuðr
    Eggtið – egg time
    Stekkið – lamb fold time

3rd month
    ÞriÞi mánuðr
    Sólmánuðr- sun month
    Selmánuðr – shieling month

4th month
    fiorÞi mánuðr
    Miðsumar – midsummer
    Heyannir – hay time

5th month	trimánuðr – double month
	Heyannir – hay time
	Kornskurdarmánuðr – corn cutting month
6th month	setti mánuðr
	Kornskurdarmánuðr – corn cutting month
	Haustmánuðr – harvest month

Misseri – Vetr

1st month	vetr – winter
	Gormánuðr – slaughtering month
2nd month	ylir – Yule
	Frermánuðr – frost month
3rd month	mörsugr – fat sucker
	Jólmánuðr – yule month
	Hrutmánuðr – ram month
4th month	Þorri – Thor's month
	Midvetr - midwinter
5th month	gói – unknown origin
6th month	einmánuðr – one month

Norse time — the Day Mark

hádegi	*midday*	*- sun position south*
undorneykt	*afternoon*	*- sun position south-west*
miðr aptan	*mid-evening*	*- sun position west*
náthmál	*night measure*	*- sun position north-west*
miðn ætti	*mid-night*	*- sun position north*
ótta	*early morning*	*- sun position north-east*
miðra morgun	*east-rise measure*	*- sun position east*
dagmál	*day measure*	*- sun position south-east*

n.b.　　*1/*　　the sun's position in the sky is referred to with the time and the place. i.e.　　*midday place* = *hádegistað*

　　　　2/　　if the sun is half way between two of the eight possible times, then the time is given by using those two times and the phrase, 'evenly near both', which is in Old Norse, '*jafn nærri badu*'

　　　　3/　　the system worked best in a familiar location, where reference points in the landscape indicated where in the sky the sun was. Each reference point would have been a day mark. Even if the sun had disappeared below the horizon the glow of sunset or sunrise would help with its position and thus give the time

Norse Numbers

Number	Cardinal	Ordinal
1	Einn	Fyrstr
2	Tveir	Annarr
3	Þrír	Þriði
4	Fjórir	Fjórði
5	Fimm	Fimmti
6	Sex	Sétti
7	Sjau	Sjaundi
8	Átta	átti, áttandi
9	Níu	Níundi
10	Tíu	Tíundi
11	Ellifu	Ellifti
12	Tólf	Tólfti
13	Þrettán	Þrettándi
14	Fjórtán	Fjórtándi
15	Fimmtán	Fimmtándi
16	Sextán	Sextándi
17	Sjautan	Sjautándi
18	Átján	Átjándi
19	Nítján	Nítjándi
20	Tuttugu	Tuttugandi
21	Tuttugu ok einn	tuttugandi ok fyrstr
	einn ok tuttugu	fyrstr ok tuttugandi
22	Tuttugu ok tveir	tuttugandi ok annarr
30	þrír tiger	Þrítugandi
31	þrír tigir ok einn	þrítugandi ok fyrstr
40	fjórir tigir	Fertugandi

Number	Cardinal	Ordinal
50	fimm tigir	Fimmtugandi
60	sex tiger	Sextugandi
70	sjau tiger	Sjautugandi
80	átta tiger	Attatugandi
90	níu tiger	Nítugandi
100	tíu tiger	(títugandi)
110	ellifu tigir	(ellifutugandi)
120	Hundrað	(hundraðasti)
200	hundrað ok átta tigir	(hundraðasti ok áttatugandi)
240	tvau hundrað	
960	átta hundrað	
1200	Þúsund	(þúsandasti)

Norse places

Adelsö	Island in Lake Malar- near to Birka
Aga	Small settlement in Hordaland
Agder	Area of Norway
Arsand	Trading village in Hordaland on Viksfjord
Birka	Great trading town on the island of Björkö (Sweden)
Byrgisey	Birsay, small Orkney isle
Björkö	Island in Lake Malar (Birch Island)
Bornholm Isle	Danish isle in Baltic Sea
Dorestad	Trading town in Denmark
Egersund	Coastal trading town in Jaeren (site of royal burial)
Eketorp	Trading town on Öland
Føroyar	Island group NW of Hjaltland (Faroe Islands – sheep isles)
Fjelberg	Trading village in Hordaland on Viksfjord
Fordefonn	Glacier above Odda in Hordland
Gokstad	Norwegian town near to Kaupang
Gotland	Island to the east of Sweden
Hedeby	Great trading town in Denmark (place of heather)
Helgö	Trading town on eastern coast of Sweden (near Birka)
Hesthamar Utne	sea village in fjord in Hordaland
Hjaltland	Island group N of Orkneys (Shetland Isles)
Hoi	Orkney isle (high)
Hordaland	Western region of Norway

Hrossey	Main Orkney Isle (Horse isle)
Jaeren	Area of Norway
Jondalsora	Trading village in Hordaland on Viksfjord
Kaupang	Great trading town south Norway (market-place)
Korshamn	Natural harbour at Birka on Björkö- (The Cross harbour)
Kugghamn	Natural harbour at Birka on Björkö- (The Cargo Boat Harbour)
Lake Malar	Expanse of water in which Birka lies – water routes converge from south & east
Leirvag	Trading village in Hordaland on Viksfjord
Lindholm Hóje	Settlement in north Denmark
Nordland	Area of Norway
Odda	Small settlement in Hordaland
Öland	Island off Sweden
Orkneyinga	Group of islands north of Bretland (Orkney Isles)
Östergötland	Area of Sweden
Paviken	Trading town on Gotland
Ribe	Trading town in Denmark
Ringerike	Southern region of Norway
Rogaland	Southwest coastal region of Norway
Ryvardenmost	Trading village in Hordaland on Viksfjord
Shapinsay	Orkney isle
Sogn	Petty kingdom, west Norway
Sundal	Trading village in Hordaland on Viksfjord
Sunde	Trading village in Hordaland on Viksfjord
Swelki	mythological svelgr (sea-mill) north of the Orkney Islands
Tjernagel	Trading village in Hordaland on Viksfjord

Uppland	Area of Sweden
Viksfjord	Fjord in Hordaland
Wollin	Small trading town in Denmark

Places in the British Isles

Birsay	Small Orkney Isle, Byrgisey (fort island)
Donemouth	Gyrwe or Jarrow
Dornwaraceaster	AS for Dorchester, Seat of the King of Wessex
Dumna	Isle of Lewis (Celtic)
Farne	AS for Farne Island
Farne Island	Small island, used by hermits from nearby Lindisfarne
Gyrwe	AS for Jarrow or Donemouth
Gyruum	AS for Jarrow
Hamton Wessex	coastal town, site of battle with pirates (787 AD) See Hamtun
Hamtun	AS for Southampton
Hjaltland	Group of isles north of the Orkneys (Shetlands)
Holy Isle	Lindisfarne (alternative name) orIona (alternative name)
Hoi	Orkney Isle with great stack of rock off it (Hoy - high)
Hrossey	Mainland Orkney, Horse Island
Inis Metcaut	Lindisfarne (ancient name – isle of winds)
Jarrow (Gyrwe) Monastery	raided by Vikings in A.D. 794 (twinned with Wearmouth)

Lindisfarne	*Holy Isle off Northumbria, site of first Viking raid (793AD)*
Lindisfarena eg	*AS for Lindisfarne*
Mercia	*AS kingdom*
Northumbria	*AS kingdom*
Orkneyinga	*Island group N of Scotland (Orkneys)*
Portland	*Town in Wessex, site of first Viking killing (787AD)*
St. Aiden's Monastery	*Monastery on Lindisfarne*
St. Cuthbert's Church	*Church on Lindisfarne*
St. Paul's Church	*Jarrow / Gyrwe / Donemouth*
St. Peter's Church	*Wearmouth*
Shapinsay	*Orkney isle*
Wearmouth monastery	*Monkwearmouth monastery twinned with Gyrwe*
Wessex	*AS kingdom south of Mercia*
Wiht	*AS Isle south of English coast (Isle of Wight)*

AS = Anglo Saxon

Glossary

Alecost	ale additive to disinfect & make bitter, (Chrysanthemun balsamita)
Alehoof	ale additive to disinfect & make bitter, (Ground ivy)
Amanita Muscara	fly agaric, red and white mushroom – toxic and psychoactive
Anchorite	hermit
Ash	mythological Norse tree that turned into man
Beserker	Norse fighter who feels no pain during combat – from bers (bear), for some combatants wore bear skins to fight in. They took hallucinogenic mushrooms to reach a state of frenzy
Bog myrtle	ale additive to preserve in especially Denmark (Myrica gale)
Bondsman	debt ridden Viking who is bonded to work to clear what is owed
Bretwalda	king of kings
Calefactory	warming room
Chip-carving	jewellery technique - hammering tiny holes into gold surface
Ciboria	chalice for religious purposes
Ciepemenn	monk trader merchants
Cloisonné	jewellery technique – inserting garnets to produce sparkling effect
Cuddy beads	ornate rosary beads, Lindisfarne made, to remember St. Cuthbert

Damascened	technique whereby alternate layers of iron and steel were folded together to produce a strong, light and flexible blade
Devil's Toenails	Gryphea – fossilised oyster-like shell
Elm	Norse - mythological tree turned into woman
Fallen stars	crinoids – fossilised sea anemone stem segment (star shape)
Filigree	jewellery technique – twisting wire of gold or silver
Fraterhouse	Refectory
Futhark	Name given to runic alphabet (1st 7 letters – F,U,T,H,A,R,K – Younger <8th Cen & Older >8th Cen -) see sections on runes & on Norse pronounciation
Hemina	measurement of wine (approx one pint)
Icelandic Spar	evidence suggests this crystal (calcite or sun stone) mined in Iceland, was used to find the sun when hidden by cloud or fog (possibly used at a later time than indicated here) – later 'discovered' and named after Eskifjord, Iceland, where it is found in basalt cavities – well known for its double refraction – the crystal may change from yellow to blue when pointed towards the sun due to it responding to polarised light – in northern latitudes it would respond better due to the fact that the best polarization patterns are produced when the sun is close to the horizon – light fog and thin clouds do not stop skylight polarization
Labora	work (Latin)
Millefioriglass	glass bead manufacturing technique – twisting rods of coloured glass then cutting off amalgam to produce multi-coloured bead

Nalbanding	*knotting wool by hand to produce a very tough woven like material*
Norn	*Pictish branch of Celtic spoken in The Hjaltlands*
Obsidian	*Volcanic glass (various colours, can be black – stone age currency, due to sharpness when chipped)*
Oghams	*Pictish script – see separate section*
Ora	*prayer (Latin)*
Pyxes	*Small circular box for communion bread (usually decorated with a cross or other Christian symbol)*
Regula	*rules (Latin)*
Runes	*Ancient written language (the futhark) – usually composed of straight strokes, carved onto stone and wood*
Runestones	*Dye like stone with rune symbols - thrown to predict the future*
Samian ware	*Type of glazed Roman table ware (terracotta colour)*
Scriptorium	*Room for copying scripts*
Snakestones	*ammonites - fossils of same shape as 'Nautilus'*
Sun stone	*see Icelandic Spar*
Tablet woven braid	*elaborate weaving technique involving rotating two tablets that were typically held in place between the weaver's belt and a solid object – the weave was highly colourful and used to decorate the edges of tunics and skirts to prevent them wearing out quickly*
Thunderbolts	*belemnites - bullet shape fossils from squid-like molluscs*
Top strake	*wooden plank at top edge of boat, fastened with iron nails*

Lightning Source UK Ltd.
Milton Keynes UK
UKHW041917070319
338695UK00001B/28/P